The Drowning Game

The Drowning Game

A Novel

LS HAWKER

WITNESS
IMPULSE

An Imprint of HarperCollinsPublishers

EPub Edition SEPTEMBER 2015 ISBN: 9780062435170
Print Edition ISBN: 9780062435187

10 9 8 7 6 5 4 3

To Layla

Chapter 1

Wednesday

PETTY

SIRENS AND THE scent of strange men drove Sarx and Tesla into a frenzy of barking and pacing as they tried to keep the intruders off our property without the aid of a fence. Two police cars, a fire truck, and an ambulance were parked on the other side of the dirt road. The huddled cops and firemen kept looking at the house.

Dad's iPhone rang and went on ringing. I couldn't make myself answer it. I knew it was the cops outside calling to get me to open the front door, but asking me to allow a group of strangers inside seemed like asking a pig to fly a jet. I had no training or experience to guide me. I longed to get the AK-47 out of the basement gun safe, even though it would be me against a half-dozen trained law men.

"Petty Moshen." An electric megaphone amplified the man's voice outside.

The dogs howled at the sound of it, intensifying further the tremor that possessed my entire body. I hadn't shaken like this since the night Dad left me out on the prairie in a whiteout blizzard to hone my sense of direction.

"Petty, call off the dogs."

I couldn't do it.

"I'm going to dial up your father's cell phone again, and I want you to answer it."

Closing my eyes, I concentrated, imagining those words coming out of my dad's mouth, in his voice. The iPhone vibrated. I pretended it was my dad, picked it up, hit the answer button and pressed it to my ear.

"This is Sheriff Bloch," said the man on the other end of the phone. "We have to come in and talk to you about your dad."

I cleared my throat again. "I need to do something first," I said, and thumbed the end button. I headed down to the basement.

Downstairs, I got on the treadmill, cranked up the speed to ten miles an hour and ran for five minutes, flat-out, balls to the wall. This is what Detective Deirdre Walsh, my favorite character on TV's *Offender NYC*, always did when emotions overwhelmed her. No one besides me and my dad had ever come into our house before, so I needed to steady myself.

I jumped off and took the stairs two at a time, breathing hard, sweating, my legs burning, but steadier. I popped a stick of peppermint gum in my mouth. Then I walked straight to the front door the way Detective Walsh would—fearlessly, in charge, all business. I flung the door open and shouted, "Sarx! Tesla! Off! Come!"

They both immediately glanced over their shoulders and came loping toward me. I noticed another vehicle had joined the gauntlet on the other side of the road, a brand-new tricked-out red Dodge Ram 4x4 pickup truck. Randy King, wearing a buff-colored Stetson, plaid shirt, Lee's, and cowboy boots, leaned against it. All I could see of his face was a black walrus mustache. He was the man my dad had instructed me to call if anything ever happened to him. I'd seen Randy only a couple of times but never actually talked to him until today.

The dogs sat in front of me, panting, worried, whimpering. I reached down and scratched their ears, thankful that Dad had trained them like he had. I straightened and led them to the one-car garage attached to the left side of the house. They sat again as I raised the door and signaled them inside. They did not like this one bit—they whined and jittered—but they obeyed my command to stay. I lowered the door and turned to face the invasion.

As if I'd disabled an invisible force field, all the men came forward at once: the paramedics and firemen carrying their gear boxes, the cops' hands hovering over their sidearms. I couldn't look any of them in the eye, but I felt them staring at me as if I were an exotic zoo animal or a serial killer.

The man who had to be the sheriff walked right up to me, and I stepped back palming the blade I keep clipped to my bra at all times. I knew it was unwise to reach into my hoodie, even just to touch the Baby Glock in my shoulder holster.

"Petty?" he said.

"Yes sir," I said, keeping my eyes on the clump of yellow, poisonous prairie ragwort at my feet.

"I'm Sheriff Bloch. Would you show us in, please?"

"Yes sir," I said, turning and walking up the front steps. I pushed open the screen and went in, standing aside to let in the phalanx of strange men. My breathing got shallow and the shaking started up. My heart beat so hard I could feel it in my face, and the bump on my left shoulder—scar tissue from a childhood injury—itched like crazy. It always did when I was nervous.

The EMTs came in after the sheriff.

"Where is he?" one of them asked. I pointed behind me to the right, up the stairs. They trooped up there carrying their cases. The house felt too tight, as if there wasn't enough air for all these people.

Sheriff Bloch and a deputy walked into the living room. Both of them turned, looking around the room, empty except for the grandfather clock in the corner. The old thing had quit working many years before, so it was always three-seventeen in this house.

"Are you moving out?" the deputy asked.

"No," I said, and then realized why he'd asked. All of our furniture is crowded in the center of each room, away from the windows.

Deputy and sheriff glanced at each other. The deputy walked to one of the front windows and peered out through the bars.

"Is that bulletproof glass?" he asked me.

"Yes sir."

They glanced at each other again.

"Have anyplace we can sit?" Sheriff Bloch said.

I walked into our TV room, the house's original dining room, and they followed. I sat on the couch, which gave off dust and a minor-chord spring squeak. I pulled my feet up and hugged my knees.

"This is Deputy Hencke."

The deputy held out his hand toward me. I didn't take it, and after a beat he let it drop.

"I'm very sorry for your loss," he said. He had a blond crew cut and the dark blue uniform.

He went to sit on Dad's recliner, and it happened in slow motion, like watching a knife sink into my stomach with no way to stop it.

"No!" I shouted.

Nobody but Dad had ever sat in that chair. It was one thing to let these people inside the house. It was another to allow them to do whatever they wanted.

He looked around and then at me, his face a mask of confusion. "What? I'm—I was just going to sit—"

"Get a chair out of the kitchen," Sheriff Bloch said.

The deputy pulled one of the aqua vinyl chairs into the TV room. His hands shook as he tried to write on his little report pad. He must have been as rattled by my outburst as I was.

"Spell your last name for me?"

"M-O-S-H-E-N," I said.

"Born here?"

"No," I said. "We're from Detroit originally."

His face scrunched and he glanced up.

"How'd you end up here? You got family in the area?"

I shook my head. I didn't tell him Dad had moved us to Saw Pole, Kansas, because he said he'd always wanted to be a farmer. In Saw Pole, he farmed a sticker patch and raised horse flies but not much else.

"How old are you?"

"Twenty-one."

He lowered his pencil. "Did you go to school in Niobe? I don't ever remember seeing you."

"Dad homeschooled me," I said.

"What time did you discover the—your dad?" The deputy's scalp grew pinker. He needed to grow his hair out some to hide his tell a little better.

"The dogs started barking about two—"

"Two A.M. or P.M.?"

"P.M.," I said. "At approximately two-fifteen P.M. our dogs began barking at the back door. I responded and found no evidence of attempted B and E at either entry point to the domicile. I retrieved my Winchester rifle from the basement gun safe with the intention of walking the perimeter of the property, but the dogs refused to follow. I came to the conclusion that the disturbance was inside the house, and I continued my investigation on the second floor."

Deputy Hencke's pencil was frozen in the air, a frown on his face. "Why are you talking like that?"

"Like what?"

"Usually I ask questions and people answer them."

"I'm telling you what happened."

"Could you do it in regular English?"

I didn't know what to say, so I didn't say anything.

"Look," he said. "Just answer the questions."

"Okay."

"All right. So where was your dad?"

"After breakfast this morning he said he didn't feel good so he went up to his bedroom to lie down," I said.

All day I'd expected Dad to call out for something to eat, but he never did. So I didn't check on him because it was nice not having to cook him lunch or dinner or fetch him beers. I'd kept craning my neck all day to get a view of the stairs, kept waiting for Dad to sneak up on me, catch me watching forbidden TV shows.

I turned the volume down so I'd hear if he came down the creaky old stairs.

"So the dogs' barking is what finally made you go up to his bedroom, huh?"

I nodded.

"Those dogs wanted to tear us all to pieces," the deputy said, swiping his hand back and forth across the top of his crew cut.

I'd always wanted a little lapdog, one I could cuddle, but Dad favored the big breeds. Sarx was a German shepherd and Tesla a rottweiler.

The deputy bent his head to his pad. "What do you think they were barking about?"

"They smelled it," I said.

He looked up. "Smelled what?"

"Death. Next I knocked on the decedent's— I mean, Dad's— bedroom door to request permission to enter."

"So you went in his room," the deputy said, his pencil hovering above the paper.

"Once I determined he was unable to answer, I went in his room. He was lying on his stomach, on top of the covers, facing away from me, and—he had shorts on . . . you know how hot it's been, and he doesn't like to turn on the window air conditioner until after Memorial Day—and I looked at his legs and I thought, 'He's got some kind of rash. I better bring him the calamine lotion,' but then I remembered learning about libidity on TV, and—"

"Lividity," he said.

"What?"

"It's lividity, not libidity, when the blood settles to the lowest part of the body."

"Guess I've never seen it written down."

"So what did you do then?"

"It was then that I . . ."

I couldn't finish the sentence. Up until now, the shock of finding Dad's body and the terror of letting people in the house had blotted out everything else. But now, the reality that Dad was dead came crashing down on me, making my eyes sting. I recognized the feeling from a long time ago. I was going to cry, and I couldn't decide whether I was sad that Dad was gone or elated that I was finally going to be free. Free to live the normal life I'd always dreamed of.

But I couldn't cry, not in front of these strangers, couldn't show weakness. Weakness was dangerous. I thought of Deirdre Walsh again and remembered what she always did when she was in danger of crying. I cleared my throat.

"It was then that I determined that he was deceased. I estimated the time of death, based on the stage of rigor, to be around ten A.M. this morning, so I did not attempt to resuscitate him," I said, remembering Dad's cool, waxy dead skin under my hand. "Subsequently I retrieved his cell phone off his nightstand and called Mr. King."

"Randy King?"

I nodded.

"Why didn't you call 911?"

"Because Dad told me to call Mr. King if something ever happened to him."

The deputy stared at me like I'd admitted to murder. Then he looked away and stood.

"I think the coroner is almost done, but he'll want to talk to you."

While I waited, I huddled on the couch, thinking about how

my life was going to change. I'd have to buy groceries and pay bills and taxes and do all the things Dad had never taught me how to do.

The coroner appeared in the doorway. "Miss Moshen?" He was a large zero-shaped man in a cardigan.

"Yes?"

He sat on the kitchen chair the deputy had vacated.

"I need to ask you a couple of questions," he said.

"Okay," I said. I was wary. The deputy had been slight and small, and even though he'd had a sidearm, I could have taken him if I'd needed to. I didn't know about the coroner, he was so heavy and large.

"Can you tell me what happened?"

I began to repeat my account, but the coroner interrupted me. "You're not testifying at trial," he said. "Just tell me what happened."

I tried to do as he asked, but I wasn't sure how to say it so he wouldn't be annoyed.

"Did your dad complain of chest pains, jaw pain? Did his left arm hurt?"

I shook my head. "Just said he didn't feel good. Like he had the flu."

"Did your dad have high cholesterol? High blood pressure?"

"I don't know."

"When was the last time he saw a doctor?" the coroner asked.

"He didn't believe in doctors."

"Your dad was only fifty-one, so I'll have to schedule an autopsy, even though it was probably a heart attack. We'll run a toxicology panel, which'll take about four weeks because we have to send it to the lab in Topeka."

The blood drained from my face. "Toxicology?" I said. "Why?"

"It's standard procedure," he said.

"I'm pretty sure my dad wouldn't want an autopsy."

"Don't worry," he said. "You can bury him before the panel comes back."

"No, I mean Dad wouldn't want someone cutting him up like that."

"It's state law."

"Please," I said.

His eyes narrowed as they focused on me. Then he stood.

"After the autopsy, where would you like the remains sent?"

"Holt Mortuary in Niobe," a voice from the living room said.

I rose from the couch to see who'd said it. Randy King stood with his back to the wall, his Stetson low over his eyes.

The coroner glanced at me for confirmation.

"I'm the executor of Mr. Moshen's will," Randy said. He raised his head and I saw his eyes, light blue with tiny pupils that seemed to bore clear through to the back of my head.

I shrugged at the coroner.

"Would you like to say goodbye to your father before we transport him to the morgue?" he said.

I nodded and followed him to the stairs, where he stood aside. "After you," he said.

"No," I said. "You first."

Dad had taught me never to go in a door first and never to let anyone walk behind me. The coroner frowned but mounted the stairs.

Upstairs, Dad's room was the first one on the left. The coroner stood outside the door. He reached out to touch my arm and I took a step backward. He dropped his hand to his side.

"Miss Moshen," he said in a hushed voice. "Your father looks different from when he was alive. It might be a bit of a shock. No one would blame you if you didn't—"

I walked into Dad's room, taking with me everything I knew from all the cop shows I'd watched. But I was not prepared at all for what I saw.

Since he'd died on his stomach, the EMTs had turned Dad onto his back. He was in full rigor mortis, so his upper lip was mashed into his gums and curled into a sneer, exposing his khaki-colored teeth. His hands were spread in front of his face, palms out. Dad's eyes stared up and to the left and his entire face was grape-pop purple.

What struck me when I first saw him—after I inhaled my gum—was that he appeared to be warding off a demon. I should have waited until the mortician was done with him, because I knew I'd never get that image out of my mind.

I walked out of Dad's room on unsteady feet, determined not to cry in front of these strangers. The deputy and the sheriff stood outside my bedroom, examining the door to it. Both of them looked confused.

"Petty," Sheriff Bloch said.

I stopped in the hall, feeling even more violated with them so close to my personal items and underwear.

"Yes?"

"Is this your bedroom?"

I nodded.

Sheriff and deputy made eye contact. The coroner paused at the top of the stairs to listen in. This was what my dad had always talked about—the judgment of busybody outsiders, their belief that somehow they needed to have a say in the lives of people they'd never even met and knew nothing about.

The three men seemed to expect me to say something, but I was tired of talking. Since I'd never done much of it, I'd had no idea how exhausting it was.

The deputy said, "Why are there six dead bolts on the outside of your door?"

It was none of his business, but I had nothing to be ashamed of.

"So Dad could lock me in, of course."

Chapter 2

THE MEN ALL exchanged glances again.

"As . . . punishment?" the sheriff said.

I sighed, weary. "For my protection."

"When did your father lock you in your room?"

"Every night since I was three," I said, and went downstairs.

While the men in Dad's room finished up, I gazed between the steel bars welded over one of the west-facing living room windows and watched dusk settle over the greening Kansas landscape. On a clear, early spring day like this the horizon seemed thirty or more miles away, nothing between me and it but cloudless sky and rolling prairie, patches of foxtail millet, goosegrass, yellow fawn lilies and blue phlox, black and brown beef cattle, and our family of five tall, sprawling oak trees, which were starting to sprout leaves.

I learned early not to praise the beauty I saw around me. Dad liked to show me how the pretty surface of things in this world always hid ugliness. For instance, the Star of Bethlehem flowers that grow like crazy by the side of the road are poisonous. And those oak trees. In the summertime they're robed in hundreds of succulent, transparent-green leaves that clap politely in the breezes like spectators at a golf match. In the fall they turn Creamsicle orange with brilliant red edges. But when the bitter winter winds strip the leaves away, you see what the trees are really made of: sinister, granite-hard bark, angry-looking and full of vengeance for having to endure the deranged Kansas weather, those extremes of heat, cold, and humidity, the relentless wind, the sleet, the lightning.

Out here in northwest Niobe County, there's little that dares stand in weather's way, to talk it down off the ledge of its rage—no trees except the five brave oaks, no other buildings. The nearest town, the one our junk mail comes to, is called Saw Pole and is fifteen miles away. Weather has peeled the paint from our house, the only one for thirteen miles in every direction, leaving the wood siding bleached gray, the color of bird crap. Memory snapshots from when I was three tell me the house was butter yellow at the time we moved here from Detroit. Now, you can still see fragments of color, remnants of someone else's life, someone who raised flowers and watered a lawn and planted crops.

Watching out that window occupied me until the crowd began to thin—first the firemen departed, then the paramedics, the police, and finally the coroner and his minions pushing Dad's black-bagged body out on a gurney. Randy King was the last one there, still standing against the wall in the living room. Something about him, that pose, made me think of Curly in *Of Mice and Men.*

"If you want to go up and pick out a suit for your daddy to be buried in, I'll take it on over to the mortuary," he said from under the hat. I was glad I didn't have to look at those pinprick pupils of his.

I went up the stairs and stopped in front of Dad's bedroom door. It was as if there was electric fencing keeping me from going in, powered by my dad's glare. But I didn't have time to psych myself up. The sooner I got the clothes, the sooner I could get this last person out of the house, and the closer I would be to having the house to myself, doing whatever I wanted, for the first time ever.

I'd never been in Dad's closet, of course. I pulled on the string attached to the ceiling bulb but nothing happened. The light probably hadn't worked for years. Out in his room was a large flashlight. I switched it on and headed back into the closet. The wide beam threw light on several pairs of faded jeans, a lot of camo wear, and a few collared shirts.

These had belonged to the only other person I'd ever really known, and suddenly I was terrified. The flashlight slid from my grip as a scream built in my chest. I covered my mouth with both hands to prevent it from escaping and stumbled forward into his clothes, which caught me with empty arms. I sank to the floor crying silent tears. Bottomless grief threatened to smother me. On my knees, I pressed the fabric to my face and inhaled, the faint scent bringing back Dad almost in full form and life. But he was gone, and I was alone.

Then I heard careful footsteps climbing stairs. From the hollowness of the sound, I knew someone was coming up from the basement. The steps were hesitant, and I realized the person was trying not to make any noise. I froze, listening. The feet were now on the main floor, walking toward the front door. I catwalked to the top of the stairs and saw Randy King holding a large cardboard box with the letters M R written on it in black Magic Marker. On top of that was Dad's laptop with its L-shaped dent.

But what was in the box? And where was Randy taking it and the laptop?

I tiptoed back into Dad's room and watched out the window as Randy carried the box and computer to his truck. He put them in the front seat and headed back toward the house.

Once back inside, he called, "Petty? You all right up there?"

I heard booted feet—decisive and confident this time—mount the stairs. I ran into the closet and pulled out Dad's three-piece suit. No way would I be trapped in a bedroom with this guy, who'd come into my house and removed things without my permission, who seemed to believe that he belonged here. He didn't. I didn't know him at all, but his presence, which felt like a sickness, seemed to take up a lot more space than it should have. I got out of the room as Randy was about to enter it and thrust the clothes at him. He took them wordlessly, turned and started down the stairs.

"You don't need to worry about funeral arrangements," he said. "Your dad left instructions with me."

Worrying about funeral arrangements hadn't occurred to me, but I nodded at the back of his descending head. At the bottom of the stairs, Randy turned and slid his hat back on. "You gonna be all right? You want me to stay with you tonight?"

I was so shocked by the question I couldn't respond. I just stared dumbly.

He shook his head and smiled a little. "Suit yourself," he said, and walked out the front door. Through the screen I heard him say, "Sorry for your loss."

Once I heard the truck start up, I went down to the living room and watched out the front window as he drove away.

And then it hit me.

I had no one to lock me in my room. Why hadn't I thought to ask one of them to lock me in? They probably wouldn't have. But how would I sleep?

Dad had left instructions for Randy King. Why hadn't he left any for me? I was the one who needed them.

One of the dogs gave a sharp yip from the garage. I'd forgotten all about them, and they probably needed to go outside and do their business. I was grateful for something to do.

Out in the garage, I raised the door and they ran for it, making a fast trotting check of the perimeter of the property. Dad had taught them to do that before they did anything else. After their tour, they relieved themselves and sat panting in front of me, waiting for orders or to be released to patrol.

I gave the hand signal to heel and walked into the garage with them following, lowered the door and locked it. Then I opened the door from the garage into the house, and they alternately studied each other and me, trying to understand what I wanted. I signaled for them to follow me into the house. Dad wouldn't like it, but he wasn't here. If I couldn't be locked in my room, this was the next best thing.

They danced uncertainly at the threshold, remembering well what Dad had taught them about going in the house, which was not to do it unless a stranger was attacking me or him. I dropped to a squat and scratched their ears.

"You're going to come in the house," I told them. "It's okay. I'm the alpha now." I walked through the door, turned and faced them, and signaled "come." They danced and whined.

"Come," I said.

It took five tries, but they finally tiptoed into the house, glancing at each other guiltily. I hoped this wouldn't ruin their training. I signaled for them to follow me into the TV room. They did, and sat. I released them, hoping they'd explore the house and get used to the idea of being inside. After a while they ventured out of the room, Sarx going left, Tesla right, like they'd been trained to do.

I sat on the couch and picked up the remote. Every sound was amplified—the dogs' panting, the prairie wind outside, my gurgling stomach—which made me want to crawl out of my own skin. I turned on the TV and surfed until I found an *Offender NYC* marathon. The dogs returned, then stood and stared at me, waiting for a command.

"Lie down," I said. They did.

THE NEXT THING I knew I was drowning in the bathtub.

I wanted to breathe, but I couldn't because I was underwater, on my back staring at the misshapen, shifting bathroom ceiling. I tried to break the surface, but it was as if I was chained to the bottom.

But I wasn't chained. I didn't see it before, but someone was holding me underwater. I couldn't quite make out the face, but I knew it was a man and he was pushing down on me with huge hands, trying to make me inhale. Talking to me, saying something I couldn't quite make out from beneath the water. The bridge of my nose burned and everything went gray, so I knew I wouldn't be conscious for much longer. Death was coming for me.

I'VE HAD THIS recurring dream for as long as I can remember. It made sense I'd dream it the night my dad died. I always wake up from it gasping for air, like I've actually been held underwater. As I surface from sleep, I can feel the heavy water sliding off me, down the hollows of my face. My eyes sting and my lungs can't expand enough to take in the oxygen I need, although I'm in no true danger. It was only a dream. But even as the nightmare fades, the irresistible force of the dream tugs on my every cell, dragging me downward into a spiral that will never end, circling the drain for all eternity.

Drowning. This is my biggest fear. You'd think it would be fire, since that's what killed my mom when I was three. But it's water. I can't take baths, only showers. I can't even stopper the kitchen sink and fill it, because I feel that weight bearing down on me, pushing my face toward the water, an irresistible compulsion to submerge my head.

The TV was still on when I woke up. Deirdre was questioning a suspect in the dingy interview room at Precinct 51 in New York City.

Stiff didn't even begin to describe how my body felt. I stretched and then led the dogs through the kitchen and out the back door. According to the oven clock, it was after nine A.M. I needed to get ready for work.

Since I'd slept in my clothes, all I needed to do was get my stuff together. I used the bathroom, washed my face and combed my hair. Then I made my lunch, put Dad's iPhone in my pocket and strapped the shotgun across my back. After locking up the house, I walked the quarter mile to the Niobe County dump.

Inside my little guard shack where I took five dollars from people to dump stuff, I kept a photograph album someone had dumped a couple of years before.

The photos I liked best were of the kids in snow forts and at backyard barbecues and Little League baseball games. None of the pictures were labeled, so I named the kids myself. There was

Justin, the oldest, and the middle sister Madison, and the youngest boy Aidan.

Since I never got to see many little kids or babies out at the dump, I loved to study the faces of those three little blond kids squinting at the camera, holding up fish they just caught or riding a tire swing with sprinklers running in the background.

Dad never knew about my album, which I paged through nearly every workday. I had every image memorized so I could close my eyes and tell myself the story of that family without even looking.

Why would someone throw away a photo album? I'd have given anything to have pictures of me as a baby, to have even one photo of my mother. All that stuff burned up with her in Detroit.

As I sat on my stool in the booth that morning, looking out over the mountain range of trash, it dawned on me that I could take the photo album back to the house now. I could go somewhere besides my house and the dump if I could get someone to teach me to drive. Maybe I'd go into Saw Pole and eat at the diner and then visit the stores. Maybe I'd go to Salina. Maybe I'd go to New York.

Now that Dad was gone, I could do anything I wanted.

Chapter 3

Thursday

DEKKER

I ANSWERED THE phone before I was totally awake.

"Dekker?"

"Yeah," I said, rubbing my eyes.

"You know I wouldn't be calling you if it wasn't absolutely necessary."

I sat up. "Chad?" I must still have been asleep, because there was no way the lead singer from my ex-band would be calling me, not after how things had ended five months ago.

"Here's the deal. We're going to give you one last chance, and we wouldn't do it if we weren't absolutely desperate. I want you to acknowledge that."

"Okay," I said, cautious. I lit a cigarette. Oma would be pissed, but these were special circumstances. No way I could take this call without tar and nicotine.

"Tell me you acknowledge what I said."

"Okay," I said, trying to keep the eye roll out of my voice. "I acknowledge."

"Acknowledge what?"

"That you wouldn't be calling if you weren't desperate. Right. Go on. What were you saying about a second chance?"

Chad snorted. "We're way past second. I don't think I can count high enough to figure out how many chances we've given you. This is your *last* chance. I want you to acknowledge that I've told—"

"All right, all right, I get it. Just get on with it, will you?"

Chad's voice changed, excitement leaking through the cracks of his hardline pose. "Disregard the 9 is going to open for Autopsyturvy at the Uptown in Kansas City eleven days from today on Monday the twenty-seventh."

I stopped breathing. Was this a dream?

"Hello?" Chad said.

"I'm here," I said. "I'm just not sure I heard you right."

"You heard me. See, our new, better, more dependable drummer who doesn't steal shit from bandmates broke his wrist skiing, and we don't have time to teach the whole set to some new guy."

New. Better. More dependable. Doesn't steal shit. Each descriptor hit me like a two-by-four with a rusty nail in it. Especially since it was all true.

"So it's up to you," Chad continued. "This is your very last chance. Ever. This is it. You either get it together and get up to Kansas City eight days from today for rehearsals, or that's it. We're done."

"I'll be there," I said.

Chad clicked off.

This changed everything.

Because just four months before, the administration at Kansas State University had strenuously encouraged me to leave and never come back after just one semester on campus. Good thing my dad had taken off when I was in elementary school, or I'd never have heard the end of it, though the old man was a high school dropout himself. Here I'd spent three years commuting to Brown Mackie College in Salina so I could transfer to K-State for junior and senior year, and I'd blown it. I'd been delivering groceries to pay for tuition for five long years, and until thirty seconds ago I'd thought delivery boy would be my permanent vocation.

But suddenly I was the drummer for Disregard the 9 again. Good thing I hadn't sold my drum kit after all. But I needed to set it up in the shed and get practicing. I lay back, set my shitty flip phone down, and smoked with my eyes closed, glad to be alive for the first time in months.

The door banged open and my grandma Oma cycloned into the room.

I opened one eye just as she snatched the cigarette from between my lips. She dropped it into a soda can and threw the whole mess into my wastebasket.

"*Aus dem Bett holen,*" she said, dashing aside the heavy curtains to reveal the anemic spring sunshine.

"*Nein,*" I said.

"*Ja.* We've got somewhere to go." She slapped my blanket-covered butt. I was still a six-year-old to her, and ever would be. My face flared.

"I've asked you not to do that," I said, rolling away from her. "It's weird."

"What, waking you up at two o'clock in the afternoon? I told you. If you're not going to go back to college, if you're going to live here, you're going to live by my rules. Which doesn't include sleeping the *verflucht* day away."

She didn't know the details of my departure from K-State. She assumed I'd dropped out, and I let her.

"It's my day off," I said, stretching. "I was up late last night. And anyway, I just got some amazing news. I'm going to—"

Oma yanked the sheets up, threatening to make the bed with me in it, and I knew she'd do it. Her massive, floppy upper arms swayed as she extracted the pillow from under my head.

"Don't be a *Waschlappen*," she said. "I need you to go with me."

She would not be interested in my good news. She would be unimpressed, so I didn't bother telling her. I sat up and dropped my feet to the floor, scratching my head with both hands.

"We've got to get that washing machine out to the dump by four o'clock."

"You mean the one that's sat in your backyard since the Ford administration?" I stood and pulled on the jeans and Gangsta-grass T-shirt I'd left on the floor the night before.

She didn't answer, just continued to bustle about the room.

"Okay," I said. "I'll bite. Why do we have to get the washing machine to the dump by four o'clock?"

Oma turned to me with a delighted smile on her face beneath the gray Berber carpet of her permed hair. "Charlie Moshen passed yesterday."

"And this makes you happy because . . ."

She moved to slap my scalp but I ducked her.

"I made his girl a ham and spaetzle casserole and a Jell-O salad. We need to take them to the dump."

She needed to say no more. I knew, like everyone else in Niobe County, you didn't drop by the Moshen place unless you wanted to be plugged full of buckshot or shredded by their legendary attack dogs. Rumor had it their property was booby-trapped with punji sticks and trip wires.

"Can I eat something first?" I said.

"Hurry."

I used the toilet, then headed into the kitchen and poured myself a bowl of Lucky Charms. Oma put her casserole and salad into a grocery bag and stood by the counter, waiting.

"I hate it when you stand and watch me eat. For God's sake, Oma, would you sit down?"

She didn't, of course, so I ignored her. When I was finished, I put my bowl and spoon in the sink.

"Would it be that hard to put them in the dishwasher?" Oma said.

I sighed and rolled my eyes. "I never know if the stuff in there is clean or dirty."

"I'll let you in on the secret: if there's food on the dishes, they're dirty."

I went into the bathroom and ran a comb through my hair, washed my face and brushed my teeth.

I'd need to figure out what I was going to wear for the gig. Go back to torn jeans and a profane T-shirt, or maybe a skinny tie and suspenders? I wished I'd thought to ask Chad.

As I followed Oma out the door to my yellow Toyota pickup truck, my thoughts turned toward the girl I'd heard about but never actually met or even seen. I knew from talking to people at K-State that every community has a weird family. The Moshens do the job not just for Saw Pole but the whole of Niobe County. They're the Satan worshipers. The cannibal family. The Radleys. Take your pick. It's all bullshit. Probably.

Charlie did odd jobs around the county but mostly kept to himself. He wore his shoulder-length graying hair back in a ponytail, and his face displayed the furrows and grooves usually seen on men decades older. His blue eyes were deep-set and haunted, and when I was little, if I saw Charlie Moshen on the street in Saw Pole, I'd cross to the other side.

Everyone spread rumors about the Moshens. Charlie was a white supremacist, a fundamentalist, a separatist. He had a concrete bunker beneath the house, he hunted humans for sport, and worse things than that.

Mostly, I felt sorry for the girl—stuck in Saw Pole, no friends, no contact at all with the outside world.

I went around to the backyard to grapple with the washing machine. I secured it in the truck bed with bungee cords, then we headed toward the county dump.

Driving the dirt road out there, my nerves got the better of me and I lit up a Camel. Oma waved a hand through the air and wrinkled her nose but said nothing. She turned the radio to KYEZ, one of Salina's country stations, and sang the whole way. I was glad for the irritation because it canceled out my case of jitters, right up until I caught sight of the little guard shack to the left of the dump's entrance. Petty Moshen was in there, along with her guns and knives.

As I slowed the truck, I watched a hand appear, palm up, from the shack window. When I pulled up to it, I saw the hand was attached to a sinewy and finely muscled arm with a gnarly scar from elbow to wrist. Then I saw her profile. She was reading a book and didn't bother to look at us or my vehicle. I sat gawking at her, this legend, this rumor, this cautionary tale. It was kind of like seeing the Aurora Borealis. You couldn't stop staring, even if you wanted to. Which I didn't. Because one of the things never mentioned in the wealth of information and rumors and stories that had circulated for years was that this girl was beautiful.

She was one of those girls you couldn't look directly at for fear of burning your retinas. You needed one of those cards used to view a solar eclipse with a hole poked through it.

Petty's neck was long and slender, and her caramel-colored hair hung carelessly to her shoulders. Her eyes were large and round and sparkling hazel, surrounded by more eyelashes than I had ever seen on a person, and I briefly wondered if she was wearing false eyelashes, then realized how ridiculous that was. When she licked her full lips, I saw a hint of dimples, which would deepen if she ever smiled.

I stared so long her head rotated toward me, shriveling my guts. I gulped.

"Five dollars," she said, looking just to the right of my face.

"Hi," I said, my mouth suddenly dry. "You're Petty Moshen, right?"

"Of course she is," said Oma, annoyed. She leaned forward and talked around me. "I'm Lena Sachs, and this here's my college-dropout grandson Dekker."

I turned to glare at her.

"Oh," Petty said. "That'll be five dollars."

"Hon," Oma said, "we were so sorry to hear about your daddy."

"Okay," Petty said, deadpan.

Okay? The correct response to this platitude was of course "Thanks," but clearly Petty hadn't been schooled in the small-town small talk like the rest of us. Which I found both exotic and slightly titillating.

Oma chattered on at my side. "We brought you a casserole and some Jell-O. Normally I'd bring it to your house, but I wasn't sure . . . what I mean is . . . I didn't know if . . ." She trailed off, waiting for this backward girl to finish a sentence she'd have no idea how to finish.

" . . . I like casseroles?" Petty said.

I couldn't help laughing.

"I never knew you were funny, hon," Oma said.

I now felt Oma and me were the inappropriate ones. This girl's dad died less than twenty-four hours ago, and here we were giggling at her social awkwardness, or so it seemed to me. I cleared my throat.

"Sorry for your loss," I said to her.

Oma nudged me. I turned as she handed me the grocery bag with the food. I passed it through the window to Petty.

"Heat that casserole on three fifty for thirty minutes or so," Oma said. "And put the Jell-O in the fridge soon's you get home, all right?"

Petty took the bag and disappeared as she set it on the floor, reminding me of the tollbooth scene in *The Godfather* where Sonny gets machine-gunned in spectacular fashion. But unlike the movie tollbooth attendant, Petty reappeared and no gunfire erupted.

A moment went by where the only sound was the idling of the old pickup's engine.

"You gonna dump that washing machine," Petty said, "I need five dollars."

I had momentarily forgotten why we'd come.

"Right," I said. I stretched out my legs and dug in my pants pocket, pulled out a folded bill and handed it to Petty. "There you go."

"Just pull on through."

"Thank you," I said.

Oma leaned forward again and said, "You let us know if we can do anything, Petty."

Her eyebrows came together. "Anything?"

"Right?" I blurted. "Everybody says that when someone passes away. 'Let me know if I can do anything.' Sure."

Petty's direct, demanding gaze and no-nonsense responses threw me into a mini-panic, and I couldn't seem to stop talking.

"Because the only thing you want is for that person not to be dead. 'Can you do anything about that? No? Okay, how about you give me some of your IQ points, because you obviously have way more than you need.'"

Oma slapped me in the head, effectively silencing me. I was almost grateful. Almost.

"*Lass den Quatsch,*" Oma said. "Petty doesn't need any of your lip." Then Oma addressed Petty: "He's a real smartass sometimes."

I rubbed my head.

"Sorry," I said, my embarrassment so intense it took near physical form, like a parasitic twin growing out of my side. "I really am sorry about your dad."

"Okay," Petty said, turning back to her book. "You can pull on through."

When we were out of earshot, Oma said, "What the hell is wrong with you?"

"I was trying to treat her like she was anybody else," I said. "And is there any way I can talk you out of smacking me around in front of other people?"

Oma made a sound like *Psh*.

Chapter 4

PETTY

I SAT WITH my eyes on my book, but I wasn't reading. I was watching Dekker Sachs and his grandma wrestle the washing machine out of the bed of their yellow Toyota pickup from my peripheral vision so they wouldn't know I was observing them.

The sniping between them seemed like an act, like the banter in a sitcom. I allowed myself a silly daydream, of being around other people like this, of talking and laughing with them. Maybe this daydream was on the verge of coming true.

After they drove away, thinking of the Sachses' easy conversation—nothing like the two-word communications between my dad and me—filled me with an unfamiliar but not unpleasant feeling. It was an expansion, pushing up through my chest and warming my face, making me want to smile. In fact I caught myself smiling, staring at nothing as a red Dodge Ram pickup pulled up next to the booth.

This made me jump off my stool. I was so deep in thought about the conversation with Dekker and the old lady, I hadn't heard Randy coming. I had violated the first OODA Loop rule: Observe. Dad and

I had drilled on this endlessly. When I was eight or nine, he'd started leaving me alone in public places to help me learn to be vigilant and ready to act. The first time, he didn't warn me beforehand. We were at Fort Hays, and he vanished from sight. I was scared at first, but then I found a place to get my back against a wall. As soon as I did that, he reappeared and explained to me that I'd done the right thing.

OODA Loop: Observe, Orient, Decide, Act. Dad had taught me to always be alert. Always be in a defensive position. Always be cataloging your options. Always be ready and willing to act. If you blow any one of the rules, you've blown them all. And I'd blown them big-time just then.

I swept thoughts of the Sachses out of my head and focused.

From my observation of Randy the previous day, I knew he didn't carry a handgun, but wore a sheathed hunting knife clipped to his belt. I'd have no trouble blasting his head off if he decided to attack me. I slung the shotgun over my shoulder.

Randy cleared his throat through the truck's open window. "I got everything all arranged."

I didn't respond.

He waited a beat before he said, "Did you want to hear about it?"

"About what?"

"We'll have the funeral at the mortuary in Niobe tomorrow at two." He paused to see if I'd have any reaction. When I didn't say anything, he went on. "Nothing fancy, short and sweet. Everything's already paid for. It'll be a closed-casket service, but after the service you'll have a chance to say goodbye."

I didn't say anything.

"I'll pick you up tomorrow at one," he said.

That meant I'd have to ride in a vehicle with this guy, which was against Dad's rules.

"I'll ride my bike," I said, though I'd never actually ridden it out of sight of my dad.

"It's twenty miles to Niobe," Randy said.

"That's all right," I said.

"Your dad wouldn't like that," he said, tipping his head back so I could see his eyes.

"Dad's dead."

He lowered his head again. "You ever use that shotgun?"

"I know how to," I said.

"Of course you do," he said. "I mean, have you ever *had* to use it?"

"Only had to show it," I said.

That dumb mustache twitched. "Your dad trained you good, didn't he?"

I shrugged.

"Your dad asked me to see after you, and I aim to do it. I'm the one he told you to call, so you know you can trust me because your dad did. So I'm going to pick you up for the funeral at one tomorrow. And then after that, I'll drive you to your dad's will reading in town."

Maybe I just wasn't used to talking to other people, but Randy seemed really pushy to me. He didn't ask me, he told me what he was going to do, and it raised my hackles. But twenty miles was too far to bike, and how else would I get to the funeral? My desire to make my own decisions almost made me want to skip the funeral altogether, but I'd go. This would be the last time anyone told me what to do, because I was going to learn to drive. Thinking of that made me feel a little better. I nodded at Randy.

"Good girl. I'll see you tomorrow at one." He revved the Ram, backed up in an arc, then put it in first and drove off down the dirt road. Once he was out of sight, I put the zippered cash bag in the lockbox for my boss to pick up, locked the shack, and walked home.

I didn't know why we had to have a funeral. Who would come? Dad didn't have any friends. For the last two years he hadn't gone anywhere or done anything but sit in front of the TV.

Another, more terrifying thought struck me. What if people showed up? The funerals I'd seen on TV shows were always crowded and stuffy. The thought of being in a place with strangers surrounding me on all sides made my stomach flip. I didn't know if I could do it, although I'd fantasized about leading a normal life since I was old enough to realize I didn't have one.

On TV shows the bereaved always have to shake hands with visitors and even hug some of them. After everything my dad had taught me, how was I supposed to be in an unfamiliar place surrounded by strangers without wondering if they wanted to kill me or rape me? Women didn't bother me too much; when I was little, Dad had said in the event of an emergency to find a woman with small children and ask her for help. But of course, he said, there were plenty of women who'd helped their men kidnap girls like Elizabeth Smart and Jaycee Dugard and the girl who was in a box under some psycho couple's bed for seven years.

Back at home, I had to coax the dogs inside again, but it didn't take as long as it had the previous day. I switched on the TV and went upstairs to my bedroom. Mine was the master bedroom of the house since it had its own bathroom. Dad had given it to me so he wouldn't have to get up in the middle the night to let me out to use the toilet. I reached under my mattress and pulled out a spiral notebook I hadn't cracked open in quite a few years, but it had a list in it I wanted to read. I carried the notebook downstairs and sat at the kitchen table.

I paged to the list and read it out loud. Now that Dad was gone, I wasn't afraid he'd find out. I could say things out loud that I never dared to when he was alive. The dogs sat next to my chair and listened, cocking their heads every now and then.

"What I would do if I had a normal life," I said. "One. Move away from Saw Pole. Two. Learn to drive. Three. Go to college. Four. Eat in restaurants. Five. Have friends. Six. Go to a movie in a theater."

I pictured these things, savored them in my mind, and for the first time almost believed they could happen. The thrill of this thought shot me through with adrenaline, which made me want to run down the road past our house—my house, now—but I wasn't quite ready for that. I read on instead, anticipation and excitement making my voice sound higher.

The next item on my list made my face hot just seeing it, but I soldiered on. "Seven. Fall in love. Eight. Go to New York City." Number eight also embarrassed me, because I knew Detective Deirdre Walsh and the 51st Precinct weren't real. But I wanted to go to the place where I'd spent much of my life on TV.

"Nine. Eat junk food." I took a big breath and let it out. "Ten. Learn to be normal."

Chapter 5

Friday

PETTY

ON THE FIFTEEN-MILE drive to Saw Pole after the funeral, I kept my eyes down or aimed at the window because I didn't want Randy to think I was interested in conversation. I was feeling as charged as a frayed electrical wire, edgy and nervous. I scratched at the bump on my left shoulder and couldn't stop thinking about Dad being lowered into the ground and dirt thrown on top of his coffin.

Randy spat tobacco juice into a brushed-metal container at regular intervals. The sloppy sound of it, the moist *ptoo*, unraveled my nerves further. After another endless night in the dark, empty house, during which the dogs had started at every little noise, and the strain of the funeral and now the will reading, I imagined opening my mouth and screaming until I passed out.

The Dodge came to a stop in front of a limestone building on the corner that housed Mr. Keith Dooley's law office. Saw Pole's main street was soupy with mud because the town didn't have the money for asphalt. Dad told me that back during its heyday the town had paved streets. But when family farms went into foreclosure and the oil wells dried up, so had town funds. The streets were never repaved.

I saw a few other cars parked on Main Street, which is a slow-down point on the two-lane state highway that cuts through town. There are signs pointing every direction, but it's as if an invisible electric fence encircles the town, and the only way out is to die. There's a little post office, a grocery store, the Farmers National Bank, a beauty parlor called Clips and Curls for Guys and Girls, and a restaurant with the name The Cozy Corner Café. I'd never been inside of any of these businesses, only seen them through car windows. To me they were just facades on the set of a not-very-interesting small-town soap opera.

Randy switched off the truck, but I needed to sit for a moment to psych myself up to get out. So I did what I normally did when I was afraid, and that was to recite the opening to *Offender NYC*, which is actually the title on a black screen with several voices saying the NYCPD's oath: "I do solemnly swear to uphold the Constitution of the United States and the Constitution of the State of New York, and that I will faithfully discharge my duties as a police officer with the New York City Police Department to the best of my ability, so help me God."

I recited very quietly with my face to the window, but Randy heard me.

"Are you praying or something?" he asked me.

I didn't answer, but got out of the truck and strode toward the office building, with Randy jogging to catch up. I knew the only way I'd get through the will reading would be to pretend Deirdre was at my elbow, my personal bodyguard, along with Detective Mandy Quirke, as if we'd just attended Captain Barrigan's funeral after he was killed in the first episode of season nine.

I opened the door and Randy tried to take it from me, tried to get me to go in first. But I held on until he got the hint to go on in, which he did with a sigh. I followed and located all the exits. OODA Loop activated. Two doors, one front, one back. Six windows. A staircase. The outer room had a conference table with six chairs. The actual office was at the back of the building, thirty feet from where I stood. Although I sensed no physical threat, something tripped my inner alarm. Was it because I was so overtired and overemotional? Or was it something else?

One of the men I'd seen at the funeral stood up from a desk in that inner office. His face had skin the texture of oatmeal and he wore a powder-blue suit. His squarish wire-rimmed glasses accentuated the rectangular shape of his large forehead. The glasses kept sliding down his nose, so the tops of the frames bisected his colorless eyes and he had to tip his head back to look at me.

"Hello, Petty," he said. "I don't know if you remember me or not. I'm Keith Dooley. I met you when you were not but yay high." He held his hand palm down at hip level.

I had no recollection of him before the funeral, but he'd obviously known the younger me. Hearing him describe what I didn't remember made me feel like a ghost, watching events and people from an alternate lifetime that never happened to me. He waited for me to respond, but I didn't.

"We'll be watching the video out there," Mr. Dooley said. "Let me grab a few things."

Video? What kind of video would we be watching? Randy sat

down at the conference table, but I remained standing, taking in the lawyer's outer office. It was dim and musty. Through the door to the inner office, I saw that Mr. Dooley's desk was U-shaped and mounded with bulging file folders, documents, and different colored papers spilling out. How could he find anything in there?

Mr. Dooley rolled a metal cart out of his office. On top of it were a TV and a VCR. He positioned the cart at one end of the table, plugged the machines' electrical cords into a wall outlet and switched them both on.

"We all ready?" Mr. Dooley said. He held up a VHS tape for us to see before sliding it into the top-loading VCR.

The tape rolled, and the image shimmied and dipped. The picture stopped bucking, and Dad came into the frame and sat in his recliner in front of the camera. I inhaled sharply, stunned by a sudden rush of emotion, seeing him. I was so glad at that moment he'd taught me how to not cry.

Obviously he'd been setting the video camera on a tripod but couldn't get it into the position he wanted it in and then gave up. Consequently, we only occasionally saw his mouth. Mostly we saw the top third of his face.

"Petty," my dad said, "this is your dad." He cleared his throat. "Today is your eighteenth birthday, and I'm making this video will. I've also typed it up and had it notarized."

Mr. Dooley held up a file folder, and I took that to mean the written will was inside it.

"I know you realize I'm not going to be around forever to take care of you. I've tried my best to keep you safe all your life. I've taught you everything I know. And I've done my best to be a good father. I know I didn't always succeed but I didn't have your mom around to help me out."

I found myself sitting up straighter, trying to see the bottom half of his face.

"I know you got tired of me telling you that we live in an extremely dangerous world. In Saw Pole, you're about as safe as you can be on this earth, and I want to make sure you stay here. That's why I bought a million-dollar life insurance policy today."

It took me a moment to realize he was speaking literally. My jaw sagged.

A million dollars?

"You're the sole beneficiary, Petty, but there are conditions. And you know I'm only doing this because it's for your own good."

Randy sat straighter in his chair and gave me a sideways glance.

"In order to get the money, Petty, you're going to have to marry Randy King—if he's alive and still single."

He said it casually, as if telling me I needed to remember to feed the dogs. My head jerked, almost involuntarily, toward Randy. He stared back at me, emotionless. It was clear he'd already known what was coming and hadn't said a word about it. Nausea dribbled into my stomach.

"And if he's not, you'll have to join the Dominican Sisters order in Bison, Kansas, and live and serve with them for twenty years after my death . . ."

I lunged forward and hit the pause button. Then I looked from Randy to Mr. Dooley and opened my mouth. A loud sound like the bleating of a wounded sheep came out, and I couldn't stop for quite a while.

It was the sound of all my treasured hopes and dreams disappearing down the drain.

This was worse than drowning. Worse than having no mother.

Worse than living with a silent crazy father. I wouldn't be free after all. I wouldn't have the normal life I'd planned.

The silence that followed was broken only by the sounds of both men's ragged breathing. Randy held his hands over his ears.

"What the hell was that?" he said.

"Now now," Mr. Dooley said.

Marry Randy King? I'd never even been alone with a man other than my father until two days before. Never been kissed. Marriage meant sex, and my dad had talked endlessly about rape and how to avoid it. And now he had sold me out for a lifetime of it.

I had to think. Was it possible to just refuse the money? If I did, I would no longer have anywhere to live. I couldn't drive. I had no skills, no friends, no family. Where would I go? What would I do?

How could Dad do this to me? How?

"I'm not . . ." I said. "I'm not . . ."

"Do you need some water?" Mr. Dooley asked.

"I do solemnly swear," I shouted suddenly, "to uphold the Constitution of the United States!"

I only got to the second line before Randy let loose an ear-splitting whistle and I stopped talking.

"Are you crazy?" he said to me.

I closed my eyes and whispered the rest of the oath to myself.

"Let's everybody take it easy," Mr. Dooley said. "I know this is a shock, Petty. You've been through a lot in the last few days. But let's go ahead and see what else your dad had to say. All right?"

I couldn't answer.

Mr. Dooley stood cracking his knuckles, watching me. He glanced at his watch and cleared his throat. "Petty, I have a four o'clock appointment. Is it okay if we go on with the tape?" He hit play on the VCR.

"I know this is unexpected," Dad said. "It might feel unfair to you, but I have devoted my life to protecting you." Dad pressed his lips together and he couldn't go on for a moment. "So I'm doing the only thing I can think of to continue protecting you after my death. Randy's a good man and he'll keep you safe. You can trust him. He runs a decent operation, he's well respected around the county, and he's a member in good standing with the Kansas State Militia.

"But if you don't marry Randy, you forfeit everything. It'll all revert to the trust, and it will all go to the sisters in Bison. If you marry and then divorce him, you forfeit the money and the house. It all goes to the sisters. You have thirty days from the time you see this videotape to make up your mind."

He focused on the camera, and it was as if he was in the room, making eye contact from beyond the grave. "I was thinking the other day about Cousin Rose. Remember her?"

For a moment I couldn't grasp what he was saying, who he was talking about. I didn't have any cousins. All my relatives were dead. But then I understood. This was how he was going to lock me away forever, one way or another.

"I know you remember what happened to her, and you know *why* it happened to her. You don't have to be like her, not if you marry Randy. If you don't . . ." Dad held up a brown manila envelope to the camera. "I've given this sealed envelope to Keith Dooley."

Mr. Dooley mirrored Dad's movements, raising the envelope in the air like a magician's assistant displaying the trick saw box. He pointed to the wax seal over the flap.

"If you don't marry Randy, Keith will open the envelope and then . . . you know what will happen. I don't want that to happen, and you don't either," Dad said.

So even if I refused the money, I'd still be trapped. He'd thought of everything.

"But I know it won't come to that," he continued. "I have faith in you, Petty. I know you'll do the right thing. I've instructed Keith to burn the envelope if you go through with the marriage. This is the only copy, so no one will ever know what's in it. Of course, I'm hoping you'll never actually see this video, or by the time you do, you're in your seventies and it doesn't matter anymore. I love you, Petty."

The screen went black.

He didn't love me. He was transferring title, that was all. He'd spent my life teaching me to defend myself, to fight, and for what? Just to be locked away again. Forever.

I couldn't get a full breath, it was as if there were a cork in my throat.

I had a brief thought of slicing Randy and Mr. Dooley to bacon strips with my blade, allowed myself to imagine the blood spatter, but it only made me feel better for a moment. I knew my life was over now.

I started making the same sounds the dogs made when they were about to yak.

"You're not going to howl again, are you?" Randy said.

"Are you all right?" Mr. Dooley asked.

My stomach convulsed, forcing more embarrassing sounds from my mouth.

"Give her a paper bag or something, Dooley, will you?" Randy said, scooting his chair farther from mine. The way he said this let me know that it wasn't out of concern for me but out of concern for his boots.

I heard Mr. Dooley clear his throat again. "Petty," he said, "I know this is a lot to take in."

Randy tapped his fingers on his cowboy hat brim, and the sound magnified in my ears. I slumped forward and put my head in my hands. There was no movement in the room, only the sound of Randy's tapping fingers. He must have noticed it too because he stopped it.

"Do you know what's in that envelope?" Randy asked Mr. Dooley.

"Nope," Mr. Dooley said, holding up his hands. "And I don't want to know." He glanced at his watch again. "I'm not trying to throw you out, but my next appointment will be here soon, so . . ."

"We'll get out of your hair," Randy said to him and stood.

"Could you drive me home, Mr. Dooley?" I whispered.

Mr. Dooley's face reddened. "I'm sorry. I can't. Randy will drive you."

I hissed at Randy like an old barn cat. Both men started a little and glanced at each other.

The effort of not crying made my head feel like it was expanding, filling the room.

"Randy, would you wait outside for a minute? I want to have a word with Petty."

Randy gave me a glance, pressed his hat down on his head and went out the door.

Mr. Dooley squatted down next to my chair but he didn't touch me. He seemed to know better. "Petty. This probably seems . . . wrong to you. But your dad had his reasons, and I believe he had your best interests at heart."

Was this supposed to make me feel better?

"Your dad knew what he was doing. He's right about Randy. Randy's a good man. You can trust him. He'll take care of you. And you wouldn't believe how many men die without giving any thought at all to what their families will do. Your dad provided for you in an unbelievably generous way. You should count yourself lucky. Now, listen. You really embarrassed yourself there. You need to do what you can to make it up to Randy, you really do. You need to apologize and be sweet to him."

That was not going to happen. Over his dead body. Or mine.

I still didn't move, and I could feel his frustration mounting.

"You'll see, Petty. Everything's going to be okay. It'll all work out."

He touched my chair and I understood I was to stand and walk out the front door and into Randy's pickup truck. Which I did. I had brain freeze because I couldn't let myself think about what had just happened.

It was a good three miles before the shock wore off and I started to notice things, like the nice leather interior of the Dodge, and the soft country music on the stereo, which didn't sound tinny like the radio in Dad's Silverado. And then I noticed, in my peripheral vision, Randy sneaking glances at me. I thought about bleating at him again, but my throat hurt from the first time.

To his credit, he didn't try to talk to me at all the whole way home, just chewed on that big ridiculous mustache of his and periodically spit tobacco juice into the brushed metal container.

When he pulled up in front of my house, he put the truck in park and cleared his throat. I reached for the door handle, but he pressed the door lock button, which shot me straight to DEFCON 2. I launched myself at the window, knowing it was useless, that auto glass doesn't break easily. I grunted and slammed into the window again.

"What the hell are you doing?" Randy shouted.

I yanked on the door handle repeatedly, once I determined a dislocated shoulder was more likely than a broken window.

"Knock it off! Stop it!"

I didn't.

"All right." He unlocked the door just as I was pulling at the handle and I tumbled out of the truck and onto the ground. The dogs came running. I looked up and saw Randy frantically pulling on the passenger door to keep them out.

I ran for the front door of my house.

Randy's voice shouted through the barely open window. "It's what your dad wanted! I'll be back, and you'd better be ready to talk."

The dogs leapt at his truck, trying to get at him, and he sprayed gravel gunning it out onto the county road. They chased him for fifty yards then loped back to me.

I led them into the house and threw myself on the couch. I banged my fists into the sofa cushions, trying to beat back the sense of betrayal I felt. My dad had sold me like one of Detective Deirdre Walsh's fellow detectives sold her out to a local drug kingpin, and got her shot and nearly killed. Sold her out for an envelope stuffed with cash.

Kind of like the sealed envelope that was now in Mr. Dooley's possession. The Cousin Rose my dad had referred to in his video will was a character in a book called *Rose-tinted Glass* I'd found at the dump. I'd read it, keeping it hidden in my room, but Dad had found it during one of his surprise inspections. He'd given me the silent treatment for days after that, and then he'd read it himself. He sat me down when he was done and told me he was glad I'd read it because it could teach me about obedience and the price of defiance.

In the book, Cousin Rose was the high-spirited, rebellious daughter of a powerful and wealthy New England family. In order to prevent Rose from embarrassing her family and jeopardizing her father's Senate bid, Rose's stepmother convinced a judge to have Rose committed to the state mental hospital.

If I didn't marry Randy, there was something in that envelope that would persuade a judge to lock me up. So the question was . . . what was it?

And how am I going to get my hands on it?

Chapter 6

PETTY

I WAS OUT back practicing knife throwing before work when the dogs tore around to the front of the house, barking. The road we live on gets very little traffic other than propane delivery trucks, so I stood and listened. A diesel engine rumbled toward the house.

The dogs' barking got more frantic as the vehicle approached. I slung the Winchester's strap over my shoulder, went into the house and looked out the front window. Randy King's red Dodge Ram pulled into the drive and sat idling. He saw me and I ducked. Sweat sprang up on my forehead as I crouched by the window, and Randy tapped his horn. I looked out the window again. He was pointing at the dogs. I crouched again, wondering if he would leave if I ignored him. The bellowing truck horn answered my question. I stood and went out the front door, the Winchester still over my shoulder.

The dogs barked nonstop. Randy pointed at them again. I sighed.

"Sarx. Tesla. Off. Come."

They reluctantly gave a few last barks over their shoulders and came to me. Randy cracked his window.

"Can I come in for a minute?"

"No," I said.

"We need to talk."

I knew this was true. I'd thought of nothing else since yesterday. I was in the process of formulating a plan to get that envelope from Mr. Dooley and escape the life Dad had mapped out for me, but I couldn't avoid Randy forever.

I opened the garage door, put the dogs inside and closed it.

Randy switched off the Ram and stepped out. He smoothed his mustache.

I moved the Winchester strap to my other shoulder.

"Listen," he said. "I wanted to come by and explain a couple of things to you. And I brought you something." He turned and pulled out a large bouquet of flowers in a cone of floral paper. He held them out toward me.

I didn't move.

"For you." His mustache twitched.

Sweat rolled down the side of my face and it tickled, but I still didn't move.

"Can we sit down?"

"Can if you want," I said, pointing at the misshapen Adirondack chairs my dad had made out of some dump-scavenged wood.

He walked over to one of the chairs and lowered himself into it. It creaked. He took off his Stetson and wiped his forehead with his shirtsleeve. "Hot one, huh?"

I nodded.

He put his hat back on and laid the flowers on the ground next to his chair.

"Petty, I wanted to tell you how this all came about. This will and everything. I take it your dad never mentioned the . . . our . . . his will to you."

Why would he include me in my wedding plans?

"I met your dad about ten years ago at the Quivera Gun Club in Salina, though we'd been neighbors for eight years. Anyway, he's—was kinda like you, not real talkative, you know, but a serious, right-minded guy." Randy coughed. "You understand what I mean by right-minded?"

I shrugged.

"A Second Amendment kind of guy. I was the one who sponsored his membership to the Kansas State Militia."

I didn't care.

He squinted up at me. "Would you mind sitting down? I admire your defensive posture, but I'm not the enemy."

But he was.

Although marrying Randy would be the path of least resistance, the dreams I'd had for myself would die with Dad. When I thought about going out into the world alone, the fear nearly convinced me to go along with his wishes.

Almost, but not quite.

Because something just beyond my reach was coming into focus. What was Dad's goal for this arrangement? To keep me caged. And what did that make me? Livestock.

That kind of thinking was not normal. That was not how a father was supposed to think of his daughter. Didn't that prove Dad had no idea what was right for me? And if he was wrong about that . . . . maybe he was wrong about how dangerous the world was too.

Maybe he was wrong that I couldn't navigate the world on my own.

This idea exploded in my brain and showered sparks, lighting everything up, and I knew Randy was wrong too. He *was* the enemy. He was the one standing in the way of my freedom.

I stood there a moment longer, then moved the other chair farther away from him and sat down, laying the shotgun across my knees.

"Thanks," he said, rubbing his neck. "I was getting a crick looking up at you." He smiled at me. At least, I think he did. It was hard to tell with that mustache in the way.

I didn't smile back.

"So anyway, when you turned eighteen, your dad told me about his plans for you. I didn't think too much about it, because he wasn't an old guy by any means. But I agreed, because he was absolutely set on making sure you were taken care of for the rest of your life. I want you to know, though, he didn't say nothing about the insurance policy."

I spat on the ground.

"Cross my heart," he said, actually drawing an X on his chest with his finger. "I was as shocked as you. But that's how serious Charlie was about protecting you, and he knew I had the same values as him." He cleared his throat again and gazed up at the sky. "All this to say I don't expect it to be your typical marriage. It would be a straight-up business deal. I house you, clothe you and feed you, and I control the money. But I'll buy you anything you want. We could even build a house that has two sides to it—one for you and one for me. Of course, your side would have to be locked up, but you're used to that."

I *was* used to that. It was familiar and safe and easy. But it wasn't normal.

So Dad and Randy had planned everything out for me. Years ago. I still wouldn't have any say in my own life. I was going to be a militia man's "wife," and that was all.

I stood. "I have to go to work."

Randy didn't move, just gazed up at me from under his Stetson. "No you don't."

"Yes, I do," I said, gripping the rifle.

Randy dug a cell phone out of his pocket and held it out to me. "No, you don't. Ask Dooley. He'll tell you all about it."

I didn't understand what he was telling me, so I didn't answer, just stood there staring. He opened the phone and pushed some buttons then held it out to me again. I felt a chill of fear, as if he were handing me a live grenade. I heard a voice coming out of the phone but still I didn't take it. Randy frowned and held it to his ear.

"Hey, Dooley, it's Randy. You need to tell Petty about her job." He held the phone out again. This time I took it and put it to my ear.

"Petty?"

"Yes," I said.

"I'm glad Randy called, because I need to go over a few pieces of business with you. Your situation is fairly complex. I certainly hope you appreciate everything I'm doing on your behalf, young lady!"

I kind of got the feeling he was expecting me to thank him, but I said, "I don't have time to talk right now. I've got to get to work."

"You don't have to worry about that anymore. I've called your boss to let him know."

"Let him know what?" My blood felt cold inside me. Randy appeared to be smiling underneath his mustache.

"That you're no longer a dump employee. Randy went and got your things—he's probably got them with him right now."

"But I don't want to—"

"And if you need a ride anywhere, Randy said he'd give it to you. You don't need to worry about a thing."

"I don't want to quit working. And I don't want any rides from Randy."

"Already done. You can just relax. Lot of ladies would kill to be in your shoes, you know that?"

I closed my eyes. "You said I had thirty days to think about it."

"But what is there to think about? It's no contest."

A phrase I'd heard over and over again in TV courtroom dramas had been trying to rise from my subconscious since yesterday, and now it did. I turned my back to Randy and whispered, "How do I contest the will?"

I heard the Adirondack chair groan behind me as Randy stood. I didn't know if he'd heard me or not. I didn't look back at him.

Mr. Dooley cleared his throat again. "You don't want to do that," he said. "It would be expensive, it could take years and you have nothing to live on in the meantime. That's not a viable option."

I turned to face Randy, who was glaring at me. I glared back.

"I'd like to do it anyway," I said.

There was a pause. "As your lawyer, I have to advise against it."

I gulped. "Then I'll get another lawyer."

Mr. Dooley laughed. "You need money for another lawyer. You don't have any, and I don't have time to argue about this anymore. Understood?"

I said nothing.

He put on a more jovial tone. "Petty, you've got a million dollars coming to you if you'll just follow your dad's wishes. That insurance policy is money in the bank."

Money in the bank.

I gasped.

"What is it? Petty?" Mr. Dooley was still talking, but I pressed the end button on the phone and tossed it to Randy, who almost didn't catch it.

"You got some stuff of mine?" I said, walking toward the Ram.

He followed me to his truck, pulled a box out of the bed and put it in my hands.

"Mr. Dooley said you'd give me rides if I needed them," I said. "I need a ride into Saw Pole."

"You going to scream or try to bust my window again?" he said.

"I'm gonna put this stuff inside first," I said, ignoring him. "Get in the truck so I can let the dogs out."

I ran the box inside then went upstairs to get my state ID. I locked up the house and opened the garage door. The dogs came tearing out and attacked the truck. Randy cracked open his window and yelled, "Get them off my rig!"

I counted to five before I made the signal for "off" and they obeyed. Then I got in the truck and buckled myself in. I studied the buttons on my armrest to see if there was a way to keep him from locking me in and saw I could lock and unlock the doors myself. He pulled onto the county road. I stared out the window. He turned up the country music station. I daydreamed until he said something I didn't quite catch, then looked in his direction.

He turned down the radio. "I said, you should go to the beauty parlor. They could show you how to do yourself up. You'd be a lot prettier if you wore makeup."

I shrugged and turned my face to the window. He didn't talk anymore. When we hit the Saw Pole city limits, I sat up and said, "Can you take me to the Farmers National Bank?"

He parked in front of the bank. "I'll wait here."

I'd never gone into a building that wasn't my house by myself. I wondered if there was an armed guard inside like I'd seen on TV. I opened the door, edged inside with my back to the wall. Found the exits. No armed guard. Two tellers. One customer at a window. I waited against the wall until the unoccupied teller called out to me, "Can I help you?"

Filled with resolve, I pushed myself off from the wall and ran to the counter. I pulled out my Kansas state identification card and gave it to the teller, a girl in a navy blue suit and a flouncy pink blouse.

"I have a savings account here, and I'd like to close it out."

Chapter 7

DEKKER

THIS WEEK, INSTEAD of cashing my paycheck like usual, I was heading straight to Farmers National to deposit it. I wouldn't buy weed and PBR, I'd bank the money to buy some new clothes for the gig and beers for my bandmates to try and make things up to them. I would be smart and disciplined this time, and I'd take whatever extra hours I could pick up at the grocery. Things were turning around—I could feel it.

I opened the glass door to the bank and walked in, and there was Petty Moshen standing at the counter. What were the odds that, after all these years of living in the same town and never seeing her, now I'd seen her twice in one week? But then I remembered what a fool I'd made of myself the last time—the only time—I'd talked to her, and the humiliation drove me back behind a pillar, hoping she wouldn't see me. But I could hear the transaction going on at the teller's window. I tried not to listen, but the tile floor magnified every sound.

"All right, hon," the teller, a girl named Britney, who was three years older than me, said to Petty. "What's your account number?"

"I don't know. My dad opened the account for me five years ago."

Not a promising start. I peeked out from behind the pillar. Britney frowned at Petty and pecked at her keyboard. I remembered that look. She'd been the type of girl who smiled to your face and talked shit behind your back. She wore pearls around her neck, paid for, no doubt, by the bank's owner—her father.

Petty probably had never been inside a bank before. She was navigating all these new things on her own, and I tried to imagine how terrifying and confusing it must be.

Britney put Petty's card on her keyboard and typed. "Okay," she said. "Your account number is 06315. I'll need you to fill this form out, sign and date it, and I'll get your cash."

I watched Petty bend forward, pen in hand, and I briefly wondered if she could actually write or if she was going to scrawl a big X on the paper. But then I felt like a dick for thinking that.

She slid the form back to Britney, who peered at it, then turned and walked away.

As if by magnetic force, Petty turned and looked right at where my head stuck out from behind the pillar.

Her eyebrows rose.

Busted. I stepped out of my hiding place and walked toward her.

"Hey, Petty." I tried to sound casual, not like I'd just been spying on her or anything.

She stared at me.

"How's it going?" I said.

"How's what going?"

"Just everything, I guess."

She shrugged.

Britney returned and opened her drawer with a key attached to her wrist. Then she counted out cash and slid it toward Petty. "There you are."

Petty stared at the pile. "I need *all* my money," she said. "Do I have to come back for it or . . . ?"

Britney looked at Petty like she had three heads. "That *is* all your money."

It was two tens, a five, a one, three quarters, a nickel, and a penny.

"You took my money," Petty said. "Didn't you? You're not going to get away with this."

I had to stop myself from laughing out loud at this. She sounded just like someone from a bad TV cop drama.

"Of course I didn't take your money," Britney said, in a puffy, insulted voice.

I needed to redeem myself for wanting to laugh, so I decided to step in. I walked toward the cage. "How much money do you have in there?" I asked Petty.

"I had almost thirty thousand dollars."

Britney and I gasped in unison, the shock deflating Britney's indignation. "What made you think you had that kind of money in here?" she asked.

"Give me my money or I'm calling the cops," Petty said.

"She didn't steal your money," I said, and stepped up next to Petty, putting my hands on the counter. "There's been some mistake."

Britney shot me an annoyed glare, obviously done here and ready to move on with her day. I could just imagine the story she was rehearsing in her mind about the spooky girl who had accused her of embezzlement. The bitch.

"She lost her dad a few days ago," I told her. "She's trying to get her affairs in order, so if you wouldn't mind . . ."

Petty's suspicious gaze made my face burn, but I didn't care. She needed someone in her corner. That's what I told myself anyway, trying not to imagine her falling helplessly in love with me or anything.

Britney wrinkled her nose like she smelled something bad, but she turned back to her computer. "Just a second," she said primly.

Petty bent over and put her hands on her knees, breathing hard. If it had been anyone else, I would have put my hand on her back. But she wasn't anyone else, so I didn't dare touch her.

"There's only been one deposit on this account," Britney said. "The original deposit of twenty-five dollars."

"That's impossible," Petty said, her words escaping between gulps of air. "My dad . . . deposited . . . all my paychecks . . . for the last five years . . ."

Britney leaned out of her window and called out, "Next."

Now, that was just unnecessary. I blocked her view and got in her face. "Let her see the monitor."

We had a staring match for a minute, and I remembered all the times back in school that Britney had overwhelmed meeker girls with her nastiness, and I'd just stood by and watched. Not this time. I wasn't going to let her do the same to Petty.

"Yes," Petty said. "Let me see the monitor."

I was surprised by the granite in her voice.

"Fine," Britney said in a hiss. She turned back to her keyboard and typed with a vengeance, fuming. She shoved her computer monitor toward Petty. I stepped away to give Petty some privacy. Britney pointed with her red pen. "See? This account was opened sixty-two months ago with a deposit of twenty-five dollars. Your account earns interest of one percent compounded daily, which means you've earned one dollar and eighty-one cents on your original deposit."

Petty's hands fluttered in front of her mouth, her eyes glistening.

Wow. What kind of an evil man had Charlie Moshen been to do this to his only kid?

"If you want to bring in the statements you've received from the bank over the past five years, we can get this straightened out," Britney said, a snotty grin on her face. She slid Petty's ID and the cash to the edge of the counter. "Next."

I blocked the next customer and said quietly to Britney, "Would it kill you to be nice?"

"Next!"

Petty ran out the door.

Chapter 8

PETTY

Outside, I couldn't seem to get enough air.

"Are you all right?" Dekker asked me.

I shook my head. I looked up and down the street and then at the steamy white clouds in the blue-gray sky, thinking.

I should be able to get copies of all the check stubs from Mr. Siebert, my boss at the dump. Dad must have deposited my checks into another account. I could prove that with the pay stubs. This money wasn't part of the trust. It was all mine. I needed to go down to Mr. Dooley's office to see if he had Dad's financial records. Otherwise, I didn't know where they might be.

Dekker stood motionless, staring at me.

"What?" I said finally.

"What are you going to do?" he said.

"I'm not sure." I turned and walked west down Main Street toward the lawyer's office.

"Um, bye," Dekker said to my back.

Randy's truck kept pace with me. His window slid down. He was not pleased. "Where are you going?"

I stopped and turned back to thank Dekker for his help, but it was too late. He was walking back into the bank.

"I'm going to walk down to Mr. Dooley's office," I said to Randy.

His eyebrows came together. "Okay," he said, but the end of it rose like a question. I ignored him and ran down the block to Mr. Dooley's office.

I burst in the door and said, "I need Dad's bank statements."

An old man in overalls sat in the inner office. Mr. Dooley half stood from his desk and said, "I'll be with you in a minute, Petty."

"How much money does Dad have in his checking account?"

The old farmer turned around in his chair and stared at me.

Mr. Dooley rose from his chair and walked around the desk. He put his hand on the farmer's shoulder. "Give me one minute, Ben."

The farmer nodded, still staring at me.

Mr. Dooley's lips were white and tight over his teeth. He went to a filing cabinet and pulled out a file. He opened it, removed several sheets of paper and slammed them down on the counter in front of me.

"Here's your father's last bank statement." He pointed at the bottom of the page.

It said $79.45.

"No," I whispered. "There must be another account somewhere."

"There's not," Mr. Dooley said in a low voice. "This is all there is."

"What happened to all my money?" I shrieked.

"Shh," Mr. Dooley said. "The fact is, Petty, you were pretty much supporting you and your dad. And paying the premiums on the life insurance policy."

"So . . . so all my money is . . . gone."

"No. It was invested in the life insurance policy." He positioned his face in front of mine. "Which you can have as soon as you marry Randy." He put on a big phony smile and said loudly, "Okay?" as if he were speaking to a particularly slow toddler.

I felt a stinging in the bridge of my nose. I was going to cry.

Mr. Dooley scrubbed his hand over his face. "Did you ever stop to think how hard all this is for me? I'm only the messenger, but I'm the one who's getting all the fallout from what your father did. Think about that for a while."

He seemed to expect me to say something. I didn't.

Mr. Dooley blew out a sigh. "Fine. I hate to have to put it this way, but marrying Randy is your best option. Deal with it."

But it wasn't my only option. I had my blade with me.

"Where is your bathroom?"

"Thatta girl," Mr. Dooley said, smiling. "Upstairs. Go freshen yourself up. Everything's going to be fine. You'll see." He winked at me, turned and went back to the inner office.

I climbed the stairs straight up, not sideways with my back to the wall like I normally did, because it didn't matter anymore. Dad had stolen my money. He had made sure I'd be trapped here forever, that I'd never have a life of my own, ever. He'd died and left me all alone, to be given away to strangers like the rest of his stuff, as if I were a pet goldfish or a tablecloth. I was nothing, and when I was gone, no one would miss me.

At the top of the stairs was a cramped hallway, piled with boxes and furniture and typewriters and adding machines. I was never going to escape. I couldn't drive, I had no money, and unless I married Randy I'd lose the house at the end of the month and have nowhere to live. I now saw that no one and nothing could help me. There was no reason for me to go on living. My blade burned against my skin. It was my way out.

I knew exactly where my jugular and my carotid were. I hoped there was a tub in the bathroom upstairs because cleanup would be a snap, as the commercial says.

In the upper hall, I picked my way through the towers of boxes, and on the other side of the bathroom door a tower was topped by a box marked M R. The same box Randy had taken out of my house and put in his truck. On top of it was a Mac laptop with an L-shaped dent in the lid. My dad's computer.

I glanced over my shoulder and then back at the box. I might as well take a peek before I killed myself. The box was stamped in several places with the warning PERSONAL & CONFIDENTIAL. I knew this warning was for me. If Dad had wanted me to see what was in this box, he would have shown me.

I looked behind me again and moved the laptop to the floor, then picked at the packing tape of the box and carefully, slowly pulled. My heartbeat sped up with each breath. I folded back the box sides. File folders. I don't know what I expected, but my disappointment had sharp edges that cut deep. I was about to the close the box back up when a flash of color between the folders and the side of the box caught my eye. I pulled it free and found it was a photo of . . . me.

I'd never seen a photo of myself. My dad didn't own a camera, and when I'd brought one home from the dump, it had disappeared. I'd asked Dad what had happened to it, but he acted like he didn't know what I was talking about. There were no photos of me as a child. As far as I knew, no pictures of me—or Dad or Mom—existed anywhere.

I brought it close to my face. I'd read the term "cognitive dissonance" and knew that was what I was experiencing right now. Because this photo had to have been taken within the last year or two, but when and where? And why didn't I know someone had photographed me? A chill stole over me as I realized maybe someone had been stalking me and taking my photo and I'd never known.

But as I stared at the picture, I realized there was something about it that wasn't quite right. I flipped the photo over, and scrawled on the back was 987.

What did that mean?

I turned it over and studied the image again, especially my face. The heart shape of it. My round hazel eyes. My dimples. But . . . not my hair. Not my eyebrows. The hair was shorter and curly, the eyebrows were thin. The eyes were rimmed with liner, shadow and mascara, which I'd never worn, had never even owned. I only knew about them because of TV commercials.

I turned back to the box and reached in to search for more photos. Where there was one, there were bound to be more.

"Petty?"

Mr. Dooley's echoing voice made me jump straight up and I dropped the photo, which fell to the floor facedown. As I bent to pick it up, I realized my thumb had covered up part of what was written on the back. It didn't say 987. It said 1987.

"You okay up there?"

"Fine," I called as I flipped the photo over once more. The photo that *wasn't* of me.

It was a picture of my mom.

While I knew next to nothing about her, I do actually remember her a little bit. I remember her in flashes and snippets, in three different mental movie clips. The first one is of me sitting on my mom's lap and Dad sitting next to us. Mom's telling me to "*Look! Look!*" And she's pointing at a little TV to our right. And just as I look, these snow-topped mountains pop up on that TV like toast, and I'm amazed. How did she do that? And she and my dad are laughing.

The next clip is of me sitting across from her and we're gliding. My mom is moving backward, and the sky and clouds and trees are bending around her face. She wears round sunglasses. I can't move my head because I'm wearing a puffy orange vest. We're in a rowboat on a lake, and it's late afternoon. My mom is rowing, and then she stops and pulls the oars into the boat. It's sunny but cool, and the sun on the water makes me squint. She gives me a peanut butter and mayonnaise sandwich and a box of juice with a straw in it. It's just my mom and me and our sandwiches on the lake.

In the last clip, Mom is lowering me into the bathtub. "You want to play the game?" she says, and then the doorbell rings.

The only images I have of Mom are the ones in my head. Except for the one I now held in my hand.

Where had it come from? I wanted to dig through that box, but I heard the front door open and the old farmer say, "Thanks a lot, Keith."

"That's all right," Mr. Dooley said. "See you in church."

The front door closed.

I slid the photo in my bra, sealed the box back up, and put Dad's Mac on top. I was sweaty and cold, and that picture burned against my skin. I felt like it was glowing through my clothes.

What else was in that box?

I came down the stairs, shaking. "I want that box in the upstairs hall," I blurted.

Mr. Dooley froze and didn't answer right away. "I'm sorry?"

"I want that box."

A longer pause. He turned to me but didn't speak.

"Did you hear me?"

"Yes, Petty, I heard you. No need to shout. That box is the property of the trust."

"So I can have it and Dad's laptop if I marry Randy," I said. "Right?"

"No," he said. "The laptop will be stored inside the box, sealed and in my possession."

"Does Randy know what's in it?"

"I couldn't say. I just know that your father instructed him to remove the box and his laptop from the home and deliver them to my office for safekeeping."

I couldn't think of anything to say. Why couldn't I speak? Why couldn't I be like Detective Deirdre Walsh and demand what I wanted? I grabbed a handful of my hair and pulled.

"I'm certain your dad had a good reason for not giving you access to these things. Best not to think about it."

My dad was still controlling everything from beyond the grave. "But—"

"You always trusted his judgment in the past, didn't you?" Mr. Dooley's sharp tone startled me. Then he softened it again, but I didn't believe anything he said anymore. "There's no question in my mind that marrying Randy is the right thing. I was reading the other day that arranged marriages are actually some of the most successful. In the old days, they happened all the—"

I turned and ran out the door. Randy was sitting in his truck and saw me come out. He got out of the truck and opened the passenger-side door for me. I got in and buckled up. I was light-headed and almost giddy as I sat staring out the window, marveling at how often and how quickly I'd gone from excitement to total despair and back again over these last two days. How I'd been committed to killing myself. Until I saw my mother's face.

"Everything all right, gal?" Randy said.

"Yes."

Randy kept the country music turned up on the drive back, for which I was grateful. All I could think about was my mother's face against my skin, and how I wanted to be home alone to think about it.

Before I knew it, we were in front of my house. Randy put the truck in park.

"I'm gonna be coming by every day to make sure you're okay," he said.

"You don't need to do that."

"Dooley and me, we discussed it and we decided I do. Now that your daddy's gone and you're all alone in this house, you need someone to protect you."

"I got the dogs."

"You can't be too careful." I wasn't sure whether this was a helpful warning or a threat. "What with your grief and all, you probably aren't thinking too straight. Just let me and Dooley figure out what's best for you."

Figure out what's best for you. Because that's what men did. What lawyers and dads and husbands did for girls. Decided what was best for us. Because we can't think straight. Because we're confused. Because we don't understand.

"So I'll be by later. Maybe you'll ask me inside for a beer."

This time he didn't pretend to lock me in. He let me go, because he'd be back later.

I shut the door of the truck and squatted down to hug the dogs, who licked my face and danced around me. They were overjoyed I was giving them affection, which I'd never done when Dad was alive. But these guys kept me safe. I went inside the house and let them in before dead-bolting the door.

I reached inside my bra and peeled the photo off my chest. My sweat had leeched some of the color off the print and my mom's face was now imprinted on my skin, which gave me an inexplicable rush of gladness. Mom's picture didn't seem to be damaged. I stood staring at it, scouring the image for clues. Her ears were double-pierced. There was a tiny scar on her left cheek. She wore a silver chain with a tiny square silver box around her neck. Staring at her, I was suddenly overcome with the feeling—the certainty—that my mother was still alive.

I set the picture on the kitchen table to dry out.

The only thing in life that mattered now was to get that box, the laptop, and the envelope from Dooley's office and then get the hell out of Saw Pole.

I DON'T REMEMBER when I realized I wasn't supposed to ask Dad about Mom. I was pretty little though. We were in Kansas and I asked him if he knew the words to a song she used to sing called—I think—"Dig Down Deep." He acted as if I'd said an obscene word or something. He was completely surprised and a little offended. It was like he'd forgotten all about her and figured I had too.

"No."

He said it in a tone that let me know I'd better not ask anymore, or I was going to get a paddling. I kind of wondered if maybe I'd made her up, if I'd imagined a beautiful, happy, laughing, smiling mother to balance out this stern, irritable, paranoid dad I was left with.

Why had Dad hogged this picture of Mom all to himself? Why had he told me there were no photos of her, and why had he never told me how much I resembled her?

I was restless, and I realized I hadn't worked out at all since Dad had passed, other than the quick mile on the treadmill. Although he'd been a slave driver when it came to training, I was glad because being in good shape made me feel easier. Since I was little, he'd tell me he wanted me to be like Sarah Connor in *Terminator II*, "except without the crazy," he'd say. *Because you've got that part covered for both of us.* I'd always thought it but never said it.

I ran on the treadmill for an hour and then lifted weights while the dogs lay on the floor watching me. I did my best thinking during workouts, and I needed a plan. No one could help me. I had to do it myself, even if it meant what I did wasn't exactly legal.

I didn't want to break the law, but the law sure wasn't doing me any favors. I *needed* to see what was in that box and on that laptop and in the envelope, and the only way to do that was to go to Mr. Dooley's office when he wasn't in and take them. But how was I going to get there when I couldn't drive? It was thirteen miles to Saw Pole. I had to find someone other than Randy to take me there.

Sarx cocked an ear and jumped to his feet, followed quickly by Tesla. They both growled and then galloped up the stairs. I toweled off and followed them, on alert. They stood at the front door barking.

I looked through the bars on our bulletproof windows, and there was Randy's pickup truck sitting in the road, idling, with only the parking lights on.

Randy stayed in front of the house for a little over an hour. I knew that most regular people would call the police, but those people didn't have a father who told them endlessly that cops were never to be trusted. While Deirdre Walsh was my hero, she was just a character in a TV show. Real cops weren't straight arrows like she was, according to my dad.

Should I send the dogs out? Should I go out there to talk to Randy myself? Talk about what? I didn't have anything to say to him.

What could he be thinking? Sitting out in the truck with the engine running did not say "protection" to me. It whispered something entirely different.

In the end, I turned on the TV, but the dogs whined and barked, paced and jumped at the door, until Randy finally moved on, long past midnight.

Chapter 9

Sunday

PETTY

I WAS ALMOST ready to execute my plan. The preparations included a lot of walking, which took me two miles down the road I had never walked, and I was assaulted by the smells of the greening hay and thistles. The sky felt so huge overhead, so limitless, with its high, wispy spiderweb clouds. The dogs came with me, following along vigilantly, barking occasionally. While we were out, the iPhone buzzed in my pocket and I pulled it out. *King, Randy,* it said. I let it ring and go to voice mail. A few minutes later it buzzed again, and again I let it go. This happened twice more, and I thought about turning it off, but instead I answered after the fifth buzz.

"Hello," I said.

"Petty, I'd like to take you out on a real date. Maybe go into Salina for dinner, spend some money on you."

"No."

There was a pause. "No?"

"No."

"Do you think you'll start talking to me after we get married?"

I didn't say anything.

"Hey," he shouted. "I'm talking to you."

"I'm not going to marry you," I said, and clicked end. Then I turned off the phone.

Detective Deirdre Walsh had a suitor who wanted to control her. She thought it was the right thing for a while, but then she realized she didn't want some man telling her what to do and how to dress, so she pulled the engagement ring off her finger, dropped it into his Chinese food, and walked out of the restaurant.

Back at the house, everything was ready for tomorrow, and I was excited as I went downstairs for my workout. I ran on the treadmill longer than I normally did to burn off some of the nervous energy, even though I'd already walked four miles earlier in the day. I got in the shower and took my time about it since I didn't know when my next shower would be. After drying off, I put on some sweat pants and a T-shirt, and sat down in front of the television. The long run had paid off, because I was sleepy as well as tired. I was about to turn on the TV when I heard one of the dogs give a sharp cry of pain out in front of the house. Then I heard another yelp and I jumped up and ran to the door. As soon as I unlocked the last dead bolt, I was knocked backward by it swinging open.

"Hi, Petty," said Randy. "Did you miss me?" His face was shiny and red, and I smelled whiskey.

I reached for my blade just as I realized I hadn't put on my bra.

He pulled a hand cannon out of the back of his jeans and

pointed it at the screen door, which poor Tesla was hurling himself at frantically. The dog's eyes were red, puffy and running.

"You pull anything, I shoot the dog," Randy said, his words slurred.

"Where's Sarx?" I choked out. "What did you do to Sarx?"

"Pepper spray," he said. "The dogs'll be all right if you listen to me. Understand?"

I nodded.

"Call the dog off or I'll shoot him." He raised the pistol and pointed it again.

"Off, Tesla," I said, giving the hand signal.

Tesla backed off, pacing in front of the door, sneezing and whining.

Randy turned to me, unsteady on his feet. If he'd only been a little drunker, I could probably have disarmed him. But as it was, he had a .357 Magnum in one hand and pepper spray in the other. So I made sure to keep my knees loose and watch for an opening.

"You listen to me," Randy said. "You're going to marry me, and you're going to show me some respect. I've put up with your silent treatments and your playing hard to get. I'm sick of it. You're going to marry me, and you're going to have my sons. You're going to start wearing makeup and dress like a real woman, and you're going to cook and clean my house."

He stuck the pepper spray in his back pocket and his gun down the back of his jeans. What came next happened in slow motion. He corralled my waist and crushed me to him, but his mistake was trying to pin my arms to my sides. I pressed my wrists together, bent my knees and slipped his grasp. He stood blinking dumbly at me for a split second before he drew the gun and fired out the screen. "I will shoot the dog. Stand still. Do it. Stand still or I shoot the dog."

My dad had always said if it was ever between me and an animal, choose me. But Randy would still have a gun, and he was drunk. So I did as I was told. He caught me around the waist again and pulled me against him, then mashed his mustache into my lips. Without any warning at all his tongue plopped into my mouth too, and then I thought I was truly and really going to vomit. I didn't crush his windpipe the way my dad had taught me, although I had never wanted to do anything more. I just stood there and took it.

"Open your mouth a little wider," he said into the side of my face before diving back in. I did. That tongue lashed around inside my mouth for a while, and that mustache went in my mouth too and up my nose and made me need to sneeze. While this was going on, he slipped his hand down the front of my sweats and between my legs. He did it so easily, as if it was nothing, as if this wasn't the one thing my father had tried to prevent my whole life. It was as if he'd cut me open, reached inside and exposed my deepest thoughts to a jeering crowd. But the move released my right arm and without thinking at all I brought my fist up and boxed his left ear. He pulled his hand out of my underwear, took hold of the neck of my T-shirt and slapped my face so hard I saw double.

Tesla went berserk outside the screen, throwing himself at the door again and again.

"You want it rough, huh?" Randy said, feeling his ear. "So do I." Then he slapped me again before shoving his tongue in my mouth. His hand traveled up to my right breast and squeezed so hard the pain and violation made me gasp. I imagined biting his tongue off and spitting it in his face. For the umpteenth time I wished I could revive my dad and kill him all over again. And then I'd put him and Randy and Mr. Dooley into the meat grinder and let the dogs eat them.

I stood limp, nauseated, until he stopped. He smiled at me as he felt his ear again, moved his jaw around. "Don't worry," he said, winking at me. "We'll save your cherry for our wedding night. I'm kind of traditional that way."

My breast, my face, and my crotch all throbbed, but I didn't move. I didn't speak. My body parts blazed humiliated red, no longer my own, no longer protectable or private. Just spoiled meat you'd feed to pigs.

"Here's what's going to happen," he said. "We're going to the courthouse tomorrow, and we're going to get married. You don't have any choice, and you know it. I'll come for you at one o'clock, so you get a dress on, and we'll go into town." He started for the door and then stopped and turned back to me. "Almost forgot. Here you go." He dug in his front pocket, snatched my hand up and put a black velvet box into it. I let the hand fall to my side. Impatiently, he took the box and opened it, holding it in front of my face. "Here's your engagement ring. Put some ice on your face. See you tomorrow."

Before he opened the door, he said, "Call the dog off."

I thought about giving the signal to attack, but I was afraid Randy'd have the chance to pull the pistol out of his pants and shoot me or poor old Tesla. So I complied. Randy winked at me again and walked off into the night.

Once he'd driven away, I ran out into the road and found Sarx wandering and bumping into the fence posts with bubbling lips, nose, and eyes, crying and whining. He must have gotten the bigger chemical dose. I led him back to the front steps and did my best to flush his and Tesla's faces with the hose. I brought them into the house, and I was able to see in the light how burned their poor eyes and noses were. I locked up then went into the bathroom.

My face was lopsided. I touched the cheek Randy had slapped, and it hurt. It would be bruised.

I would never forget this. That had been my first kiss. It was something I'd daydreamed about since I was twelve or so. I always imagined it would be in the moonlight, underneath a willow tree, maybe with music in the background. I looked at the picture of my mom, her smiling, happy face, and imagined her first kiss had been wonderful, magical. I could never do it over again. It was done.

I knelt in front of the toilet, stuck my finger down my throat and puked then spit several times. I brushed my teeth and rinsed my face.

Then I let myself cry.

As I inspected the photo of my mom again, I felt stronger. I imagined finding more pictures of her. Finding out what her name was. Finding out why my dad had done what he did. The answers to these questions must lie in the city we left when I was three: Detroit. After I got the box, the laptop, and the envelope, that's where I was going, and anyone who wanted to stop me would have to do more than slap me around. They'd have to kill me.

Chapter 10

Monday

PETTY

THE SWELLING IN my face had gone down, but my left cheek was bruised and still hurt. Worse was how my brain felt foggy and disjointed, which made me nervous. I needed to be sharp, and I couldn't wait another day.

I checked out back. Everything was set for the dogs. Now it was time to make the call. If just one domino in the sequence fell too early, the whole plan was ruined. I closed my eyes and prayed everything would work.

The iPhone's keypad sang out notes as I pressed the numbers to the supermarket in Saw Pole. "I need some groceries delivered," I said when a lady answered. "How soon could you get them to me?"

"How far are you?"

"Fifteen miles on County Road 167."

"Within the hour," she said. "Dekker just got back from lunch. Dekker?" She shouted the name away from the phone receiver.

"Dekker Sachs?" I said, aghast. It was the boy who'd brought the washing machine out to the dump my last day of work, the boy who'd tried to help me at the bank.

"You know any other Dekkers? 'Cause I sure don't."

"Do you have any other drivers available?"

The lady laughed. "Honey, he's our only driver. Where do you think you are, New York City?"

This was a monkey wrench I hadn't accounted for. I didn't want the driver to be someone I knew. But it was too late to back out now. I read the lady my list of canned goods. She repeated it back to me and said Dekker would be here soon. Then I erased the records of the calls I'd made, turned off the phone and smashed it with a hammer. I buried what was left in the yard.

I waited out front, keeping an eye out for the red Dodge pickup. Randy might decide to come by early, so I kept running inside to check the oven clock. It was 11:28 when I looked out the door and saw a cloud of dirt-road dust moving toward me. The vehicle that had caused the cloud pulled up to the house. It was Dekker's yellow pickup truck. The dogs attacked the truck, of course, and Dekker looked concerned behind the dusty windshield.

"Off," I yelled and signaled. They reluctantly backed away and sat, snarling and growling.

I scratched both their ears, feeling sentimental. Then I lifted the two bags out of the bed of the truck. Dekker rolled his window down an inch. "Can I carry those in for you, Petty?"

"No," I said. "I got it. But can you hold on a sec? I got something I want to ask you."

I took the canned goods inside, put them on the kitchen counter, and took one last look around. Then I went outside and locked the door.

The dogs were still sitting and growling, and Dekker's window was still cracked open.

"I wondered if you could take me into Saw Pole. I have an errand I need to run, and I can't drive."

He stared at me. "Really?"

"Yes."

"Sure. Get in."

"Just a minute." I turned away and squatted down to scratch the dogs' ears. I hugged them both. "Thanks for taking such good care of me," I whispered to them. "Sorry about the pepper spray."

They sat, panting and smiling at me as I got in the pickup truck. I was hit by the smell of cigarette smoke, and Dekker waved his hand through the air as if to make it disappear.

"Sorry about that," he said. "Wasn't planning on having a passenger. I'll roll down my window."

A scrunched pack of Camels sat on the console along with a lighter. I watched out the back window as we drove away, and I felt that sting behind my eyes.

"Those are some intense dogs," Dekker said.

I'd never been alone in a car with a boy my age. Dekker was so tall, the tips of his hair brushed the ceiling of the little truck, and he had big brown eyes. He had long fingers too and a large, pointy Adam's apple.

He pulled out onto the county road and drove west toward Niobe. "How've you been? How you holding up?"

"Okay," I said, my face to the window.

He turned down his music, as if he expected to have a conversation or something.

I kept looking out the window, my heart pounding with nerves.

"I was surprised when Candace told me who I was delivering to," he said. "Guess I didn't realize you'd never learned to drive."

I didn't say anything, so he went on.

"How come you didn't? I got my license the day of my sixteenth birthday. I couldn't wait, man. I mean, it's not like you can't walk wherever you want to go in Saw Pole, but just the idea of it, you know? The freedom. The idea I could drive to California if I wanted to . . . of course, I've never had the money to do anything like that, but . . ."

I stared out the window.

"Am I talking too much?"

"Yes."

"No one's ever answered that honestly before," he said. "Hey. I always wanted to ask you . . ."

I looked at him then and cringed. I could only imagine the kinds of things people wanted to ask about me and my dad.

His face fell. "Never mind."

We drove in a silence for a beat.

He drummed on the steering wheel to the music on the radio. "So did all your relatives roll into town for the funeral? You have a houseful?" He squeezed his eyes closed briefly. "And I'm going to shut up now. Sorry. Didn't mean to be nosy."

I kept my eyes on the right shoulder, looking for the little green Mile 211 sign.

"Stop," I said when I saw it.

"I will. I tend to talk too—"

"No. I mean pull over and stop the truck."

He braked to a stop. "Wow. This is unprecedented. I promise I'll shut up. You don't have to get out."

"Can you wait here?" I asked.

"Um, yeah?"

I jumped out of the truck and ran down into the ditch. I breathed a sigh of relief. The camouflage I'd arranged the day before on my walk had done its work. I brushed it away and lugged my bundle out of the ditch, and hoisted it into the bed of the truck. Then I got back in the cab.

Dekker looked through the back window and then at me. He blinked. "Is that a suitcase?"

"Yes," I said.

He shrugged and put the pickup in gear. "Okay." He continued drumming on the steering wheel.

We drove on, and I could feel Dekker's curiosity eating him up, his desire to talk dissolving his insides. It was kind of weird. I needed to focus so I let it go. He drove for five minutes before he spoke again.

"Where are we going?"

"Mr. Dooley's office," I said.

"The attorney?"

"Yeah."

"Okay. That's cool. Awesome. It's kind of great when I can get away from the grocery store because no one else our age works there. You're, like, twenty-one, right? It's all old ladies. I'm only working there until I can get enough money together to go back to K-State. People probably told you I flunked out, right? But I actually ran out of money, so . . ."

Who was he talking to? What "people" would have told me anything about him?

He rolled his eyes. "Sorry," he said. "You make me nervous."

"No, I don't," I said. He couldn't possibly know about my knife or Baby Glock, so what about me made him nervous?

He did a double take, a little smile on his lips. "No, you definitely do. You're just . . . I don't know. It's not you. It's me."

He shut up when we hit the city limit and I started scanning the streets for the red Dodge.

Dekker watched me. "So drop you off, or . . ."

"Could you wait for me?" I asked. "I'll only be a few minutes."

"Yeah. Sure. No problem."

He parked and I got out. I reached into the truck bed, unzipped the side pocket of the suitcase and removed a collapsible bag. I glanced up and down Main Street twice. It was deserted. I walked to the door of Mr. Dooley's office, which was unlocked. I was actually kind of disappointed; I wouldn't get to use the key he kept hidden under the windowsill.

I poked my head in the door and called out, "Hello? Mr. Dooley?"

No answer. It was straight-up noon, so as I'd hoped, he was gone, probably to lunch at the Cozy Corner. I went inside and closed the door behind me.

I ran into the inner office. On the desktop were piles of loose papers and stacks of file folders, and I despaired of finding mine. Where was it? I lifted several, afraid to upset the delicate balance of the folders, and finally I saw it.

I grabbed the folder, flopped it on top of everything else and opened it. There was the envelope. I shoved it into my bag, closed up the file, and put it back where it had been. As I ran through the outer office toward the stairs, a shadow darkened the front shades. I waited for Mr. Dooley to come in, but the shadow passed on by.

I took the stairs two at a time. The box and laptop were where I'd left them. After I shoved Dad's laptop into my bag, I pulled the tape from the top of the box and folded back the sides. I lifted everything out and set it on another box. On top was a photo album, which I stuffed into my bag, feeling prickles of excitement all over. More photos! Underneath was a stack of letters rubber-banded together, typed addresses on the envelopes. I shoved them in the bag too.

Below that lay coiled a silver necklace—the same necklace, I realized with a tingling chill, that Mom was wearing in the photo. Hanging on the chain was a silver box with polished gems on the sides and a hinged top. I felt like I might float to the ceiling. I examined the clasp and rather than try to figure it out, since I'd never worn any jewelry, I put it in my jeans pocket. I wanted to open the little box and look inside, but I had to hurry. *Later.*

There wasn't much room left in my bag, but all that was left in the box were longer, brownish-green file folders, the hanging kind. The top one was labeled BELLANDINI.

As I reached for it, I heard the front door of the office open.

Chapter 11

DEKKER

As I SAT waiting in my pickup, I kept thinking about all the things I might have said when Petty got in with me. "Third time's the charm," or "If you wanted to go out with me, you just had to ask," or "Fancy meeting you here!" and cringing at my utter lameness. I'd only had two girlfriends in my life, one in high school and one during my Brown Mackie days, so I wasn't exactly a player. I wouldn't allow myself to linger on the thought that kept rearing its pathetic head: all these chance meetings had to mean something. Right. Like we were destined to be together. Petty was beautiful, but she was also odd to an astonishing degree.

I lit up a Camel, ready to chuck it out the window the moment she appeared in the doorway. The clock on the dash told me I needed to be back to work in eighteen minutes. My boss Candace was a stickler for timed grocery runs, which was stupid because you never knew how long it would take. She claimed she'd clocked every possible route and knew exactly how long each one should take. She talked about this accomplishment as if it were exceptionally noteworthy, like climbing K2 or memorizing the phone book.

While I watched Dooley's office door, I tried to figure out a casual, conversational way to bring up the gig opening for Autopsyturvy. But two things occurred to me—no matter how I brought it up, it sounded like bragging. And secondly, it would mean exactly nothing to Petty. She'd have no idea how big this was. Then I allowed myself to imagine inviting her to the concert so she could see it for herself. That would be miserable for her—in a crowd with strangers, loud music. But this didn't stop me from picturing her standing in the front row, an expression of rapture on her face at my drumming brilliance.

Just then, Keith Dooley ambled down the sidewalk, in no hurry to get back to work after lunch at the Cozy Corner. Which struck me as weird. Why hadn't Petty come out when she realized Dooley wasn't there?

PETTY

MR. DOOLEY WHISTLED tunelessly between his teeth as he walked leisurely across the office floor. As quietly as I could, I stacked the file folders back in the box, closed it up and replaced the tape.

I remembered how creaky the stairs were, but I placed my feet on the outer edges of them where they were less likely to make noise. They weren't sound-free, but it was better. It didn't hurt that Mr. Dooley kept his radio going all the time. Down I went, little by little, until I got to the ground floor. Now I had to get out the front door without him seeing me. I got on my back and reverse-army-crawled toward the door, my bag on my stomach.

When I got there, I took my time getting to my feet. I crouched behind the three-foot-high counter until his phone rang.

"Dooley," he said.

I put the bag strap over my head, filled my lungs with air, exhaled and slowly depressed the thumb button on the door handle in increments, pulling the door toward me in slow motion—

Which rang the bell over the door, something I'd somehow forgotten about in just four minutes.

I heard Mr. Dooley get to his feet.

"Come on in," he called.

I slipped out the door and walked toward the yellow pickup truck.

DEKKER

PETTY LOOKED UP and down the street once after exiting Dooley's office and then got in the truck.

She had a soft briefcase-type bag with her, and it was bulging.

"What's that?" I said.

"A bag," Petty said.

I glanced over my shoulder to back out of the space, then looked forward as the door to Dooley's office opened once again and Dooley himself appeared with his phone pressed to his ear. He twisted his head left then right, his mouth moving the whole time. I turned to ask Petty where she wanted to go just as she ducked her head, as if searching for something she'd dropped below the seat.

"Um, Petty?" I said.

Without really moving her lips, Petty said, "Go."

"Go?" I echoed stupidly. What did she think I was doing? But then I saw Dooley walking toward us, a grimace on his face, and suddenly I knew.

"What were you doing in Dooley's office?" I reached for the bag.

She covered her face with her hand and said, "Go, Dekker, please."

"Not until you tell me—"

Suddenly, Petty removed a handgun from inside her zippered hoodie and shoved the muzzle into my hip.

"Go," she said.

Waves of panic spread from the place on my leg where the pistol touched, and my muscles locked up. And all I could think was, *I knew it.* What I supposedly knew, though, I couldn't have said. I stared at Petty, outraged.

"I didn't want to have to do this," she said through gritted teeth. "Go now, before Mr. Dooley sees me, or I'll shoot you. Believe me. I'll do it."

I believed her. With more calm than I felt, I smoothly backed out of the space then put the truck in gear and drove the twenty-five-mile-an-hour speed limit toward the cemetery.

Spots pulsed at the edges of my vision. The center of my universe was that quarter-inch round spot on my hip. When I thought I could trust my voice, I said, "I'm going to drive you out to Highway 16 and I'm going to let you out. I won't tell anyone anything. I don't know what kind of trouble you're in, but I'd rather not get involved."

This had to be some kind of weird militia shit, some mission she was carrying out on behalf of her insane dead father.

In my rearview mirror I saw Dooley standing on the sidewalk, talking into his phone and gesturing. I refocused through the windshield on a red Dodge Ram driving toward us. It looked like Randy King's. Beside me, Petty folded in half, her face to the seat.

"What the hell, Petty?"

"Keep going," she said.

I trained my eyes on the road, grinding my teeth.

"Is that red pickup gone?" she asked.

My eyes flicked to the rearview mirror. "Yes."

Petty sat up. "Drive me to Salina."

"You want to rephrase that as a question?"

It was clear from her expression she had no idea what I was talking about.

"How about a please, at least?"

Still, she said nothing.

"Fuck you," I said. "I'm not doing shit for you after you . . ."

I'd never, in my twenty-two years, ever said "fuck you" to a girl. Not even in jest. My hands shook with rage and fear, my face was hot and my eyes watery.

"I didn't want it to be you," Petty said. "When I called the grocery I didn't know it would be you."

"Well, that makes two of us."

"If you'll take me to Salina, I'll give you every cent I have. I've got twenty-six dollars. I need to pawn some things and then get on a bus out of town."

"What?" I wiped at my eyes, but I didn't care that I looked like I was crying. "Everybody was right. You and your old man are fucking bat-shit insane. I mean, here it is, in living color. Holy shit. I can't believe this."

"Please, Dekker. I am *begging* you."

"Women and drama. They go together like—like—I'm doing just like I said. I'm dumping you off at 16 and good fucking riddance to you, you psycho."

She withdrew the gun from my leg and pointed it at my head.

"Drive me to Nick's Pawnshop in Salina. I'll sell my stuff, I'll pay you for your time and gas, and then you can go. Do it, or I will shoot you. I'm fucking bat-shit insane, and I will shoot you."

I hated the ragged, desperate sound of my own breathing, but I hated her more. It felt like the flesh of my face had been drained of blood, tight against my cheekbones. If I hadn't been clutching the steering wheel so tight, my hands would have been shaking hard enough to knock me to the ground. I should drive her straight to the cop shop over in Niobe, but she'd know where I was going, and I believed she wouldn't hesitate to blow my head off. I cursed myself for trying to help her in the bank yesterday, helpless in the presence of a pretty girl. So I kept driving, unable to do anything else.

My phone buzzed, startling me, making me jump, and I was afraid the movement would make Petty's gun go off. I started to reach for it, but Petty said, "Don't answer that."

"It's my boss," I said.

She pushed the barrel into my temple again. "Don't."

"Okay. Shit."

After a bit, Petty's gun was no longer aimed at my head, but it was close enough to take care of business if necessary. I drove five minutes longer as waves of nausea rolled through me. When I couldn't hold it any longer, I pulled to the side of the road.

"What are you doing?" Petty said, raising the gun again.

"Permission to vomit, please," I said, then threw open the door and threw up.

Chapter 12

DEKKER

"Let's go," Petty said.

"Hurff," I said. The wind blew and the occasional car or semi rushing by intensified it.

"Come on," Petty said, nudging me in the back with her gun.

I was in no position to have a conversation at this point. I held up a hand as I spat and rubbed my mouth with my sleeve. I closed the door, staring out the windshield.

"I think you should get out of my truck," I said.

"You'd better—"

"You're not going to shoot me," I said. I hoped saying it would make it true. "Get out of my truck. I don't care where you go, but you're not going there in my truck."

"Go now!"

"Get out of my fucking—" As I turned, I saw a red truck pulling up behind us. Curiosity quelled my anger temporarily. Hadn't it been going the opposite direction down Main Street only moments ago?

"Hey," I said. "Here comes Randy King's—"

Petty dove to the floor of the cab, curled into a smaller ball than I would have thought possible, and pulled her bag on top of herself.

"Petty, why—" I looked up in time to see Randy pull up beside me, the passenger window level with mine. In the seat was Keith Dooley. He rolled his window down and grinned expectantly at me. I was ready to signal with my eyes that Petty was on the floor of the Toyota, because surely she wouldn't shoot me in front of two witnesses. But something stopped me.

"Hey," Randy said around Dooley. I'd always known who Randy King the Militia Man was but had never actually met him.

"Hi, Dekker," Dooley said. "How are you today?"

"Fine," I said out the window, my tongue thick and abraded from puking. I wondered if the lawyer could smell the fresh vomit on the road directly below his face, and the thought horrified me.

"Was that Petty Moshen I saw in your truck earlier?" Dooley asked.

"Yeah," I said without hesitation. "She needed a ride."

"A ride? From where? To where?"

"From her house to . . . town, I guess."

Dooley glanced over his shoulder at Randy, whose mustache twitched.

"And what happened when you got to town?"

This was strangely reminiscent of TV court cross-examinations, and my guts started rolling again. "She got out of the truck."

I watched Dooley rise almost imperceptibly in his seat, trying to see into the Toyota. Maybe Stockholm syndrome had already set in, because I was careful not to shift my gaze, not to look at my passenger hiding on the floor, and my eyes watered with the effort.

"Where is she now?" Randy asked me.

I shrugged. "I don't know."

"Where'd you leave her off?"

"On Main Street."

"On Main Street," Randy said, almost mockingly. "Where on Main Street?"

"Son," Dooley said. "You need to know something about Petty Moshen. She's not well. She's not right in the head. Sad but true. I advise you to not take any more delivery calls from her. She's unstable. You might have heard about the incident a few years back at the dump. She can be dangerous."

Of course I remembered the incident at the dump. Everybody did. Justin Pencey and a few of his brain-dead pals went out to the dump to torment her but got more than they bargained for. Justin had told everyone that she'd attacked them for no reason, but no one who knew Justin actually believed this. Still, it hadn't stopped everyone from embellishing the story to paint Petty as a monster freak.

So "dangerous" seemed a bit of an overdramatic interpretation. "Defending herself" was more like it. This further put me on alert.

"She's actually retarded or autistic. Something like that," Randy put in.

Dooley looked back at Randy, annoyed. "In any event," he said, "if you know where she is, you need to tell us so we can help her."

Randy put his hand on Dooley's arm. "We're wasting our time," he said. "Don't worry. We'll find her. She can't get far."

His weird confidence seemed to confirm my intuition. I knew Petty was strange, but it wasn't like she hadn't been provoked that day at the dump. It wasn't like that behavior came out of nowhere. And I got a major bully vibe off Randy. Plus Dooley was a lawyer. So fuck them.

My phone buzzed again. Candace would be throwing a rod back at the grocery, wondering where I was, what was taking so long.

"Aren't you going to answer that?" Dooley said.

"Nope," I said.

We stared at each other until the phone quit buzzing.

"Well," I said, taking a Camel from the console, lighting it up and blowing a lungful of smoke into the Ram. "I don't know what to tell you. I'm just out making a delivery. So I'm going to go on ahead now. Good luck to you." I rolled up my window and, without letting my eyes drift downward, accelerated out from the roadblock of the Dodge Ram and back onto the two-lane highway.

Neither of us spoke for several minutes, and Petty didn't rise from the floor.

"So what kind of trouble are you in?" I said. "Come up here. The coast is clear, or whatever."

Petty climbed up in the seat and looked out through the back window. She turned, sat and buckled up.

"That was, like, beyond weird," I said.

Petty was silent.

"Do you want to hear what they said?"

"No."

Why didn't she want to know? I'd never met someone so un-talkative. So literal and awkward. So uninquisitive. I, on the other hand, was burning with curiosity. But I held off for a while. Finally, I said, "Why is . . . Randy King so interested in where you are?"

Petty winced.

"I mean, he really, *really* wants to know where you are. I mean, really."

"I know."

I finished my cigarette and flicked it out the window. I drove silently for several minutes, thinking about all the possible reasons two men with as little in common as Dooley and Randy King would be hunting an awkward, isolated, grieving girl, and couldn't come up with anything. If she'd killed someone or robbed a bank, they would have flat-out said so. And actually, the cops would be the ones out searching. My sense of injustice was ruffled, so I turned my head toward Petty and said, "You can put the gun away. I'll take you to Salina. But then I want you out of my truck. I don't know what kind of shit you're mixed up in, but I don't need it. My life is starting to turn around, and I don't need any drama to fuck it up. Okay?"

"Okay," Petty said.

"Good."

Another fifteen minutes went by before I spoke again. "You burglarized Dooley's office, didn't you? That's what it is, right?"

But if that's what it was, why was Randy King involved?

"No."

"What's all that shit in your bag? You didn't go into his office with it."

Petty sighed. "Things that belonged to my dad."

Weirdness on top of weirdness. "Why did Dooley have them?"

"Long story," Petty said.

PETTY

"WHERE IS THIS pawnshop?" Dekker asked as we drove into Salina an hour later.

I gave him the address. I kept an eagle eye out, because I didn't know whether he was going to drive me straight to the police station. But he pulled into the parking lot of a corrugated tin-shed-type building with the sign NICK'S PAWNSHOP on the front. I was disappointed. I'd hoped for a pawnshop like those I'd seen on TV. A storefront in an old New York City brick building with the crisscrossed bars over the windows. This building stood alone and seemed fairly new. It also looked so flimsy it would crumple if you leaned on it too hard.

"Can you help me get some stuff out of my suitcase back there?" I asked. "I need to pawn it."

"So you said."

"Will you help me?"

"Why not," Dekker said. It was not said kindly, more like he didn't really mean it. But then he smiled. It was going to take me a while to decipher what different tones of voice and facial expressions meant in the real world. I wished I had a chart or something.

We got out of the truck. I felt stiff and slow after all the stress of the afternoon. I unzipped the suitcase and surveyed my dad's and my guns. It was the story of my life in firearms.

"Holy shit," Dekker said, stepping backward with his hands in the air. "So your dad really was survivalist guy, huh? A John Bircher?"

"Dad always said it was a dangerous world," I said. I carefully considered what I wanted to sell and what I would need to keep and use. "Which do you think will bring the most money?"

Dekker kept his hands up and said, "I don't know shit about guns."

Finally, I chose the 9mm Sig Sauer P226, the Stoeger Double Defense shotgun, the Bushmaster AR-15, and the AK-47. I'd packed each with its registration papers. I left the Winchester rifle, the Mossberg 590 Mariner, and the Weatherby SA-459 TR.

"What about the one you got in your holster?" Dekker said. "You gonna sell that one?"

"No," I said. "That was the last thing my dad ever gave me."

"Just a sentimental fool, wasn't he?"

Dekker picked up the AK and the AR and held them like they might explode spontaneously. He went to the door and held it open for me, but I shook my head. He shrugged and went in. I followed, back to the wall, found the exits, located the security cameras, evaluated the threat level. The building had the smell of old dust. I pictured in my mind the kind of guy who would be behind the counter—a short, round Italian guy with a cigar in the corner of his mouth wearing a Hawaiian shirt. I was of course disappointed again. The guy behind the counter was tall and thin and very white, like most people in Kansas, and he was wearing a blue button-down shirt.

Dekker laid the guns carefully on top of the glass. I set the dump diamond ring next to them and pulled out the black jewelry box with my engagement ring. I was happy to be rid of the thing—it felt dirty and evil. If I didn't need the money so badly, I'd use it for target practice.

I set the ring box on top of the Bushmaster.

Dekker raised his eyebrows but didn't say anything.

I reached inside my pocket and felt my mom's silver necklace chain. No way would I pawn this, even if it were worth anything.

The clerk surveyed the collection of stuff, looked up at Dekker and then at me. "Shotgun wedding?"

"That's a rifle, not a shotgun," I said. "There's a difference. See, a rifle has a—"

Dekker burst out laughing. I turned to him, confused, and then saw the clerk was laughing too. He gathered up the gun papers and the rings.

"Take a look around. I'll be right back." He disappeared through a doorway.

"Did Randy King give you those rings?"

"One of them," I said. "The other I found at the dump."

"So . . . you're a runaway bride, is that it?"

"Not exactly."

I heard buzzing coming from Dekker's pocket.

"Go ahead," I said. I figured it was safe now because he wasn't acting like a hostage anymore. He was acting how I'd always imagined friends might act.

He dug out the cell phone, glanced at it then flipped it open and held it to his ear. "Hello?"

The clerk came back, both rings on his right pinky. "I can give you thirty-five hundred for everything."

That was more than I'd hoped for. It would get me to Detroit and hold me over until I got a job. I thought. I wasn't completely sure, but it was a lot better than twenty-six dollars.

"Okay," I said.

The clerk nodded and produced a carbon copy form for me to fill out and a pen. He then lifted the Stoeger Double Defense. "They ain't loaded, right?" he said.

"'Course they are," I said. I pulled it out of his hands, broke it and grabbed the shells as they popped out. I handed everything back to him. "There you go."

Dekker and the guy stared at me for a few beats before the pawnbroker said, "Be right back with your cash," and went in the back room again.

"So Dooley called my boss," Dekker said. "Wanted to know what time I took the groceries out to you, what time I got back to work." His eyebrow quirked. "I told her I took your groceries out to you, then gave you a ride into town and let you off at the cemetery so you could visit your dad. Then I went home because I got sick."

I pressed my lips tight together. The cemetery story was pretty good.

The clerk reappeared and gave me an envelope with my money in it. "Count it, please," he said. "Then initial this and sign here."

I did and then put the money in my pocket.

"Thank you," Dekker said to the old man.

We walked outside and got in the truck.

"Do you have the bus terminal address?" Dekker said.

I gave it to him. "And then you'll be rid of me," I said.

The terminal wasn't far. When we got there, Dekker got my suitcase out of the bed of the truck and set it on the sidewalk. "Are you in the witness protection program or something? I gotta tell you, I am—"

"Thank you very much for your help," I said. I pulled some of the pawn money from my pocket and held it out to him.

He backed away from it. "I'm not taking—"

"It's definitely the least I can do," I said, stuffing it in his shirt pocket. "I put you through a lot today. I'm sorry. And I really appreciate your help."

He stood staring at me. I picked up my suitcase and headed for the terminal door.

I didn't look back.

DEKKER

BACK IN MY truck, I felt enormous relief at being rid of that strange girl. It was just my luck to be kidnapped at gunpoint. It was like

I had a fiery red arrow pointed at me that attracted the notice of every zombie freak goon out there. As I adjusted the rearview, I found myself rehearsing in my mind how I was going to tell the story to my bandmates when I got to Kansas City.

But the conversation with Dooley and Randy King kept rolling through my mind. Something was fishy here. Petty could obviously take care of herself, but she was more alone than anyone I'd ever met.

I put the truck in gear and pulled out onto Broadway before pity could overwhelm me. I switched on the radio, hoping to wash away the picture in my mind of that lone girl and her sad suitcase. My life was turning around, and I didn't need any complications. No matter how beautiful she was.

At a stoplight, I pulled the cash she'd given me from of my pocket and fanned it out. Ten one-hundred-dollar bills.

A horn honk from the rear startled me into hitting the gas and moving forward, but I was so rattled by the wad of bills that I had to pull off the road.

Traffic whizzed past me as I wrestled with what was left of my conscience. A thousand dollars would get me to Kansas City, and buy some great stage gear and plenty of good feelings from my bandmates. But Petty had given me nearly one-third of all the money she had in the world. Surely she didn't mean to give me that much—maybe she'd thought they were tens instead of hundreds.

On the other hand, maybe this was the universe's way of telling me the band thing was going to work out, of urging me on toward stardom. Maybe this was a karmic gift for helping out the town weirdo.

But even as I thought this, I knew it was bullshit. I knew it was a justification to rob this girl who was truly desperate in a way that I would never experience or fully understand. She was going to need every dime she had. This was not my money. I had to go back and return it.

I made a U-turn, cursing the angel on my shoulder.

PETTY

I BOUGHT MY ticket, pushed open the restroom door and, after I'd investigated every stall, walked into the last one. Luckily it was large. I wedged my suitcase between the toilet and the wall then sat on it. Unless someone got on his knees and looked under the door, I was invisible. From my bag I pulled a paperback and started reading but saw I'd become too engrossed and my OODA Loop would disappear entirely. I put the book back in my bag and promised myself I'd get it out once the bus crossed the Nebraska state line.

It was going to be a long night. I sat listening, turning over in my head what I would do if Randy King came busting in there. My back ached from sitting awkwardly, but I hoped it would help me stay awake and alert.

Twenty minutes later the restroom door opened and I heard high heels on the linoleum. Then I heard the stall doors being pushed open one by one. And finally:

"Petty Moshen? Are you in here?"

I held my breath, sitting silent and still. More clicking high heels coming toward my stall. A tinny knock on the stall door. A female voice Randy couldn't fake. "Petty Moshen?"

"No," I said.

"Aren't you the one who just bought a ticket to Detroit?"

"No."

"Yes, you are," she said, irritation peppering her voice. "Come on out here. There's a man who wants to talk to you."

How had he found me?

"Please," I said. "Please tell him I'm not here."

"Come on out of there, now."

"Please," I whispered.

"He says he has something of yours."

Has something of mine?

"Does this man have a big mustache?"

"No."

"Are you sure?"

"I think I'd probably notice if he did. This kid doesn't look like he could grow any facial hair at all."

Dekker?

The woman huffed. "Now come out of there. I need to get back to work." Her shoes made brisk sharp sounds as she walked across the linoleum and out the door.

I got to my feet and unlocked the stall. I went to the restroom door and peeked out. A blur of passengers—all ages, sizes, and races—trooped wearily past carrying suitcases and backpacks. In the midst of this migration stood Dekker.

"Come out of there," he said.

I scanned the crowd once more. "Is anyone with you?"

"It's just me."

"What do you want?"

He rolled his eyes. "Would you just come here?"

I hesitated, then walked into the lobby, keeping an eye out for Randy or Mr. Dooley.

"Nobody's here," Dekker said.

"Why did you come back?"

"I was at the last stoplight on the way out of town," he said, "and I started wondering." He lowered his voice. "What could make a girl so desperate she'd kidnap a delivery boy and then turn around and give him a thousand dollars? And all day I kept thinking you had a smudge on your face, but then at some point you turned your head and I saw what it really was."

I put my hand to the cheek Randy had slapped.

"So I had to come back and return your money and make sure you were going to be okay."

In that moment I had an odd sensation in my chest and arms. They were tingling. I realized what it was. I wanted to hug Dekker, and it was very nearly a physical pull. Which set off alarms.

"I'm fine," I said. "And I won't take that money back. That's yours. You earned it. I threatened to shoot you."

He seemed to mull this over. "When does your bus leave?"

"Tomorrow morning at ten forty-five."

"What are you going to do until then?"

"Sit in the bathroom," I said.

"How about you come with me instead?"

I looked at him and then away. My muscles all seemed to loosen then, while my stomach simultaneously contracted. Everything jumbled in my head, the signals in my body contradicting each other, jockeying for control. What was going on? "Come with me" sounded comforting, thrilling, and terrifying at the same time. My dad hadn't trained me for this.

"I don't know if I can trust you," I said.

"I didn't take you to the police, so that should tell you something right there."

"Maybe that's where you're going to take me right now," I said, but I didn't really mean it.

"I know a place you can stay tonight, and it's not the county jail."

"I don't think I should—"

"It's safer and more comfortable than a bathroom. Come on."

I thought about how Dad had said I could trust Mr. Dooley, and I could trust Randy King. But he'd also said, "You judge a man by his actions." The way those two acted was not honorable. Dekker, on the other hand, had come back for me, and tried to give back the money.

These were trustworthy actions.

It seemed Dad hadn't been the best judge of character. Maybe I could do better. Maybe I could figure out who to trust all on my own. I went in the bathroom, got my suitcase and hauled it out to the lobby.

Dekker picked it up.

"Let's go," he said.

I followed him out the door.

Chapter 13

DEKKER

As I LED Petty out of the bus station, I wondered if I was making yet another mistake. But I felt confident that for once I was doing the right thing. It didn't have anything to do with how good-looking she was.

We got in the truck.

"Just don't ask me any questions," Petty said.

"Deal," I said. "And don't threaten me with bodily harm."

"Deal," Petty said.

"This girl I'm going to call I haven't seen in over a year." I opened my phone and dialed. "But we're old pals. She's from Saw Pole too. Did you ever know Ashley Heussner?" I shook my head. "No, of course you didn't."

A raspy voice said, "Hello?"

"Hey, Ash. It's Dekker. I'm in town and I wondered if me and a friend could crash there tonight."

A prolonged squeal made me pull the phone away from my ear. Petty's face showed alarm, so I covered the mouthpiece with my hand and said, "Everything's okay. This is her way of saying she's happy to hear from me."

"Dekker! I've missed you so much! Why haven't you called? I can't believe it's really you! Yes, yes, yes! Come to my place and we'll catch up! It'll be so much fun!"

I kept trying to interrupt and cut the call short, but Ashley made it impossible. "Okay—okay—when's a good—"

"Just come on over. We'll go out and get shit-faced. You're buying, right? You owe me! You know you owe me!"

"Okay. We'll see you soon." While she was still talking, I clicked end, pocketed the phone and said to Petty, "You have to do that. She'll keep talking. She's probably still talking."

Then I pulled out the wad of hundreds Petty had given me. "I can't take this." I held the bills out to her.

"Yes, you can," she said. "I'm not taking it back. I can't tell you how sorry—"

I held up a hand. "Let me explain how this whole apology-slash-forgiveness thing works. You say you're sorry, and you really mean it. I say that's all right, but, like, please don't point a gun at me ever again. And you say I won't, and you really, really mean it. And then we move on. But please take your money back."

"No." She turned away and looked out the windshield.

"All right, then," I said, but I felt like I was taking the last remaining vial of a diabetic's insulin. "I'm taking you out for dinner, and you're going to order whatever you want to eat and drink, and I'm paying."

The silence that greeted this made me turn toward Petty, whose lips were trembling.

"You okay?" I said.

"Yes."

"You have any favorites? Places you like to eat?"

She shook her head and turned it toward the window.

"Ashley said to come on over. Would it be cool with you if we made a stop? I need to get some more cigarettes if we're going to Ashley's. She only smokes OPs."

"OPs?"

"Other people's."

"That's fine," Petty said.

We pulled into a Walgreens lot, parked and got out. I remembered not to wait for Petty to go through the door first and walked inside past the automatic sliding door toward the beverages. I turned to say something to her and realized she was not beside me. I backtracked to the front of the store, where I found her standing and staring with her mouth open.

"What is it?" I said.

She gestured. "This," she said. "I've never been inside a store before."

"Never?" I said, a little too loudly. I wondered what it would be like to see a place like Walgreens for the first time, dazzled by all the products and colorful packaging in real life instead of on TV.

She was so awed, in fact, that she turned in circles—she must have been so happy to be out in the world that she was twirling. I hoped she'd stop soon, because it was a little embarrassing.

"You want anything?" I asked her. "Soda? A snack?"

"I'm thirsty," she said.

I led her over to the drink case and she stared at the rows of energy drinks, sports drinks, flavored teas, sodas and water.

"You want a Coke?"

"Never had one," she said.

Had she ever eaten Twinkies or Doritos or any of the staples I grew up on? I didn't want to ask, to draw more attention to her weirdness.

"How about a bottle of water?" I said.

"Okay."

I handed her a chilled bottle of Aquafina. Up at the counter, I asked the clerk for two packs of Camels and paid for everything with my new cash.

"Thank you," Petty said as we walked out the door.

I nodded. As we stepped onto the sidewalk, two guys on skateboards whizzed toward us at high speed. I reflexively reached for Petty's arm to pull her out of the way.

What came next happened so fast I barely had time to process it. Petty brought her arm up whip-smart, instantly and painfully breaking my grip on it, then bounced backward with her fists up. Just as quickly she dropped her hands in front of her, embarrassed when she saw the skater boys and realized I was only trying to keep her from getting creamed.

"Whoa!" I said, impressed. "Do that again!" My finger and wrist bones rang from the force of her movement.

Petty shook her arms out and avoided my eyes. "No," she said.

"Do you know like kung fu and stuff like that?" I couldn't disguise my admiration, didn't want to. This girl was a straight-up badass.

"Listen," she whispered. "I'm not used to having people touch me."

Before I could stop myself, I let this sink in too far and felt the girl's loneliness and isolation so acutely I wanted to run from her.

"It's cool," I said. "Don't worry about it."

I led Petty back to the truck and unlocked her door. Then we drove to where Ashley lived, a large, old brick house with a patchy front yard.

Petty followed me up to the front door, next to which were five mailboxes.

"Why does she have all these?" she asked, pointing.

"They aren't all hers," I said. "The house is divided up into apartments." I smiled. "You know, hanging out with you is a little like hanging out with E.T."

"Who?"

"Don't tell me," I said, incredulous. "You've never seen *E.T.*? E.T., the extraterrestrial? You know, 'E.T., phone home!'" I said that last bit in my best approximation of E.T.'s voice, but it came out sounding like Donald Duck.

"I know what it is, but I've never seen the movie."

"The whole world has seen it," I said.

"My dad wasn't real big on kids' movies. *A Clockwork Orange*, yes. Disney, no."

A Clockwork Orange? Wow. "You have a lot of catching up to do." I looked at the mailboxes and pointed at the one labeled HEUSSNER. "She's in 1A." I opened the door, and inside was a stuffy tiled foyer divided by a staircase. Somebody's TV was blaring behind one of the doors on either side the stairs, 1B to the right and 1A on the left. I knocked on 1A.

The sound of the TV lessened. "Yeah?"

"It's Dekker," I called.

The door flew open, drawing with it a billow of smoke which then rebounded outward. The smell hit me like a two-by-four to the face. But then the sight of Ashley's face whacked me even harder. It was just a skull covered in scabby skin. She was shockingly thin, and her hair was greasy and dry at the same time, yellow with brown roots. Her eyes shone unnaturally bright.

I'd made a huge mistake bringing Petty here.

Ashley lurched toward me and clutched my arm with her skeletal, nail-bitten hand. "Dekker!" she squealed, and pulled me toward her. She planted a big kiss on my mouth with flaky, dry lips. Her breath smelled like nail polish remover and cigarettes.

Just as quickly and before I could stop her, Ashley pushed me away and reached for Petty, who jumped backward.

Ashley rolled her eyes at me and then said, "Hi, Petty."

I didn't like the way she said Petty's name, like she was spitting out some gristle. This was not the sweet girl I remembered. This was somebody else. I knew Ashley had heard the stories about Petty's strangeness, but the old Ashley would have acted more charitably toward someone like Petty. Even though Ashley was somewhat competitive with other girls, she'd never been nasty like this.

It was going to be a long night.

Petty fixed her eyes on me. "You didn't tell me she was a methamphetamine addict." She turned to Ashley. "How long have you been using?"

The flicker of rage on Ashley's face appeared and disappeared like a haunted house black-light flash of lightning.

"Whoa!" I said. "What a kidder this girl is, huh?"

Petty said, "I'm not—"

"Jeez, Ash, crack a window," I said, taking Ashley by the shoulders and twirling her away. Petty couldn't know that in real life, unlike on TV, you never called out an addict unless you had a van and a cot waiting. You pretended she wasn't an addict, even with clear evidence staring you in the face. I'd never actually put words to this phenomenon, but it was as if Petty had been put on earth to expose everything that would show up on a bullshit meter.

I glared over Ashley's shoulder at Petty and shook my head, hoping she'd get the hint. She looked bewildered.

Ashley took a big drag of her cigarette and blew directly in my face then laughed. It wasn't the laugh I remembered. She literally laughed—"Ha ha ha, ha ha ha"—her voice brittle and rough.

"Come on in," she said with an arm sweep. Then she ran around the cluttered living room snatching up piles of clothes, which she pitched through a door on the other side of the room. "I was just picking up." She emptied ashtray after overflowing ashtray into a paper sack. "Gotta save these," she said as she went. "I have to save them and get the leftover tobacco out of the butts to roll some more. I can't afford to buy any right now, and it's not like I'm going to give it up."

While she was doing that, I watched Petty turn in a slow circle, her eyes scanning every inch of the room.

Ashley picked up stacks of magazines and carried them through the kitchen doorway. "I wasn't expecting you so soon," she called.

The sound of water running and dishes clanking came from the kitchen. Petty bent and looked underneath the couch.

"You told us to come on over," I called back through the doorway, wondering what exactly Petty was searching for.

Ashley laughed. "That's right. Time got away from me, I guess."

"Can I help with anything?" I asked.

"No, no, you two make yourselves at home. I'm going to finish up in here and then we can go out and get a beer."

"Listen," Dekker said. "You sure it's okay if we stay here?"

"Of course," Ashley called above the splashing and clattering.

"Thanks," I said. "We can't stay out too late because Petty's got a bus to catch in the morning."

"Whatever," Ashley said. The water turned off. "I'm going to get cleaned up and then we'll be off."

She disappeared again and I heard the shower turn on.

"Do you think she'd mind if I changed the channel?" Petty asked, pointing at the TV.

"Go ahead," I said, and went into the kitchen. The counters were piled with crusted dishes, food from possibly weeks ago. The smell was gag-inducing. I could almost hear the cockroaches in the walls scratching to get out and feast. I opened some of the cabinets and found nothing but spices and a few cans. In the refrigerator was mustard, a bowl full of green fuzzy mold, and a carton of milk with an expiration date of two weeks ago.

The sound of changing television channels drifted in through the kitchen doorway until I heard the familiar minor-key theme song of *Offender International*. I returned to the living room and found Petty standing with her back to the wall, eyes riveted on the TV.

"You okay?" I asked her.

She shrugged. I could tell she didn't feel safe here. I probably should have taken her to another of my friends' places in Salina, but they were all guys, and I didn't think she'd be comfortable in a man cave. Ashley was the only girl I knew in town.

I sat on the couch and watched the show until Ashley reappeared looking like a whole different person, almost like her old self. She wore jeans and a jeans jacket, had on makeup, and her hair was curled. She was almost pretty.

"So let's go, let's do this," Ashley said, lighting a cigarette.

"You ready to go, Petty?" I asked.

She didn't move, her eyes on the TV.

Ashley took a drag off her cigarette and stared in Petty's direction.

A glance at the clock on the wall told me that about three minutes remained in the episode.

"Hey, Ashley," I said. "Do you have your yearbook from my senior year handy? I want to show Petty our pictures, show her what she missed."

Ashley squealed. "It's in my room. I'll go get it."

She went into her bedroom and closed the door behind her.

On the TV, Detective Mandy Quirke was telling the killer how she knew it was him. The killer sobbed into his hands. As the uniforms handcuffed him and led him out of the interview room, Mandy's partner said something clever and the black screen that says "Created by Bob Blaine" appeared. Petty turned off the TV.

I stuck my head in the door Ashley had disappeared through. "Never mind," I said, "we can find it later. Let's go. I'm hungry."

On the way out to the truck, I asked Ashley, "So where you working?"

"Well," Ashley said, dragging on her cigarette before crushing it out on the walk. "I was working at Schwan's, but I got laid off."

Right. Laid off. I turned my face away so she wouldn't see my skepticism. As if she'd notice. I unlocked the pickup. Petty opened the passenger door, pushed the seat forward and sat on the little shelf seat behind the buckets, letting Ashley have shotgun. I totally understood why Petty didn't want Ashley to sit behind her. Ashley probably struck her as the kind of girl who was handy with a garrote.

"Where we going?" I asked.

"Knucklehead's," Ashley said, pulling a cigarette out of her pocket and lighting it up. She held it to my lips and I took a grateful hit.

"You're gonna have to tell me where to go," I said, pulling away from the curb.

"I'll tell you where to go, all right," Ashley said. "Ha ha ha, ha ha ha. It's on Pacific and Third."

It was only a few blocks away. The bar was a cinder-block building the size of a small ranch house. I parked on the street and Ashley swiveled the rearview mirror to look at herself and fluff her hair before getting out. Instead of holding the seat forward for Petty, she let it clunk back into place and walked ahead of us to the bar. I sighed and yanked the seat so Petty could get out. As Ashley disappeared inside, Petty froze up.

"I can't go in there," she said.

"Sure you can," I said. "You got your ID, right?"

"No, I mean . . . I . . ."

Once again, pity for this girl washed over me. What must it be like to be so paranoid? Still, observing Petty side by side with Ashley made me admire her more, because unlike Ashley, Petty hadn't chosen her circumstances.

"I'll stay right by your side," I said. "There's nothing to be nervous about."

"I think I'd better wait in the truck."

"Listen," I said. "Let's go in there for a little while. I think we—I should buy her a beer or two since she's letting us stay at her place for free. I'll make sure you're sitting against the wall, away from the window. I will not leave your side. Okay?"

Petty breathed deeply, clearly psyching herself up.

"You want me to get your gun out of the truck? Would that make you feel safer?"

"It's not in the truck," she said, and opened her hoodie to show me her holstered pistol.

The sight of it made my stomach clench. I stopped walking. "Wait. You can't wear that in there."

"But you asked me if I wanted you to—"

"I know I did, but I was just . . ."

Why had I said that? I'd never really thought about all the ordinary, weird conversational and behavioral tics everybody used; the casual lies, the empty offers, the figures of speech.

Petty awaited my answer.

"That's just how people talk."

"Why?"

"They just do," I said.

"So why can't I wear the gun in there?"

"You got a concealed carry permit?" When in doubt, divert, distract, or avoid the subject altogether is my motto.

"I'm not going in there without it," Petty said.

"You're not going to threaten anyone, right?"

"Not unless someone threatens me first. Or you. Or even Ashley."

The people I knew who toted guns around with them—who was I kidding? The guys I knew who carried were usually overcompensating for their shortcomings, ready to yank out their piece and wave it around like a flag. Petty was the first person I'd ever met who actually carried for self-protection. I couldn't help but feel admiration for this strange girl.

"Okay," I said.

Instead of holding the door for her, I led the way inside, where the sharp *whock* of colliding pool balls punctuated loud classic rock. Just beyond the door, Petty stood with her back against the wall and scanned the room.

Ashley, who had her arms draped over two guys' shoulders,

waved at me. I pointed to a table in the corner, which would be a perfect place from which to view the entire room.

Petty led the way over to it, turning in a circle, then sat on a stool with her back against the wall. Ashley came dancing over to the table, an unlit cigarette between her lips.

"You want a beer?" Ashley asked me, then turned. "You want a beer, Petty?"

Petty glanced at me.

"You need his permission, or what?"

"Is that how you ask permission?" Petty said. "By looking at someone?"

Ashley burst into laughter.

"And why would I need permission?"

My head spun. No way could I explain to Petty that Ashley was insulting her in order to assert her queen-bee status. That this new, fucked-up Ashley perceived her as someone too weak or too stupid to make her own decisions.

Thinking about all the head games involved in a normal social interaction depressed the shit out of me. I definitely needed a beer to stop the editorial bubbles from appearing over every communication. I dug out my wallet and handed Ashley five twenties. "Buy a pitcher and keep the rest to get yourself a couple of packs of smokes and some groceries."

Ashley screamed and threw her arms around me. "I love you!" she shouted, and returned to the bar.

I leaned close to Petty, but she leaned away.

"I wanted to tell you something," I said, "to whisper it to you, so I need to get close to your ear." I felt like a foreign exchange student host, having to explain American customs.

Even in the dim bar light, I could see her face redden, embarrassed at her ineptitude.

"But nobody will be able to hear it anyway," I said loudly. "I was going to say we probably should have crashed at Mike Zang's, but I thought you'd be more comfortable at a girl's house. Ashley's changed a lot since the last time I saw her."

Petty didn't look at me. She kept her eyes on the careening mass of people before us. Ashley danced over to our table and set down two red plastic cups of beer. Petty pushed hers away, but then seemed to reconsider. She picked up the cup and took a sip.

I watched.

"My first beer," Petty said, holding it up in a toast.

I clicked my cup against hers. "How about that. I had my first beer when I was ten."

She tipped up the cup and drained it.

Out of the corner of my eye I watched Petty as she watched people, until two guys by the pool table started arguing loudly.

"Don't worry," I said, in my best Batman growl. "I'll protect you."

"From those two guys? I could take them both, easy."

I felt a thrill. She probably could. I smiled at her and she smiled back, her dimples deepening, and I realized this was the first time I'd seen her smile. It was a sight to behold, and it sent blood rushing through me before I could stop it. That was all I needed, to be crushing on this gooney girl who could probably snap me in half.

"Until you pulled that wicked jiu-jitsu move in front of Walgreens, I wouldn't have believed you," I said. I sat up straighter. "Who else? Who else could you take?"

As soon as it was out of my mouth, I was afraid she'd say, "You." But she didn't. She glanced around and said, "The guy on the far right of the bar, the bartender, the waitress, and the guy in the hunting vest."

"And who'd you have trouble with?"

"The stout guy in the slipknot T-shirt at the bar and the guy in camo."

"And we're talking strictly hand-to-hand, right?"

She nodded. "It's Ashley I'm most worried about, because she's wiry and unpredictable and meth heads sometimes have super strength. Plus I'll bet she cheats."

"Right?" I said. "Listen, I swear I didn't know she was doing drugs. She was such a sweet girl. It sucks."

A giggle escaped Petty, but she sobered immediately. "That's not funny. I don't know why I laughed."

"Because it's your first beer and you haven't had anything to eat. Don't worry about it."

She giggled again.

Ashley came back to our table. "You need another one?" she asked.

"I think we're good, Ash," I said.

"Okay. I'll be right back."

She went back to the two guys in baseball caps she'd been talking to. She would talk and talk then throw her head back and laugh, then glance in Petty's direction. The two guys kept smiling at each other, smiles that said, "We're getting laid tonight."

PETTY

DEKKER ORDERED US some nachos. I felt clearer after I had some food in my stomach, but the beer made me warm and relaxed, which alarmed me. Ashley spun over to us every once in a while. She didn't eat anything, which didn't surprise me. By eight o'clock the place was standing room only, and Dekker told Ashley it was time to go.

"She wants to stay," Dekker said when she walked away from the table again. "She said to go back to her place and she'll catch a ride with her new 'friends' later. She gave me the key." He held it up.

That was fine by me. But looking around at the packed bar, I felt jumpy. No way I'd get out of here without making physical contact with a bunch of people.

Dekker said, "I'll go first and clear a path for you."

"Okay," I said.

He turned his back to me and I followed him out into the dark night. I took a huge gulp of the clean-smelling night air.

"Why do people hang out there?" I said.

"To get laid," Dekker said, and then turned toward me, a horrified expression on his face. "I'm sorry. That was rude."

I shrugged. I was sure he was right. All the movements and facial expressions and sounds inside the bar had been cartoonishly exaggerated, like the acting in bad TV movies I'd seen over the years. It was like mating week on Animal Planet or something.

We got in the truck and Dekker said, "Ashley told me there are two twin beds in her room, and you can have one of them. I'll sleep on the couch in the living room."

"I don't know if I'll be able to sleep at all," I said. "I've never slept anywhere but my house. Ever."

It must have been hard for Dekker not to shout out *What?* every time I revealed another facet of my weird life.

"I've always had a tough time when I'm away from home too," he said instead. "When I first got to K-State, I had a hard time falling asleep. Unless I was toasted, of course."

It would also be hard to sleep because there would be a man in the apartment, plus a girl I didn't trust at all. I thought this but didn't say it. When we got to Ashley's neighborhood, Dekker circled the block twice looking for parking. We had to park a block and a half away.

I reached for my suitcase but Dekker said, "Maybe you ought to leave that here." I guessed he didn't exactly trust her either. He put it in the cab, then locked the doors.

Inside the apartment, the smell of smoke was now old and stale, so Dekker opened some windows. He went into Ashley's bedroom and flipped on the lights. I looked under the beds and in the closet. The bed I was supposed to sleep on was piled high with dirty clothes. Dekker swept it off for me.

"There you go." He yawned and stretched, and he was so tall his knuckles scraped the ceiling. "I'm going to watch some TV."

"Good night," I said. He closed the bedroom door behind him. I heard the TV switch on in the living room as I sat on the bed. I wished I'd brought the photo album into the apartment so I could look at it, because I was sure I wouldn't be able to sleep.

I wondered why Dad had told me there weren't any photos. I thought about how he never wanted to talk about Mom, and I started to wonder if maybe the house fire was set by some criminal syndicate my dad was mixed up with and we were in the witness protection program like Dekker had said. I lay on top of the covers and closed my eyes anyway to get some rest.

I didn't know how much later sharp voices startled me out of sleep. I grabbed my bra knife from outside my shirt and held onto it. At first I thought the voices were coming from the TV, but then I heard Dekker shout, "What?"

Ashley's slurry drunken voice half cried and half whined, but I couldn't make out what she was saying. Every word Dekker said, though, was as clear as if he were sitting next to me.

"That's bullshit. I don't believe you. You're full of shit."

I sat straight up, straining to hear more, but I suddenly knew I had to get out of there. Right then.

"Oh, shit," Dekker said. "Oh, no. Oh, no."

It was as if I had X-ray vision, because I saw Dekker heading toward the bedroom door. It opened and he said, "Petty, come out here." It wasn't a request.

"What's going on?" I followed him out to the living room.

Ashley was lolling on the couch, her hair covering her face, but Dekker stood, staring at the TV, his bottom lip pinched between his thumb and forefinger. He saw me looking at him and pointed at the TV. I turned toward it and saw a picture of me side by side with a picture of Dekker. For a moment I thought Ashley and Dekker were playing a trick on me.

"How—"

"Ssshhh," Dekker hissed. "Listen."

" . . . Moshen is five-eight, one hundred thirty pounds, brown hair, hazel eyes," the anchorwoman said. "Moshen and Sachs are considered armed and dangerous and were last seen in Saw Pole, eighty-five miles northwest of Salina. If you have any knowledge of their whereabouts, call Crimestoppers at 825-TIPS or text SATIPS to CRIMES (274637). You may receive a cash reward of up to one thousand dollars. Remember, you don't need to give your name to receive the reward."

Dekker turned toward me. "You fucking *did* rob Dooley. You took more than your dad's stuff. You robbed him, and now they think I robbed him too."

"I took what was rightfully mine," I said.

"It doesn't matter. You took something from his office. And now they're looking for us, you lunatic." He collapsed onto a chair, his head in his hands.

"I'll go," I said.

"It doesn't matter if you go, Petty," Dekker shouted. "*My* picture was on the TV too."

I looked away from the TV and my eyes landed on the glowing screen of Ashley's cell phone, held casually open in her hand, displaying the numbers 911.

"Dekker," I whispered, pointing.

Ashley hid the phone, but not before he'd seen.

"You . . . what's wrong with you? You want the cops to come here and find the meth you bought with the money I gave you?"

"I had to, Dekker!" She sobbed and wailed. "I can't even buy food!"

"Maybe you could if you didn't spend all your money on drugs." He stood. "We're out of here."

"Don't go!" she cried, trying to stand. "I'm sorry! I had to! I need that reward money!" She snatched at Dekker, who shoved her away, and she lost her balance and tumbled to the floor. "Owww! Ow! Ow! You have to wait here, Dekker! You have to wait here!"

Dekker pulled me out of the apartment and through the house's front door. I didn't ask any questions, just followed him.

"We need to get to the truck as fast as we can," he said. "We've got to stay out of the light. You see a car coming, you get in the bushes."

I nodded.

"We're not going to run, though."

We walked down the sidewalk, on full alert.

"I should have thrown you out of my truck when I had the chance," Dekker said.

A car was coming our way driving slowly and Dekker stopped and watched for a moment before he said, "Bushes."

We got behind a hedge that bordered a house's yard as the car drove slowly past. Once it was out of sight, we began to rise.

"Don't move." An old man stood in the doorway of the house, aiming a shotgun at Dekker's head.

We both raised our hands.

"I've already called the police. They're on their way. You need to stay right where you are." The old man's voice was shaky and frightened.

"Sir," Dekker said, "we stepped behind your hedge to—"

"I know what you were going to do, you were going to break into my house. I'm sick to death of you kids breaking into my house. You stay right where you are until the cops—lookee there! Here they come now." The old man's face fell as they drove right on past, red and blue lights flashing. He came down the stairs, watching them go.

Dekker stood frozen with his hands up and eyes wide, and I could see that he would be no help whatsoever. We didn't have much time. My terror of cops, pounded into my skull by Dad, pumped up my adrenaline.

I took advantage of the old man's divided attention and, when he got close enough, bumped the shotgun barrels upward with the heels of my hands then yanked the gun away from him and tossed it into the bushes. While he was still frozen in shock, I pressed my advantage and twisted his hand behind his back, incapacitating him.

"We're going to be on our way now," I whispered to him.

He grunted. I released him and he fell to the ground, clutching his shoulder.

"Run," I said to Dekker. I couldn't see his face in the darkness but he turned and did as I told him. I took off too, jogging next to him. We were about a half block away from the truck when another police car turned the corner and Dekker pulled me behind a large oak tree in front of a dark house. The police car was driving in the direction of Ashley's apartment, and from where we squatted we could see it double parking on the street.

We went on running. Just as we reached the truck and Dekker opened his door, another cop car drove by, lighting us up. We both froze as it slowed near us. But then the car moved on. Dekker got in, reached over and unlocked my door. I got in and buckled my seat belt. Dekker tried to get the key in the ignition but his hands were shaking so hard he couldn't do it. I took the key from him, stuck it in and cranked it.

"Take it easy," I said.

I looked at my own hand and saw that it was steady. This surprised me, but it shouldn't have. My training had kicked in. Not only that, but I was outside of my house, out in the world, living. I was exhilarated in a way I'd never felt before.

He nodded at me in the dark and pulled out onto the street. I looked right and left, behind and in front of us, over and over. We came to an intersection, and Dekker got in the left-turn lane.

A car pulled up beside us. I started to turn my head when Dekker said, "Don't. They're looking at you."

"Are you sure?" I said.

"I can't tell if they're just checking you out or . . . oh, shit. Guy's got a cell phone. He's trying to take a picture—"

I turned then and, sure enough, the guy snapped a photo.

Even though we had a red light, Dekker gunned it into the intersection, narrowly missing a white SUV. Outside a convenience store across the street, a cop jumped into his driver's seat and flipped on his cherry lights and siren.

"Dekker! What are you doing? There was a—"

"Shut up," he said. "I'm not talking to you. Just keep your mouth shut."

He steered through the sparse traffic. I faced backward, watching for the police car to make it through the intersection.

"Turn now," I said, "before he gets out to where he can see us."

"There's nowhere to—"

"Turn!"

He hooked a hard right into an alley, his tires kicking dust from the rough, hard-packed dirt.

The siren grew louder.

"Don't stop," I shouted as we neared the cross street.

His head hunched into his shoulders and he hit the street without slowing, bouncing up over the dip and into the next alley. Suddenly, a car backed out perpendicular to us, and Dekker jammed on the brakes.

I looked back over my shoulder and saw the blur of red and blue cherry lights whiz by.

"Back out," I said.

"Quit telling me what to—"

"Do it!"

With a furious look, he complied before throwing the truck into first gear and stomping on the accelerator.

"We have to get rid of this truck," I said.

"I'm not getting rid of my truck," he said, wiping sweat off his forehead and weaving around the few slow-moving vehicles in front of us. The traffic signal ahead turned yellow and he slowed.

"Run it! Go!"

He did.

Chapter 14

DEKKER

THE STEERING WHEEL was slick with sweat for the second time that day, and I could no longer tell which direction the sirens were going or how close they were. I couldn't believe I'd run red lights and evaded police. I'd known guys in high school who were into that sort of thing, but I wasn't one of them. And it was all because of this girl. I should have taken her money, headed straight back to Saw Pole and never given her a second thought. I cursed my softheartedness and, yes, my growing attraction to her.

Yet, at the same time, I couldn't help but think that teaming up with a fuck-up like me would spell certain doom for her. I was a shit magnet, and she would be better off without me, in every possible way. But she was stuck with me—for now anyway.

We had to get out of town. If we could get to US 40, which I hoped was just a ways up ahead, we might be able to get away. I hoped the cops would concentrate their search on the interstate instead of the little two-lane highway.

As soon as I thought I could trust my voice, I said, "Fucking Ashley. She was over at the bar, and this guy comes up to her and says, 'Hey, isn't that the girl and guy you came in with?' Pointing at the TV. Ashley sees a news bulletin." I shook my head. "Dooley must have filed a police report that says you robbed his office, and I'm your accomplice."

Petty didn't say anything.

"You like that? I'm your accomplice. Your *accomplice*. Who you threatened with a gun."

Petty continued looking out the window silently.

"The report said your *fiancé*, Randy King, is *desperate* to get you back. So now there's a statewide bulletin out for us."

"Just drop me off on the side of the road," she said. "Then you can—"

"Then I can what? Take the rap for what you did? That is not going to happen."

"No, you can go back to Saw Pole and explain that—"

"Oh, yeah. They're totally going to listen to me," I said, my voice rising. The pounding in my head threatened to break it open, and I lost all control of myself, no longer caring if I hurt her feelings. "When Dooley and Randy stopped me on the road this afternoon, you know what they said? That you're retarded. That's right. That's what they said. Or autistic, or something. And that you're disturbed and deranged."

She turned her face to me, her lips parted.

I was sorry I'd said that, even as pissed off at her as I was. I didn't believe she was retarded—not mentally, anyway.

She turned back to the window. "Just take me to a bus station."

"Are you fucking kidding me? We can't go to an exit point like that. They'll be waiting for us."

"But I have to get to . . ." She trailed off.

We drove in silence for a long while after that. There were few cars out on the two-lane. It was a moonless, dark night, with no sight beyond the headlights' beams. I kept wondering why in the world Randy King and Keith Dooley were so hell-bent on finding Petty.

Finally, I couldn't contain myself anymore.

"Petty?" I said. "What is going on? Why is all this shit happening? Will you please tell me?"

She stared out her window at the dark. "Yes. I'll tell you."

PETTY

"THAT CAN'T BE legal," Dekker said after I'd finished explaining about Dad's will, Randy King, the trust, the photo of my mom.

"You'd think not," I said. "But apparently if you put your money in a trust, you can attach any conditions to it you want. I have thirty days to marry him, but obviously he doesn't want to wait. That million dollars is burning a hole in his pocket."

"Creepy," Dekker said, shuddering.

"Where are we going?"

"We can't go back to Saw Pole."

"I didn't mean to get you in any trouble."

"You did, Petty."

"Nobody forced you to come back to the bus station," I said. "You did that all on your own."

"Because I'm a fucking idiot!" He smacked the steering wheel. "I should take you to the cops and go home, but—"

"You forget I have a gun," I said.

"What I was going to say," he said, irritated, "is that I can't do it because this deal with Randy King is sketchy as hell. He hit you, didn't he?"

"And he pepper-sprayed my dogs," I said. I didn't mention how he'd grabbed my privates. It was too humiliating.

"I think we need to find you a real lawyer. The only thing to do is call my uncle in Wamego."

"Is he a lawyer?"

Dekker snorted. "No," he said. "He is definitely not a lawyer."

"Then why—"

"Let's say he's a guy who knows how to get out of trouble."

"I'm not sure I'd like to get to know any more of your friends," I said.

"He's my uncle, and as an added bonus, he's not a meth addict. But out of all the people I've ever known, he is the most trustworthy. He's my mom's younger brother. Her favorite sibling. I was named for him."

"You said his name was Curt," I said.

"Right. Curt Dekker. Mom's maiden name was Dekker. When she died—"

"Your mom's dead too?" I said, before I thought it through.

"When I was in junior high. Cancer."

"Cancer?" I said. "Your mom died of cancer and you smoke?"

He stiffened. "It wasn't lung cancer. It was pancreatic."

"Still," I said.

"Anyway," Dekker said. "My dad left us when I was in grade school, and then when Mom died, Uncle Curt took me in. It was probably the best summer of my life. We hunted arrowheads on his land and went to Echo Cliffs and Science City—he's the one who got me interested in geology."

"Geology?" I said.

"Yeah. That's what I was going to college for, thanks to him. After that summer I went to live in town with my dad's mom, my Oma, who you met at the dump, because I wanted to go to high school with my friends."

A car accelerated around us.

He looked down at the dashboard. "Ah, shit," he said. "I need gas."

"We can't stop," I said, my uneasiness making me alert. "We'll be recognized."

"If we don't, we'll run out of gas."

"Keep going," I said. "Don't you dare stop."

His enraged face appeared demonic in the light from the dashboard. "What are you going to do? You going to shoot the truck if it doesn't keep going?"

"Why would I—"

"I was being sarcastic!" he yelled at the ceiling. "You are such a Neanderthal. Listen to me. Without gas, we will be stuck in the middle of Kansas. Do you understand?" He talked loud and slow, enunciating everything.

"Yes," I said quietly, feeling stupid.

"We're going to Council Grove. It's a tiny town and nobody who's out this late is going to recognize us. Okay?"

"Okay," I said, but I didn't believe that.

He drove east on US 56, which led us into Council Grove, a little town that was dark except for a Phillips 66 gas station. Dekker pulled up to a pump, grabbed a hat out of the backseat and put it on, yanking it down over his eyes.

"It's only midnight?" he said. "Feels later. Do you think it's safe to use my cell to call my grandma?"

"Better not," I said. "They might be able to track us. You might want to turn it off altogether."

He pulled it out of his shirt pocket and powered it down. "I'll pump the gas. Do you need to use the restroom? Either way, put your hood up and keep your head down."

I yanked up the hood on my sweatshirt and got out of the truck. I was stiff from sitting. There was no one else at the gas station, and the door to the restroom was outside, so I wouldn't have to go inside the cashier station. When I came back out of the bathroom, Dekker was standing at the pay phone, smoking and talking. I didn't get too close because I wanted to give him privacy.

When he hung up, he said, "I'll be right out. Get in the truck."

I got in, closed the door, and leaned my head against the window. I was so tired, but now at least we had a place to go. A stray dog trotted by the truck, and I wondered if Sarx and Tesla were all right. I'd slit open a giant bag of dog food and left it for them, and there was a pond out back of our property, so I thought they'd be okay.

But nothing else was going according to plan. Mr. Dooley had come back from lunch too early. I should have been out of the office before he'd even finished his coffee over at the restaurant. Dekker would have driven me to Salina without me having to threaten him, without being blockaded on the highway by Mr. Dooley and Randy, and they wouldn't have even known I'd left Saw Pole. I would be waiting at the bus depot without looking over my shoulder. I'd have never met that awful Ashley, and the cops wouldn't be after us. I'd have gotten on that Greyhound bus in the morning and never seen Dekker again.

There was one aspect of how things actually happened that I did like. I enjoyed being with a person who talked to me, even though he was angry. I didn't blame Dekker. His anger and the way he expressed it stood in stark contrast to how my dad had gotten mad. While Dekker yelled and lashed out, Dad had grown dangerously silent and sometimes wouldn't talk to me or even look at me for days. I preferred Dekker's way, as it turned out.

Still, I regretted leaving the bathroom in the bus depot and coming with Dekker, because now I didn't have any idea how I was going to get to Detroit.

I was startled by a tap on the window. I turned and saw a large man standing there. Adrenaline flooded my system. The man didn't smile, but motioned for me to roll the window down. I reached into my hoodie and put my hand on Baby Glock. I shook my head at him. He made the motion again.

Where was Dekker?

The man tapped again.

I rolled the window down about an inch.

"Hey, gal, your seat belt's caught in the door."

"Oh," I said. "Thank you."

He nodded and walked away. I saw my seat belt was indeed trapped in the door. Dekker was on his way out of the store, his hat tipped low over his eyes, walking casually toward the truck. I took my hand off my gun, opened my door and yanked the seat belt inside. Then I slid down in the seat, my heart flopping around in my chest at the thought of being recognized, of being caught and arrested—and then sent back to Randy.

Dekker got in.

"Let's get out of here," he said. "Uncle Curt says we should drive over to Council Grove Lake and the Neosho Park recreation area off Lake Road. There's a loop there, and he says we need to leave the truck. He'll come get us."

"Lake?" I said. "Why a lake?" Even the thought of being so close to a large body of water spooked me, as if the water would sense me there and erupt out of its banks and drown me, but I wasn't going to tell him that.

"Nobody will be out there this time of year," he said, "so there's no chance of us being spotted."

Pulling off Lake Road and toward the lake itself, I could see the spiky skeletons of tall poplars and expansive oaks ringing the lake. The water sparkled, in constant dark motion, making my heart race in a way that running from the cops never would.

The roads and parking lots were deserted. We didn't see a single vehicle. He drove off road and pulled the truck behind the tree line so we couldn't be seen from the parking lot. The clock on the dashboard said 12:44.

Dekker shook a cigarette out of his pack and lit it up. Then he said, "I'll do this outside if it bugs you."

"It does."

He made an irritated noise and got out of the truck. I watched the lit end of his cigarette glow as it arced through the air to and from his mouth, but the dark water kept drawing my eyes. Dekker finally tossed his cigarette away and got back in the cab.

"Chilly out there," he said. He blew on his hands and rubbed them together. Within a few minutes Dekker was snoring softly against his window. My OODA Loop and I kept watch.

About an hour later I heard a rumbling and looked out the back window. A vehicle with its lights off rolled slowly into the empty parking lot, then stopped a distance away. Dekker jumped when I nudged him.

"What's up?" he said, then yawned and stretched.

I pointed out the back window.

"That's him," Dekker said.

"How do you know?" I said.

"Who else is it going to be this time of night with the lights off? Cops don't drive rag-top Jeeps and sneak up on people."

He opened his door and walked across the grass to the edge of the lot where the Jeep sat. I watched out the back window and saw a man with long hair get out of the driver's side and throw his arms around Dekker. When he let go, the passenger side door opened and a thin figure in a Unabomber hoodie jumped out, ran at Dekker and jumped on his back.

An ambush!

My stomach heaved and I reached for Baby Glock. But then the figure hopped off him and Dekker turned to embrace it. I heard a loud female voice. It was a girl. She walked quickly toward me. My breath quickened and I kept my hand on my gun.

Dekker trotted to catch up and stopped her. He put his arm around her, bent his head and talked for a while, probably explaining about the weird girl in the truck. The long-haired man joined the powwow and listened to Dekker's monologue.

Then the three of them came at me again, slower this time.

"Come on out here, Petty," Dekker said. "I want you to meet my Uncle Curt and Cousin Roxanne."

While I knew I wouldn't be any safer in the truck, probably less so in fact, I couldn't make myself open the door. I stared at the two unfamiliar smiling faces for so long their grins started to fade. I blew out hard, trying to steady myself. Dekker opened my door.

"Roxanimal, Uncle Curt, this is Petty," Dekker said.

"Petty," Curt said.

I couldn't look at him.

The girl said, "Hi—let's start over. My name is Roxanne—like the song. Dekker's the animal." She had short maraschino cherry-colored hair and smelled like vanilla.

He slugged her, not hard, because I could tell he liked her.

Dekker got closer to me and said, "I'm serious. We're safe with Uncle Curt."

I had my blade on my bra and my Glock in my holster, and

that was all the safety I truly believed in. But there was something about this man. Maybe it was how different he seemed from Dad—unguarded, peaceful but strong. He wasn't afraid. He wasn't sad or angry. I wanted to believe the smile in Curt's bright blue eyes.

Dekker got my suitcase out of the truck and I carried the bag with my treasures over my shoulder.

Curt and Roxanne led us to the Jeep, where two dogs waited, dancing on the backseat. There was a white, chesty bulldog that made sounds like a wet cough and a little fluffy dog that barked beside him. Roxanne never stopped talking, and everything she said was punctuated with exclamation points, although I was so jumbled the words might as well have been in French.

Uncle Curt made sweeping motions at the dogs. "Back up, fellas," he said. "Make room for Petty and Dekker."

I couldn't seem to make myself get in the Jeep. I didn't know these people. There were too many of them, too close to me. Dekker got in and scooted over to make room for me by pulling the fluffy dog onto his lap. Curt still stood at the passenger door, waiting for me to get in, his hand on the door frame.

I shifted from foot to foot.

"Dekker told you our girls are all about your age, right?" Curt said. "Chloe's twenty-four, and Rox and Layla are twenty."

"Oh," I said, not looking at him.

"I guess what I'm trying to tell you is, if you want to be safe, be in a car with a man who's raised three daughters. That's all I'm saying. You're safe with us."

Roxanne stared at me and my face burned.

"Get in, Petty," Dekker said.

"Yeah. Get in and tell me why you were named Petty," Curt said. "Which is, by the way, maybe the coolest name I've ever heard." He walked around the Jeep to the driver's side, got in and closed the door.

My face got hotter. He was asking me about myself, something no one had ever done before. I'd seen people talk to each other like this in movies and on TV, but I didn't believe anyone did this in real life. Dekker had asked me questions, but they were more about my circumstances than about me. I couldn't get my mouth to work.

The bulldog sat on the seat, smiling up at me, panting, waiting for me to get in so he could get acquainted. His face was so funny and full of anticipation—what I needed to break down my paranoia. I climbed in the back and let him investigate me. He smelled Sarx and Tesla on my pants. I wondered if they were going crazy trying to guard the house without me there.

Curt started up the Jeep. "Rox wouldn't let me leave her at home," he said, rocketing down the road toward the highway.

"Yeah," Roxanne said. "I was supposed to go to Padre for spring break, but I figured driving with Dad to pick up a couple of fugitives from justice would be much more fun."

Dekker smacked the back of her seat.

"Excuse me," she said. "I meant 'little lost lambs.' Not fugitives." She smiled back at me. She wore a lot of black eyeliner around eyes that were the same color as her dad's. "We brought provisions," she said, producing two bottles of water and a bag of Cheetos. I'd never actually eaten them, but I'd seen about a thousand commercials for them over the years. She passed the snacks back to us.

I opened my water bottle and drank it down without stopping. Dekker dug into the Cheetos. The bulldog leaned hard into me, and I rubbed his head. He made these funny wet grunting sounds and worked his jowls like he had something important to say but couldn't quite get it out.

Dekker pointed at the lump of fur in his lap and said, "This is Bob. The bulldog is China Cat Sunflower."

"After the Grateful Dead song," Curt said over his shoulder.

Dekker smiled and shook his head.

"Okay," Curt said. "Let's have the story. Out with it, nephew. I want to know what I'm dealing with here."

Dekker told him about Dad's will and Randy King and Mr. Dooley. Roxanne kept interrupting until Dekker told her to shut up. She did, but she wasn't happy about it. Throughout the story, she turned in her seat and gave me horrified looks. It took me a little while to understand that Roxanne was outraged on my behalf. Unlike Ashley, Roxanne was interested in what I had to say. I wondered what it would be like to have a friend like this.

"Wait, wait, wait," Curt said. "Randy King? I don't know if Dekker told you or not, but I grew up outside of Niobe, and I knew Randy. He's about ten years younger than me, but he's too old for you, girl. Is that even legal, or are you just pulling my lariat?"

"Her dad was—no offense, Petty—fucking crazy," Dekker said.

Then he recounted how I'd kidnapped him—although he didn't use that word—and about the bus station, and Ashley, and the cops. He left out the part about me pulling a gun on him. I wasn't sure whether he was trying to spare me or himself.

"So what you stole from Dooley's office should be yours anyway, right?" Roxanne said.

"Yes," I said.

"Why didn't your dad want you to have the photo album?" Curt asked. "Are there pictures of him in lingerie, or what?"

"I don't know," I said. "He always told me there weren't any pictures. But I found a photo of my mom in a box and it led me to the album."

"So you two can't go to the cops until we get you a lawyer," Curt said. "You want to get as far from Keith Dooley as possible. He and I went to school together in Niobe, so I've known him most of my life too. When my buddy Bill's grandpa passed away, Dooley handled the estate. He handled it so much, in fact, nobody in the family got a dime."

"That's bullshit," Dekker said.

"No, that's a fact. Dooley sits on estates and says he can't get in touch with any of the heirs, and his 'expenses' bleed off the money a little at a time until everything's gone. So I'm telling you, if Dooley's this interested in getting you to marry that guy, there's some scratch in it for him. He wouldn't have called the cops on you otherwise, not for going into his unlocked office to get a photo album and some letters."

All this talking had the opposite effect on me that it usually had. I felt more relaxed than I had since this adventure began. I'd never been in a group discussion before, and it made me long for a real family of my own. These people genuinely liked each other, listened to each other, respected each other. I yearned to be part of a family like this.

"So, my point is," Curt said, "we gotta get you a decent lawyer."

"I can't afford one," I said. "I've got twenty-four hundred dollars, but I have to live on that for as long as I can."

"You're in luck," Curt said. "It so happens one of my best friends is a lawyer in Topeka. I'll give him a call first thing."

"Uncle George," Roxanne said, fist in the air. She turned around in her seat and said, "When I was little I always used to tell people he was my favorite uncle, which didn't sit very well with the ones who were actually related to me."

"It doesn't matter," I said. "I can't pay him."

"You won't have to," Curt said. "George owes me big-time. Even if he didn't, he'd take your case. That's the kind of guy he is."

I didn't believe a lawyer who'd never met me would take my case for free, but I didn't say so.

"He really is," Roxanne said, as if reading my mind.

"You were going to ride the bus to Detroit," Curt said, changing the subject. "Why Detroit?"

"That's where my parents were from," I said. "I want to find out about my mom. I have this weird feeling that—" I stopped myself.

"Feeling that what?" Curt said.

I felt bashful because I'd only just met these people, and here I was, babbling on about my innermost thoughts.

"This is definitely a tribe you can share weird feelings with," Roxanne said. "Believe me. When I went off to college, I didn't realize that people don't usually just say what they think, or share their dreams, or confess stuff to each other like we do."

"Well," I said, "I have this feeling my mom . . . might be alive. But I don't have any evidence to back it up."

Curt and Roxanne glanced at each other.

"So, either way, I want to know. I want to see if I have any extended family." I said to Curt, "Could you drive me to a different bus station?"

"Since you two are considered armed and dangerous, all the bus stations and airports are going to be on the lookout for you."

"Maybe we can stay at your place for a bit," Dekker said.

"Nope," Curt said. "The cops will be out to the house by tomorrow. They'll go to your grandma's in Saw Pole too. Petty, I'm going to let you borrow one of my cars to drive to Detroit while my buddy George works things out for you here."

Why would this man do that? He'd only just met me. I didn't say this. "But I can't drive."

"I didn't mean just you," Curt said. "Dekker's going with you."

Dekker stared at the back of his uncle's head. "Yeah, no I'm not."

I sucked in my breath. While I wasn't sure I wanted Dekker to go with me, his vehement reaction surprised me.

"Yes, you are," Curt said. "Like I said, the cops are going to be crawling all over our property, so you can't stay with us, and where you gonna go? You need to get out of the state *toot sweet* until George gets things handled here."

"Uncle Curt," Dekker said, "I have a potentially life-changing opportunity coming up in eight days, and I—"

"You'll be back in plenty of time," Curt said.

"What if I'm not? Like I said, this is potentially—"

"It's hard for me to imagine any way I'd let this girl go to Detroit by herself."

"Yeah," Roxanne said. "It's a good thing Detroit isn't, like, the most dangerous city in America, or anything."

Dekker pointed his finger at Roxanne. "You shut up."

"I can take care of myself," I said, trying to defuse the situation.

"Trust me," Dekker said. "She can."

"Dekker," Curt said.

"If you're so worried about her," Dekker said to Roxanne, "why don't you go with her?"

Curt pulled the Jeep to the shoulder of the highway and stopped. He got out and stuck his head in the door. "Dekker, can I have a word with you out here?"

Dekker didn't move.

"Get out of the Jeep," Curt said with a sharp finger snap. "Now."

Dekker groaned, pushed the driver's seat forward and climbed out, closing the door behind him.

Since it was so late and we were on a two-lane highway, there was no traffic, and I was able to hear the sound of their voices, if not the words.

Roxanne climbed into the backseat next to me and strained to see out the windshield to where her cousin and dad stood. I was able to pick out Curt's words "selfish" and "that poor girl" and "so help me." The only thing I heard from Dekker was a whiny tone of voice, and I wondered if I'd be better off without him.

"Dekker can be such a d-bag," Roxanne whispered. "But Dad is unbelievably persuasive." She turned her head toward me. "Wow. You have the shiniest hair I've ever seen. What do you use?"

I leaned away from her. "What do you mean?"

"Shampoo? Conditioner? Other product?"

"Product?" I echoed stupidly. "Whatever's on sale at the Saw Pole grocery store, I guess."

"Whatever's on sale," she said in a whisper and kept right on looking at me. "Amazing. Plus you don't have a zit or a bump or a freckle anywhere. It's just so wrong."

This made me happy, though I could not have said why.

DEKKER

"LET ME EXPLAIN," I said in a lowered voice.

Self-pity hardened like cement in my arms and legs as I stood with Uncle Curt on the soft shoulder of the road. The stars were bright overhead out here in East Bumblefuck Nowhere.

I'd seen Uncle Curt mad maybe three times in my life, and because it was such a rare event, it was kind of terrifying. The old hippie stood with his arms crossed, his mouth in a rigid line. My sweat glands started up and I instantly felt clammy.

"I'm listening," Curt said.

"I have the opportunity to get back in the band."

Although pleased surprise showed on Uncle Curt's face, I could see it wasn't enough to win his approval.

"But it's not just that. They're—we're going to open for Autopsyturvy."

My uncle remained silent.

"Autopsyturvy is a Kansas City band that just signed a major label—"

"I know who they are." He said nothing else.

"This could be the big break," I said.

"You'll need to drive fast, then," Uncle Curt said, "so you can get back in time."

"It's one thing to rescue her from the bus station," I said. "It's a whole other level of commitment to drive all the way to fucking Detroit, Michigan."

"It's an eleven-hour drive," Uncle Curt said. "Nothing to it."

My patience snapped. "Here's a fun fact that I haven't told you, because I wanted to protect her, but this girl actually forced me at gunpoint to drive her to Salina."

"She—what?"

"Yeah. And then we got chased by the cops, because she took that stuff from Dooley's office. So I think I've already gone above and beyond for her."

"Wow," Uncle Curt said. "How desperate would you have to be to do something like that? Poor girl."

"Poor girl? What about poor Dekker? I'm the one who could have been shot, who had to abandon my truck, who's wanted by the law through no fault of my own, and for what?" I turned to walk back to the Jeep, but Uncle Curt caught my elbow and yanked me backward, almost knocking me off my feet.

"So you're just going to walk away, is that the plan? Going to be a selfish coward bastard like . . ."

"My dad. That's what you were going to say, wasn't it?" I snatched my arm back, my face hot with embarrassment, and I hated Uncle Curt at that moment.

"I didn't have to say it," he said. "When your mom got sick—"

I turned away, but he got in front of me. "You're going to listen to this," he said. "When your mom got sick I promised her I'd keep an eye on you, make sure you grew up right in spite of that son-of-a-bitch of a fucked-up dad. I'm sorry. I can't let you off the hook. I can't let you desert that poor girl."

I didn't move. I mirrored Uncle Curt's crossed-arm posture and tried not to appear shaky.

"All right, then," Uncle Curt said. "That's how you want to play it, you'll have to find your own way back to your truck, and when we get to the house, so help me, I'm calling the cops on you."

"You wouldn't do that," I said.

"Look. You don't know Randy King and Keith Dooley the way I do. They want Petty's money, and they will do anything to get it. And I do mean anything."

He was as serious as I've ever seen him.

"I don't understand why you're being such an asshole about this," he said. "This isn't about the band or making it big or anything like that. Tell me what's going on."

I hated that he could see right through me. I hated that I couldn't hide from him. He knew me too well.

I looked down at my feet. "I'm like Charlie Brown," I said. "Everything I touch turns to shit. This is serious, grown-up business. It's this girl's *life*. What if I fuck it up?"

"You won't," Uncle Curt said, throwing his arm around my shoulders. "Because you're not your dad. I have the feeling that this may just be the most important thing you ever do. And you won't regret it."

Chapter 15

PETTY

CURT AND DEKKER got back in the Jeep.

"Dekker would love to accompany you," Curt said. "So that's settled. We all need to get home and get some sleep because you've got a long drive ahead of you tomorrow."

It was three-thirty in the morning when we got to Wamego and Curt's farmhouse, which was in the middle of a cornfield in the middle of nowhere.

Curt pulled the Jeep up to the barn and told Roxanne to open the doors for him.

"Dekker, you gonna sit there or be a gentleman and help me?" Roxanne said.

He groaned but got out with her and each of them swung a barn door open. Curt pulled the Jeep into the barn as lights came on.

The dogs both leaned on me; they were so friendly and silly it made me nervous. They were nothing like my dogs, and if someone attacked us, they'd be worthless. Dekker opened the passenger door and they hopped out before trotting over to separate dog beds and flopping down.

Aside from the beams, the inside of the barn didn't look like a barn at all. The floor was painted, textured concrete, and the walls were covered with vivid paintings. One-quarter of the barn was an art studio, but the rest housed some classic cars, parked in two parallel diagonal rows.

Curt switched off the Jeep, pulled the barn doors shut behind it and locked them.

"Aunt Rita asleep?" Dekker said.

"She's in Houston on a job interview."

While they were talking, I studied the paintings on the walls, and ended up in front of one that was three-quarters finished, sitting on an easel. It was a massive canvas depicting a little girl running through a wheat field toward a giant rising moon. I smelled Roxanne's vanilla scent, felt her appear at my side, and took a step away automatically.

"I'm so excited for him to finish this one," she said, her eyes on the painting.

"Who?" I said.

"My dad."

"Your dad painted this?"

"All of them," Roxanne said, waving her arm at the colorful canvases around the room. "He's been doing this my whole life. Other dads play golf. Mine makes art."

"Although I golf too," Curt said as he and Dekker joined us in front of the easel. "This one is of—"

"Wait," Roxanne said, snatching at his hand. "I want to tell it this time."

He squeezed her to his side. "Oh, all right."

"When my twin Layla and I were but a twinkle in our father's eye, our oldest sister Chloe and my folks stayed up late to see the supermoon. My parents are science nerds, you know—"

"Told you," Dekker said.

"So they stopped at this wheat field where there weren't any trees," Roxanne continued, "and they had a great view of the sky and they saw the supermoon rising. My big sister, in all her infinite three-year-old wisdom, decided the moon was close enough that she could—"

"'Hurry, Daddy,' she says, 'let's jump on!'" Curt interrupted. "Ain't that some shit?"

"Dad," Roxanne said. "Language."

"Sorry. *Isn't* that some shit?"

Dekker laughed. Roxanne went on. "So she started running toward it, but when she reached the edge of the field, there was a barbed-wire fence she couldn't get over, and when my parents caught up to her, she was crying. She was so mad because she thought it was their fault. If they'd gotten there in time to lift her over the fence, she would have made it on to the moon."

I watched Uncle Curt out of the corner of my eye as Roxanne told this story, and his lips moved ever so slightly as she spoke, as if he were a ventriloquist. The look of pride on his face was unmistakable. When she neared the end of her story, he took her by the shoulders and shook her playfully, trying to knock her off balance just so he could stand her upright again, but it didn't stop her from talking.

All their touching and tickling made me nervous, but I found this story amazing on several levels. A little girl walking outside at night with her parents. Her parents letting her believe they could actually jump onto the moon. A girl and her parents having fun together.

A girl with a mom.

Dekker and Curt led the way out the door, and I tried to drop behind Roxanne, but she was determined to walk by my side. We followed them out of the garage and across the breezeway to the house.

"It's a good thing I didn't go to Padre, huh?" Roxanne said. "Since Dad's here all alone, and I got to meet you!"

I didn't answer her. I didn't know what to say. All this buddy-buddy stuff made me suspicious. What did this girl want from me? Dad had told me that people always have ulterior motives. Of course, he mostly meant men being nice to get sex. So why was she being so friendly? I was too tired to think too hard on it though, so I just let myself pretend that Roxanne was my friend.

Curt slid open a glass door that led into the house. I was the last one inside.

"To bed, everyone," Curt said, yawning. "We'll figure out your plans first thing tomorrow."

I was so sleepy I couldn't even argue. We all trooped up the stairs, and Curt carried my suitcase to one of the bedrooms. "Petty gets Chloe's room so she can have her own bathroom. Rox, you want to get Petty settled in?"

Before I knew what was happening, Roxanne took my hand and yanked me toward the end of the hall and into the last room. She went through an interior doorway and turned on a light. "Bathroom's in here," she said, opening a cabinet and pulling out two plush white towels. "You need a washcloth too?"

I shook my head, dazzled by the gleaming lime-green glass tile of the countertop, the matching walls and multicolored abstract painting across from the toilet. The light and color were so radiant, I could almost taste citrus.

"Is there a lock on the bedroom door?" I asked.

Curt appeared in the bathroom doorway. "Yes," he said, "and the whole house is alarmed. Plus we've got the dogs. Holler if you need anything."

"Thank you," I said.

"Good night, Petty," Curt said, and walked out.

Roxanne pretended to leave the bedroom, then came back around the door with a huge grin and said, "Now we can go downstairs and stay up all night watching trashy movies and—"

Her dad reappeared, lifted her over his shoulder and she screamed.

They were both laughing. Roxanne gasped out, "Good night, Petty. Sleep tight. Don't let the bedbugs bite."

"See you in the morning light," Curt said as he carried my new friend away. Did it always work this way? Was it really this easy to be friends with another girl? I wouldn't have thought so after my interaction with Ashley, but it felt to me like I'd known Roxanne my whole life.

"We don't really have bedbugs," she called.

After locking the door, I got ready for bed and looked at photos on the wall of Roxanne and the girls who must have been her sisters. They all resembled each other but Roxanne didn't look enough like either of them to be a twin. There were ribbons on the walls too, along with medals for science fairs and trophies for tennis and golf and go-cart racing. A soft stuffed bear sat on the pillows wearing a knitted navy-blue striped sweater that said, *Mr. Wugglesby*.

I let myself imagine that this was my room and that Uncle Curt was my dad. But I imagined my real mom was just down the hall, maybe knitting sweaters for my other stuffed animals, ready to come running if I called out to her in the night. I closed my eyes and whispered, "Good night, Mom. Sleep tight. Don't let the bedbugs bite."

I imagined her saying, *See you in the morning light.*

Tuesday

A KNOCK ON my door woke me with a start.

I leapt to my feet and took hold of my blade. The bedside lamp was still on although sunlight streamed in the window.

"Petty, it's me, Roxanne."

I stealth-walked to the door and listened.

"Breakfast is ready."

It was a female voice, and it did sound like the girl I'd met just a few hours ago. I unlocked and opened the door. There she stood with a steaming blue mug in her hand. She gave it to me, turned and walked toward the stairs.

"Come on," she said.

I took a sip of the coffee, smelled bacon frying downstairs and decided to follow her.

Down in the kitchen, Dekker and Curt were putting away groceries from cloth bags.

"How are you this morning, lady?" Curt said to me.

"I'm fine," I said, feeling bashful. Curt talked to me as if he knew me, as if I were one of his kids. I realized that the previous night's easy camaraderie among family members was not just a show or a figment of my imagination.

"Have any weird dreams you want to report?" he asked me.

"I don't think so."

"I did. I dreamed my wife had facial hair. She took real good care of it, kept it clean and trimmed and everything, but walked around like this was totally normal. I love my wife, you know, but I think I'd really have to draw the line at a beard. She's been telling me for years it's just a matter of time. She's Greek, you know."

"Oh," I said.

"Thanks for the visual, Dad," Roxanne said.

I looked around at everyone and was struck by how easily and completely they'd invited me into their lives, without any hesitation. I felt like I owed them a glimpse inside my head, my life, which was a terrifying proposition. But I wanted to be real friends with them, and this sort of sharing seemed to be the currency around here.

I mustered up my courage. "Actually," I said, "I've had this one dream over and over."

Curt and Roxanne both stopped what they were doing and their eyebrows rose.

I told them about my drowning in the bathtub dream.

"Wow," Curt said. "That's intense."

"What do you think, Rox?" Dekker said. "You ever take psych?"

"Yeah, but no dream analysis," she said.

"It's obvious to me what the dream means," he said. "It symbolizes the control your dad had over you. He held you down, held you back, and you felt like you were suffocating, like you were drowning."

If dreams really meant something, then his interpretation seemed logical. But the dream didn't feel symbolic to me. It felt like what it was—drowning. But what did I know?

"So maybe you won't have that dream anymore," Roxanne said. "Because you're free now."

"Sort of," I said.

Roxanne pulled two boxes of hair dye out of one of the grocery bags. "I told you, Dad, dyeing Petty's hair is like killing a unicorn. I can't let you do it."

"I'm not going to," Curt said. "You are."

"On the one hand," she said to me, "I'll be complicit in desecrating this work of art, but on the other I'll get to play with your hair."

We didn't have time for this. This was TV-movie stuff—not what real people did if they were on the lam. What if Randy and Mr. Dooley came driving up while we were playing dress-up? Curt said himself that the cops would be on their way at some point. Probably sooner rather than later. If you were on the run, that's what you did. You ran. Not dye your hair. I didn't think I could sit still long enough.

"Wait," I said. "We have to go. We don't have time for—"

"It won't take long," Curt said. "Plus I need to get the car gassed up and ready to go for you."

Dekker held up a box of dye. "I still think it's a dumb idea."

He seemed so unconcerned I felt the muscles in my neck knot up.

"If you want to get out of Kansas and stay out of jail, you'd better do it," Curt said.

"I'm going to look so emo," Dekker said.

I actually started to wonder if they were keeping me here on purpose, that they'd called the cops themselves to get the Crimestopper money. But remembering the car collection in the barn and looking around this beautiful house, I realized my faulty reasoning.

Roxanne took my hand and pulled me toward the stairs. Over her shoulder she said to Dekker, "I'll do Petty first, because hers'll take longer to process. Wait for me in Mom and Dad's bathroom." To me, she said, "We've got time. Just relax."

I tried to do as she said, but I listened hard for sirens.

I followed her up the stairs and into Chloe's bathroom. Roxanne opened the window and a warm breeze blew in, then she switched on a clock radio by the sink.

I looked out the window, out over the cornfield, the long, uniform rows rolling up over the hills. A cluster of huge old oaks like at home stood by the dirt road. The sun was behind a thin layer of silver-white cloud, and birds called to one another over the corn.

The song ended on the radio and the DJ said, "We're getting severe weather warnings from the National Weather Service, so when you're out and about today, keep an eye on the sky and we'll do the same. Stay tuned to KQLA for weather updates."

"Take off your shirt," Roxanne said, opening up the box and pulling bottles and tubes and gloves and instructions out of it.

"Why?"

"You'll need to get in the shower after we're done to rinse out the dye, and you won't be able to pull the shirt over your head without getting bleach on it."

"That's all right," I said.

"No, really. It'll be a mess. Take your shirt off. I've got an old robe you can wear. Doesn't matter if we get bleach on that."

She stood staring at me expectantly and I went cold all over. But I knew this was the kind of thing girlfriends did all the time. I'd seen it on TV. So I pulled my shirt over my head and handed it to Roxanne. Her eyes bulged.

"Holy shit," she said.

"What?"

"Are you a body builder? You're so ripped. Wow."

"I work out," I said.

"That's not working out," Roxanne said. "That's Israeli Special Forces Navy SEAL type training. Wow." Then she saw the zipper scar on my left arm. She touched it and I tried not to flinch away. "What happened here?"

"When I was seven years old I fell in a window well and split my arm open from my wrist to my elbow. Dad sewed it up with catgut."

I pulled my arm away and she pointed to the bump on my left shoulder. "How about this one?"

"Scar tissue," I said, and scratched it.

She didn't say anything, but helped me into the ratty old bathrobe then read the dye directions.

"According the National Weather Service," said the DJ on the radio, "a thunderstorm cell is picking up power over the central part of the state. We're watching out for you at KQLA."

After Roxanne brushed my hair, she put on plastic gloves and opened a bottle, squeezing a tube into it before shaking the mixture up. Then she squeezed the goo onto my head and the smell was overwhelming. I held the towel to my face but it didn't help.

"Dekker says you never learned how to drive."

"No," I said.

"How come?"

"I'm pretty sure it's because Dad didn't want me to escape, but we were in a serious car accident when I was about thirteen. We both walked away without a scratch, but the truck was completely destroyed. He decided in addition to everything else, cars were just too dangerous for me to ride in, much less drive."

Roxanne looked up, her eyes alight. "If you were going to stay a couple of days, I'd totally take you out on the country roads and teach you to drive—that's the only way to do it."

She tied my hair up in a little clear plastic hood and clipped it, then peeled off the gooey gloves and stuffed them in the dye box. "Let's put the goo on Dekker and then we can all go downstairs while it processes," she said.

"You go ahead," I said. "I'll be in the kitchen."

I cursed myself for letting them talk me into the whole hair-dyeing thing. I ran down the stairs, clutching my bra knife through the robe, and looked out the front windows, scanning the road for police cars or a red Ram pickup.

Chapter 16

PETTY

"MAYBE WE SHOULD dig into the loot you stole from Dooley's office while we're waiting," Curt said. "Might answer some questions."

Did I want to share my stuff with these people? They'd opened their home to me, their lives, and the truth was I didn't want to have to wait to look at the stuff, however briefly. I went upstairs and brought down the letters and the photo album. I left the envelope and the laptop in my suitcase.

"Let's go in the dining room so we can spread some stuff out," Curt said.

"There's also this," I said, pulling the silver chain from the neck of the robe and holding out the little silver box on it.

Curt walked right up to me and took the silver box in his hand. He was so close I could smell him. I felt dizzy and breathless with him this near. Even my own dad had never invaded my personal space the way Curt and Roxanne did. They thought nothing of it.

"So beautiful," Roxanne said, her arms around her dad's neck from behind him. He turned the box over and then closed his fist around it, looking into my eyes with his bright blue ones.

"Your mom's, you suppose?" he said.

I nodded.

"What's in it?"

"I don't know," I said. "We've been kind of busy."

"Let's find out," he said.

I nodded, holding my breath. What if there was nothing in there? I knew I'd be disappointed.

He opened the lid and turned the box upside down. A tiny zigzag of folded paper tumbled into his palm.

"May I?" Curt said.

I nodded again and he unrolled the paper and held it up. "Wow. We might need a microscope." He handed it to me.

I read the miniature text out loud. "'But those who hope in the Lord will renew their strength. They will soar on wings like eagles; they will run and not grow weary, they will walk and not be faint.'"

"This is magic," he said. "This is treasure. It's good luck."

"Yes," I whispered.

He smiled at me then sat at the dining table, looking around at the stuff from the box.

"I have to see these pictures your dad didn't want you to see," Curt said. "But you first."

I pulled the album toward me and opened it. My head felt fuzzy, my breathing was so shallow. Old photos, the colors faded, the clothes like something out of the *Mad Men* promos I saw on TV—cat-eye glasses and short poufy hair with side curls on the women, polyester shirts and sideburns on the men. There was everyone from infants to elderly folks. I looked closely at the people in the photos but I didn't recognize anyone. I thought my heart would pop out of my mouth, my chest felt so tight.

I guessed that these people must be my extended family, that or

Mr. Dooley had put a decoy box up in the hall. I turned a few more pages and it was a completely different family, but the same time period. I got halfway through and decided to start at the beginning again. Some of the people in the photos had started to look familiar. I couldn't figure out if this was because I'd just moments before looked at the photos or if I truly recognized them. Then I came upon a photo of a little boy with the skinniest arms and legs and this hilariously proud look on his face. I knew that face, and it filled me with joy.

I paged forward until I saw an image of this face as an older adolescent, and sure enough, it was my dad as a teenager. He had surfer-guy hair and high-waisted jeans and a black T-shirt that said *Scorpions Virgin Killer* on it. Dad was standing by another guy with similar hair and the two of them were obviously laughing really hard. My dad was smiling like I'd never seen him smile, and I wanted to cry. He may have been nuts, he may have been paranoid, but he was the only human being I'd ever had any kind of relationship with, and I missed him.

I wiped my eyes with my sleeve then paged forward to a picture of a teenage girl with braces and skinny legs with long light brown hair and dimples. She was wearing a swimsuit and eating a popsicle that was dripping red down her hand and arm. There were more pictures of the same girl, getting older, looking more and more like me. My mom.

Then the pattern hit me: two pages of Dad's family and then two pages of Mom's, showing them both growing up and finally as a couple. I examined all the faces throughout the album again, imagining all of us as the roots of a tree, branching off into infinity, and something clicked inside me. I'd had a family. These people and I all had the same blood in our veins. We were connected. I felt a quiet bittersweet happiness at this idea.

I flipped to the last page, and there was an eight-by-ten of Mom and Dad in winter jackets, bright sunshine in their eyes, standing in a gazebo frosted with sparkling snow, their smiles looking like they might burst right off of their faces. I was struck with the eerie feeling that someone had replaced the happy, smiling, mischievous man in these photos with the empty, somber Dad I'd known all these years. Did losing Mom in the house fire take all the fire out of his eyes? Was that what had happened?

Stuck in the very back of the album was a wedding invitation with names I didn't know, maybe friends of my parents.

I looked up to see Roxanne, Curt, and Dekker counting the rubber-banded letters in the stack.

"One hundred forty-seven," Dekker said.

"Let's divide them up," said Roxanne, handing me the top quarter, Curt the second, herself the third, and Dekker the bottom of the stack. I pushed the photo album toward Curt, knowing I'd come back to it again and again, and opened the topmost letter off my stack.

My dearest love,

The first time I saw you, everything changed for me. I can't eat. I can't sleep. I can't do anything but think about you. I have never felt like this before, and I make this vow to you that every day for the rest of my life, I will love you like no one else on earth ever could. I will spend every day working to deserve you and your love.

All my love,

M

That was a weird way to sign the letter. Why would Dad use his last initial?

Curt studied the pages of the photo album. "So how did you end up in Saw Pole? Usually people move away from Kansas, not to it."

I explained about my mom and the house fire.

"Did your folks vacation in Colorado a lot, or what?"

"What do you mean?" I said.

"Every one of these pictures was taken in Colorado." He flipped pages and pointed. "That's Mount Evans right there." He went forward a few pages. "That's Casa Bonita. And there's Red Rocks. Got to see Neil Young and Crazy Horse there one time, and it was totally kick ass. It was during the . . . which tour would that have been?"

"We're from Detroit," I said, much louder than I'd intended.

"That may be, but these pictures were taken in Colorado. And your folks got married in Colorado." He flipped to the back and pointed at a wedding announcement.

I yanked it out of the album.

Mr. and Mrs. Bart I. Davis
request the honor of your presence
at the marriage of their daughter
Marianne T. Davis
to
Michael D. Rhones
son of
Mr. and Mrs. Dwight N. Rhones
on Saturday, July 28, 1990, at seven o'clock in the evening
at Cherry Hills Community Church
Greenwood Village, Colorado.

"No," I said, my reality suddenly threatened. "It must have been some friends of theirs, because I don't know those names." I didn't want to consider that Dad had lied to me about . . . everything.

"What were their names?" he said.

"I don't know what Mom's name was," I said.

Roxanne gasped. "You didn't know what your mom's name was? How could you not—"

Dekker silenced her.

"Dad's was Charlie Moshen."

"M-O-T-I-O-N?" Curt asked.

"No. M-O-S-H-E-N."

Curt pulled the invitation from my hands and stared at it for so long I wasn't sure if he was still awake, except that his eyes were open. Then they widened. "Rox," he said.

"Yeah?"

"Go get Scrabble, will you?"

Her face lit up, but I didn't understand why. Were we going to play a game? She left the room. Curt's eyes never moved from the invitation. Roxanne appeared with a brick-colored box, which she put on the table. Curt set the invitation down, opened the box and started pulling letter tiles out and laying them in front of him. When he found all the tiles he wanted, he arranged them so they said CHARLIE MOSHEN.

His eyes grew wider and he looked at me. I didn't understand until he rearranged the tiles.

"Holy shit," Dekker said. "Check it out, Rox."

"Oh, my gosh," she said, picking up the invitation and holding it next to the tiles.

Which now spelled MICHAEL RHONES.

The box I'd taken from Mr. Dooley's office had the initials M R on it. *M R for Michael Rhones.* "The letters are signed 'M,'" I said.

"M for Michael." I picked up the wedding invitation and studied it again.

"My mom's name was Marianne," I said, more to myself than to anyone else. "Why . . . did Dad change his name? I don't understand. And if we weren't from Detroit, why did Dad say we were?"

"Maybe you're in the witness protection program," Curt said.

Dekker backhanded Curt's shoulder. "That's what I said!"

They high-fived.

"I don't think you're going to Detroit," Curt said. "I think you're headed to Denver. Just my two cents."

"That's great!" Dekker said, his face and voice full of enthusiasm. "That's so much closer than Michigan!"

"You need to find these people, the Davises and the Rhoneses," Curt said. "You may have some family still there."

"Dad said his parents were dead," I said, a tingling sensation starting on my scalp and spreading down my arms.

Why had Dad changed his name?

If he'd changed his name . . . did he change mine?

What was *my* real name?

"Your dad also told you he didn't have any siblings, and you can tell that guy standing with him in the pictures is his brother," Dekker said.

"Maybe they're cousins."

"I guess my point is that your dad said a lot of stuff which is turning out not to be true. So I think Denver is the place to start. In fact," Curt said, "what do you say we try to find these folks right now?" He picked up the phone receiver and held it out to me.

I couldn't move. My throat was dry. "Could you do it?" I said in a small voice.

He nodded and punched some numbers on the keypad. "Denver, Colorado," he said into the phone. "Dwight N. Rhones." He spelled it out and listened. "Oh? That's a bummer. Can you look up another one for me? Bart I. Davis." He listened again. "Sure. Give me that one. Do you have the address too? Thanks." He found a pen and a pad of paper and scribbled a phone number and address on it. "Thank you. Have an awesome day." He hung up the phone and slid the paper in front of me. "That's Mrs. Bart I. Davis's info right there."

I stared at it, and the tingling covered my entire body. Was I actually looking at the contact information of my maternal grandmother? It couldn't be. Dad said I didn't have any relatives. I folded the piece of paper and put it in my pocket.

Curt rubbed his hands together. "Rox, how much longer we got until the timer goes off?"

She craned her neck. "Dekker can wash off now," she said. "Petty's got fifteen more minutes." She peeked under my plastic head covering.

Dekker went upstairs and I heard the water turn on.

Roxanne, Curt, and I all continued reading from our stacks of letters. I opened the next letter on my pile, which was a lot like the last one I'd read.

I've never felt this way before. I can't live without you. You're my everything.

"Uh-oh," Roxanne said, looking up from the letter she was reading. "They're in a fight. Apparently your mom hasn't spoken to your dad in two whole days, and he's 'dying' on the inside."

Curt laughed.

We were all quiet for a while as we read. Dekker came downstairs rubbing his head with a towel, sat back down at his stack and went on reading. Every letter of mine was signed the same way: *M*.

When I was a kid, I found a box turtle in the road and I brought it home. I wanted to keep it in the backyard but I didn't want it to run away, so I drilled a hole in the turtle's shell and chained it up. I went to school the next day and came back that night to find the thing cooked in its shell.

I shivered, reading this. That was weird. Who would do something like that? And why was Dad telling Mom this in a love letter?

The timer dinged. I stood and stretched. Roxanne stood too and we went upstairs.

"Get in the shower," she said once we were back in the bathroom. "Be sure not to get any of the dye in your eyes. Rinse and then use this conditioner." She handed me a tube.

After my shower, I got dressed in jeans, a T-shirt, my holster, Baby Glock, and my hoodie. Roxanne beckoned me back into the bathroom and told me to straddle the closed toilet again. Then she used a blow dryer on my hair and a round brush. I kept my eyes closed to keep the hair out of them. When the dryer went off I opened them. My hair was golden blond, full and fluffy and almost glamorous, and while I didn't look like me anymore, I could still see my mother's face in my own.

Roxanne put her hands on my shoulders and set her chin on my head. I couldn't move. It was like having a butterfly land on me. I didn't want to scare her away.

"If it's possible," she said, "you look even prettier. Let's go down and show you off."

When we got downstairs, Dekker, Curt, and the dogs were

gone. I felt a stab of dread. I reached for my bra knife and looked in the dining room.

"Oh," Roxanne said. "They're out back."

I glimpsed Curt and Dekker through the kitchen window having an intense conversation out on the back deck. Dekker held his head in his hands. Curt waved his arms in the air. Dekker gestured with his right hand, and I could tell he was talking loud and fast. Curt grabbed Dekker's shoulders and talked louder.

I looked at Roxanne, who was watching them, motionless, her eyebrows drawn together.

I walked silently to the door, trying to hear what they were saying without being seen.

"You have to tell her, Dekker," Curt said. "It's her folks. We have to tell her."

"No," Dekker said. "It's not going to help her. It's not going to make things better for her. It's not going to change anything."

"If you won't tell her, I'll have to," Curt said.

"Fuck that! This is bullshit. This is—I had no idea that—I didn't know that—"

I drew the sliding glass door open, and they swung around to look at me and Roxanne.

Dekker's intensity alarmed me in the same way my dogs' sharp barks used to. I'd seen him angry and scared before, but this was different. This was a full-blown freak-out.

"What do I need to know?" I said, a painful dark chill covering my skin.

Dekker paced, Bob at his heels, back and forth. "Give us a minute, will you, Petty?"

This infuriated me. This was like Randy and Mr. Dooley discussing my life without my presence or consent. "Don't treat me like a child. What do I need to know? What did you find out?"

"Let's go in and sit down," Curt said.

"No. Tell me now," I said. My hands were numb and I was shaking with rage. "What is it? Tell me."

Dekker looked at Curt and Roxanne and then at me.

"Petty," he said. "Your dad . . . was not your dad."

Chapter 17

PETTY

ROXANNE GASPED AND put her hands over her mouth, her black-rimmed eyes huge.

I didn't know what Dekker meant. "My dad . . ."

He nodded. "Charlie Moshen. Michael Rhones. He's not your father."

"What are you talking about?"

"I'm reading along," Dekker said, "and it's kind of the same lovey-dovey stuff over and over so I start skimming until a phrase catches my attention. I see this sentence: 'How could you cheat on me?'"

He paused, letting those words sink in.

"Mom cheated on Dad?" I said. Why? Had he turned into the sad, strange person I knew, forcing her into the arms of another man? Had his craziness, his silence, driven her away? I couldn't blame her for that. I'd dreamed my whole life of getting away from him.

Or was it the other way around?

"Yeah," Dekker said.

"Maybe that's why he went nuts," Roxanne said.

"Yeah," Dekker said. "Your mom had an affair with a guy she and your dad worked with. And . . . she got pregnant."

I held my breath. Dekker continued.

"Your dad wrote that he didn't know if he could ever forgive her for getting pregnant with another man's child."

I could feel Roxanne and Curt's anxiety like an electromagnetic field.

"He told her if she got an abortion, it would be easier to forgive her. So your dad keeps writing to your mom about how hurt he is that she cheated on him, how she betrayed him and all that, but you can tell he's still completely in love with her. He finally says he forgives her and he'll do anything to make it work . . . he'll even raise the kid as if she's his own. That kid is you."

I sat down on the ground hard. Roxanne immediately plopped down next to me, followed by Dekker.

My dad . . . wasn't *my* dad. I flashed through a thousand memories of Dad barking at me to get him a sandwich. Dad yelling "Faster, faster, dammit! You can run faster than that, I know you can! You're goldbricking!" Or sitting motionless as I tried to tell him something and him saying, "I'm not in the mood to talk tonight, Petty." But in the last five years, he was never, ever in the mood to talk. Dad sitting in his chair, staring blank-eyed at the TV, nonresponsive. *Dadnotmydad.* My whole, miserable life, spent with . . . this *man*. Not related to me. Nothing to do with me. Not my father.

Lightning split the sky, close enough to us that the thunder following it shook the ground I sat on.

"Petty, we need to go in," Curt said. "Lightning."

It was as if I'd left my body for a time and then reentered it. I didn't know how long I'd been sitting there. I didn't know when the sky had gotten so dark, or when the temperature had dropped. The thick, solid charcoal-colored ceiling of clouds was moving closer.

"Petty." Roxanne stood and held out a hand to me. I took it and let her pull me to my feet and lead me into the house.

"Dekker, there's a blanket in the hall closet," Curt said.

Roxanne put me in her dad's leather chair and sat on the arm. "Oh, sweetie," she said. "I'm so sorry."

Dekker ran and got the blanket, and put it around me. Curt squatted down in front of me and rubbed my blanket-covered shoulders. "Let's get you warmed up here. You're gonna be all right."

I couldn't stop shivering. Roxanne slid down the arm, wedged herself into the chair with me and put her arm around me, her head on my head.

Curt brought me a glass of water, which I gratefully drank.

Dekker sat on the couch. "Petty, do you realize what this means?" he said. "Your real dad might still be out there somewhere. He might still be in Denver."

"And my mom really might still be alive," I said, and as I did, goose bumps sprang up on my arms, setting me to shivering all over again.

My mom. Marianne. I pictured her and my real dad in a house a lot like this one, warm and cozy with pretty paintings on the walls and a refrigerator full of food.

Curt went into the dining room. I could hear him gathering the letters. "I know Michael Rhones did some crazy, shitty stuff, no question," he called. "But, I gotta tell you. If Rita had cheated on me and had a baby . . . I kind of feel sorry for the guy, you know?"

I didn't. Curt hadn't lived through what I had with this person who wasn't my father after all. Curt was just a kindhearted man who didn't know any better, so I let this slide. He walked out of the dining room, rubber-banding the letters back together.

"Wait," I said. "I want to read them for myself."

"Later," he said. "We've wasted enough time today. I know you're shell-shocked, but you gotta get on the road. Run and get your stuff together and I'll pull the Challenger around to the front of the house."

"Dad," Roxanne said. "You never even let me drive the Challenger to the grocery store." She crossed her arms and pouted.

"Sorry, Rox," Curt said. "It's the newest car I have. It's got GPS and satellite radio, and it's fast." He hugged his daughter and kissed the top of her head. "I promise when Dekker brings it back, you can drive it." He went out the front door.

Roxanne stuck her tongue out at Dekker. "You better not screw that car up," she said. "I mean it, now." She pulled me up out of the chair and the blanket fell from my shoulders. "Let's go get you packed."

I followed her and Dekker up the stairs and went into Chloe's room. I opened my suitcase lid, which blocked the bottom half of the cracked-open window. I could still see the tops of trees, which were being whipped by the wind. My cash was in my suitcase but I decided to put it in my front jeans pocket so I'd have it on me.

"I wish you didn't have to go," Roxanne said from behind me.

"Me too," I said.

Before I could react, she wrapped her arms around my waist and pulled me to her, hugging me tight. I hugged her back, and tried to understand how she could so easily express herself and so casually show affection. If this was what having friends was like, I wanted a lot more of it.

"Okay," she said, letting me go. She looked in my suitcase and gasped. "That's a lot of guns."

"Yes," I said.

I heard Curt pulling the Challenger up out front, rubber tires crushing gravel. I shut the lid of my suitcase, and with a jolt I saw it wasn't the Challenger. It was a blue-and-white. State police.

"They're here," Dekker said from his room. "They're here." He ran into the room. "The cops just pulled up. We gotta hide!"

"If they've got a warrant, there's nowhere to hide," I said. "We have to get out the back door. Now." I reached for my suitcase.

"You won't get very far dragging a fucking suitcase full of guns," Roxanne said.

"I need them," I said, unzipping it.

She looked out the window. "Go, Dekker," she said. "Out the back door. Go."

He ran for the stairs and I heard him racing down them.

"Leave the suitcase," Roxanne said.

"How are you going to explain this?" I said. "You'll get in all kinds of—"

"Listen to me," Roxanne said, taking me by the shoulders. Though she was much smaller than me, she shook me and I stopped fighting. She was right; I had to leave the suitcase. But I was taking the laptop.

"There's a little door to the attic in the back of my closet," she said. "I'll put the suitcase and guns in there. When you come back—and you will—they'll be waiting here for you. Now go."

She hugged me briefly, the laptop squeezed between us, spun me around and pushed me toward the door. I ran. When I got to the bottom of the stairs, I caught a glimpse of Curt standing on the front porch talking and gesturing, his back to the door, the cops advancing.

I crouched and ran toward the back door where Dekker waited for me.

"The letters!" I hissed.

"Leave them," Dekker said.

"But—"

"Let's go!"

I saw them sitting on the coffee table and darted for them, but I couldn't get to them before I heard the front doorknob turning and Curt's voice. I ran for the open back door. Dekker was already outside. I slipped through the sliding glass door sideways as he closed it behind me. We ran for the copse of trees near the road and stopped there. The dark clouds boiled above us, and Dekker breathed noisily beside me.

"Quiet," I said.

"I can't help it."

"Try."

"I am trying!"

"That's what you get for smoking, you know," I said.

He gave me a furious look. "Nobody can hear anything we do over this wind. Should we wait here, you think?" Dekker said. "Wait until they've gone?"

"I don't think so," I said. "They'll search around the property once they're done with the house."

"How are we supposed to get out of here?"

I peeked around the tree.

Roxanne came out the back door and said over her shoulder, "Dad, I'm going to wait out here while they search. Come get me when they're done, okay?" She closed the door behind her. Nonchalantly, she made an away motion with her hands.

I spied a tractor out near the road. "Can you drive that?"

"If it has keys," Dekker said. "But those things only go about twenty miles an hour."

"We just need to get a few miles away and then we can hitchhike."

I looked around the tree again, and Roxanne threw a glance over her shoulder and repeated the shooing motion with her hands.

"Let's go," I said, clutching the laptop to my chest. I ran for the tractor, which was about a quarter of a mile away. Multiple forks of lightning sliced the sky into silver ribbons, followed by quick bursts of thunder. The dark clouds were moving fast, and I saw a vast column of heavy rain headed our way.

When I got to the tractor, I went around the far side of it, crouched low and waited for Dekker as the first drops of rain began to fall. It took him another thirty seconds to get there, and I watched, praying no one would come out the back door and see this tall gangly guy running like a scarecrow. He got to the tractor and stopped in front of it, doubled over, his hands on his knees.

The sliding glass door opened. I dove beneath the tractor and yanked Dekker's feet from under him, knocking him to the ground.

"Don't move," I said.

He froze, as much as he could, gasping for air the way he was.

"Okay, now slowly crawl underneath to the other side of the tractor," I whispered.

He shoved my hands off him and army crawled. We sat up against the large tire, Dekker getting his wind back.

Forked arrows of lightning trisected the sky in every direction almost continuously. Each clout of thunder burst sooner than the one before and tapered off with a threatening growl that crescendoed into the following explosion.

"Don't ever do that again," he said.

"I will if I have to," I said. "They would have seen you."

"You could have just told me to get down."

"Can we argue about this later?" I looked around the tire. Curt had joined Roxanne on the deck along with a police officer. "There's a cop out there with Curt and Roxanne."

Dekker looked. "Okay. We'll wait until he goes back inside and then I'll try to start this thing, because it's going to make a lot of noise."

"What difference does it make? It's farm machinery on a farm."

"But no farmer would be out in his tractor when it's raining."

"Do they know that?"

He made a growling noise. "I wish I'd called in sick yesterday."

"Me too," I said. "Then I wouldn't have to listen to your endless whining."

"If I had, you'd be on your way to Detroit. Or in jail."

I peeked around the tire again. Another cop car had pulled up to the house. The cop on the back deck stayed put, even though the rain was getting heavier. Roxanne went in, and Curt beckoned the cop inside the house, but he wasn't going anywhere.

"More cops," I said. "We have to go *now*."

"No. Not until he goes inside."

"He's not going inside!"

Dekker growled again and looked for himself. "Shit."

He got to his knees and tried the door on the tractor. It opened.

He slowly crawled into the cab. "Shit," he said again. "No keys. And it only has one seat."

I hoped the rain would prevent the cops from walking the property, or we would have to crawl away from here. I noticed the sky, how it was closer now and moving fast with oddly lace-edged, charcoal clouds spinning end over end.

I slid Dad's laptop onto the floor of the cab.

"Who gives a shit about the laptop! I told you there are no—Oh." I heard the jingle of keys. "They were up in the visor." Dekker exhaled. "Okay, get in here on the floor, although I don't know how you're going to fit."

My shirt was already soaked through from the rain and my hair was dripping. But I crawled in as far as I could, getting tangled in Dekker's long legs.

"Put them to the side," I said.

"I have to run the pedals."

"I'll do it by hand," I said. Still, I couldn't get all the way in. My butt and legs stuck out of the opening. "You're going to have to hold onto the door."

He did.

"Okay," I said. "Start it up."

"I hope this is a direct injection engine," Dekker said. "Push down the clutch, the leftmost pedal. Once the motor starts to turn, push on the rightmost pedal. That's the gas."

I shoved the left pedal to the floor and held my breath as Dekker stuck the key in the ignition and turned it. The diesel engine came to life as I pushed on the gas pedal and let go of the clutch. The tractor jerked forward and died.

"You can't let go of the clutch until I tell you," Dekker said, with more patience than I would have expected. "Let's try it again."

We did. I kept the clutch pushed in until he put it in gear. Then I let go too fast and the tractor lurched forward again but kept going.

"The cop's looking this way," Dekker said.

"Don't look at him," I said. It was so tight and humid inside that tiny space, sweat ran into my eyes and dripped off my nose. It itched like crazy but I couldn't do anything about it. Not being able to see what was going on was torture, but Dekker narrated for me.

"Okay, I'm heading for the road," he said. "Oh, no. The cop is walking toward us."

"Don't look at him!"

"I'm not. I can see him in my peripheral vision."

"Drive."

The sound of the rain on the roof changed from a pleasant piano solo to rocks in a cement mixer. The wind outside shrieked. I felt a creeping dread.

"Holy crap," Dekker said. "Where are the windshield wipers on this thing? I can't see a thing."

"Just go forward."

"I am!"

My butt and legs, still sticking out the door, were soaked. I heard a plink, and then another.

"Of course," Dekker said. "Hail."

The plinks accelerated and soon my back end was being pelted painfully with hailstones. Dekker kept going.

"Can you see the cop?" I said.

"I can't see anything," Dekker said grimly. He reached toward the dashboard and switched on the radio. The only sound was the rhythmic buzzing of an emergency broadcast. "Oh, fuck. Fuck."

"The National Weather Service has issued a tornado warning for Pottawatomie County until four-thirty Central Daylight Time. At three-thirty, National Weather Service Doppler radar indicated a severe thunderstorm capable of producing a tornado. This dangerous storm was located ten miles southeast of Wamego moving northeast at thirty miles per hour. Large hail and damaging thunderstorm winds are expected..."

Dekker seized me around the waist, dragged me onto his lap, banging my head on the ceiling, and yanked the door shut with some difficulty. The tractor died and Dekker put on the hand brake.

"It's right over us," he said, squeezing the air out of me, his face in my neck. Anxiety set in, but not because of the storm. It was the close contact that was giving me vertigo and tunnel vision.

"I do solemnly swear," I whispered, "to uphold the Constitution of the United States..."

I heard a tornado siren in the distance, which the wind outscreamed in volume.

"We have to go back," Dekker shouted.

"Where's back?" I said.

"We have to get in Uncle Curt's shelter."

All I could see was gray water pouring down the windshield backed by a weird green glow. Thunder sounded all around. Darkness devoured us. The pressure in my ears alternated painfully as the buffeting winds forced the tractor to rock tire to tire. Hail pelting metal sounded like gunfire. Only the continuous lightning broke up the blackness.

"No, no, no, no," Dekker said, and the terror I felt, the certainty we were about to die painfully, swallowed up my conscious mind and I began screaming.

The air raid siren deepened in pitch until it was no longer a sound but a vibration that could burst eardrums and eyeballs and peel your skin off. The rocking accelerated until it seemed as if the tractor was trying to run away.

Then we rose in the air.

Chapter 18

DEKKER

THE FIRST THING I thought when I woke up staring at the sky, a wedge of brownish light at one end and black angry clouds at the other, was that I wanted a cigarette. I reached up to scratch my nose and came away with a handful of glass slivers and cuts. In fact, my hand was covered with blood.

I was trapped beneath a dead weight pinning my pelvis to the ground. I lifted my head. It was Petty, lying crosswise over me, her face in the mud.

With a jolt of terror-fueled adrenaline, I reached forward and shoved, rolling her across my knees and feet, sending missiles of pain up my legs. She ended up on her back, her face clotted with blood and mud. She gasped a gulp of air and her eyes flew open as she sprang to her feet, looking around wildly.

"Dad?"

"Petty." I got to my feet just as she charged at me. "Petty, it's me. Dekker."

She stopped and bent sideways, clutching her side and groaning. "What happened? I feel like I've been hit by a truck."

"Tornado," I said. "We gotta get out of here."

The tornado siren was still blaring in the distance. I turned in a circle and saw that the tornado had moved us a good fifty yards closer to Uncle Curt's house, which was still standing, thank God. No doubt Uncle Curt and Roxanne had herded all the cops down into the tornado shelter. Their cruisers were still parked, undisturbed, in front of the house.

The tractor lay on its side ten yards away, the windshield and windows shattered, the metal twisted and crumpled like tinfoil. Its deformed shape gave me the shivers. Petty and I stared at each other in amazement.

We should be dead.

Petty ran toward the tractor and I ran after her. Now that I was up and moving, I felt specific pains. My ankle was the worst, but my right elbow and my neck hurt too.

"What are you doing?" I said.

She looked in what was left of the tractor. "Where is it?"

"Where is what?"

"The laptop." She ran in ever widening circles. "The laptop!" Her tone was frantic.

"Never mind," I said. "We've got to get out of here before the cops come out of Uncle Curt's house."

"I need that laptop!" she screamed.

"Why?"

"Stuff about my mom's on there. I have to—"

"No you don't! We have to go! Now!" I grabbed her arm and made her walk alongside me, and she only fought me a little bit.

"I'll call Uncle Curt and tell him to go look for it." Though I knew it was probably destroyed anyway.

I patted my pocket. "Shit," I said. "My cell phone's gone."

Petty didn't respond.

We trotted toward the road, me glancing over my shoulder at Uncle Curt's house every few feet. To my heightened senses, everything appeared sharp and vivid, as if I were looking through a magnifying glass. The red of the tractor. The silver edges of the still-morphing black clouds. The green of the clumpy grass.

I reached into my shirt pocket for a smoke and pulled out the waterlogged and squashed pack. I kept my disappointment to myself, though, because Petty wouldn't be sympathetic at all. I crushed the pack and threw it on the ground.

A silver pickup truck appeared beside us as if by magic. There was nowhere to hide. The driver's side window rolled down.

"You okay? Are you all right?" The man's voice was high and tight, no doubt goosed by adrenaline. "Good God, look at you two. Let's get you to the hospital."

"We're okay," I said. "Just a little shook up."

"Can I give you a ride, then?"

Petty shook her head no, but I squeezed her arm. "Thank you, sir, that would be very helpful."

I opened the passenger door then shoved Petty toward it. She resisted, and I hissed in her ear, "This is how we're going to get out of here. Get in the fucking truck. And wipe your face off. You look like a goon."

She did.

"Can I call your people for you?" the driver asked once we were inside, his cell phone at the ready. With a large but well-kept beard, pink cheeks, and glittering blue eyes, he'd be a dead ringer for Santa Claus in another ten years or so.

"No, that's all right," I said. "If you could drive us down to I-70, that would be great."

The driver gave me a strange look. "I-70?"

"Yes sir," I said. I couldn't think of any believable reason why we'd want to be let out at the interstate, so I didn't try to give one.

"I'll take you right up to your door if you tell me where it is," the driver said.

"That's not necessary," I said, and stared through the windshield, feeling the driver's eyes on me. The silence stretched, and I had to suppress my babbling reflex.

"So what happened to you all?" he asked, putting the truck in gear and accelerating forward.

I exchanged a glance with Petty.

"We were out walking when the storm hit," I said, "and truthfully, I don't have any idea what happened after that."

"I'll tell you this—you're lucky to be alive. Apparently the tornado was on the ground for about a tenth of a mile."

"Any houses hit?" I said.

"Nope, but a barn was taken out. Haven't heard of any fatalities."

"That's good," I said.

"I'm a storm chaser, you know," the driver said.

"Is that right," I said.

"Whereabouts did you say you two are from?"

"I didn't say," I said, then clamped my lips together.

"You doing okay?" the driver said over my head to Petty.

Petty seemed not to have heard anything, just kept glancing out the window at the side mirror.

"She's kind of traumatized, you can imagine," I said.

"Sure, sure," the driver said.

I prayed the bearded man wouldn't say anything to Petty to make her draw her gun, if she still had it on her.

We got to I-70 and two cars were parked under the overpass.

"Thank God, Jenny, look, they're already here," I said, pointing in the direction of the cars.

Petty glanced over her shoulder, probably looking for "Jenny." Then her mouth dropped open with realization.

"Those your people?" the driver said skeptically. I knew he'd seen the uncomprehending expression on her face.

"Yup," I said. "Thanks a bunch for the ride. We really appreciate it."

He pulled over and put the truck in park. Petty opened the door and hopped out. The driver grabbed my arm. I stared at the hand and then at his face.

"You should go get her checked out," he said. "I think she's in shock. She might have a concussion."

"I will, sir. Thanks again."

The driver didn't let go.

I bit my lip. "Thanks again, sir." I slowly pulled my arm away without looking into the man's face, got out of the truck and closed the door. The truck stayed put.

I took Petty's arm and we ran across the road, my ankle feeling loose and sore.

"Don't look back," I said.

The truck remained, idling at the side of the road.

I walked up to a silver Nissan and tapped on the driver's side window. I turned my head and waved at the truck. Still, it didn't move.

The window rolled down. "Did you see that?" the woman in the driver's seat asked. She was obviously still shaken by the tornado, her eyes immense. "You musta got hit! Look at you!"

"Any chance we can get a ride?"

"Well, I, uh—"

I lowered my voice. "Listen. That guy who dropped us off is harassing us. I'd appreciate it if you'd let us get in the car for a minute."

"Well—"

"Please. I'll give you fifty dollars."

The locks popped. I opened the back door, pushed Petty in and got in myself.

"Is he still there?"

The driver looked. "Yes."

"Give the lady fifty dollars," I said to Petty.

She pulled a wet wad of bills from her pocket and counted out two twenties and a ten.

"How about now? He still there?"

Petty handed the money wordlessly over the front seat. The lady took it. "He's leaving."

"Is there any chance you can give us a ride on westbound I-70?"

"I'm headed east," the lady said, but I could tell she was lying. I didn't blame her. Here were these two mud monsters, one of them a mute, who were trying to get away from Santa Claus Junior by sitting in her car and ruining the upholstery.

"Okay. We're going to wait another five minutes or so, and then we'll get out."

The driver never spoke, but kept shooting worried glances at us in the rearview. We sat in silence until I couldn't stand it anymore.

"Thanks," I said.

We got out of the car and walked to the westbound on ramp.

PETTY

DEKKER AND I stood under that overpass by the on ramp and stuck our thumbs out. My ears were filled with a high, metallic-cricket chirping backed by a low buzz. I kept moving my jaw and putting my hands over my ears.

"Your ears ringing too?" Dekker said.

"Yes," I said. "Were we actually in the tornado?"

"I don't know. I can't imagine we were, or we'd be dead. I think it came awfully close though."

I heard the traffic humming overhead, sparse but steady. I was antsy because I couldn't imagine a police car wasn't about to happen by. The rain began falling again and within five minutes we were mud-free and drenched.

We stood there for another fifteen minutes before a Peterbilt semi-trailer truck drove toward the on ramp from the north. It geared down, pulled over behind us and stopped. The door opened and a guy shouted, "Need a ride?"

"How far you going?" Dekker called back.

"Colorado. You're welcome to ride along. Plenty of room."

"What if he recognizes us?" I said.

"My own grandma wouldn't recognize me like this," Dekker said. "Let's go."

I got a good look at the driver's face—it was round and pink and smooth. He didn't even look like he shaved. He wore jeans and a T-shirt and a billed cap that said *Bad to the Bone*. He was a smiley, laughy person. I was grateful Dekker got in first and sat in the middle between us.

"Did y'all get caught in the tornado? I saw it from a ways away, but wow. Name's Ray," he said, holding out his hand to Dekker, who shook it. Ray kind of saluted me, but I turned away.

"I'm Ted," Dekker said. "And this is Jenny."

"Jenny. I like that name," Ray said.

"You don't by chance have any water in here, do you?" Dekker said.

Ray pointed over his shoulder. "There's a cooler behind the seat there. Help yourself."

Dekker pulled out two bottles of water and handed one to me. I opened it and drank it down without stopping. I hadn't realized how thirsty I was. Ray leaned forward, giving me a smile. I looked away again.

"We appreciate you picking us up," Dekker said.

"This is the best part of my job, picking up folks like y'all." He laughed to himself. "Y'all like jokes? What's the hardest part about eating a vegetable? Putting her back in the wheelchair when you're done!"

That one didn't even make any sense. I decided right then I wouldn't talk to Ray or even glance in his direction at all.

"How long you been driving a truck?" Dekker asked him.

"Couple years now. It was great when I started, but then they put the GPSes in the trucks so you can't make as much money anymore, you know what I'm saying?"

"Sure," Dekker said. "That's too bad."

"So what do you call a thirteen-year-old girl from Missouri who can run faster than her six brothers? A virgin!" Ray laughed at his own joke.

Dekker smiled politely and rubbed his eyes.

"Does she ever talk?" Ray said, pointing at me.

"It's been a tough day," Dekker said.

"She don't need to talk, I guess," Ray said. "That's fine. That's fine. Want to hear a joke about my dick? Never mind, it's too long." He laughed some more.

I was so sleepy. The gentle vibration of the truck, the comfortable seat, the droning of Ray's voice. I shook my head trying to stay awake, trying to stay vigilant, but my eyes were so heavy, I felt like I could fall asleep with them open. Ray and Dekker chatted, and the last thing I remember is Ray saying, "You know why they call it PMS? Because Mad Cow Disease was already taken!"

That was the last thing I remembered before the slowing motion of the truck woke me up, and it was ungodly bright. I figured we must have slept through the night and into the afternoon, but then I saw the blazing fluorescent lights overhead.

I needed something to eat and to go to the bathroom.

Dekker's head was on my shoulder. I shook him. "Wake up," I said.

His eyes fluttered open and he smiled at me and stretched.

Ray was alternately watching us and out the windshield as the truck rolled to a stop. We were parked between two other semi trucks.

"Just gonna make a little stop," Ray said. "Just a little stop. Whyn't y'all come inside?"

"What time is it?" Dekker asked him.

"About three A.M.," Ray said.

I opened the door and climbed down, and Dekker followed.

"You fell asleep like immediately," Dekker said, yawning.

We followed behind Ray, who kept glancing over his shoulder at us, as if he was afraid we weren't going to go in or maybe rob his truck or something. Bright light emanated from a glass door that Ray held open for us.

Chapter 19

DEKKER

I'VE ALWAYS BEEN slow to wake up, and Oma loved to make fun of my morning zombieness. She knew never to tell me anything important within thirty minutes of rising. I was especially reluctant to wake up now because I'd been dreaming I was onstage at the Uptown, playing the drums to cheers and applause.

I was reliving the dream as I led Petty through that side door, and it took me a good twenty seconds before I realized what I was looking at.

It was a giant sex toy store.

Blockading us on every side, floor to ceiling, were brilliantly lit displays of neon colored dildos, vibrators, fetish stuff, DVDs, books and magazines. There were boobs and genitals everywhere. Truckers browsed magazines and checked out toys, glancing surreptitiously at Petty from beneath their cap brims.

My instant panic felt like the flu—surreal, delirious, feverish. I had to get Petty out of here before she realized what she was seeing. This might really and truly send her over the edge, and if she pulled a gun in a store like this, we were really and truly fucked.

I hoped since she'd probably never experienced anything like this, none of it would register.

Petty blinked in the unforgiving fluorescent light, and she had that unfocused look she got when she wasn't really present. But it couldn't last, because sooner or later her eyes would light on a big veiny cock and she would figure it out.

Ray watched her face, confused by her seeming indifference. So I stepped into her sight line.

"Petty," I said in as calm and quiet a voice as I could muster, "this is a sex shop. Let's go right back out the door."

"It's a what?" she said, in a normal tone of voice. Heads swiveled toward us.

"We need to leave."

"But I have to use the bathroom," Petty said. "And I need a—"

And there it was. Her gaze had landed on who knew what, and her eyes grew round and enormous. Now she saw everything. She turned in a circle, surrounded by the truckers' barely concealed boners.

She ran for the door with me close behind her. In the parking lot, I now saw the sign we had missed on the way in, groggy and exhausted as we were, declaring ADULT SUPERSTORE!

Petty paced in front of Ray's semi truck.

"What was that? What was I looking at?" Petty said. "What *was* that?"

I held my hands up as if trying to calm an angry animal. "Take it easy, Petty. I'm sorry you had to see that."

She paced some more. "Why would they have all that naked . . . the little statues of . . ." She shuddered.

Ray walked out of the door, a big grin on his face. "See anything in there you liked?" he asked Petty.

He reached out to tickle-squeeze her waist.

"No!" I shouted, but it was too late.

Petty spun around and lunged at the guy. Whip-quick, she was behind him, had him tipped backward with her arms restraining his. Ray looked completely astounded, a *How did I end up like this?* expression on his goofy redneck face.

"See if he's got any weapons," Petty said to me.

No more giggling or guffawing from Ray. Only stupefied gasping. "What the fuck?" he said.

I was rooted to the spot, afraid any sudden movement would trigger a violent slash-fest on Petty's part.

"Frisk him!" Petty said, wrenching Ray's arms as she did so.

He grunted in pain, and his pleading eyes rolled in my direction. I almost felt sorry for him. Almost.

"You shouldn't have touched her," I said.

"What the hell kinda whore are you anyway?" Ray choked out.

Petty's head swiveled toward me, her eyes demanding an explanation or a reason not to kill this trailer-park Casanova. And then it hit me.

"Ray, I think you got the wrong impression about us," I said. "We're students. We just needed a ride. We're not in *business*. You understand what I'm saying?"

"But you got no bags or nothing . . ."

Petty's mouth dropped open, but she didn't loosen her grip. "You mean—he thought I was a prostitute? Is that what he thought?"

I nodded.

She squeezed him tighter and he squealed. I held up my hands palms out and almost said her real name. It was automatic. I had to concentrate. "It's a misunderstanding. Let's just go."

"Not until this guy apologizes."

"Okay." To Ray, I said, "How about you apologize to the lady?"

"Sorry," he said hoarsely.

"Satisfied?" I said.

"I should cut your throat, you sicko," Petty said to him.

Ray's knees buckled, and the only thing keeping him on his feet was Petty's iron grip. Just then another trucker came walking out the building's side door. He had a large bag of goodies in his hand, which he dropped on his foot when he saw what Petty was up to. He plucked up the bag then reached for his phone.

"Drop it," Petty said.

He didn't.

"I said drop it."

He held up the phone to focus the camera.

Petty let go of Ray, yanked her gun out of its holster and pointed it at the guy with the phone, who hadn't gotten his shot framed the way he wanted it yet. He froze with his phone out in front of him.

Ray collapsed to the ground.

"Drop . . . the . . . phone."

"But—but it'll break . . ."

"Drop it!"

He did, and it did.

"We're leaving now," Petty told them. "We didn't hurt anyone. Don't call the cops, or I'll come back here and finish the job."

Ray and the phone man both nodded dumbly, slack-jawed and glassy-eyed.

Petty backed away, aiming the gun with both hands, back and forth, between the two guys. Once we reached the edge of the parking lot, she stuck the gun in her holster and ran.

I could not believe how fast this girl could run. I couldn't possibly hope to keep up. I didn't want to admit it, but a pack a day of Camels had really cut my lung capacity. We ran on the soft shoulder, the cross-country trucks blasting by us. Petty held out a thumb as she ran.

It seemed like hours had gone by, but I knew it couldn't have been more than twenty minutes or so. I couldn't keep going, in any case. I had a stitch in my side and my ankle was throbbing, so I sat down well back from the shoulder in the soggy, shallow ditch. It was another ten minutes before Petty came running back.

"Why are you sitting? Let's go."

"I can't keep up with you," I said.

"We can't stay here," she said.

"Can we walk?"

"All right."

We walked the shoulder.

"Petty," I said, choosing my words carefully. "You can't just pull your gun on someone because he pisses you off."

"I was defending myself. I was defending us."

"From what?"

"He was trying to take our picture." She stopped walking.

I stopped too. We stood facing each other.

"But he didn't threaten you. And Ray *thought* you were a prostitute, but he didn't *do* anything. He's a moron being an asshole. You don't shoot people for being stupid assholes, or the human race would be extinct."

Petty didn't say anything for a moment. "Well, you just stood there and didn't do anything."

"Right," I said. "There was nothing for me to do. If he'd threatened you physically, I would have—"

"You'd have what? Run away? Slowly?"

"We're trying to keep a low profile," I said, stung and defensive. It hadn't occurred to me that I was the weak link in this partnership, but she was right. I wouldn't have done anything. At least I had a grip on how the real world worked and didn't think I was living inside of a cop show where pulling your piece had no actual consequences. "And Ray was harmless and pathetic. But he and that other fat fuck will never forget you. They'll tell their buddies, and sooner or later one of them's going to decide he wants that Crimestopper reward, and I hope to God we're off this road by then. In the meantime, you need to stop acting like Sarah Connor or you're going to get us caught—if you don't kill someone first. Like me." My voice rose throughout my tirade until I was shouting that last bit.

"Fine," she shouted back.

I followed several yards behind her in silence. I was tired. I was pissed at getting roped into this. Then rain began falling. Perfect.

To distract myself, I ran through Disregard the 9's set list in my mind, playing my part on imaginary drums in front of me. I needed some rehearsal time and badly. I could not screw this up. I had to be on time, I had to be easy to work with this time and not roll my eyes when Chad wanted to play songs I hated.

Not a single vehicle even slowed as they went by. We walked so long I wondered if we'd have to walk the entire way to Denver. We walked so long I began to wish for a cop car to stop and take us to a nice dry jail.

"Petty," I called.

She trudged on.

"Come on, Petty. I'm sorry, okay?"

She didn't stop.

"Come on. You've got to forgive me."

She slowed but continued on.

Just before sunrise, taillights pulled to the shoulder ahead of us. Petty slogged resolutely on past it, giving the car a wide berth. But I heard a woman's voice calling out of the open window. "What in the hell are you two doing? You're going to get killed, walking on the shoulder of the interstate!"

I stopped and looked in the open window of the Chevy sedan. The dashboard lit up the driver's face. She was in her sixties at least, with glasses and graying hair in a ponytail.

"You get in this car right now," she said.

I stood straight and shouted, "Jenny!" Petty kept walking. She obviously didn't remember the fake name I'd given her earlier. "Jenny!"

She stopped and turned.

"We've got a ride."

Petty put a hand on her hip.

"Come on, it's raining. This nice lady wants to give us a ride." Petty stood thinking for a moment then walked back. She whispered, "If she takes us to one of those shops, I'm pulling weapons again. I'm just saying."

"Fair enough," I said.

I got in the front seat and Petty got in back.

"Where y'all headed?" the driver asked.

"Denver," I told her.

"Me too," she said. "Going out to sit with my grandbabies while their folks go on a cruise. You can ride all the way if you want."

She pulled back out on the highway.

"Car break down?" she asked.

"Yeah," I said. "I'm Ted and that's Jenny."

"Debbie," she said.

"Where are we?"

"Just past WaKeeney," she said. "About three hundred miles from Denver."

Wednesday

PETTY

I WOKE UP in the backseat of Debbie's Chevy, thinking about Detective Deirdre Walsh and how I'd never gone more than a day without watching an episode of one of the *Offender* shows. I felt the way I imagined normal people felt when they were away from family for a period of time—disoriented, detached, homesick. Then I saw something that made me shout.

"Dekker!"

The car swerved. "My word," Debbie said, her hand over her mouth. "What did you say, Jenny? Are you all right?"

Dekker turned in his seat to look back at me. "Yeah, *Jenny.* What did you say?"

I couldn't say anything then, because I realized I'd used Dekker's real name. Luckily, Debbie didn't know what I was talking about.

"Did you have a bad dream?" Debbie said.

"No," I said. I pointed between the front seats at the windshield.

"What is it?" Dekker said.

"The mountains! *The mountains!* There they are!"

"Give us some warning before you freak out next time, will you?" Dekker had his hand on his chest as if he were trying to keep his heart from popping out.

"I'm sorry, but . . . the mountains!" They really were purple, and the tops of them really were frosted in snow, though it was late April. I'd never seen anything so beautiful, not in real life.

"Yes. Mountains. Shit. You're going to get us killed."

I was so excited I couldn't stop bouncing in my seat, and Dekker finally started to smile. "Pretty cool, huh?"

"Let's stop in Limon," Debbie said. "We can get food and use the restroom. Then it's another hour and a half to Denver."

AT THE TRUCK stop there were dozens of semi rigs, and I was afraid Ray might be there and get us in trouble. Dekker looked worried too. But then in the parking lot he pointed at a white Buick with a FOR SALE sign in the window. It said $900 and *See manager inside.*

A half hour later the manager signed over the title for just $800, and we gave Debbie fifty dollars for gas and said goodbye to her. Then we spent another $125 in the convenience store. We bought some fruit, toiletries, a couple of T-shirts, a new zip-up hoodie for me, and a map of Denver. We had $2500 left between the two of us, but I had no intention of letting Dekker spend any of his share.

The truck stop had showers, so we both paid to use them. I didn't want us to show up at my maybe-grandmother's house looking like drowned rats. I felt much fresher as I exited the shower room with my dirty clothes in a plastic sack.

"I need to find a pay phone and call Uncle Curt and let him know we survived the tornado." He tossed me the keys. "You can wait in the car, if you want."

I carried our purchases out to the Buick and put everything in the backseat then got in the front. The seats were deep and comfortable, not like any of the other vehicles I'd been in. It was like riding on a sofa. Maybe Dekker could teach me to drive once we got to Denver.

He startled me by opening the driver's side door and getting in.

"Boy, Uncle Curt was pissed," he said.

"Why?"

"Said he's been out of his mind with worry. Didn't know if we were alive or dead. He actually said we should turn around and come home and hide in his basement. I said this was the first time we've been anywhere near a phone. He told me call him when we get to Denver."

I pulled the folded paper out of my pocket, the one with Mrs. Bart I. Davis's address on it, and read it over again. Was this actually kin of mine, and if so, what was she like? Dekker's grandma popped into my mind, her and her casserole and the way she put Dekker in his place, and I hoped that mine was like her.

Dekker unfolded the map. "Can you navigate?"

"Yes," I said. "Dad taught me how to read maps almost as soon as I could read."

Every time I used that word—Dad—it hit me in the chest. Charlie Moshen, Michael Rhones—who had he really been? He was obviously much more disturbed than I could ever have imagined, taking me away from Mom and my real dad.

Dekker handed me the map. I looked at the address Curt had written for us and found where it was located on the map within a few minutes.

Dekker started up the car and drove us to I-70.

An hour and a half later we pulled up in front of Mrs. Bart I. Davis's address, which looked like a run-down hotel. The paint was faded and peeling, the lawn in front sparse. It was called the Village at Xanthia.

And now that we were here, I was suddenly immobilized by

fear. What if Mrs. Bart I. Davis didn't want anything to do with me? What if she was a mean old lady?

What if she wasn't my grandma at all?

DEKKER

I FOLLOWED PETTY up to the building and through the front door to a desk. My heart sank. I'd been expecting an apartment complex, but this was a nursing home. The place seemed cheery enough, but there were several old folks in bathrobes sitting in wheelchairs, staring at nothing. Underneath the floral air-freshener scent, I smelled urine. The clock, to my surprise, said three P.M. No wonder I was so tired and hungry. I'd been driving nonstop since breakfast.

A fleshy woman in scrubs sat behind the reception desk, talking on the phone. She held up a finger to us.

We waited until she hung up and turned to us. "How can I help you?"

Petty opened her mouth to speak, but nothing came out. I came to her rescue.

"We're here to see Mrs. Bart I. Davis."

She consulted a notebook. "Jeannie Davis?"

"Yes," I said with authority.

"And who are you?"

Petty and I glanced at each other. We couldn't give our real names, of course.

"We're her grandniece and nephew," I said.

The nurse looked suspicious. Or maybe I only thought she did.

"Is Mrs. Davis expecting you?"

"No," I said. "She definitely is not expecting us. We're in town from Nebraska. We promised our mom we'd visit."

"You'll need to sign in and print your license plate number here." She pushed a clipboard with a sign-in sheet on it toward us.

"We took the bus," I said.

But she'd already turned away to attend to other business.

I wrote on the sign-in sheet: *Bill and Melinda Gates.*

"Where can we find Mrs.—Aunt Jeannie?" I asked the back of the nurse's head.

"She's in room 3B."

I led the way down the hall. Petty avoided eye contact with the old people. Most of them were like droopy statues, and the rest moved with painful slowness. Petty probably didn't have any experience with old people, where I'd had a lifetime of it. After I went to live with Oma, I accompanied her Meals on Wheels runs and her weekly visits to the Sunset Nursing Home in Niobe. Every Thursday, Oma baked cookies and other goodies for the old folks.

"Here it is," I said, pointing to an open door. Many televisions up and down the hall competed with each other, most of them death-metal loud, and one of them was in the room we were about to enter. "I'll go in first, okay?"

Petty nodded, her face ashen

Inside were two old ladies. One sat up in bed, the other in a chair. Only the lady in the chair turned when Petty and I entered.

"Hello," I said.

"Good morning!" the lady in the chair said cheerfully. "Are you here for my bath?"

"No, we're here to visit. Are you Mrs. Jeannie Davis?"

"Oh, no, honey. I'm Zelda Krantz. I'm her new roommate." She whispered, "Her last one passed away."

"I'm sorry to hear that," I said.

I glanced at Petty, who couldn't take her eyes off the lady in the bed, her possible grandma, who hadn't taken her eyes off the TV.

"We're some relatives in from Nebraska," I said. Then I said to Jeannie, "Hello, Mrs. Davis."

Her head turned slowly, and her eyes traveled from my belt buckle to my face before her eyes narrowed in what might have been confusion or suspicion. She didn't answer.

"How are you today?"

She kept staring at me.

"She's having an off day, I think," Mrs. Krantz whispered. "She has the Alzheimer's, you know."

"No, I didn't know," I said, deflated. This was a major setback. Would Mrs. Davis be able to provide any information? Would she even be able to talk to us?

Petty backed up against the wall.

"She was very lively this morning," Mrs. Krantz said, looking at the TV. "Very talkative."

"What did she talk about?" I asked Mrs. Krantz.

"About when her children were little, mostly," she said. "She has her good days and her bad days. You should go ahead and talk to her anyway. Even if she doesn't answer, you can talk to her."

I tried to catch Petty's eye, but she was frozen in place. I imagined she'd even stopped breathing. I got as close to her as I dared and whispered, "Talk to your grandma, Petty."

"What do I say?"

"Just . . . say hello." I thought I could see some resemblance to the lady in the photo album, but maybe I just hoped I could. I turned back to Petty. "Don't make her strain to see you," I whispered. "Go over by the bed, look her in the eye and talk to her."

Petty detached herself from the wall with some effort and

walked to the bed. Mrs. Davis's eyes were still on me. Petty cleared her throat, and the old lady's watery eyes slowly tracked over to Petty's face.

"Hello," Petty said.

Mrs. Davis's cloudy old eyes gazed into Petty's, and I could actually see her pupils dilate. She must recognize Petty! A low growly noise came out of Mrs. Davis's mouth. "Ma. Ma. Ma. Ma. Ma. Ma."

"Is she saying 'Mama'?" I said.

Mrs. Davis's veiny old hand came up off the blankets and wavered, but it looked like a shooing motion to me. She kept her eyes on Petty's face, her eyebrows drawn together. "Ma. Ma. Ma." It was creepy, the way she drew the syllables out, how her voice was pitched so low. I knew this voice would haunt my dreams.

"She must be way back in her childhood now," Mrs. Krantz said. "I feel for her, I do. I hope it's not contagious. Not a thing wrong with my mind, not a thing. Sharp as a razor!"

Petty shocked me by reaching out and taking Mrs. Davis's hand. Once contact was made, Mrs. Davis stopped making any noise at all. She continued staring at Petty until her eyelids got heavy. Then they closed and she snored softly. Petty set her hand back on the blanket.

"Does she ever have any visitors?" I asked Mrs. Krantz.

"I've only been her roommate for about a week now, and she hasn't had any in that time. I've had two, though."

"That's great," I said.

"Do you want to try again tomorrow?" Mrs. Krantz asked. "She might be a little clearer. Then again, she might not."

"But you'll be here, won't you?" I said. "We can talk to you then, can't we?"

"Of course you can!" Mrs. Krantz's dried apple-doll face lit up, and I could see that she'd once been very pretty.

"Is there a special treat we can bring when we come back tomorrow?"

"Can you bring me some chocolate-covered cherries?"

"We can," I said, "and we will."

Chapter 20

DEKKER

"WE DROVE BY a motel for twenty-nine dollars a night," I said. "That's probably as good as it's going to get."

What I didn't say was that it was called Motel 9, which I took as a good omen because it was so close to Disregard the 9. I didn't want her to think I was superstitious.

When I snapped out of my mini-daydream, Petty was staring at me. "We're going to a motel?"

"We need a place to sleep," I said. "What were you thinking we should do?"

"I didn't think about it," Petty said. "I guess I thought we'd come to town, we'd find my grandma, she'd tell us who my real dad is and we'd go there. I didn't think about . . . nights."

The way she'd said it, "going to a motel" sounded extra special sleazy. Suddenly my stomach felt like it was tumbling in a clothes dryer.

"If we stayed at a nice place," I said, feeling my face glow red, "it would be over a hundred a night, easy."

"That's not exactly what I was—"

"It'll only be for a night or two."

She went quiet and stared out the window, to my relief.

We pulled up to the motel, which was made of tan brick. MOTEL 9, said the sign. *Best Rates in Town. WiFi. Cable. Phones. Fridge.* What looked like old blue terry-cloth towels hung behind some of the windows while others were sealed up with slabs of particle board. The rooms surrounded the parking lot in a U, and all the doors were red. We got out of the Buick. There were cigarette butts all over the ground, so many of them it almost looked decorative.

"Maybe we should gather all these up for Ashley," I said.

"That's a joke, right?" she said.

I couldn't help but smile as I nodded. "That's a joke."

We stood gazing at the motel.

"Do you feel weird?" Petty said.

"Yeah," I said. "But our cash stash is going to go a lot quicker than you think, so I think we need to stay in the same room."

"No," Petty said. "I mean I'm having a hard time getting enough air, and my heart rate's way up." She held two fingers against her jugular.

Oops. I tried to recover quickly. "That's the altitude."

I led the way into the front office. A wall of what was probably bulletproof glass stood between us and a dried-up old man shaped like a parenthesis. He wore pants belted just under his armpits and his voice squawked out of the mouth-high metal speaker embedded in the glass.

"Room?" His teeth were the color of maple syrup.

"Yes, sir," I said. "We're not sure how long we'll be here, so maybe we should—"

"Twenty-nine dollars a night, one forty-nine a week."

"Right. You have a room available for, I don't know, like three nights?" I glanced at Petty to see if this seemed reasonable. She had no reaction.

"Pay up front," the old man said. "Cash only. No check. No card. Cash only."

I could imagine he'd been saying this speech dozens of times a day for the last sixty years in exactly the same way. A metal drawer popped out and knocked Petty in the hip. Inside of it was a pen and card to fill out. I removed them and started writing. Petty reached into her pocket, pulled out five twenty-dollar bills and put them in the drawer, which retracted.

"No pets." The old man counted the cash as he talked and never looked up at us. "No smoking in the rooms. Outside only. Hundred dollar fine we catch you smoking in your room."

It was funny he was saying all this, because the inside of the office smelled a lot like Ashley's apartment. But I figured Petty was glad I'd have to smoke in the parking lot.

"Here's your key," he said, and the drawer popped out again. This time Petty got out of the way. She pulled out the change and the key.

"Thirty dollars if you lose the key," the manager said into the metal speaker that made his voice sound like a robot's.

"Gotcha," I said.

The old man put his mouth up against the metal circle and shouted, "And no drugs!"

Petty jumped at the sound.

Outside, I parked the car in front of the door to Room 5, our new home for the next couple of days. As I tried to unlock the door to the room, a woman peeked out the window next door. She had crispy yellow hair and sleepy eyes that rolled in my direction, but she looked through me. I snorted. No drugs my ass. I unlocked the door, opened it and went in first. Thousands and thousands of cigarettes had been smoked in that room. The brown carpet resembled felt and was worn to the floorboards in some places.

Petty glanced in the bathroom, under the double bed and the couch, then she stood staring at me.

There was only one bed. Every motel room I had ever stayed in had two double beds. I'd thought there would be two. My skin got hot and I couldn't look at her, because I had a flash of the two of us lying in it together.

"I'll be right back," I said, and walked out the door.

I pulled a cigarette out of my pack and lit it up, gazing up at the sky, which was blue and thin and high. I walked back to the office and rang the bell. The old man came out of the back office and just stared at me.

"I'm in Room 5, and I wondered—do you have a different room available with two double beds?"

"No."

"Could you check?"

"Don't need to."

"Well, then I'd like my money back so we can go someplace with two double beds."

He pointed at a sign on the back wall before disappearing into the back room again.

NO REFUNDS.

Maybe we should've gone somewhere else, just eaten the hundred dollars, but I didn't want to make a big deal out of it, for fear Petty would pick up on what I'd been thinking.

This was going to be torture. Having Petty so close, staying in the same room. I hoped Mrs. Davis would be semi-lucid tomorrow and tell us where Petty's real dad was. I would drive her to him, there would be a tearful reunion, then I would get on the road tomorrow to Kansas City with five days to spare. I was suddenly acutely aware of the attraction that had been building. Now that we'd be sleeping in the same room, that attraction hit critical mass. I'd need to practice not thinking about her.

No way I could sleep in the same bed with her and expect not to have a reflexive physical reaction. I'd have to sleep on the couch.

I finished my cigarette and went back in the room.

Petty hadn't moved from the spot she'd been standing in when I left.

"Wow," I said. "This is a shithole, isn't it? This place makes the motels I stayed in as a kid seem like palaces. I'm going to use the bathroom."

"Okay." Petty sat on the couch, the middle of which sagged into a crater, and dust rose. She sneezed.

I went in the bathroom and tried to shut the door, but it wouldn't close. It was too big for the frame. Perfect.

"I'm going to turn on the TV," Petty called. I was grateful to her for that. I heard the television switch on.

Rust ringed the tub, and the corners of the room were packed with pubic hair. There seemed to be a film of ancient filth on everything. So. Gross. I sighed.

PETTY

DEKKER CAME OUT of the bathroom and reached for the tan-colored phone. He punched some buttons. "Hey, hippie," he said. "We're here . . . it was fine . . . it's called Motel 9, and it's a real shithole, but it's cheap. We're in room number five." He listened for a minute. "Yeah, we saw her about an hour ago. She's got Alzheimer's . . . I know. We're going to try again tomorrow morning . . . I don't know . . . She's doing good . . . Okay. Hold on." He held the phone out to me.

I felt a deep flush spreading over my neck and face. Curt wanted to talk to me? Why?

"Hello?" I said.

"How you doing, Petty girl? How do you like Denver?"

"It's big. And loud. And dirty."

"You feeling overwhelmed?"

"Yes," I said.

"Whatever you find out there, be bold, and mighty forces will come to your aid. And tell your granny hi for me. I'll talk to you soon. Give the phone back to Dekker, will you?"

I handed the phone over. He'd just wanted to say hello, which confused me and made me glad at the same time.

"Yeah, it's not exactly what she's used to," Dekker said. "I'll call when I find out anything new. 'Bye." He hung up. "We have to find a place to buy chocolate-covered cherries for Mrs. Krantz and some groceries so we don't have to eat out. I mean, eat in restaurants."

His face got red, but I didn't know why.

In the nightstand was a smudgy phone book he paged through until he found what he was looking for and wrote on a little pad of paper. He called the number and asked for directions from Motel 9, which he also wrote down.

Once we were back in the Buick, I read off the directions while Dekker drove the Denver streets. When he parked in front of the Walmart, I said, "I've never seen one in real life. Just on TV."

I followed him through the automatic doors. This place was ten times the size of the Walgreens in Salina, and it made me feel dizzy and untethered. The aisles were packed with slow-moving people who all seemed to be talking at once, and loudly. Not long after we got inside, we got separated by the throng and I started hyperventilating. I stopped walking and backed into the shopping carts, making a racket above the general noise. Dekker was taller than most people, so I could see the back of his head. But he turned and saw I wasn't there and pushed his way back through the crowd. He grabbed a shopping cart and put my hands on the push bar then got behind me, not touching me but staying close enough to make me feel safe.

We pulled out into the human traffic. I turned and looked up at him. "Thank you."

We navigated through the aisles to the stuff we needed. We each had to buy some clothes—luckily, Walmart's stuff was pretty cheap. I got a pack of underwear, pajamas, two pairs of jeans, and three T-shirts for less than fifty dollars.

Dekker insisted on using his own money to buy his clothes. I insisted on buying the food.

I was so glad to get out of there.

Back at the motel, Dekker put the food away then flopped on the bed with the TV remote.

"I'm going to get ready for bed," I said. I took my Walmart bag into the bathroom, then brushed my teeth, washed my face, and put on my pajamas, feeling shy about Dekker seeing me like this. But I couldn't sleep in the tub.

"My turn," Dekker said, and took his stuff into the bathroom.

I found an old blanket on a plywood shelf above the little fridge. I spread it out on the couch and took one of the lifeless pillows from the bed. Then I crawled into my couch bed, lay on my side and faced the wall.

I heard the toilet flush, the bathroom door open and the light go off. "Petty, where are—what are you doing?"

I turned over and looked at him. "What?"

"Why are you on the couch?"

"We can't sleep in the same bed."

"Yes, we can," Dekker said. "I'm not going to—I'd never—you don't have to worry about me."

"I know you wouldn't do anything on purpose," I said. "But as a guy, you have certain reflexes you can't control." I was glad my back was to him, because my face flamed with embarrassment.

"What does that mean?"

"My dad told me boys can't help overpowering girls. It's something their bodies are programmed to do. It's not your fault. But I can't be in the same bed with you."

"That is so sick," Dekker said.

"I know, but you can't help it."

"That's not what I mean. What your dad told you was a lie. It's not true. Anyone is capable of self-control. Nobody is 'programmed' to 'overpower' anyone else."

"Of course you're going to say that," I said. "You can't help it."

"I can help it! If you don't believe me, look it up on the Internet."

I sat up and faced him.

"Your dad," Dekker said, "Charlie Moshen, Michael Rhones, whatever the hell his name was—was a total skeev. He made it his life's mission to fuck with your head. He lied to you about—well, about everything, as far as I can tell. You need to understand that. I'll sleep on the couch."

"No," I said. "I'm already here, and you're too tall. Now go to bed." I turned over again.

He sighed, exasperated, and got in bed.

Thursday

IT WAS A restless night. There were lots of sirens, howling dogs, people yelling in English and Spanish. Plus the smell of rot, ancient cigarette smoke, mildew, and B.O. was so ingrained in every fiber of the room, I couldn't escape it. I also couldn't stop hearing my grandmother's creepy low voice in my head saying, *Ma ma ma ma.*

My disappointment at not being able to ask Jeannie a ton of questions was heavier than I would have expected. I hoped today would be different. I had a whole list: What was my mom like as a kid? How did they get along? What was I like as a baby? What exactly happened between Michael Rhones, my mom, and my real dad?

I guess I'd expected to feel some sort of instant connection with her, but all I'd felt was fear and revulsion. This person meant nothing to me, and I wondered what life would have been like had Michael Rhones not taken me away. I wondered if I'd have spent time over at my grandma's house, baking cookies and coloring and sewing like I'd seen on TV.

I knew about Alzheimer's disease, but I'd never seen it in real life. It was scary and life-shattering.

I woke up earlier than Dekker and tried to go back to sleep, but my back hurt and my legs were stiff from being bent all night. Plus my sinuses and throat were so dry they ached. I got up and went to the bathroom. When I came out, Dekker's eyes were open.

"Good morning," I said.

"Hey," he said, sleepy.

"You ready to get going?"

He rubbed his eyes. "Something you need to know about me," he said. "I wake up slowly. You need to give me about thirty minutes before you try to talk to me."

"Okay," I said.

I was antsy, anxious about going back to the Village at Xanthia. I couldn't just sit there and wait, so I got over my self-consciousness and did push-ups, sit-ups, squats, lunges, tricep dips.

"You make me feel lazy," Dekker said.

"Nineteen," I said, "twenty, twenty-one . . ."

I was halfway through my strength exercises before I realized that I'd dreamed Dekker and I had been lying on that bed, kissing for hours. I was appalled by how uncontrolled my brain was—why hadn't Michael Rhones told me about this, trained me to manage my subconscious?

Suddenly, I was afraid Dekker could read my thoughts, see into my head, and shame engulfed me like a tidal wave. I'd only ever had dreams like that about actors on TV, never a real person. It was as if I had violated him, done things to him without his permission, like when Randy had attacked me a few nights before. I knew it wasn't the same thing, but I was still disturbed and felt like apologizing to him. But I knew that would be inappropriate.

Would Dekker be able to tell that I'd dreamed about him? Would it show on my face somehow?

And did I want to kiss Dekker?

I pushed this thought out of my head and went back to my workout, pushing myself, doing more reps, imagining Michael Rhones shouting at me to try harder. Even so, I could feel I wasn't getting the oxygen I needed, because I hit muscle failure long before I normally did.

"How does anyone breathe this air?" I said. "There's nothing to it."

Dekker stretched and yawned. "Yeah, but isn't it kind of nice not feeling moist all the time?" He startled, as if he'd said something wrong. "I mean, feeling like you're wet? The humidity, I mean. I don't miss it. That's what I'm saying."

I took a shower before dressing in the bathroom, and then Dekker took his turn in there while I watched TV. The thought of visiting my grandma again made me fidgety and nervous. What if she still couldn't talk? How were we supposed to find my real dad? This whole trip would be for nothing, and then what would I do?

I reached for Mom's silver necklace and realized I'd forgotten to put it on. When had I taken it off? It must have been the night before. But where did I put it? I couldn't remember. The necklace wasn't in my shoes, the Walmart bags, or in any of my pockets. I felt around on the bed and peeled back the sheets and blankets, then felt around on the floor. I brought the lamp off the nightstand and looked under the bed for it. It was gone.

Dekker came out of the bathroom, bringing a cloud of steam with him. "What are you doing?" he said.

"My mom's necklace," I said. "It's gone."

"I'll bet you lost it in the tornado," he said as he folded yesterday's clothes.

"No," I said. "I had it after that."

"Are you sure? Maybe—"

"Yes. I had it yesterday."

I was annoyed that he didn't seem to understand how important this was to me. The necklace was the only thing of my mother's I had, and I'd only had it for two days. I mourned its loss.

"It'll turn up," he said. "You ready for this?"

We walked out the door. It was chilly, but the dazzling morning sunshine made me squint. Frost covered the Buick.

I walked to the passenger door then stopped and stared.

"Did you roll down my window?" I said.

"What?" Dekker said. "Why would I—oh, shit. Oh, no."

When he got to the driver's side, he went limp then started jumping up and down. "Shit! *Shitshitshit!*"

I went around to where he stood and saw that someone had scratched CRAKER into the paint on the door. I looked around the parking lot and saw faces peeking around terry-cloth curtains, shaking their heads. I went back to the passenger side of the car and opened the door. Glass dropped to the ground and there was more on the seat. I brushed it off before I got in.

Dekker sat rocking in his seat, pulling his hair with both hands. It was then that I saw that the glove box was open and empty.

"What does 'craker' mean?" I said.

He banged the heels of his hands against his forehead.

"Did they mean to write 'cracker,' like white trash?" I thought about the run-down, jerry-rigged house I'd grown up in and the crappy trailer homes in Saw Pole, and I figured the key artist was pretty accurate.

"Will you shut up?" Dekker said. "Don't you see what happened here? We were robbed!"

"We just need to find some cardboard and duct tape to shut up this window."

"No! They stole my money!"

"Your money?"

"It was in the glove compartment."

Why had he put his money in the glove box? "What? How much of it?"

He didn't say anything.

"How much, Dekker?"

"All of it."

Chapter 21

PETTY

WE GOT OUT of the car.

Dekker paced. "Why me?" he wailed at the sky. "Why?"

"Because you left all your money in the glove compartment of a fairly nice car in a terrible neighborhood," I said. "I've got just fifteen hundred left."

He glared at me.

"You know," I said, "I may not know a lot about how the real world works, but I know enough never to leave a thousand dollars in a—"

Dekker strode toward the motel office. I followed him. He threw the door open and banged on the bell on the counter. "Hello?"

The old man came out of the back. "Can I help you?"

"Yeah, you can help me," Dekker said. "Somebody broke into my—our car last night and stole some cash. And then they keyed the door."

The manager pointed to a typewritten sign fastened to the wall with scotch tape: NOT RESPONSIBLE FOR VANDLE OR LOSS IN CAR.

Dekker didn't say anything for a moment before turning to me. "Was that there yesterday?"

"I didn't see it," I said. Regardless, this was Dekker's fault and no one else's.

He stormed back out the door to the Buick as he lit a cigarette, and I followed him.

"The no-refunds sign was there yesterday," I said. "I remember it, so—"

"Shut up! That's not helpful."

Why was he mad at me? I actually was trying to help.

He slumped. "I'll pay you back. Whatever expenses for the rest of this trip, I will reimburse you."

I shrugged. "I'm just sorry you had your money stolen. Let's forget it."

We drove back over to the nursing home with the chilly, dry wind blowing in through my window.

A different nurse was at the reception desk, and Dekker used a different set of names for us to sign in with. Today it was Richard and Elizabeth Burton.

I had all kinds of plans for our visit today. I'd watched hundreds of hours of interrogations on cop shows, so I felt like I knew the techniques pretty well. Obviously I wouldn't start yelling and throwing furniture if she didn't give the answers I wanted, but I thought I could get the job done.

We walked down the hall to Room 3B, and Dekker knocked on the open door. Mrs. Krantz was sitting in her chair, but Mrs. Davis's bed was empty, and I got a pang of fear.

"Mrs. Krantz?" Dekker said.

She turned her head and smiled when she saw us. "Back again, eh? Come on in! Did you bring me my treat?"

She was sharp, just like she'd said.

"We sure did," Dekker said, holding out the box to her.

She clasped her veiny old hands together and reached for the box. "Thank you, dears." She carefully opened it, pulled out one of the candies and ate it. "Would you like some?"

Dekker and I shook our heads.

"Where's Aunt Jeannie?" he said.

"As I predicted, she's much better today, so she's down in the TV room socializing."

"How are they?" Dekker asked, pointing at the open cherry box.

"Nothing tastes as good as it used to," Mrs. Krantz said. "But they're still pretty good." She looked at me. "Doesn't this one ever talk?"

"She's very shy," Dekker said.

Before the last few days, I'd never been required to talk to people other than to say "That'll be five dollars" to dump customers, and in fact had been discouraged from it. I obviously needed to say the kinds of things I'd seen on TV and heard Dekker say to people.

"Hi," I said. "How are you today?"

"My arthritis is acting up. I can always tell when a change in the weather's coming. My arthritis tells me."

"Sorry to hear that," Dekker said. "We're going to go down and say hello to Aunt Jeannie, and then we'll pop back in afterward. Do you need anything? Can I get anything for you?"

She held up one of the cherries and waved him away.

"Which way to the TV room?"

She pointed. We walked out in that direction. My heart fluttered as we walked down the hall. I heard a television up ahead and saw many old folks sitting in chairs around the large screen. I scanned the old faces and then I saw her. Today her hair was done and she was wearing makeup and a nice pink pantsuit. She stood and walked toward us, and I was afraid I would faint. It was like she was a different person altogether.

"There you are," she said. "I've been waiting. Let's get away from this loud TV so we can have a real conversation." She strode farther down the hall. Dekker and I shrugged at each other and followed her.

She stopped at a table and hugged us both. We all sat just as she reached out to touch my hair. I drew back. Impatiently, she made a beckoning gesture with her hand. So I leaned forward again, and she touched my hair.

"What did you do different?" she said.

"I—I don't know what you—"

"You know I don't like your hair hanging in your face, but I like the new color."

"Thank you," I said, a flash of unreality surrounding me, as if she actually knew I'd dyed my hair two days ago.

She looked around and then leaned forward and whispered, "We need to talk about Glenn."

"Of course we do," Dekker said.

"Who is—"

Dekker squeezed my leg under the table, and I knew he meant for me to shut up and go along.

"Your father's tried. He told Glenn if he doesn't propose soon, Michelle is going to leave him for good. But you know him. He's the expert. So I'd like you to talk to him. Sometimes he'll listen to you when he won't listen to anyone else." She turned to Dekker. "Or maybe you. Maybe he needs to hear it from a man his own age."

"Sure," Dekker said. "I'm happy to do it. I've always liked Michelle."

She sat back, satisfied, her arms crossed, and then she sat forward again, looking around and under the table.

"Does Annie have preschool today?" she said.

I looked at Dekker, wondering who she was talking about. Luckily, he was good at thinking on the fly.

"Yeah," he said. "We knew you wanted to talk about Glenn, so we wanted to be undistracted."

"All right," Jeannie said. "But next time, bring her. Yes?"

Dekker and I nodded.

She nodded too, like it was all settled.

"Yes," she said. "Good. Now . . . I wanted to tell you something but I can't remember what it was."

"About Glenn?" Dekker said.

She pressed her fingers to her lips, shaking her head.

"About . . . Annie?"

"No, but do you have any new pictures for me?"

Dekker patted his shirt pockets and held up his hands. "We gave you one last week."

"That's right," Jeannie said. Then she smiled at me. "Do you remember what you used to say when you wanted me to tell you stories about when I was a girl?"

Dekker squeezed my leg again.

"No," I said.

"Series one ladle."

I sneaked a glance at Dekker. I was irritated with myself for being so tongue-tied. Here I'd thought I would be such a smooth interrogator because I'd spent my life watching TV. This proved I didn't really know how to do anything, not even talk to my own grandmother.

She laughed, reached across the table and grasped my hand. I had to force myself not to pull away. "What you meant was 'stories when little.'"

Dekker and she laughed. "Say, Jeannie," Dekker said. "Why don't you tell the story again of when she was born?" He pointed at me.

"There was a blizzard when I went into labor. I was at home and Bart was out of town—he traveled for work of course in those days—so I had to get Mrs. Fletcher to drive me to Porter Hospital, and it took three hours with the roads the way they were. When we got there, I was ready to push."

She smiled at me. I stopped breathing.

"You were almost born out in the parking lot, Marianne."

Chapter 22

DEKKER

"And what did she look like?" I asked Jeannie.

"Full head of black, black hair," she said. "Came out squalling. She was mad she'd had to wait, I guess."

"When did Bart get there?"

"It wasn't until three days later he could get a flight in." She reached out and touched Petty's face, and to Petty's credit, she didn't pull away. "You had him wrapped around your little finger from the first moment he saw you."

"What about Glenn?" I said.

"He was a hard one, since he was my first," Jeannie said. "We didn't think he would ever come out. Two days I was in labor. They wanted to use forceps to pull him out, but I screamed. I wouldn't let them because of what the forceps did to Cousin Erin's face. I suppose that was all the incentive I needed to push him on out!"

I wondered who Cousin Erin was and where she was now. I wondered how many relatives were out there that Petty might never be able to find.

"Do you remember when Annie was born?" I said, taking a

stab that she meant Petty. Michael had changed his name; it only made sense that Petty wasn't her real name either.

Petty looked askance at me.

Jeannie shoved at me girlishly. "I do. Do you?"

I laughed. "Of course."

"One of the best days of my life. The most precious baby. Wouldn't make a sound, not a peep! Quiet as a church mouse, remember? Full head of black hair, just like you," she said to Petty. "They had to slap her feet so many times to get her to cry, remember, Michael?"

"I remember," I said. "She was beautiful, that's for sure."

Petty blushed.

I forced myself back into this interrogation disguised as conversation. "Do you still have the photos we gave you?"

Jeannie looked at me like I was crazy. "Of course I do."

"I'd love to see them again," I said. "Wouldn't you, Marianne?"

"Sure," Petty said. Her face was very white, and I hoped she could keep it together. I hoped I could.

"Where are they, Jeannie?" I asked her.

"They're in my room, of course."

"Shall we go down there and take a look?"

"That woman might be in there."

"Mrs. Krantz? That's all right. She's very nice."

Jeannie rolled her eyes. I rose and helped her to her feet. I threaded her arm through mine and looked back to make sure Petty was following us. The three of us walked down to Jeannie's room.

"Thank God she's not here," she said.

"Now, where are those pictures?" I said.

"What pictures?"

"Of Annie when she was a baby."

"Oh, that's right," she said. She opened a cabinet and pulled a photo album out.

Petty's eyes shone, her expression hungry.

Jeannie sat in her chair and held the album on her lap. Petty and I pulled up two chairs side by side. Jeannie handed the photo album to me, and on the cover was a photo of an infant with black hair and a thin, birdlike face. Below it, it said, *Anne Marie Rhones.*

I read it aloud. Petty had been named after her mother. I got chills, looking at it.

"Oh," Petty said, but it was more like a sigh. She smiled at me, a sad smile, and I felt my sinuses back up.

I opened the album, and it was a shock to see a picture of some-one who looked just like Petty, sitting on a hospital bed, holding a newborn baby, with a huge proud smile. And next to her, a young, beaming Michael Rhones. Which confused me. In the letters, he'd been furious that Marianne was pregnant with the other guy's baby, although he also said he'd raise the baby as his own if she'd just come back to him. It appeared that they'd reconciled. Maybe the birth had brought them close again. I'd heard of that sort of thing. Still, it seemed odd.

I turned the pages, looking at the photos of baby Petty lying on the floor with toys around her, Marianne reading colorful board books to her, baby Petty with bunny ears on her first Halloween, Petty smiling dimply and toothless. This was shocking too, be-cause I'd never seen her smile like that. Toddler Petty with water wings in a swimming pool, Michael Rhones pulling her around by her arms, Petty squinting against the bright sunlight.

So when had Marianne finally left Michael for Petty's real father?

"That's weird," Petty said. "Dad and I never went to the pool. I never did learn how to swim."

"What are you talking about?" Jeannie said, indignant. "You were on the swim team, for God's sake! And your father took you to the pool hundreds of times when you were little. You don't remember?"

"Oh, right," Petty said. "I meant that—it just seems so long ago, that's all."

"Do you have any other photo albums?" I asked Petty's grandma.

Jeannie got up and pulled a wedding album out of the same cabinet. She handed it to me.

I opened it up and there was the same photo of Michael and Marianne under the snow-covered gazebo that was in the album from the box in Dooley's office. Petty nodded at me, obviously recognizing it too. On the next page was another eight-by-ten of them standing on the altar of a church with a big cross behind them, Marianne looking up at Michael. She had on a large sweeping white dress with a long train, and she was absolutely beautiful, radiant.

"He looks so . . . normal," Petty murmured.

"Who does?" Jeannie asked.

Petty smiled at me and said, "Michael does."

We went through the album, Jeannie commenting on this or that detail. She pointed out Glenn, Marianne's brother, and I remembered Michael had lied to Petty about that too—he'd said neither he nor Marianne had siblings.

I wondered how deep the lies ran.

"Tell us your favorite memory of our wedding," I said. "What was the best part?"

"The expression on your face when you saw Marianne walking down the aisle on Bart's arm. I never saw a happier couple, and that's the truth. I was so mad when they wouldn't open up the terrace for the reception, remember? Just because it had rained."

Petty nodded, in a daze.

Then Jeannie's face darkened. "But why you had to go and invite that man to the wedding, Marianne . . . What were you thinking?"

My spidey sense tingled. "What man?"

"Don't pretend you don't remember," Jeannie said to Petty, as if she'd been the one who asked. "The ex-boyfriend."

"Right," I said, looking at Petty. "The ex-boyfriend. The one we both worked with, right?"

Jeannie glared at Petty. "I don't want to talk about it."

"Everything's okay," I said. "I can't seem to remember his name. Can you remember it?"

It was like performing delicate heart surgery. I took the photo album out of Petty's hands and set it in Jeannie's lap. I needed to proceed with caution.

"I'd like to look at his face to remind myself how smart Marianne was for choosing me over him. Are there any pictures of him at the wedding?"

Jeannie stared down at the album. "At the wedding?"

"Right. Remember? Marianne invited him. Are there any photos?"

"I—I don't know. Did he come to the wedding?"

"I thought that's what you said," I said, feeling as though my patient was slipping away, flatlining. "Maybe I was mistaken."

"Did I dream that, do you suppose?" Jeannie said. She looked down, frowning, and was silent for a while. Then she smiled at

Petty. "Your bridesmaids were all in navy blue. I wanted you to wear a veil, but you had to have everything your way. It was *your* day, you kept telling me. And I kept reminding you who was paying for *your* day. You wanted to wear red nail polish! So tacky. But I couldn't stop you from doing that, could I?"

Petty shook her head, her eyes glazed.

Jeannie turned again to me. "And I didn't like you at first, Michael. Remember?"

"How could I forget?" I said. "But you never did tell me why."

She glanced around and leaned in to whisper, "Of course it was all that mental illness in your family."

I looked at Petty then back at Jeannie. "Mental illness?"

"Don't play coy with me, young man! You know exactly what I'm talking about. The suicide. The insane asylum. All those things."

Whose suicide? What insane asylum? I wondered. That would explain a lot about Michael Rhones. I wanted to ask more about it, but I knew it would seem strange. I decided to go back to the ex-boyfriend again.

"Jeannie, can you help me remember that ex-boyfriend's name? The one Marianne invited to the wedding? We can't remember his name. Can you?"

Jeannie stared and then wrinkled her brow. "The ex-boyfriend? You mean Marianne's ex-boyfriend?"

"Yes. You said you didn't know if he had actually come to the wedding or not, and you know me, I can't remember what I had for breakfast this morning. So I wondered if you remembered his name."

Jeannie stared. "If he's the one I'm thinking of, it was an Eye-talian name."

Petty jerked beside me. Her mouth dropped open. "It wasn't . . . Bellandini, was it?" she said in an airless voice.

Where she'd pulled that out of, I could only guess.

"Yes! That's right!" Jeannie said. "I remember, because I told Bart it was a ridiculous name. A wop-greaser name." After the initial excitement at having remembered something important, Jeannie's face fell. She covered her mouth with her hands and stared.

"I'm sorry," Petty whispered.

"I don't want to talk about it," Jeannie said from behind her hands. "How could this happen to *our* family?"

"It's over," I said. "It's all right."

"How could this happen to our family?" Jeannie repeated in a whisper.

It appeared that Jeannie knew something horrible had happened but couldn't quite remember it. So the question remained: Where was Petty's mom? It wasn't like we could ask Jeannie, since she thought Petty was Marianne, and that Petty was a toddler, and that it was nineteen-ninety-something.

Tears filled Jeannie's milky eyes. "Where did it go?"

Where did what go?

"I'm sorry," Petty said again.

I reached for Jeannie's hand. "It's all right. It's all in the past."

"All in the past," Jeannie echoed. "I'm so tired."

"Why don't we leave now and let you get some rest." I stood, and Petty did too.

Jeannie sat staring for a moment more, then went and sat on her bed. She had nothing more to say.

"We'll see you soon, Jeannie," I said as she lay down, turning away from me and Petty.

"Goodbye," Petty said.

I led the way into the Colorado afternoon and immediately lit a cigarette. I thought about asking Petty if she wanted one to calm her nerves but knew she'd throw a rod. So I leaned back against the car and smoked while she paced in front of me, her fingers at her lips.

I waited until we were buckled in the car. "Where in the hell did you get the name Bellandini? How did you know? Did you remember from when you were a little kid, or what?"

"No," Petty said. "When I was in Mr. Dooley's office going through the box, there was a file folder marked 'Bellandini.' Now I wish I took it."

"Your dad—I mean, Michael Rhones—kept a file on him? Now, that's twisted."

"Yes."

"She thought you were your mom," I said, excited. "Yesterday, she wasn't saying 'Mama.' She was trying to say Marianne."

"I know."

"Bellandini has to be your dad's name."

"Right."

"What's the matter? Why aren't you as excited as I am?"

She didn't answer right away.

"I am," she said. "But there's all this other stuff going on inside me. Like—and this is going to sound crazy—I feel bad for my dad. For Michael Rhones. He loved my mom. You could see it in the pictures. You could feel it when you read the letters. And it drove him insane."

I stayed quiet, even though I wanted to dance around. We'd done it. We'd cracked the code. And it was largely thanks to my steering Jeannie in the direction we wanted her to go. No way could Petty alone have gotten the information we needed.

As soon as I thought this, I realized how selfish my excitement was. It wasn't about finding Petty's family, it was about my clever-ness. But this wasn't a puzzle, it was Petty's life. The seriousness of this situation hit me, that and how ill-equipped I was to handle it. Shame washed over me.

"Petty, this must be awful for you."

"What if this Bellandini guy is worse than Michael Rhones?" Petty said. "I don't know what I'll do. I really don't."

"But there's only one way to find out. We've come this far. Let's go back to the motel and we'll call information."

I started up the Buick and drove to Motel 9. When we were in our room, Petty paced up and down, wringing her hands.

There was a knock on the door, and she looked at me, alarmed.

I went to the door.

"Who is it?" I called.

"Management," came a voice, but it didn't sound like the old guy.

"What is it?"

"There's a problem with the water. Can you open up?"

I did.

A tattooed young man stood there.

"Hi," he said. "We have to turn the water off until tomorrow morning, so you won't be able to shower or flush until then. Okay?"

"Okay," I said. "Thanks."

The guy held up a hand and walked to the next room as I shut the door.

"No flushing," I said to Petty.

"That's weird," she said.

I picked up the phone and dialed information. The recording asked me for city, state, and name, to which I replied "Colorado. Bellandini. Can I get the address too?"

"One moment, please," the recording said.

Petty sat clutching a pillow and staring at me.

A live person came on the line. "Spell the name for me," the operator said.

I did and heard clacking computer keys. I held my breath.

"There's a Mitchell Bellandini in Paiute, Colorado, but no phone number," the operator said. "But his address is 33 Timbervale, Paiute, Colorado. May I help you with anything else, sir?"

I couldn't speak.

"Sir?"

"No other Bellandinis in Colorado?"

"No, sir."

"How do you spell the town name?"

She spelled it and asked again if there was anything else she could help with.

"No," I said. "Thank you very much."

I hung up the phone and wrote the name and address on a pad of paper before I forgot it.

"That's your dad's address," I said.

"My dad," she said, staring at the paper. Her eyes welled up and ran over.

"Hey," I said, reaching for her.

Petty pulled away and covered her face with her hands. "Don't," she said.

"I'll just get the map out of the car so we can figure out how to get to Paiute," I said, and went outside to give her some time alone.

I walked around for about ten minutes then knocked before reentering.

Petty was squatting by the fridge next to my folded pajamas, and suddenly I knew she'd found her mother's necklace. My stomach seemed to collapse in on itself.

She turned her head and I saw the look of betrayal on her face. She stood and held up the necklace.

"Where'd you find it?" I said, stalling for time, the map clutched in my sweaty fist. I had to think of a plausible explanation.

"Right here," Petty said, her voice crackling with anger. "In your pajamas."

"How did that get in there?" I said. "You must have bent over and it—"

"It didn't fall off my neck. It's clasped. You took it."

I could think of nothing to say.

"Why would you take the only thing of my mom's I own?"

"I wasn't going to keep it forever," I said.

"What does that mean?"

"I don't know."

She stared at me, as if trying to divine from my face the answers I couldn't verbalize. Then she put the necklace on.

"Keep your hands off my stuff." She went in the bathroom and closed the door.

I went and leaned my head against the door. "I'm sorry, Petty," I said.

She didn't answer.

"Listen," I said. I had to tell her the truth, or most of it, anyway. "I need to tell you something."

It was silent in the bathroom. I took a deep breath, closed my eyes and plunged in.

"I didn't leave college because I ran out of money," I said. "I was asked to leave because I got caught stealing stuff from the other guys in my hall at the dorm."

She opened the door, causing me to lose my balance and stumble toward her.

"What?" she said, her face red.

"That's right," I said.

"Why?"

"I don't know," I said. "I mostly blame it on the dead mom and the asshole dad. But the truth is, I was pissed at all these guys who had so much money, so much stuff—laptops and iPads and iPhones, expensive clothes and great cars—and I had shit. I figured they wouldn't miss little things, and if they did, they could run out and buy five more."

"So they kicked you out of college."

I nodded. "Yeah. And I also used to be in this band called Disregard the 9 and I stole stuff from my bandmates too." I explained about the upcoming band gig in Kansas City, which was why I'd been reluctant to bring her to Denver.

"Didn't you like your bandmates?" she asked.

"Well, yeah, but—well, I sometimes steal stuff when I'm stressed out. Like now." But I couldn't admit to her that this was not exactly what was going on here.

"That's messed up," Petty said.

"I know. I didn't mean to hurt you. I'm really sorry."

"You said you stole from the guys in your dorm because they had better stuff than you."

"I know, but—"

"I'm not one of those rich guys," Petty said. "I don't have *any-thing* but this necklace."

"I told you—I'm totally stressed out and—"

"When I'm stressed out, I run," Petty said. "You might want to try it. Of course, you'd have to quit smoking."

Maybe it was the crack about smoking. Maybe it was getting caught doing something stupid and careless and preventable. Whatever the cause, I snapped. "When have you *ever* been stressed out? What would you have to be stressed out about? Because you can't find an *Offender* episode on TV? Because somebody accidentally made eye contact with you at the dump? You don't know anything about stress! You've never lived in the real world, never had to deal with . . ."

I ran out of gas as Petty's expression became icy steel and she walked toward me. I backed up until I hit the wall.

She poked me in the chest. "I never knew my mother. I was kidnapped by her husband. I've been locked in my bedroom every night for my whole life. I almost died of the flu because my dad wouldn't take me to a doctor. I've been assaulted at the dump and had to fight for my life. I was attacked by Randy King. I'm on the run from the law. And now I'm having to drag a whiny *boy* along with me so I can find my real father. So don't tell me I don't know about stress, you sheltered, spoiled brat!"

She yelled the last part and slugged me hard in the arm. It hurt.

A voice shouted from inside the motel. "Shut the fuck up!"

"*You* shut up!" Petty shouted back.

I stood rubbing my arm, wishing I could redo the last thirty minutes, realizing that she was right. I was a sheltered, spoiled brat.

"Petty, I'm sorry. I won't take anything of yours ever again."

"If you do? I'm going to do more than slug you." She touched the knife beneath her shirt.

My nose twitched but I didn't say anything. The air in the room seemed chillier now. Her wall of suspicion had returned, and I'd built it for her. I'd blown it.

"Petty . . ." I said.

She ignored me, walked to the couch and lay down with her back to me.

PETTY

I'D THOUGHT DEKKER was my friend, but now I didn't know anymore. Although my dad—or the man I'd thought was my dad—had been silent and sullen the last years of his life, he'd been solid, dependable, always there.

I wanted to talk to Deirdre Walsh. I wanted her to be real and to be my true friend. But the picture of Deirdre in my mind morphed into Roxanne. Roxanne and her cherry-pink hair, her big, black-rimmed eyes. Roxanne, who didn't want anything from me. She was my friend. She'd said so, and I believed her. I held on to that picture of Roxanne in my head with all my strength, and I felt a little better.

I sat up on the couch. Dekker started, sitting there on the bed, like I was going to jump up and cut him.

"So we're going to Paiute first thing tomorrow, right?" I said.

"Yes," Dekker said. "Whenever you want."

"Do you mind if I turn on the TV?" I said.

"No," Dekker said. "Do you want me to go get you a snack or something? Are you hungry? Thirsty? Just say the word."

He was trying to make it up to me. It didn't exactly excuse what he'd done, but it seemed to me he really was sorry. Hearing about the rock show in Kansas City changed something inside me. That was the reason he hadn't wanted to bring me to Denver, not because he didn't like me. This revelation loosened the tension in my jaw and chest, giving way to relief, which made me want to forgive him. Eventually. For now I figured he could squirm a little so he'd know his behavior was unacceptable.

"Maybe we could go get some ice cream in a little bit," I said.

"Sure," he said in an eager voice. "I think I saw a Dairy Queen not too far from here."

I sat on the chair and faced the television. He flicked on the remote and handed it to me. I channel surfed, not really seeing the TV, thinking about my baby pictures and my real name. Anne Marie Rhones. Maybe when I found my real dad, I'd change my name back. Anne Marie Bellandini. It sounded exotic, like the name of someone who traveled a lot and wore big hats. I pictured my new name, my new family, my new home, my new life—maybe in Paiute, Colorado.

I woke with a start. I must have nodded off. The motion and sound on the TV remained the same, Dekker's position in the chair hadn't changed. But my OODA Loop activated. Something was different. I listened. Glanced quickly around.

Someone was outside the door.

I jumped off the bed, startling Dekker. "What the—"

I held my finger to my lips and grabbed onto my knife, listening for sounds beyond the room, sounds hidden by TV noise.

Fright stiffened Dekker's shoulders as he stared at me. An urgent knock at the door jangled his limbs.

"Gas leak," shouted a familiar voice. "We need everybody out in the parking lot immediately."

I shook my head at Dekker but he leapt to the door as if he couldn't see me.

"The water and now the gas," Dekker said. "A real palace I picked out for us, huh?"

In my mind I shouted *NO!* but he reached for the doorknob as I dropped to the floor and rolled under the bed. I heard the knob turn just as the door was kicked inward. The sounds of Dekker straining to close the door were drowned out by the voice on the other side.

"Open this door, you son of a bitch!" Someone repeatedly threw himself against the door. It slammed against the wall and there was scuffling.

I heard Dekker gargle, as if someone held his throat.

"Where is she, you little bastard?"

It was the voice of Randy King.

Chapter 23

DEKKER

I STARED INTO the furious face of Randy King, who slammed the door shut before throwing me onto the bed, knocking the wind out of me.

How did Randy find us? It wasn't possible.

"Where is she?" Both of Randy's fists were balled up and ready to rumble.

"Who?" I said. I hated how high my voice sounded. I tried and failed to pull it into a lower register. "It's just me here."

"Bullshit! The old man in the office said there was a tall boy and a skinny girl in here." Randy strode to the bathroom and threw the door open.

A plausible explanation popped into my head.

"All right, I had Ashley Heussner in here," I said. I sat up slowly so as not to attract another body throw. "But she took off with some meth dealer, I guess." I tried to put on a companionably masculine *Women, huh?* face, but it probably looked more like constipation.

"Bullshit. Where's Petty?"

"I don't know," I said.

"Don't you lie to me, boy."

"I put her on a bus to Detroit."

Randy sneered at me then walked over to the dresser and began opening and closing drawers. I knew it was just a matter of time before he bent over and looked under the bed. He pulled a pair of panties out of Petty's drawer. "These yours?"

"I told you. Ashley was here. She left all her stuff."

I hoped Petty couldn't get at her gun. I wasn't sure what she'd do, cornered like this so close to her goal.

Randy paced, pushing his cowboy hat back on his head. Finally he sat on the couch, and I willed him not to look down.

"Tell me where she is, and everything will be all right," Randy said, obviously switching gears to Good Cop. "Dooley can get the charges against you dismissed. He seriously can do it. Tell me where Petty is. I'm doing you a favor, because you don't know what you're dealing with here."

He was right about that. I couldn't speak, because I was afraid I was going to puke.

Randy's eyes narrowed. "Listen," he said. "It's like I told you the other day. Petty is very disturbed."

"Do you expect me to believe that?"

"I don't give a shit if you do. I'm telling you as a courtesy."

"Get out of my room," I said.

Randy walked to the edge of the bed and bent down, his face within an inch of mine. He drew a very large pistol out of his jacket pocket. "Or you'll what? Call the cops? Go ahead." He smiled.

I tried not to blink. I held Randy's stare until I couldn't anymore.

"That's what I thought," Randy said. He sat back on the couch and put his gun back in his pocket.

I was sure he'd only pulled it out to make me aware of its presence.

"We can help each other out here," Randy said. "And we can help Petty in the process. See, Dooley is working on drawing up commitment papers right now. She needs to be in a mental hospital, and I'm going to see that she gets there."

"Is that a joke?" I said. "You can't do that."

"Watch me. I got the law on my side. You got shit."

My voice shook. "I don't know why Petty's dad picked a douche like you to—"

"Douche? I'm a respected man in Niobe County. I'm an Elk and a Lion. I'm a great guy. Everybody knows it. And you're nothing, a thief and a liar. A grocery boy. You're a fugitive, and so is she."

I said nothing.

"Why do you think her dad kept her locked up all those years, huh? Did you ever stop to think about it?"

I couldn't help myself. "Because her dad was crazy."

"Because he was crazy?" Randy said, "Or is she?"

This was a twist. She was odd, no question. But crazy?

"She almost got put in the mental ward after she tried to kill Justin Pencey at the dump."

"She didn't try to kill him," I said. "She was defending herself. Justin and those kids ambushed her."

"Right," Randy said. "That's the official story, but nobody attacked her. Those kids went out there to dump something, and for no reason at all *she* attacked *them*. Put Justin in the hospital, if you'll recall. Dooley and Charlie concocted that story, and

Charlie had to pay those kids and their parents off to go along with it."

That couldn't be true . . . could it? I knew what kind of an asshole Justin Pencey was. He'd brag about having sex with girls after they passed out from drinking too much. He tormented smaller boys in the school locker room. I'd always figured he'd deserved the ass-kicking that he'd received from Petty, that he'd provoked her or even snuck up on her in her little dump guard shack. But she was a volatile person with some weird ideas. Who knew what was really true?

"You're so full of shit," I said, but my confidence was wavering. Maybe Randy knew Petty was in the room, and he was saying all these things to provoke her. I hoped she wouldn't rise to the bait—if that's what it was.

"Listen. I'm going to make this easy for you. You bring Petty to me, I'll give you a share of the insurance policy. I'll give you one hundred thousand dollars."

I inhaled sharply. For a split second I let myself imagine what it might be like to have that kind of money. To go back to college. To blend in with the rich kids. I shook my head, as if to dislodge the idea from it. I couldn't possibly even entertain the idea of betraying Petty like that. Except I already had.

And maybe it was truly the best thing for her . . .

"If she's so dangerous, how come her dad let her work at the dump? With a shotgun in her booth?"

"It wasn't loaded, numb-nuts. Charlie let her think it was. As long as she wasn't around people that much, she was okay. He kept her locked up so she wouldn't hurt anyone else. And look what it got him."

"What's that supposed to mean?"

"I saw the coroner's report. Her dad didn't die of a heart attack. *Someone* held a pillow over his face. He was smothered to death."

PETTY

"Bullshit," Dekker said, sounding even more uncertain.

"Dooley's planning for her to plead not guilty by reason of insanity. I'm guessing you know about the sealed envelope that Petty stole from Dooley's office. There's a report in there from a psychiatrist that says she's a paranoid schizophrenic."

That's what I had feared was in that envelope. After that day at the dump, a lady had come to the house and we'd sat out front while she asked me all kinds of questions. Things like did I hear voices, and did I think that everyone was out to get me. She'd written my answers on a clipboard and then went away. I'd never heard any more about it.

But Randy's words: Delusional. Paranoid. Suspicious. Odd.

That was me.

"He's appointing me as her guardian," Randy continued. "She'll spend some time in the nuthouse, but we'll get her the medication she needs, and then she'll come home with me."

I'd dreamed of killing Dad thousands of times. Of waiting until he fell asleep and taking a pillow and slowly lowering it over his face. Of getting comfortable with holding it down, with waiting until he started to fight. Of not being surprised when he didn't.

Of imagining my life outside of his house.

Did I really only imagine it? Or had I killed the man I'd thought was my father? The man who trained me to kill?

How had I let myself believe in the last few days that I deserved to be around normal people?

Maybe Michael Rhones and Randy King knew what was best for me. Maybe I didn't.

Because I didn't know whether I had done the things he said I'd done, whether I was what he said I was. I felt like I was falling, tumbling through space, with nothing and no one to catch me. I'd seen shows about people who couldn't tell the difference between what happened on television and what happened in the real world. And now this thought spiraled in on itself. Had I watched so many crime shows that I could no longer distinguish between what I'd seen on TV and what I'd done?

Not knowing made me desperate to get up to Paiute, to meet my biological father and discover the truth about myself and my past. To find out if my mother was up there with him. If I could just look them in the eye, somehow I would know the truth about everything.

"I'm getting tired of all this talking," Randy said. "I've been driving all day. Now you're going to tell me where she is."

There was silence, and I pictured Dekker mouthing the words, *She's under there*, and pointing at the bed. But instead he said, "I'm not going to tell you."

Above me the box springs sagged as Randy added his weight to Dekker's. I heard struggling, grunting, fists making contact with flesh.

I had to get out of there, get up to Paiute now. I unholstered Baby Glock as I rolled out from under the bed, and saw Randy's hands fastened around my friend's neck, Dekker's eyes bulging and limbs flailing ineffectually like a beetle on its back. His helplessness enraged me. I pulled back the slide on my gun and pushed the barrel against Randy's temple. Somehow his Stetson remained on his sweaty head.

"Get off him," I said. "I'm crazy. I will shoot you." I hated the fact I was using the exact same words I'd said to Dekker a few days ago. But the slack surprise on Randy's face as he loosened his grip on Dekker's neck gave me a thrill. Dekker pushed him off and straightened, panting and gagging.

"I know you've got your hand cannon," I said. "Put it on the nightstand."

Randy glared at me and pulled the .357 Magnum out of his pocket. He laid it on the nightstand. I picked it up and ejected the clip, which I pocketed.

Dekker's nose and mouth were bleeding and he had a knot on his forehead. The skin on his neck was bright pink.

"Get up," I said to him.

Dekker rolled off the bed, wiping blood from his face, and Randy tried to stand.

"Not you, Randy. You stay where you are."

He did.

"You all right, Dekker?"

Dekker nodded, his hands bloody, his face smeary and swollen.

"Petty," Randy said.

"Take this," I said to Dekker, holding out the Magnum butt first. "Then get our things together. We're leaving."

He took the gun, shoved it awkwardly into the waistband of his jeans, and started packing up.

"Petty, I'm talking to you," Randy said.

I so wished I could take another shower after lying in the underbed filth, but it would have to wait. Dekker threw clothes and toiletries into the plastic Walmart shopping bags.

"Don't forget the stuff in the bathroom," I said.

"Petty!" Randy shouted. "I promised your dad I'd take care of you. I'm not going to stop coming after you. I won't stop until I bring you home."

I got in his face. "Randy, you didn't promise my dad anything. Because Charlie Moshen wasn't my real dad. In fact, his name wasn't Charlie Moshen. It was Michael Rhones. And you can go to hell along with him."

"Well, whatever his name was, you knew him and what he was willing to do to keep you safe."

What did that mean?

"He made it so he could find you if you were ever kidnapped. Trust me. I will find you *wherever* you go." The smile on his face was insane—triumphant and gleeful.

"What are you talking about?"

"That bump on your left shoulder. He told you that was scar tissue from a fall, right?"

My scalp began tingling, the blood in my veins rushing and expanding. How did Randy know about the itchy little bump on my left shoulder? I felt it with my right hand. It now seemed to throb under my touch.

Randy held up his iPhone. On the screen was a pulsing yellow dot on a map. "Your dad implanted a microchip under your skin. Got it from the vet. Works like a charm. So you can run, Petty, but I'll find you."

DEKKER

I COULD NOT believe what I was hearing. Surely Randy was bluffing. The microchips for pets that I'd heard about were just for identification, they didn't have GPS capabilities—that was science fiction stuff.

Petty stripped off her hoodie and stared at her own shoulder, her mouth open, horrified, as if it were covered in boils or slugs.

"You're full of shit," I said to Randy, and my voice was shaky and hoarse. "The technology doesn't exist."

"Fine," he said. "How did I find you, then?"

A flash of light and movement in my peripheral vision drew my attention. Petty held a small knife on a clip in her hand, the same one she'd threatened Ray the truck driver with.

"You cut me and you're going to the nuthouse or jail," Randy said. "Your choice."

But Petty clearly had other ideas. She slashed the blade across her shoulder. The knife was sharp enough that it easily sank into the flesh.

"No!" I yelled, reaching for her, but it was too late.

Sweat ran down her face as she gouged into the skin of her shoulder with her fingers, which were now coated with her own blood.

The hole in her shoulder widened, skin and muscle tearing as she dug. I watched her teeth sink into her bottom lip until blood appeared as she grunted and gasped through her nose. I stopped breathing, watching this, unable to help, afraid I might throw up.

With a final push, Petty pinched her fingers into her shoulder and withdrew a capsule, not much larger than a grain of rice, from the ragged fissure she'd made. With her shaking, gore-slicked hand, she held it out to me. But I couldn't move, I was so horrified by what she'd just done to herself.

"Flush this," she said in a quivering, ghostly voice.

When I didn't take it from her, she seized my hand with hers and pressed the bloody microchip into my palm. I stifled my gag reflex and did as I was told, and even had the presence of mind to bring out a towel with me. Petty clutched it to her shoulder while I tied it clumsily in place. She pulled her hoodie on over it.

Randy sat staring in horror, gasping as if he'd been underwater for a long time. He wiped his face with his sleeve and gaped at Petty.

PETTY

RANDY FOUND HIS voice at last. "See? She's crazy."

I felt light-headed and nauseated, but we had to get out of there and make sure Randy didn't follow us.

"It doesn't matter what you think," I said to him. "You're not going to remember any of this anyway."

I wound up—using all the power in my hips for force—and punched through his temple with my right fist, knocking the hat from his head and the consciousness from his mind. He dropped over on his side.

Dekker stood staring, his mouth fallen open. "You killed him," he said.

"He'll be fine. Let's go."

I withdrew the .357 from Dekker's jeans and laid it on the pillow next to Randy's head.

"Don't we want to take that?" Dekker said.

"I'm not stealing the guy's gun," I said. "That wouldn't be right."

"Have you lost your mind?"

"I'm starting to think I never had it in the first place," I said.

THE SUN WAS setting as we drove west. Along the sides of the highway, massive red rocks were strewn about like a giant's carelessly discarded Legos.

"Petty," Dekker said, his eyes on the road.

"Yes?" I was busy applying pressure to my shoulder, which felt hot and sore, and really itched now that it had mostly stopped bleeding.

"I'm only going to ask this one time," he said, his voice chapped, whether from recent trauma or fear, I didn't know. "Did you kill Charlie Moshen? Michael Rhones? Your mom's husband?"

The shadowy boulders started to look like giant, angry faces in the dark.

"What difference does it make?" I said.

"Did you?"

I didn't answer. We were silent for a long while, driving up and up into the mountains.

"I'm wondering," I said, "if you're thinking hard about that hundred thousand dollars."

More silence.

"I remember that day," Dekker said.

At first I thought he meant the day my dad died. But then he went on.

"I remember the day it happened. It was around Halloween, I remember, because the sky was dark and there were construction-paper pumpkins and Kleenex ghosts in the school halls. I remember Justin's face when he came back to school."

"Let me explain," I said. I couldn't bear to think of that horrible day, to remember my terror, what it had felt like to be attacked and forced to maim another human being.

It was as if he hadn't heard me. "I remember every Halloween from then on we all talked about you, about how you were cursed and lived in a haunted house. Everyone had a Petty Moshen story. You were an urban legend. You were the boogeyman. We all talked about how you tried to break into our houses at night to kill us."

I'd never had any sense of myself outside of my house and the dump. I'd never realized the town knew what I was—a mentally ill freak.

"I was feeling like we'd kind of gotten to know each other over past couple of days, but I've been sitting here thinking back over our conversations, and I realize it was always me talking. I don't know what you think about anything, I don't know who you are at all, so I don't know what to believe about what Randy said."

"I guess I'm not sure either."

Dekker groaned, clearly frustrated. He didn't say anything for a moment. "That doesn't make me feel better."

"What do you want me to say?"

"I want you to answer my question."

I turned back to the window. "It doesn't matter."

We drove in silence, endless headlights cutting bright streamers into the dark. I grieved for the trust that had been shattered on both sides. My heart felt like it was shredding itself because something had been lost. Randy King had taken it. I wanted to talk to my friend about how scared I was about meeting my real dad, but I didn't think he could hear me anymore.

Between two mountains, we came over a rise into a flat valley cut in half by a glittering river.

I had cotton mouth, and I wished I'd thought to bring some of our bottled water. I wished Randy had showed up earlier in the day so we wouldn't be sneaking up on Mitchell Bellandini after dark like this. I rubbed my sweating palms on my jeans. What if he wasn't interested in meeting me? What if he was like my other dad?

Dekker missed the turnoff and we had to double back. Then we took a steep dirt road to the top of a hill that overlooked the valley. We almost didn't see the little cabin all by its lonesome back there in the midst of the pine forest. There was a light on inside though.

I was afraid I was going to be sick. Plus we were now at a higher elevation, which had me gasping for air again.

Dekker pulled the car over to the side of the dirt road, which was twenty feet below the cabin. "Are you ready?"

"I guess," I said.

We found a place to climb up, and as soon as our heads cleared the embankment, brilliant light flooded the yard and a big black dog came tearing out of the darkness, followed quickly by the black silhouette of a man with a rifle.

"Who the hell's in my yard at nine o'clock at night? Show yourself or I'll blow your head off."

Chapter 24

DEKKER

OH, YEAH, I thought. That's definitely her dad.

Petty and I held our hands in the air, trying to simultaneously shield our eyes from the blinding lights. I froze so the dog wouldn't attack us, but Petty kept making some sort of signal with her right hand.

"Stop it," I hissed. "What are you doing?"

"It's the hand signal for sit," Petty said. "But this dog hasn't been trained at all."

It was all over the place, snapping at us with a menacing bark.

"Dekker," Petty said. "Don't make eye contact with the dog, and don't smile. Okay?"

"No problem," I said.

"Who's out there?" the man on the porch yelled.

I wasn't sure what to say. *This girl is the product of your affair with her mother twenty-two years ago?*

"Could you put the gun down?" I said.

"Not until you tell me who you are and what you're doing here in the middle of the night."

"Mr. Bellandini?" I said.

"Who the hell wants to know?"

"Did you know Marianne Rhones?"

Silence.

"You get the hell out of here, you damn kids! Out! I'm giving you until the count of three!"

"Mr. Bellandini, let me explain," I said, one hand still in the air and the other blocking the light. "This girl here is Marianne's daughter."

A pause. "What did you say?"

"This is Anne Marie Rhones."

The rifle clattered to the wooden porch.

"Your daughter."

Mr. Bellandini rocked on his feet, then his knees buckled and he sank to the porch beside the gun. "*My* . . . what? How . . . I don't understand what—"

"Michael Rhones took Anne Marie and moved to Kansas and changed both their names. He raised her as his own and never told her about you. We don't want anything from you. She just wanted to meet you. Michael passed away a couple of days ago, and we found all this out by reading his letters to Marianne."

"His . . . ?"

"Right," I said. "Michael sent her a ton of love letters. Like a hundred and fifty of them."

"Is she here?" Petty said.

"Marianne?" The shadowed form on the porch covered its face with its hands. The dog ran to his side and sniffed him.

"Yes," Petty said.

I felt a little choked up, in spite of all the shit that had gone down between me and Petty in the last two days.

"Can she—can you uncover your face?"

Petty dropped her hands to her sides and squinted at the dark figure.

"Oh, my God," he said, his voice full of wonder. "You could be Marianne."

"Is she here?" Petty's voice was vehement.

The noises coming from the porch sounded like Mr. Bellandini was trying not to cry and failing.

Petty took a step backward, and I wondered if she was going to bolt.

"Where is my mom?" she asked.

"I've searched for years," he said. "I never stopped." He wiped his face and hoisted himself up.

"For my mom?" Petty said.

His hands dropped to his sides. "What?" he said.

Nothing anyone was saying made any sense at all at this point. I could not imagine how the stress of this situation must feel to these two people.

Petty's breath hitched and she started to fall. I caught her before she hit the ground.

"Please," Mr. Bellandini said. "Bring her inside."

I led Petty up to the porch and Mr. Bellandini held the door open for us. He was even taller than me—around six-foot-five maybe. I was still a little blinded from the klieg lights outside, so it took a minute to adjust. The cabin was rustic, a little dingy, but better by far than Motel 9.

"I'm sorry," Mr. Bellandini said. "I think I'm in shock." He pointed in Petty's direction. "Her too. Let me get her a glass of water."

I helped Petty sit on a green couch. She had a dazed, faraway look in her eyes, and my heart broke for her. She seemed smaller now, deflated.

Mr. Bellandini returned from the kitchen with a glass of water, which he held out to Petty. His hands were huge, the backs of them covered in black hair.

Petty didn't move, just stared, so I took the water for her.

"Poor thing," Mr. Bellandini said. He had thick lips that covered small teeth. His black hair was wavy, and he wore gold-rimmed glasses with chunky lenses that miniaturized his eyes, making them look almost artificial. The contrast between the tiny eyes and teeth, and the giant proportions of the rest of him, was striking. There was absolutely no resemblance between father and daughter that I could see.

He let out a big breath and sat down in a chair. "I always knew we'd be reunited one day," he said. "I knew that nothing could keep us apart." He stared at his hands. "How did you find me?"

"It's kind of a long, convoluted story," I said, "but the upshot is we found Petty's grandmother in a nursing home in Denver."

He sat forward again, the expression on his face sharp, as if I'd said something insulting.

"You know she has Alzheimer's," I said.

"Oh, of course," Mr. Bellandini said, casting his eyes downward again. "Jeannie."

Hearing him say that name had the same effect on me as biting on tinfoil with a metal filling. A painful shock jolted through me, because it was all true. This was Petty's father.

Shit just got real.

Mr. Bellandini did not look at Petty, but I could tell he wanted to. Maybe he believed she was a mirage he could only see out of the corner of his eye. It must have seemed like a dream to him.

"So . . . Jeannie couldn't have told you where I was, am I correct? With her condition, she didn't remember me. Did she?" Mr. Bellandini snuck a glance at Petty then looked back at his hands.

"She remembered your last name, that's all," I said. "She only remembers that something sad happened, not that—well, that Petty is your daughter, and not Michael Rhones's."

Mr. Bellandini let out another big gust of breath. "Well. Yes. It's probably better for Jeannie that she doesn't remember." His eyes only briefly met mine, and then they flitted up.

I felt Petty's body shake violently beside me. I turned to her and saw that her face and eyes were a deep shade of red, as if she'd been holding her breath this entire time.

Mr. Bellandini noticed too.

"Is she all right?" He rose from his chair.

Petty shrank back. He was so large and overwhelming, I understood this involuntary reaction.

The big man now stared openly at his stolen daughter. "Where have you been all these years?"

She opened her mouth, but nothing came out. Petty of course needed time to adapt to these new circumstances before she'd be able to talk or even process what was going on. It would be like the slow rise from the ocean floor to avoid getting the bends.

"Kansas, sir," I said.

"Call me Mitch," he said, sitting back down. "And who are you?"

I introduced myself.

"And you're her . . ."

I didn't know this man, and it was obviously an emotional moment, but he sounded wary.

Embarrassment heated my face. "Her friend, sir. I'm just her friend."

Mitch shifted his gaze to Petty and said, "Is that true?"

She nodded.

"And how old are you now?"

She cleared her throat. "Twenty-one."

"That seems right. She was about three the last time I saw her." Before Michael Rhones whisked her away.

Mitch was still staring at her, looking her up and down. "You're taller than she was."

Petty squirmed under the scrutiny.

"But of course you are," he said, with a big smile. "I'm your dad! You're just a chip off the old block." He chuckled, although it sounded a little forced. He must not have any other kids, because the words *I'm your dad* seemed unnatural coming from him.

"Well," I said. "We're sorry for coming here so late, but circumstances kind of forced us to. Would it be all right if we came back tomorrow and spent some more time with you?"

"You have a place to stay?" Mitch said. "You know people up here?"

"No sir," I said.

Mitch decisively rapped both arms of the chair. "You'll sleep here. Dekker, you take the guest room, and you can have my bed, Marianne. Anne Marie, I mean."

"My name is Petty," she said, in a tiny voice, startling me.

"I beg your pardon?" Mr. Bellandini said.

"I'd never even heard that other name until today," she said, her voice stronger. "My name is Petty."

Mitch snorted. "Petty. That's not a name. It's an adjective."

I was shocked by this pronouncement, and his casual denigration of Petty's name irked me.

Petty bristled. "It's my *name*," she said, sounding like herself again.

"Oh, well," Mitch said. "My apologies. In any event, you'll stay here."

He wasn't wasting any time taking control and telling everyone what to do. The thought of spending the night in that cabin helped me understand how Petty must have felt when faced with the prospect of sleeping at Ashley's place. Disoriented. Uneasy.

"We don't want to impose," I said. "I'm sure there's a motel nearby."

"Oh, no you don't," Mitch said. "No daughter of mine is going to a motel with a boy!"

He gave a laugh, but I knew he was deadly serious. It would be a bad idea to tell him that we'd stayed in a motel together already.

"I work the night shift, so you can sleep while I'm gone. I'm a security guard at the old Black Star mine." He glanced at his watch. "Let's go move your car up to the house and get your luggage." To Petty, he said, "The bathroom's just down the hall if you want to freshen up."

Petty shook her head. "I'm fine," she said, wrapping her arms around herself.

I rose and followed Mitch out the door. The dog came running, but I realized this one wasn't like Sarx and Tesla. He didn't know how to attack; he was just an outside animal, aggressive and out of control. So I ignored him and sniffed the air—which was filled with the scents of pine and wood smoke—and gazed at the dark sky overhead. I'd never seen such brilliant stars. Once we hit the yard, they were drowned out by the blinding motion-sensor lights.

I walked down the embankment to where we'd left the Buick on the access road, got in it and drove up to the front of the house where Mitch waited. I got out and opened the trunk to get our stuff from it, and handed a few of the Walmart bags to Mitch.

"Mr. Bellandini—Mitch—why did you come out of your house with a gun?"

Mitch paused for a minute in the alpine chill, the bright light behind him obscuring his features. "We've had a lot of vandalism and theft up here in the past year or so," he said. "Had to buy a gun and a mean dog. People out creeping around in the middle of the night make you jumpy." He set the bags on the ground. "So tell me. Are you a student? A working man?"

"I've been saving money to go back to school," I said.

"Ah," he said. "What's your major?"

"Geology."

"Geology! How would you like to tour the Black Star mine tomorrow?"

"That would be epic," I said, and I meant it.

"So you're saving money to go back," he said. "What do you do?"

This was Petty's dad I was talking to, so I didn't want to answer "delivery boy." I wanted to sound more impressive.

"Well, actually," I said, "I'm the drummer for a band and we're playing at a big show in Kansas City in about a week."

"Really? So you'll need to leave soon?"

"Yes, sir."

He tilted his head toward the sky before turning back toward me.

"Tell me something. Anne Marie seems a little . . ." He made circles in the air with his hands, seeming unable to reach for the right words.

"Yeah," I said. "She is."

I told Mitch a little about Petty's life in Kansas under lock and key. He frowned and nodded as I talked, as if this confirmed everything he knew about Michael Rhones.

"He could never love Marianne the way I did," Mitch said. "He thought he owned her."

"He was looney tunes," I said. "His letters were totally obsessive and crazy."

Mitch seemed to get taller, but I couldn't see his face with the light behind him. "Well, I'm sure they sound strange to an unintended audience. Imagine how personal love letters *you've* written would sound to Michael. Or to *me*."

I couldn't decide if I was suddenly flooded with shame because I'd read letters that weren't addressed to me or because maybe Mitch sensed how I felt about Petty. Was it that obvious? The whole father-daughter-potential-suitor dynamic hadn't occurred to me. I felt chastised, which pissed me off and intimidated me at the same time.

"I need to hear more," he finally said, looking at his watch, "but it'll have to wait. Can't be late for work." He picked the bags back up and walked toward the house.

I followed him up to the porch and into the cabin. Petty sat staring on the couch exactly where we'd left her, and I hoped she hadn't heard our conversation. I tailed Mitch down the hall to the bedrooms. Mitch switched on the light in what appeared to be the guest room and set down my bag, then led me to his own bedroom. I set down Petty's bag and left Mitch alone to get ready for work, joining mute Petty in the living room.

I walked to the fireplace mantel, on which some "Precious Moments" figurines were arranged, big-eyed sad kids doing cheesily adorable things. This was more than a little weird. What bachelor collected Precious Moments? Creepy. Of course, maybe they'd been Marianne's.

Mitch reappeared wearing a blue wool jacket and a matching cap. He had a utility belt on with a flashlight, a huge brass key ring, and a small-caliber pistol.

"I'll be back around six-thirty A.M.," he said, glancing again at his watch. "You kids get some sleep." He kept his eyes on Petty, but his hands looked like they didn't know what to do with themselves. Finally he shoved them in his pockets and turned to the door. "Guess I'll be going. Good night."

Mitch closed the door behind him, and Petty sat staring, an unfocused look in her eyes. I hoped her shell shock would wear off by tomorrow so she could find out what she needed to know and we could leave.

"You okay?" I said to her.

She shrugged. "Would you help me find a real bandage for my shoulder?"

We walked down the hall. Bathroom on the right, guest room on the left, master past the bathroom. I went in the bathroom, turned on the light then opened the linen closet, where I found a first-aid kit with some large Band-Aids, cotton, and disinfectant spray.

Petty pulled off her hoodie and the towel came off with it, starting the wound bleeding all over again.

"Great," she said. "I'll just bleed all over my dad's bathroom."

I squirted disinfectant on the cotton, swabbed the ragged cut and placed the big Band-Aid over it.

"Would you mind sleeping in Mitch's room?" she said. "It feels a little weird to me."

I was relieved she felt the same way I did.

"Absolutely," I said.

While she used the bathroom to get ready for bed, I stowed the bloody towel in my Walmart bag, switched my stuff to Mitch's room and hers to the guest room. Then I snooped around a little. The guest room was dusty but looked like it had never been used—the bedspread pristine, still with the creases from the package it had come in.

I checked out the rest of the house, and when I returned to the living room, a thought hit me. There were no pictures on the walls. No landscapes or paintings, or portraits or plaques. I walked around once more to be sure, but all the walls were perfectly bare.

This struck me as odd, but I realized something else bothered me more. Mitch had never answered Petty when she'd asked where her mother was.

Chapter 25

Friday

PETTY

I DIDN'T KNOW where I was. I tried to position things in my mind so that I was in my room in Kansas, but it was all wrong. Was I in Motel 9? And then I remembered. I was in my father's house in the Colorado mountains, six hundred miles from my prison.

In the house my mother had lived in.

As I lay staring at the ceiling, I remembered that Mitch hadn't answered my questions about Mom. It must mean she was dead or had left him. It had been foolish to get my hopes up. Now I had to bundle all my hopes and pin them on Mitch. Maybe he had some other children—some siblings for me, maybe some other grandparents. Maybe I'd still get to have some sort of family. I had to focus on that.

But for a little while I let myself imagine my mom cooking breakfast in the cabin's little kitchen. I imagined her waking me up for school. I imagined us watching *Offender NYC* together and eating popcorn. This lovely daydream was interrupted by the fact that, try as I might, I couldn't picture her with Mitch. I immediately felt guilty at this thought, because I'd only recently been able to picture her at all. Mom must have loved him, and I was the result.

I sat up and looked out the window. Sunrise was a ways off, but I could make out mountains and trees. I smelled wood and pine in the sweet, clean air. It was chilly in the room, but I liked it. Not like Kansas, where your sheets and towels never feel quite dry. Maybe I wouldn't go back to Kansas at all. Maybe I'd stay here with Mitch for a while. I could cook and clean for him like I did for Michael Rhones. I could make a home for us.

But that was a crazy thought. I'd only just met him.

Maybe he could get me a job at the mine, or maybe there was a shop down in Paiute where I could work, waiting on tourists. Maybe I'd make friends with some of the local girls. Maybe I'd go to movies and shop in the supermarket.

Did I really think Mitch would just invite me to move in with him? Did he believe I was his blood? Maybe we should get a DNA test to confirm our relationship so he wouldn't think I wanted anything from him. I needed to find out about my mom, but did I want more than that? What exactly did I want from Mitch?

I knew what I needed—more time. But Dekker needed to go back, and the pressure to find out everything I could as quickly as possible was giving me vapor lock.

Plus how would Mitch react to all the drama surrounding me? The theft and murder warrants? The commitment papers Mr. Dooley had so thoughtfully drawn up? If Mitch knew everything . . . anybody in his right mind wouldn't want me to stay. He'd be afraid I'd kill him too.

I walked to the bathroom, closed the door and checked the shower and the closet before using the toilet. A clock sat on the vanity, saying five-fifty. Mitch would be getting off work in ten minutes, and then he'd be home. Realizing this, I had an over-whelming urge to wake Dekker up and talk to him.

I went into the hall and turned the master bedroom doorknob slowly before pushing the door open. Dekker was sprawled on the bed, and I looked at him for a while—his unruly dyed black hair, his big Adam's apple, his long fingers. I remembered the dream I'd had at the motel, about Dekker and me kissing. Maybe it was just hormones, but I couldn't help feeling attracted to him at this moment. It was gratitude too. He'd put up with a lot of crap from me this past week. He'd let me into his world but never made me feel like a freak. Well, hardly ever.

His eyes opened, focused exactly on me. I started.

"How long you been standing there?"

"Awhile," I said.

He sat up and scratched his head. "Petty, you know you're not supposed to talk to me right when I wake up." Dekker swiveled toward me and put his socked feet on the floor. "Holy shit, it's cold," he said. "You suppose it ever gets warm up here?"

I shrugged.

He sat blinking. "What time is it?"

"It's almost six."

"Mitch will be coming home soon."

"Yes." I wanted to talk to Dekker about all the things I was feel-ing, but I didn't have the words.

"It's kind of hard to believe we actually did what we said we were going to do," he said. "Other than you kidnapping me at gunpoint, and me finding out you actually killed Michael

Rhones and everything, this has been a pretty amazing road trip."

I didn't say anything, stung by Dekker's words, remembering how he'd characterized me the day before—the boogeyman. I couldn't help grimacing.

"That was a joke, Petty," Dekker said. "You need to start getting used to that sort of thing. I don't really believe you killed your dad. Or, the guy you thought was your dad. The guy who raised you."

Even though I now knew Michael Rhones—Charlie Moshen—was not my father, I felt a pang in my stomach. He was the only dad I'd ever known. He was the one who'd trained me to disarm the old man with a shotgun in Salina. He was the one who'd taught me how to knock someone out with a punch to the temple. He was the one, as Dekker said, who'd raised me. That counted for something, no matter how crazy he was, no matter how strange.

"Dekker," I said. "I want you to know how much I appreciate everything you've done for me. How grateful I am that you're my friend."

His eyebrows rose in surprise. This was the first time I'd said anything so personal, and it felt as strange to me as it looked like it felt to him. But being around his family, even for such a short time, had shown me how friends act toward one another.

"Even though I had to kidnap you to make you my friend," I added.

He laughed. "There you go," he said. He reached for his jeans and pulled them on. "You might get the hang of this joke thing yet."

Of course, I hadn't been joking. Not at all.

"I'm starving," he said. "Let's go see what's in the fridge."

After we ate cereal, we washed our dishes by hand since there was no dishwasher. While Dekker showered, I looked around to see if there were any magazines or books, but I found none. I wished for the one I'd left behind with my suitcase and guns.

A weathered red Ford Taurus drove up and parked in front of the house, and the dog barked. I didn't see how you could keep a dog outside with how cold it got up here, but he obviously wasn't allowed in the cabin. Through the window, I saw Mitch get out of the car and walk to the house with the dog close behind. My palms got sweaty again, waiting for Mitch to unlock the door, and I couldn't figure out why. Was I afraid he was going to reject me? Ask me to leave? That this trip had all been for nothing? Or was it just because I didn't know him at all?

He came in, closed the door behind him. "Good morning," he said.

I gripped the arms of the rocking chair, my heart pounding. I wished Dekker would come out of the bathroom already.

"Where is your friend?"

"He's taking a shower," I said.

"Good," he said, sitting on the couch. "I wanted to talk to you alone."

My hands got clammier and I rocked a little faster.

"I certainly appreciate his bringing you to me." Mitch didn't look directly at me. He jabbed up his glasses. "I'd like to repay him. He told me about the show coming up."

For a second I didn't know what he was talking about but then I remembered Dekker's drumming job in Kansas City.

"I'd like to see that he makes it back in time to rehearse, but I'd also like us to have more time together." Mitch reached out and took hold of my chair arm, halting the rocking motion. I had to force myself not to brace my feet and push against his restraining grip.

"Okay," I said, moving my hand that was nearest to his to my lap.

He fixed me with an intent gaze. "But I think he's hesitant to leave you here. He's willing to miss the show just to make sure you're safe—and I appreciate that about him—but I think if you tell him he can go ahead and leave, he'll understand that you're okay staying here by yourself." With every emphasized word he jerked the chair a tiny bit closer. "What do you think?"

I didn't think I was ready for that. But when would I be?

"How will I get back there?" I said. Even though earlier I'd been thinking about living here with Mitch, the reality of it made me nervous. I reached up to scratch the bump on my shoulder and dug into the injury by accident, forgetting the bump had been replaced by a laceration. It hurt.

"I'll just put you on a plane when you're ready," he said with a smile, his tiny eyes crinkling at the corners. "But I don't want to lose you again."

"I don't know," I said.

"Well, you need to put others before yourself sometimes, don't you agree?"

I nodded slowly, trying to discern why his words made me anxious. What he said was the truth, but I couldn't help but feel accused somehow.

"When he comes out of the bathroom," Mitch said, "why don't you tell him I'm taking you all on a tour of the mine. And then you can tell him you want to spend some alone time with dear old dad, and he should go on back without you."

I wished I could talk to Dekker about this alone, but I didn't know when we'd get the chance. I didn't say anything. Mitch gave my hand a squeeze, patted it and rose from the couch. I fought the desire to wipe my hand off. His was spongy and moist, nothing like Michael Rhones's callused ones.

"I'm going to make some coffee." He smiled at me and went in the kitchen.

I didn't really care about seeing a mine, but if it was important to him, it was important to me. I knew from TV that people liked to show other people stuff as a way of explaining themselves, what they liked, what made them who they were. I wanted to know who he was because he was my father. I just needed to get used to him.

DEKKER

MITCH HAD A cup of coffee waiting for me when I came out of the bathroom. I sat next to him on the couch.

"So tell me," he said. "How did Michael Rhones die?"

"He had a heart attack," Petty said.

"Heart attack," Mitch said, shaking his head. "So young. So sad. But it's brought you to me, so it's not all bad, is it?"

It seemed to me then that maybe Petty had inherited some of her social awkwardness from Mitch, because who would say such a thing? I decided to steer the conversation in another direction.

"Why don't you tell Mitch about Randy King and all that?" I said to Petty.

She told him about the forced betrothal, but she didn't mention how much money there was. She also didn't mention the arrest warrants or any other unpleasantness. As she talked, Mitch's eyes went flat and his expression hardened.

"That bastard," Mitch said. "That coldhearted, manipulative bastard."

"Yeah," I said. "That's Randy."

"I meant Michael," Mitch said.

To my confusion, I was strangely offended by this little outburst. "Michael thought he was taking care of Petty," I said. "I think your . . . relationship with Marianne drove him completely over the edge."

The look Mitch shot in my direction chilled me. But he brightened again when his eyes focused on Petty. "We'll make sure this Randy King doesn't bother you." Mitch stood and drained his coffee cup. "Are you ready to see the mine?"

We followed Mitch out to his Taurus, where he clipped dark protective lenses over his glasses. Petty surprised me by getting in the front seat. She was obviously determined to try harder today. But there was no legroom in back, and I had to wedge my knees in behind the passenger seat.

Mitch drove the dirt road west. "Every once in a while I get to give tours of the mine, so I'm going to give you my whole spiel. Is that all right?"

"Sure," I said. Honestly, I was more interested in how he ended up in this solitary job, living alone, collecting Precious Moments. But I didn't want to be rude. I figured we'd get to all that eventually.

He cleared his throat. "The Black Star mine opened in 1869. Over a million tons of pyrite were taken out of the mountain before it closed in 1963."

"What's pyrite used for?" Petty said.

Mitch's head jerked toward her, apparently pleased that she'd formed an entire sentence. "Lots of things."

"Gunpowder, for one," I said. "Paper production. Crystal radios before vacuum tubes. Now it's used in lithium batteries and solar panels and jewelry."

Mitch's tired face clouded in the mirror, and I berated myself for stealing his tour-guide thunder.

"Why'd they close the mine down, then?" Petty asked Mitch.

He didn't answer for a minute, and I wondered if he was waiting for me to answer this question. I remained silent.

"Because of nineteenth-century mining practices," Mitch said, "the whole mountainside is contaminated. Now it's a ghost mine."

He drove us up switchbacks lined with towering pine and aspen trees. I saw no other houses or cabins, and few cars, just massive boulders breaking up the forest. The sky was a deep blue and the sun bright. At the top of the pass there was an expanse of level unwooded land, where Mitch pulled off and stopped the car. "You ready?"

"Sure," Petty said. We got out. There were some old, rusty buildings and piles of crushed rock, as if they'd just stopped mining that morning.

"Over there is where the original opening was," Mitch said, pointing. "In those days miners used a technique called longwall mining. It was all picks and shovels, digging into the earth and making rooms. They put timbers in there to prevent cave-ins. Miners at the turn of the century worked twelve hours a day, six days a week. They were paid three-fifty a day, and children who sorted the ore were paid fifty cents a day."

I tried to imagine what it must have been like to be a kid back then, not going to school, working in a dark hole day after day for just fifty cents. Petty appeared to be contemplating this too.

"The mine was automated in 1952," he went on. "More than five hundred men lost their jobs. Paiute's population decreased by almost half."

We walked along, looking up at the barren mountain. No vegetation anywhere. Just dirt and rocks, and some ancient timbers. The openings had all been filled in—likely to keep adventurous kids from tumbling down the shafts.

I'd never seen a mine from the 1800s before, and it was an awesome sight. I wished I could spend more time there, but I needed to get on the road tomorrow morning at the latest. With this thought, I had to push away my nagging conscience. Petty would be fine without me.

We walked around the buildings. Planted in front of an old shaft covered in barbed wire was a sign depicting a stick figure falling down a hole accompanied by rocks. It said: DANGER! ABANDONED MINE! STAY OUT! STAY ALIVE! I wished I had a camera with me, or even a cell phone.

Mitch continued his canned speech. "In 1972," he said, "the mountain fractured, which means it collapsed on itself, and many of the shafts disappeared. It's unknown how many miners were trapped in the shafts. The mine finally closed down completely after that."

We walked around a little longer before Mitch said, "Back to the car."

I followed behind him and Petty and got in the backseat. Mitch drove about a mile down the mountain and then turned off at another dirt road, which led to a huge body of water in a valley. A finger of land, a berm, maybe ten feet wide and several hundred feet long, jutted out into the middle of the lake. Mitch parked. We got out of the car again and stood looking down at it.

The water at the lake's center was blue, but near the edges it was rust-colored in some places, tannish in others. Twenty feet from the shore stood an ancient wooden sign with the faded word FORBIDDEN handwritten on it.

"That's the tailings pond," Mitch said.

"Pond?" Petty said. "Back home we call that a lake." Then she nudged her shoulder into me, something she'd never done before, and it sent tingles up my arm, to my annoyance. I didn't want to feel that way about her. A certainty that we would soon part ways and probably never see each other again filled me with gloom.

"Break it up, you two," Mitch said, jovially, but with an edge. He was the proverbial dad with a shotgun on the porch.

"What's tailings?" Petty asked, her face red.

"It's what's left over after the ore has been processed," Mitch said. "This tailings pond is special, if you can call it that. It's one of the deepest in North America at over seven hundred feet, so you can imagine how long it took to build that berm out there."

"What's the pond for?" Petty said.

"To collect the contaminated runoff from the mountain," Mitch said. "What you're looking at is some of the most acidic water found on earth."

"Why's it taken so long to go into remediation?" I said.

"Money, of course," Mitch said. "Lawsuits have gone back and forth to see who's responsible."

"What does remediation mean?" Petty said.

"Cleanup," Mitch said. "Water is released a little at a time through that treatment facility over there. See it? It will take a long time to clean this up. It's a very delicate operation. But that's job security for me."

He started toward the water. "Let's walk down by the pond."

I followed several steps before I realized Petty hadn't moved. I turned.

"You two go on ahead," she said, loitering by the sign.

I recognized but didn't understand the fear in her eyes. I walked back to where she stood. "Come on," I said.

She shook her head.

"It's okay."

"I'm not going down there, no matter what you say," she said.

"Everything all right?" Mitch called.

Petty's hands were shaking.

"Okay if we just go back to the cabin?" I said to Mitch. "This altitude is kind of getting to me."

"Oh," Mitch said. "All right." He looked disappointed but began trudging toward the car.

Once we were all buckled into the Taurus and driving down the mountain, Petty said, "I didn't care about coming to see the mine, but you're right, Dekker. This is pretty interesting."

Petty was agitated, eager to please her dad, I could see. I felt embarrassed for her.

"How long have you worked here?" I asked Mitch.

"Almost twenty years." He pointed at a little building a ways from the tailings pond. "There's my office, such as it is. Gets pretty lonely up here."

"I'll bet it does," I said.

We drove in silence for a while, and I watched the towering pines slice the sky through my window. This would be an amazing place to live.

"When we get back to the cabin, I'm going to take a nap," Mitch said.

"And I'd like to go for a run on that dirt road by the cabin," Petty said.

"A run?" Mitch said.

"Yes, sir—Mitch. I run every day I can."

"If Michael Rhones had let her go to public school," I said, "she'd have been the star of the track team."

The back of Petty's neck got red.

"Is that right," Mitch said. "I don't think that's a good idea. We've got a bit of a wildlife problem—bears and mountain lions."

"Where would be a safe place I could go around here?"

Mitch stared at her. "There really isn't one, darling."

This term of endearment, seemingly out of nowhere, disturbed me, but I didn't know why.

We pulled up to the cabin.

"Do you have any pictures of my mom?" Petty asked.

Startled, Mitch said, "Of course."

"How about family photographs?" I said.

He fixed his small eyes on me from the rearview mirror. "What do you mean?"

"You know," I said. "Of you and Marianne and Petty."

"Oh. Yes."

"How come you don't have any of them hanging up in the cabin?"

His eyes went flat and he didn't answer right away. Then a big cheery grin replaced the look. "Well," he said. "Aren't you quite the interrogator?"

He didn't answer the question, but I let it drop. It was always weird to me what different people thought was too personal.

Mitch got out of the car, and Petty and I followed. She was the last one through the front door.

Mitch stood in the hallway and stretched. "I sleep with a box fan going year-round, so don't worry about being quiet on my account."

"Okay," Petty said.

"But no funny business, mister," he said, wagging his big finger at me.

I tensed.

He glanced at his watch. "It's eleven now. See you around four. Then I'll make you all a nice dinner."

He went into his bedroom and closed the door.

I sat staring at my hands, trying to untangle everything that was going on in my head. I needed to leave, but I was uncomfortable leaving Petty here alone with Mitch. We still didn't really know anything about him. Just because he was Petty's father didn't make him a good man.

What I needed was an impartial assessment from someone I trusted who didn't have these confused and possessive feelings about Petty.

"Hey," I said in a low voice, even though I heard the box fan turn on in Mitch's room. "I have an idea. Why don't you come to Kansas City with me, see the concert, and then we'll pick up Uncle Curt and Aunt Rita, and they can come back here with us."

"Why would we do that?" Petty asked.

"I don't feel right about leaving you here alone."

"Actually, I think maybe you ought to go on home without me." She didn't look at me as she said this.

I was taken aback. "But I have a couple of days before I need to be in KC. I don't mind hanging around."

"That's okay," she said.

"But didn't you notice he doesn't have a TV? How would you survive?" I looked at my hands. "And the truth is, you don't know anything about this guy."

"I know he's my father," Petty said. "What else do I need to know?"

"Where's he from? Does he have any family? Did he go to college?" I gulped. "Does he have a police record?"

"*You* have a police record, and I've been hanging around with you for a week."

I slumped.

More gently, Petty said, "It's going to take a little time to find all this stuff out."

"I'd think you'd want to know a little more about him before you decide you're going to move in here."

"I didn't say I was going to move in," Petty said. "But I want to understand why my dad—why Michael Rhones—was the way he was. I want to understand why I'm the way I am."

I glanced toward the hall and lowered my voice. "No, I get that. But I can't help feeling that there's something he's not telling us." I hadn't known I felt this until it was out of my mouth.

She frowned at me. "I'm sure there's plenty he hasn't told us. We've been here less than twenty-four hours."

"I guess it's just me," I said, realizing I was losing the argument, "but don't you kind of wonder . . . what kind of a man . . . goes after another man's wife?"

"People marry the wrong people all the time," Petty said. "Your mom did."

It was as if she'd slapped me across the face. "Thanks, Petty."

Mitch's bedroom door opened and he stepped out into the hall. "I'm sorry," he said. "I couldn't help but overhear."

Petty's face went a deep shade of red. I felt as if we'd been caught smoking crack or making a pipe bomb.

How had Mitch heard us with his box fan going? He must have been standing right behind his door, listening. I felt a pang of unease.

"Anne Marie, of course your friend is going to be worried. He's right. You don't know anything about me. But think about it, Dekker. You two show up in the middle of the night unannounced and come in here claiming that this girl is my daughter. You could be robbers or worse, but I opened my home to you. I didn't question you. I trusted you, and I don't think asking you to trust me in return is asking too much."

"I'm sorry, sir," I said, feeling chastened. He was right. I'd met plenty of slightly odd people in my life. I was even related to some. I was just feeling possessive of Petty. "We've been through a lot in the last few days."

"But having said that, you were right about something else. There is something I haven't told you. And I suppose I should go ahead and tell you now. I won't be able to sleep unless I do." He sat on the rocking chair and stared down at his hands, which he wrung together. "Your mother didn't die in a house fire."

My heart seemed to stop in my chest.

Petty sat straight and alert. "She didn't?"

"Your mother was murdered. By Michael Rhones."

Chapter 26

PETTY

"Murdered," I said, the word reverberating in my ears.

Tears ran down Mitch's face behind his glasses. "He also tried to—tried to . . ."

"What?" But I wasn't sure I wanted to know.

Mitch wiped his eyes, stood and went to the mantel, moving the figurines around. "He came to our house to take Marianne away while I was at work, and she wouldn't go. So he held you underwater in the tub until you almost drowned and she agreed to go with him."

I couldn't breathe. My mom, the woman I'd never known, had sacrificed herself for me. It had been my life or hers. Suddenly I was on my back staring at the misshapen, shifting bathroom ceiling, trying to breathe, unable to because someone was holding me underwater. My dream was no dream. It had really happened. And now I could make out the face. It was Michael Rhones, and he was pushing down on me with huge hands, smiling down at me as if we were playing a game, saying something I couldn't make out, trying to make me inhale. Death was coming for me. And his name was Michael Rhones. My mother had chosen to die rather than let me die.

My mom was dead because of me.

A high, shrill siren of a noise filled the cabin. It was coming from my mouth, pouring forth like a volcano, and I couldn't stop it. And then I was sobbing, my face to the ceiling.

I don't know how long this lasted, but it seemed to go on for a very long time. All the despair and grief of my stolen life streamed out of my mouth and eyes and nose, and everything and everyone around me disappeared until I could cry no more.

I got up and staggered to the bathroom. Weirdly, understanding my drowning dream, where it had come from, made me feel better. And the truth was, it wasn't that surprising Michael Rhones had killed my mother, after all the other crazy things he'd done. It actually made a lot of sense. I blew my nose, then splashed cold water on my face and used the toilet.

Back out in the living room, Dekker was saying, "So he killed her and took Petty and changed their names and disappeared."

Mitch nodded.

I reseated myself on the sofa.

"Why didn't Michael just divorce her?" Dekker asked.

"He said if he couldn't have her, no one could," Mitch said, moving the mantel figurines to their original positions before turning toward us. "Michael framed me for the murder. He planted evidence and I was put on trial in Denver."

Nothing surprised me anymore.

"I was acquitted. That's a matter of public record, but it ruined my life. Not only because Marianne was gone, but because I've been hounded by the press since. I moved to this cabin to escape it all, but the teenagers up here like to dare each other to 'touch the murderer's house.'"

"That's why you came out with a rifle," Dekker said.

Mitch went on as if he hadn't heard. "The media turned me into a monster. It was hell. Of course, all this happened before the Internet, so your mom didn't know Michael had a history of stalking women. He'd been in prison for raping and disfiguring a woman he was obsessed with. This was in another state—Ohio, I think—and he had several aliases. I don't even know if Rhones was his real name."

He came toward me in two long strides, fell to his knees and grabbed mine, making me jump. "Someone like him, Petty, doesn't kill just once. And he doesn't rape just once, so . . . I have to know, Petty. Did he . . . ?"

Dekker's head whipped toward me.

"Did he . . . what?" I said, barely able to get the words out.

"Did he violate you? Did he have sex with you?" Spit flew from his mouth as he said "sex" and it landed on my cheek.

I shoved Mitch's hands off my knees and got to my feet. "No!" I said. "He never touched me."

"Are you sure? Sometimes—I've read quite a bit about the subject—when children are molested, they suppress the memory. They bury it, but it sometimes comes out in dreams. They become withdrawn and introverted and depressed."

Dekker looked at me as if I were roadkill. Horrified. Disgusted. Probably thinking to himself, *That describes Petty to a T.*

I paced. "I'd remember," I said. "I know I would."

"No," Mitch said. "You might not. Michael was a violent, sadistic rapist and murderer. When the authorities found Marianne's body, it was mutilated. He'd cut off her—"

"Stop," Dekker said. "Don't. Don't say it. Stop."

He'd cut off her what?

"She needs to hear this."

Dekker rose, trembling, and stood between me and Mitch. "No, she doesn't."

Mitch frowned at Dekker, gave him a flat stare for a moment, then his face cleared.

"Of course, you're right. I apologize. You're absolutely right." He sat back in the rocking chair, took off his glasses and rubbed his eyes. "I've carried this burden by myself for eighteen years, and I guess I'd hoped we could carry it together. But it was selfish of me."

Dekker and I sat on the sofa. Mitch gave me a pointed look that I couldn't figure out. It was as if he was waiting for me to say something, but I didn't know what.

Then his shoulders dropped. "I'm so tired. I'm going to go to sleep now. We'll talk more when I get up." He leaned over me and kissed my forehead and squeezed my shoulder. Then he turned to Dekker. "I don't know when you were planning to leave, but there's snow in the forecast, and we get snowed in up here pretty good."

Dekker looked at me, and I shrugged.

I'd told him he should leave, just like Mitch had suggested. But I didn't want him to go. I felt—what was the word?—safe with him, and I couldn't figure out why. He didn't know how to shoot a gun, or how to fight, and he sure couldn't run. What did it mean?

Mitch hadn't made a move toward his bedroom.

"So be off with you, then!" he said to Dekker with a forced laugh.

"All right," Dekker said. He gave me a blank look and went into the guest room.

Mitch turned to me and gave me a big grin and the okay sign with his hand.

I was paralyzed between my desire to have Dekker stay and my desire to please my father. I felt so raw after finding out that Michael Rhones had tried to kill me, I'd wanted to talk it through with Dekker while Mitch was asleep. Now I wouldn't have a chance to do that, and it made me feel unsteady.

Dekker came back out of the guest room with his Walmart bag full of stuff. Since Mitch was standing right there, I tried to use my face to tell him that I didn't want him to go.

"Are you sure you'll be all right?" Dekker said.

Mitch watched my face.

"Sure," I said, angry at myself for wanting to leave with Dekker, because I wasn't being fair to my dad. It was all just too much.

Dekker pulled the car keys out of his pocket and studied them. "Well," he said. "I guess this is goodbye."

Mitch stuck out his hand to Dekker. They shook hands, and Mitch said, "I can't thank you enough, young man."

"I'll be back," Dekker said, surprising me. "I've got to bring your car back to you."

My disappointment at his reason for returning embarrassed me. "You can keep the car. I can't drive, remember?"

His face fell.

I stood up and we stared at each other for a moment, my kissing dream filling my head. I had to look away from him.

"Hey," he said. "Can I borrow some money? I'll need gas and I'd like to get a new shirt for the show."

I pulled my money from my back pocket and counted a thousand dollars, leaving myself five hundred. I held it out to him.

"I don't need that much," he said.

"Take it," I said. "Have a good show. I wish I could see it. I'll bet you're going to be great."

He took the money out of my hand and put it in his pocket. "You gonna be okay?"

Mitch held open the front door.

I stuck my hand out to Dekker. He took it in both of his. I looked into his brown eyes and I started to shake. He pulled me toward him and it felt like my bones were melting.

"All right you two, break it up, break it up." Mitch made a karate-chop motion between us.

Dekker let go of my hand, turned to the door and picked up his Walmart sack. Mitch held the door open for him once more.

"Goodbye, now," he said.

"Goodbye, Petty," Dekker said over his shoulder. And then he went out the door.

DEKKER

As soon as the cabin disappeared from my rearview mirror, I lit a cigarette and inhaled. What a relief to be able to smoke in the car! No more nagging about how bad it was for me, about how she was in such better shape than me. No more drama.

Still, I felt low-level trepidation at leaving, because I could tell Petty wasn't ready for me to go yet. But Mitch had been more than eager to push me out the door. In fact, he'd taken on the father role pretty quickly after meeting Petty, as if he'd been waiting to do it for a long time.

I turned on the radio and flipped the dial until a station came in semiclear. It was playing an Autopsyturvy tune. I pounded the steering wheel, letting out a shout of exultation, then I drummed along with the song.

But the farther I got from the cabin, the less excited I became at the prospect of rejoining the band. It was the reverse of what I expected. But I'd made a commitment, and I needed to honor it. So why did I feel so lousy?

The problem was pretty much everything reminded me of Petty.

I hit Leadville about a half hour later. My fuel was near E, so I drove into a Conoco and paid for a tank of gas with the cash Petty had given me. It was cooler out than it had been earlier, the sky filled with low, gray clouds. While the pump clicked and whooshed, I went inside to use the restroom and buy some junk food. There were a few people in line ahead of me, so I glanced at the newspaper on the rack in front of the counter.

AURORA RAPIST GETS FIFTEEN YEARS, a headline read.

A rapist like Michael Rhones. Petty had lived in a house with a rapist and a murderer for eighteen years, the man who'd tried to drown her. I wondered if what Mitch had said about kids who were molested—that they couldn't remember the abuse—was true. I wondered if Michael Rhones had raped Petty.

Even as the idea entered my head, I punted it right back out again. Petty was suspicious and paranoid, but she didn't exhibit the anxiety and depression that I'd seen in the two girls I'd known who'd been raped. Petty was a trained, fierce warrior, not a PTSD sufferer. She was a female Jason Bourne. I smiled at the thought.

I tried to pull my mind back to Kansas City and Disregard the 9 and Autopsyturvy, but one of the semi drivers in line was wearing a cap like Ray's, the poor dumb trucker bastard who'd thought

Petty was a hooker. I grinned at the memory now, how Petty had put that guy in his place.

I hoped she'd be okay. I missed her.

I walked out the door just in time to see a flash of red traveling west.

It was a Dodge Ram pickup truck with Kansas plates.

Chapter 27

PETTY

I HAD SPENT much of my life alone—out at the dump, in the old farmhouse, when Dad was uncommunicative. But I'd never felt loneliness like what I felt when Dekker drove away.

I decided I'd go for a run out on the dirt roads. It would make me feel better. It always did. I went to the bathroom first, and as I was rising from the toilet, Mitch walked in. Instead of turning around and walking out apologizing, he stood in the doorway.

"Take your time," he said, keeping his eyes on me.

I struggled to get my pants up, my face burning, and flushed the toilet.

When I didn't say anything, he said, "Don't be embarrassed. We're family."

I wanted to tell him that he needed to knock before busting in the bathroom, but this was his house. I was a visitor. Plus I'd walked into Dekker's room this morning without knocking, so maybe this was normal.

"So I was thinking," Mitch said, cheery. "After my nap, I'll run into town and get us some steaks and a bottle of wine, some candles, have a nice dinner. I'll cook for you and we can really get to know each other now that the boy is gone."

Every muscle in my body was rigid with awkwardness and humiliation. The bathroom felt close and too warm, but Mitch was gripping the doorjambs with both hands.

"I'll get out of here so you can use the bathroom," I said.

Mitch didn't move, didn't say anything for a moment, deep in thought.

I walked toward him, assuming he'd back through the doorway and let me out. Instead, he shifted his hips, keeping his hands on the jambs, and left a narrow space for me to squeeze through.

I tried to exit the bathroom but he caught me in his arms.

"Oh, Marianne," he said, holding me tight. He kissed the top of my head repeatedly, and I stood frozen to the spot before I pressed my wrists together, bent my knees and slipped his grip. His face clouded over.

"Mitch, you need to understand something," I said, breathless, in the same coaxing tone I'd always used when Michael Rhones was agitated. "I'm not used to people touching me, not at all. I need a little time to get used to everything. And I've told you. My name is Petty. It's not Anne Marie, and it's definitely not Marianne."

The hurt on his face tugged at my conscience.

"I'm sorry," I said.

"No, I'm sorry," Mitch said. "I guess it's too much to hope for that you'd love me the way I love you." He hung his head, his hands dangling loose.

Even though we were related by blood, it seemed strange for him to say he loved me. "I don't know you yet," I said. "Maybe you ought to take your nap and I'll go for a run. Then we'll both feel better."

His head snapped up. "I told you no. And that's that."

"I've got a gun," I said. "You don't have to worry about me."

"Oh, but I do," Mitch said, smiling at me. "I'm afraid I'm going to have to put my foot down, young lady."

I wondered how Detective Deirdre Walsh would react to this, being told she couldn't do something. She wouldn't put up with it, that was for sure. But I had nowhere else to go. I couldn't afford to upset Mitch. This was familiar territory. I'd had to walk on eggshells around Michael Rhones those last years of his life to keep him from giving me the silent treatment.

"Okay," I said.

"Instead, why don't you get prettied up for dinner while I'm asleep."

"Prettied up?"

"You know. Put on your makeup and do something with that hair. That's not your natural color, is it?"

My hands tugged at my hair, the hair that Roxanne had been so complimentary about.

"We'll want to dye it back," he said. "I'll bet you could actually be sort of attractive if you did yourself up."

"I don't wear makeup."

He looked away. "That explains it."

"Explains what?"

"Oh, nothing," Mitch said.

What did it explain? I suddenly felt awkward and unattractive, although that word had never been part of my vocabulary until this moment.

"I'm going to try to sleep now. But first, come give your dad a hug." Mitch held his arms out.

I forced myself to walk to him and let him pull me into his

arms again. He rubbed his huge hands up and down my back, stopping just short of my butt.

"Mmmm," he said into the top of my head. "I just want to eat you up."

I stood there, not wanting to think about why I needed to breathe through my mouth when he was near. He finally let me go.

He blinked at me. "Do you think you'll ever warm up to me?" His tone was petulant, whiny, and it made my skin crawl.

"I think it's going to take a little longer than eighteen hours," I said, forcing a smile, wishing he'd leave already.

He brushed the tip of my nose with his knuckles and said, "You have no idea how badly you hurt people, do you?"

I almost looked behind me to see who he was talking to. Ever since he came into the bathroom, I'd had the sense that it wasn't really me.

He smiled sadly, went into his bedroom and closed the door.

I felt stung and guilty all at the same time. Conflicting emotions swirled through my brain, making it feel swollen. I needed to run to calm down. As soon as I could assume Mitch was asleep, I didn't care what he'd said, I was going running. He needed to understand I was an adult and I could take care of myself.

I walked resolutely back to the guest room and sat on the floor next to my Walmart bag. Out the window, high in the sky above the pines that stood guard, the clouds rolled in. They weren't as dark or threatening as the Kansas tornado clouds, but thick and gray, blotting out the sun. I hoped I could get in a few miles before the snow started falling, because I hated running in the snow.

I opened the plastic bag and dug through my clothes. I reflexively reached inside my hoodie for my gun, even though I knew it wasn't there. I hadn't put on my holster that morning, because

I'd been afraid that Mitch would see it and think I was here to rob him.

But it wasn't on the floor or under the bed.

Baby Glock was gone.

Dekker had promised he wouldn't steal anything more from me, but he couldn't help himself.

This thought froze me where I sat.

Dekker would never take my gun, I was sure of it. He knew I needed it to feel safe. And if he didn't take it . . .

Silently, I stood, walked lightly to the front door and turned the knob.

Nothing happened.

I twisted and rattled it, but nothing. I couldn't get the door open. I walked to the back door and tried it—same thing. Although I tried to convince myself there was some problem with the doorknobs, I knew better. There were dead bolts on both doors that unlocked only with a key, inside and out.

My scalp prickled and my stomach dropped. I was locked in. Just like at home.

DEKKER

THREE CARS SEPARATED me from Randy King's red truck. I wished I knew Mitch's phone number so I could call and warn them that Randy was on his way. Why hadn't I thought to write it down before I left? Because I was in such a hurry to get to rock god stardom, that was why. I cursed myself as I tailgated the SUV in front of me.

One by one the three cars turned off the road until I was right behind Randy's pickup. But now I didn't know what to do. Honk and flash my lights? Smash into the back end of the truck to get him to stop? I had no weapon, so what good would that do? Randy had his gun, and I was sure he had more ammo than the clip Petty had taken from him.

Still, I followed him up to the access road, where he pulled over, got out, and climbed the embankment toward the cabin.

I felt faint and breathless. As soon as he was out of sight, I counted to three and hurled myself out of the car, running up the slope and throwing my shoulder at Randy's knees, knocking him to the ground. My surprise at having accomplished this energized me. I got up and flung myself on top of him, trying in vain to pin his arms. And then what?

Randy managed to draw the pistol out of his pants and I grabbed for it. He twisted my arm painfully, forcing a grunt from me. So I concentrated on pinning his shooting arm to the ground with both hands. Randy was much denser than I was, and it was like trying to fight bags of wet clay.

He lifted his other hand and slapped me in the face, which was both humiliating and painful. What exactly was I going to accomplish here? I tried to punch him in the face but he easily blocked me, then just as easily shoved me off him.

"Stop it," he said. "Listen to me, you stupid bastard. You didn't read all the letters, did you?"

PETTY

I HEARD SHOUTING out in the yard. I turned on the sofa and peered out the window, and to my astonishment, Randy King and Dekker wrestled there.

I screamed and pounded on the window. "Randy! Let him go!"

Randy straddled Dekker, one hand squeezing Dekker's throat and the other pressing his Magnum against Dekker's forehead. Randy's mouth was moving, his face blazing furious red.

And then I heard the gunshot.

Randy's face went slack, and it appeared he realized what he'd done. And then he pitched over to the side, off of Dekker.

I pounded on the window, screaming, and through it I watched Mitch dash out of the house, a smoking rifle in his hands. I hadn't heard him come into the room, or open the door, or fire the rifle out of it.

Randy lay on his back, his legs at odd angles. His shirt had a ragged bloody hole in it.

I don't know how I got there, but suddenly I was in the front yard too.

Dekker bore down against Randy's bullet wound with bloody hands.

"Call an ambulance," he said to Mitch. "Quick."

Mitch stood staring, still gripping the rifle. He set it down on the porch.

"Mitch," Dekker said.

"He would have killed you," Mitch said, calm and stoic.

"Call an ambulance! Now!"

"I don't have a phone." Mitch was serene, almost in a trance, and it chilled me.

I couldn't stop staring at Dekker's hands.

"I'll have to drive him down the mountain, then," Dekker said.

Randy moaned. His voice was full of blood, octaves lower than normal—a wounded animal's voice. "In my truck," he said.

"You don't know where the hospital is," Mitch said to Dekker. "I'll take him. You two stay here. I'll send the police up. You have to tell them Randy was attacking you, Dekker."

"Pack in my truck," Randy said.

"Hold on, Randy," Dekker said. "Mitch is going to take you to the hospital. Just hold on."

Randy worked his mouth like a goldfish out of its bowl. Blood appeared on his mustache, and I knew this was a very bad sign.

He gasped for air, his eyes gazing at the sky, unfocused, unblinking.

I looked at Dekker and he shook his head, his lips set in a grim line. He pulled one hand away from Randy's side and swiped at his own forehead, leaving a red slash there in the sweat.

"Give me your keys," Mitch said.

Dekker pulled them out of his pocket and tossed them to Mitch, who ran down the embankment and reappeared driving the Buick. He hopped out, the motor still running, and opened the vehicle's back door.

"You take his feet," Dekker said to me.

Dekker took Randy's hands and placed them on the gunshot wound, but his strength was gone and they fell away. I looked into Randy's eyes, but it was as if his spirit was receding deep inside and would soon dissipate altogether.

We lifted Randy, and Dekker crouched low, backing into the car. He laid Randy's head on the seat and I bent Randy's knees.

I saw he'd voided his bladder when he was shot, and for some crazy reason I felt embarrassed for him. I wanted to say something to him, but I couldn't find my voice. So I backed out of the door and Mitch closed it.

"How far is the hospital?" Dekker asked.

"About eighteen miles. Stay at the house. I'll send the police,"

Mitch said. Then he lunged at me and pinned my arms to my sides in a big bear hug. "Oh, sweetheart. You're safe now. You're safe."

He nuzzled my ear and his wet lips slid over my cheek. I broke his grip and stepped back, disconcerted. He got in the Buick and drove down to the road.

DEKKER

THE FIRST FLAKES of snow fell. I watched Petty hold out a bloody hand to catch them.

"That was a little . . . weird," I said. "I know we're all freaked out, but he's your . . . dad."

Before I could look away, her eyes met mine. To my surprise, she charged at me and clung on, her arms around my waist, her face buried in my chest.

"I'm sorry, Petty," I said. "I shouldn't have left. I never should have left. I'm sorry."

We held onto each other as the snow floated down around us in large fat clusters.

I let go and wiped my eyes and nose on my sleeve.

Where Randy had lain, no snow accumulated thanks to the lingering warmth of him, like a chalk outline.

Randy. He'd said . . .

"Petty," I said, as we went back into the cabin, "Randy said something weird when we were fighting out front. He said, 'You didn't read all the letters.'"

Petty sat on the sofa and stared quizzically at me. "How would he know about . . . wait. *Did* you read them all? All the ones in your stack?"

"I read most of them," I said. "I guess I stopped reading when I realized Charlie Moshen wasn't your dad."

"So there *were* some letters you didn't read." No longer rattled by the shooting, she was alert and focused.

I prickled. "I guess I'm just the guy who always lets you down, so—"

"No, that's not it," Petty said. "Why would it matter that you didn't read all the letters? And how would Randy know that?"

My puzzlement over this deflated my indignation. "Before Mitch took him away, Randy said, 'Pack in my truck.'"

"What does that mean?" Petty said.

"Maybe I ought to go down and see."

I ran out of the house and down the hill. When I reached the Ram, the door was unlocked and I got in the driver's seat. A fancy spit container was in one of the cup holders next to a bottle of Mountain Dew. He'll never see the inside of the truck again, I thought, and then chided myself. Randy needed to live if for no other reason than to go to jail.

Sure enough, on the passenger seat sat a rust-colored backpack. I nabbed it and carried it up to the cabin.

By the time I returned, Randy's outline in the yard was filled with snow, as if he'd never been there at all.

PETTY

DEKKER RETURNED WITH a rust-colored backpack, breathless and flushed. He unzipped the pack and pulled out several sheets of copy paper.

I watched his eyes track back and forth as he read.

Then his face turned as white as the thick snow falling outside the window. He looked up and the stack spilled from his hands, a cascade of paper littering the floor. His mouth moved but nothing came out.

"What is it, Dekker?"

A thin high sound came from his throat. Syllables poured out but I couldn't understand them because his lips weren't moving. Sound but no meaning. His pupils were pinpricks.

"What?" I said.

Finally, the noises resolved into words. "Michael Rhones didn't write those letters."

The blood seemed to evaporate from my veins.

"Who did, then?"

But I already knew.

Chapter 28

PETTY

I PITCHED FORWARD onto my knees and scrabbled like a crab toward the papers on the floor. I read the first one I saw, dated that day.

09:27 a.m.
FAX transmission
To: Motel guest Dekker Sachs, Room 5, Motel 9
From: Curt Dekker
DEKKER! As soon as you get this, call me IMMEDIATELY. DO NOT GO TO PAIUTE. Mitchell Bellandini is NOT Petty's dad. See attached. COME HOME NOW!

"Randy must have stopped by the office at Motel 9 to see if the front desk guy knew where we were going," Dekker said, taking the paper from my hand.

"This is a trick," I said. "Randy obviously wrote this to—"

"Petty, listen to your instincts. You're not wrong about Mitch.

You think there's something weird about him too, I know you do. A dad doesn't kiss a daughter the way Mitch kissed you. He doesn't call her by her mom's name."

"But maybe—"

"Here," Dekker said, shoving another piece of paper at me. It was a photocopy of a *Denver Post* article from eighteen years ago. BELLANDINI NOT GUILTY, the headline read.

Three days of deliberations in the murder trial of Mitchell Bellandini, accused of killing coworker Marianne Rhones, concluded today when the jury returned a verdict of not guilty.

Michael Rhones, Mrs. Rhones's husband, reported her missing on January 12 of last year. Mr. Rhones told police he suspected Mitchell Bellandini of Arvada of kidnapping his wife. He produced letters implicating Bellandini. According to Mr. Rhones, before they were a couple, his wife had briefly dated Bellandini, who subsequently stalked her for three and a half years until she disappeared.

The Rhoneses and Bellandini were coworkers at the accounting firm of Bendel and Bendel. Mr. Rhones alleged that Bellandini broke into their home more than once, although he was never charged. Marianne filed for a protection order against Bellandini.

"What didn't come out at trial, but should have, is [Bellandini's] history of stalking and an Ohio rape conviction in the 1980s," Mr. Rhones said. "He served time at the Ohio State Penitentiary before moving to Colorado."

No body has been recovered, and this key piece of evidence is the main factor in Bellandini's acquittal.

Another article, dated three months after the last one, had a headline that read: MICHAEL RHONES, TODDLER DAUGHTER RE- PORTED MISSING; BELLANDINI QUESTIONED.

Michael Rhones and his three-year-old daughter, Anne Marie Rhones, were reported missing Saturday by Scott Rhones, Michael's brother. . .

Pictures that I recognized from my grandmother's photo album of Michael Rhones and me as a toddler accompanied the article.

"When we first got here," Dekker said, "Mitch didn't offer any information. We fed him information about you. We told him who you were, who we *assumed* he was."

I thought back to the signature on the letters I'd taken from Mr. Dooley's office. "I'm so stupid," I said. "M is for Mitch." I wanted to scream. This mistake, fueled by my desperation for a new family, could end up costing us everything.

Dekker rolled his eyes. "I'm just as stupid," he said. "I didn't put it together either. Which means that Michael Rhones didn't kill your mom. Mitch did."

There was something just beyond my consciousness demand- ing to be heard that I couldn't quite latch onto.

I picked up the article that said BELLANDINI NOT GUILTY.

The subhead beneath it read: *Jury Cites Lack of Body, Evidence.*

"The body was never recovered," I said. "Mom's body was never . . ."

Dekker's eyes got big. "That's right. Mitch wanted to tell you what your mom's body looked like when the authorities found it, that's what he said."

"But there was no body," I said.

We stared at each other. Goose bumps raged up my arms and scalp. My heart beat like a hummingbird's wings.

"He said I could be Marianne," I said, nausea rising in my throat.

"What?"

"When he first saw me. I thought he meant I looked like her. But now I think—"

Dekker's eyes grew wider. "He was saying you could take her place. You could be his new . . ."

Horror at the real picture threatened to paralyze me. The very thing Dad had tried to prevent was on the verge of coming true.

"Mitch isn't my dad," I said. "Is he." It wasn't a question. I knew this to be the truth.

"We have to get out of here," Dekker said. "Now." He stood.

I gathered up the papers and started to put them in the backpack.

"Leave them," Dekker said. "Leave the pack. Let's go."

He was right. It didn't matter if Mitch knew we were on to him. I dropped everything and stood. A dog howled some distance away, and it was then that I realized Mitch's dog had disappeared. The dog hadn't come running when Randy showed up. The dog was gone. Dead probably.

My biological father, my real father, was Michael Rhones, who'd trained me to stay out of danger. I'd let my desire for a different family and a different life override all those years of training, the sacrifices my dad had made. I had destroyed all that in just a few short days. I'd betrayed him and myself, run toward the one place and person Dad had never wanted me to go. But I didn't have time to mourn right now.

I'd been ignoring my OODA Loop, but it kicked in now, picking up a car door opening slowly, quietly, down on the access road.

I touched Dekker's shoulder.

"What?" he said.

I held one finger to my lips and took his arm. I pulled him toward the front door. "He's coming," I whispered. "He's going to try the front door. We can't go out the back because it's locked from the outside. We need to wedge something under this door to force him to go around to the back." I hit the floor and crawled to the fireplace, removing the poker. I made it to the front door just as I heard a creak on the porch.

Dekker stood glancing around frantically, probably wondering how he could help. I motioned him over beside me.

The click of metal contacting metal, the key seeking entrance to the doorknob lock.

I took a few practice jabs before spearing the poker into the soft wood of the bottom doorjamb. It stuck a split second before Mitch got the door unlocked. He pushed on the door then made a surprised and exasperated noise when it didn't open.

I braced my back against it. Dekker did the same. Mitch threw all his considerable body weight against the door. Between me, Dekker, and the poker, it remained closed, but Mitch threw himself at it twice more.

Now he would go around to the back. At least I hoped he would.

Dekker's eyes were wide and frightened.

We had to time this right or we were going to run into the business end of Mitch's rifle. I held up my hand and pantomimed to Dekker pulling out the poker while he opened the door. He nodded.

I held up a fist and listened. Mitch was still there, listening too. Finally he walked to the edge of the porch and jumped down. Dekker lunged for the door but I stopped him. I counted silently to ten as Dekker twitched and fidgeted beside me. Then I made the "advance" motion, but Dekker frowned and threw his hands up, performed fake sign language to indicate he didn't understand, then shrugged furiously at me.

I didn't have time or the ability to explain what I wanted, so I drew the poker out of the jamb like King Arthur pulling Excalibur out of the rock. Dekker slowly opened the door and went through it. I followed and closed it.

We ran down the hill to the access road where Mitch had parked the Buick. Dekker carefully opened the driver's side door and slid into the seat. I went around the car and got in the passenger side. As my door clicked closed, relief flooded my body, making me feel rubbery and weak.

"Let's go," I said, almost giddy. I fixed my eyes out the window, keeping a lookout for Mitch and his rifle. It took me a moment to realize we weren't moving, that the motor wasn't even running. I turned toward Dekker, who sat staring straight ahead.

"What are we waiting for?" I said.

"I gave the keys to Mitch," he said. "Remember?"

The words hit me like a blast of January wind.

"Let's see if Randy's keys are in the truck," I said.

"Even if they are," Dekker said, still inert, "I locked the doors after I got the backpack."

I fought the despair that threatened to paralyze me. "We'll have to run for it, then," I said.

"I can't."

"You have to," I said. "You have to go to Kansas City and be a big rock star."

"I'm not kidding," he said, turning his head toward me. "I won't make it."

I slapped his face. Hard. "We have to go. Now."

It was as if he'd been asleep, because he jumped and shook himself. I opened my door as quietly as I could and crouched behind the car. Dekker did the same, crawling around to squat beside me.

The sun's fading light seemed trapped in the frozen atmosphere. Snowflakes continued to fall thickly in the silent, windless air, muffling all noise so everything sounded closer than normal. At least our footprints had already almost been wiped out by the falling snow. I was grateful for that.

An outcropping of boulders sat to the east, and I signaled for Dekker to follow me to it. The protection was better there.

I pulled Dekker's head close to mine.

"I am going to run west, up the hill toward the mine, and find a telephone. Mitch's little office building must have one, and I'll call the cops."

"But we're still wanted," Dekker said.

"Listen," I said. "Mitch is going to kill you. I'd rather go to jail than watch you die."

Dekker nodded, his trembling lips pressed together.

"When I start off," I continued, "I'm going to make a racket. Mitch will hear me, and he'll come after me. You know I'm fast. He won't catch me. When we're gone, you get down to the road and head straight east to Paiute, and don't stop. Just follow the road. Do not stop, no matter what."

Dekker shook his head violently. "But he'll shoot you," he whispered.

"No, he won't," I said. "He wants me alive, remember? He wants me to take Mom's place. That's the whole point." I let him go and turned toward the slow and quiet swish of the front door opening.

It sounded, in this silent storm, like Mitch was just feet from us when he shouted, "Randy's going to be fine," startling us both. "I took him to the hospital in Leadville, and he's in surgery right now. Where are you?"

I breathed slowly into my sleeve so the vapor cloud wouldn't give away our position, and signaled for Dekker to do the same, but he was panting like a draft horse. I lifted his arm against his mouth.

Mitch was taking his time, because he knew these woods. He knew the snow and the altitude and the cold.

I got down to double-knot my running shoes and pull up my socks, then stood.

Dekker leaned into me. "I need to tell you something," he whispered.

"Tell me later," I said, making sure my knife was secure on my bra, my thoughts already elsewhere. "We don't have time right now."

He gripped my shoulders and drew me close.

"There might not be a later. I need to tell you right now. I stole your mom's necklace because I wanted to be a hero and find it because I can't do anything else for you. I'm sorry."

In the midst of this wild crisis, his declaration filled me with joy. "There will be a later. That's a promise. There will be."

The terror in his eyes broke my heart. "But—"

I drew his face to mine and kissed him on the lips. Then I pressed my forehead to his and looked in his eyes. "I need to tell you something too," I said. "I'm not crazy. And I didn't kill my dad."

"I know," he said.

"Thank you for everything," I said. "Now go. This is not how it ends for you."

I let go of him, pushed off and ran.

Making as much noise as possible, I purposely stepped on branches and panted loudly. My chest felt like it was in a vise, and the lack of oxygen made my leg muscles burn. But I ran as fast as I ever have in my life.

Look for a fixed point and memorize it.

Michael, my real dad, had told me this dozens of times when we practiced direction.

Mark it by the angle of the sun. Run to it then find your next point.

The sun was nearly gone now, but a fixed point loomed in the distance. I ran toward the barren and ruined mountain on which the Black Star mine sat. I knew if I ran straight, I would hit the mine, and hopefully a telephone. If there was no phone, I'd head east on the road, and then nothing could stop me. Except a gunshot.

The light faded, and suddenly, as if someone had dropped a curtain, it was night. But the snow had a glow all its own, and I could see. Which meant I could be seen.

The road was just a half mile in front of me. I couldn't run as fast on this forest ground, but I was going to make it to the road. Some low branches wrenched hair from the side of my head. I felt the cold of air on blood. Another branch snagged my pants, and another struck me full in the face, stunning me for a moment. But on I ran.

Silently, I thanked my father for making me run.

I glanced back to see if Mitch was following me. No Mitch.

The fading thrum of a car's engine—likely Mitch's Taurus—told me the car was heading away from me, which meant east. Was it really, or was this landscape playing audio tricks on me? I stopped and listened. A squeal of brakes. A shout.

The road snaked away, a river of asphalt in the dim reflected light. Here came the Taurus. Mitch had reversed direction and was headed west now. I crouched and watched the car drive past.

Dekker was in the backseat, his face pressed grotesquely against the window. I couldn't tell if it was the weird light, but his face appeared to be bloody.

Where was Mitch taking him?

But then I knew.

To the mine. To the tailings pond, one of the deepest in North America.

Chapter 29

DEKKER

I THOUGHT I must have the flu, my head hurt so much, and that my mom was driving me to the doctor in the middle of the night during a snowstorm. The cool of the window glass felt good, but it did nothing for the strain I felt in my shoulders and the sharp pain in my wrists. My nose itched. I tried to scratch it but found I couldn't move my arms.

As my eyes focused, I knew I wasn't going to wake up from this nightmare, safe and cozy in my own bed. This nightmare was real, and it was not going to end well.

I was in the backseat of Mitch Bellandini's Ford Taurus.

And my head didn't hurt because of the flu. It hurt because Mitch had hit me over the head then tied my hands together behind my back so tightly my fingers were numb and tingling.

Where was Mitch taking me? Where was Petty?

I tried to remember what had happened. I remembered running through the pines and out to the paved road, the relief I'd felt when I got there. I remembered hearing a car drive up behind me then swerving into my path on the shoulder. But that's all I remembered.

Now, Mitch was driving slowly uphill on snow-slicked switchbacks. Finally, the Taurus slowed and turned off the road. Fear flooded my system, and I was afraid I might piss myself or worse, every part of me felt so loose.

I had to get the car door open and jump out—and I'd have to do it with my mouth. I got my teeth on the door handle and pulled. Nothing happened. I could see there was no lock on the front passenger door either. While I'd been able to open the car door earlier when we toured the mine, I hadn't noticed there were child locks on the damn doors, unlockable only from the driver's seat.

No way to get out, just like the cabin.

Terror shrilled down my spine.

The car stopped and the ignition switched off. The driver's side door opened, and I felt the car rise as Mitch got out. The door closed and I heard him walking around the car. I quickly moved away from the door so I wouldn't pitch headfirst out. I closed my eyes. If I pretended to still be unconscious, maybe I could run once Mitch pulled me from the car. I didn't believe he would shoot me inside the Taurus, because that would leave evidence. He was too smart for that, and I hoped that would work in my favor.

PETTY

How would I ever catch up? I couldn't compete with a car, but I had to try. So now I really ran. My best time for a mile was 5:37. But that was on a treadmill at low altitude. I'd have to beat that and then some if Dekker was going to live.

And I would have to do it going uphill in the snow at ten thousand feet above sea level.

The words inside the silver box around my neck bubbled up into my consciousness. *They will soar on wings like eagles; they will run and not grow weary.* I let them repeat in my head as I ran, spurring me on.

My eyes watered unceasingly. I kept my elbows in, back straight—I pretended Dad was timing me and shouting instructions. *Knees up! Tuck your butt in!*

My sinuses burned. My lungs felt like they were collapsing, my calf muscles like they were being shaved from my bones. But I ran, because Dekker's life depended on it. My clothes were wet inside and out, sweat and snow conspiring to throw me into hypothermia the moment I stopped running. But I couldn't dwell on that. All I could think about was getting to Dekker and a phone.

The tall pines that lined the road had gathered snow, now just white flashes as I ran past them. My quads knotted and cramped.

Every third breath or so made me feel as if I would overinflate and explode, because I couldn't wring enough oxygen out of this air. But I kept on. Switchback to switchback. The only sounds were my ragged gasps for breath and my shoes pounding the pavement.

Pain exploded in my left leg as part of my left calf muscle ripped loose. The sensation made lights sparkle in front of my eyes, but I couldn't stop. Not now.

Dizziness rose as the Black Star mine, dark and dead, swelled up in the near distance.

DEKKER

I HOOKED MY right foot under the seat in front of me as the car door opened and a whoosh of cold air filled the Taurus. Mitch grabbed my shoulders, tipped me sideways and tried to lift me out of the car, but made an exasperated sound when he couldn't.

When he bent to dislodge my foot from under the front seat, I tensed and brought my opposite knee up, hitting him in the face.

He grunted, wound up and threw a punch, but I turned my head and the blow glanced off my ear.

"Get out of the car," he said, pulling me by the hair.

I fell out headfirst, driving rocks and gravel into my scalp, making my already aching head ring. Mitch closed the car door and yanked at the wrist restraints, which bit into my skin and forced a yelp from me.

PETTY

I SLOWED TO a limp at the crest of the hill, above the tailings pond. There sat the Taurus, parked and running, throwing billowy fumes into the air. I couldn't swallow, my throat was so dry. I had to recover, and quick. My eyeballs felt as if they'd shrunk and my field of vision was narrowed almost to the point of blindness.

I rubbed them and gasped for air, trying to determine if Mitch or Dekker were in the car. It appeared to be empty. Where were they? At the bottom of the slope, by the edge of the water, I saw two mounds of black, like two bears foraging slowly along the rocky ground. Was I hallucinating? But then I saw it was Mitch, dragging Dekker's motionless body toward the deep lake.

The only possible thing to do at that point was run down to the mine and the office building to find a phone, because there was no way I could go down to the lake. Even as exhausted as I was, the thought of being that close to the water petrified me. The few times I'd been anywhere near a river or lake, I'd felt this weird compulsion to throw myself in, coupled with a terror that I'd be knocked in, that I'd drown.

I was frozen with indecision and wasting seconds standing there. But then Mitch began backing toward the finger of land that jutted out into the center of the pond, dragging Dekker, which snapped me back to the present. I had to do something. But by the time I got to a phone, Dekker would be drowned. I had no choice now. I had to go down there, down to the water.

DEKKER

THE WET AND the cold enveloped me as Mitch dragged me out on the berm. I'd recovered enough to try to dig my heels in, to stop his progress, but the ground was frozen. I knew Mitch wanted to drop me off the tip of the berm where the contaminated water was deepest.

In desperation, I twisted my body back and forth, attempting to somehow get on my feet and run.

But Mitch stopped dragging me and forcibly threw me to the ground like a basketball. I had no way to stop my own downward momentum. My entire body weight dropped onto my bound hands, wringing a wail of pain from me. But I tried again to stand.

Mitch pulled at a strap on his shoulder and I now saw it was attached to his rifle. He gripped it like a baseball bat and swung, smashing me in the skull.

The next thing I knew, my face was covered in snowflakes, and Mitch was dragging me again, the rifle back in place over his shoulder, my head thrumming and throbbing.

And then I heard a coyote howl in the distance.

Maybe not a coyote.

"Mitch! No!"

PETTY

MITCH DIDN'T SEE me at first, but when he did, he straightened so fast he let go of Dekker's head, which clunked on the ground.

I screamed. "Mitch!"

I was still panting but I limped toward them, feeling dizzy with the fear of running toward water, my left leg shrieking with pain every step I took. Mitch was so surprised to see me there that he stood motionless, staring with his mouth open. Now that I was close enough, I saw Dekker's face was swollen, bloody, bluish.

Terror chattered away in my brain, fear of the water, fear of Dekker's death. Fear of my mother's murderer raping me over and over again, for the rest of my life.

But then something weird happened. I didn't know if it was hypothermia, but all of a sudden my mind got quiet, and I knew what I was going to do.

"How did you get up here?" Mitch said. "How did you do that?"

I walked slowly toward him. The water beyond seemed to glow.

"Nobody's going to come between us," Mitch said. "Not ever again." He pulled the rifle from his shoulder and pointed it at Dekker's head. Dekker wasn't dead. Yet.

I walked closer. I was at the edge of the berm. The only thing standing between me and them—and the water—was the FORBIDDEN sign.

"Nobody's going to come between us," I said, limping around it, a rocket of pain shooting upward with each step. "That's right. So let's get him to his car so he can go back to Kansas."

"No," Mitch said. "He might come back again. You want to be with him, don't you?"

"I don't," I said, walking out on to the berm, feeling faint, nausea pushing bile up my throat. "It's you I want. Why do you think I was running west? I was running away from him."

Mitch didn't say anything, just stood gazing down at Dekker. I moved a little closer, the water now on both sides of me, only feet away.

"Let's get him out of here," I said. "If you're planning on dumping him in the pond, I don't care how deep it is, they'll find him. Let's let him go. Then you and I will be together. Forever. You don't have to—"

"You'll try to get away," Mitch shouted.

"I'm here," I said, holding my arms out, walking closer still. I tottered a little, feeling the pull of the water. I forced myself to look at him. "I came to you, remember? You didn't find me, I found you."

Mitch blinked behind his frosted glasses.

"I've come home. If Dekker goes in the pond, he'll be between us forever." I couldn't look at Dekker.

"He won't," Mitch said, "because—"

"Because I'll be dissolved within a couple of days," Dekker said in a hoarse voice. "Remember how he said this is some of the most acidic water on earth? Pyrite plus oxygen plus water makes sulfuric acid."

I didn't understand what he was saying. "Acid?"

"Don't go near it, whatever you do," Dekker said.

My heart dropped to my feet. I was surrounded by acid, millions of gallons of it, and the ground beneath my feet seemed to ripple, to quake, threatening my balance.

Mitch smiled hopefully at me. "He'll just disappear," he said. "As if he never existed to begin with."

Like Randy.

"If you put him in there," I said, edging nearer, "I'll have to go in after him. If you let him go, you and I will go back to your cabin and we'll be together." I was shaking violently.

It seemed to me that one way or another, I was going to end up in that lake, and it was going to hurt. Badly.

"Your choice, Mitch," I said. "He goes in, I go in." I held my arms out. "Or you can come to me right now. Come to Marianne."

Mitch's tiny eyes were unfocused, distant.

"Marianne?"

"Yes," I said. "It's me. Hold me. I'm so cold."

Mitch stepped over Dekker, his feet inches from the acid. I hoped Dekker had the presence of mind not to make any sudden moves, because if Mitch went in, at the very least Dekker would be splashed with acid and there would be no way to help him out here.

Mitch walked toward me. He still held my Glock. I kept my arms out toward him, locking eyes with him. I slid my arms around his waist inside his open jacket.

He groaned, an animal sound. "Wait," he said, and moved away, settling the rifle strap over his shoulder. Then he wrapped his arms around my waist and bent down to kiss me on the lips.

Chapter 30

DEKKER

THE REVULSION I felt as Mitch touched his lips to Petty's made me light-headed. I couldn't feel my hands anymore, which were crushed beneath me on the hard snowy ground, but I had to get free somehow. I struggled to a sitting position but my dizziness remained. If I stood, would I be able to keep from falling over, possibly into the acid?

Suddenly, Petty reached for the rifle.

"No, Petty!" I shouted. Mitch was too big for her to overpower, no matter how much training she had.

They each clenched it with both hands, parallel to the ground. Petty suddenly let go, causing Mitch to stumble backward, then unleashed a mighty high kick, dislodging the rifle from his grasp. He was stunned, watching it fly and land with a *plop* in the pond. While Mitch was preoccupied, Petty turned and kicked his knees forward, dropping him onto them.

As he fell, he got hold of her ankle. She grunted and caught herself before her face hit the ground. Mitch grabbed the other ankle and flipped her onto her back, her left hand inches from the water.

He straddled her. "You lied to me."

I rocked from side to side, trying to move forward, frantic to stop what was happening. I tried to pull my knees under me but only succeeded in moving closer to the acid.

"Get off and I'll go to your cabin with you," Petty said.

"I'm not falling for your lies anymore. I'm not going to wait that long," Mitch said. "I'm going to take you right here, and then you're mine for good."

To my horror, he pinned her arms with his knees and began unfastening his belt. I bucked, desperate to do something, anything. Was Mitch really going to do this here? Outside? In the cold and snow?

He leaned forward, trying to get his pants undone with one hand while pinning Petty with his opposite elbow. She wheeled her arms and legs, at once trying to pull her bra knife loose and get a punch in, but she had no leverage. He was so large and heavy it must have been like trying to fight a boulder.

"No! Stop!" I yelled. I'd never felt so helpless, so useless, in my life.

Mitch fumbled with his zipper. "I need to show you," he said. "You are mine."

PETTY

IT WAS A trick of the light, maybe—or the snowflakes in my eyes had warped my vision—but suddenly I was in a bathtub with huge hands pinning me underwater.

And just like that it came to me.

Of course it hadn't been Michael Rhones who'd tried to drown me. It was Mitch and his huge hands. To get my mom to go with him. I saw it all now, heard it all. Mom screamed in the background, "Let her go! Let her go!"

"Let's play a *new* game," Mitch was saying to two-year-old me. "Let's play the drowning game."

DEKKER

PETTY STOPPED FIGHTING.

"No!" I yelled. "Petty, this is what your dad trained you for, all those years, your whole life."

Mitch lifted his head and smiled victoriously at me.

"Petty," I said. "This is the moment. This is your moment. Your mom couldn't stop him, but *you can*."

Mitch licked his lips and turned his attention back to his fly. As he did, Petty thrust her hips upward, knocking him off balance. He scrambled to regain his stability, but he rolled forward onto his right shoulder, and then Petty was on top of him, one of his feet dangerously near the water.

Suddenly Petty let loose. And it was glorious to behold.

She drove her elbow into Mitch's nose. Fine droplets of blood burst outward, misting in the frozen air before Mitch covered his face with his hands. I'd seen fights before, and somehow the punches had always seemed restrained. Not this time. Petty pounded his face so fast and hard, I couldn't count the blows. One of the lenses of Mitch's glasses was suddenly gone, the frames bent.

But once Mitch recovered from the surprise of the broken nose, he was able to collar Petty's throat with both bloody hands and squeeze. She punched his elbows, but he wouldn't let go. Petty rose to her knees and threw her weight straight down into his midsection. As she forced the air out of him, his grip loosened on her throat. Then she punched him in the Adam's apple, and he made a loud *heeeeeeee* noise as he tried to inhale. She finally got hold of her bra knife and held it to his throat.

"I'm not going to kill you," Petty said. "I'm taking you to the police. You're going to pay for what you did to my mother. Now get up."

Mitch recovered enough to struggle to his feet. He shuffled toward her, his right hand covering his nose, blood dripping off his chin.

"Give me that knife, young lady," he said through his hand.

"Walk back to the car," she said to him.

Mitch turned toward the lake's shore and lifted his hands into the air. His pants fell down.

Petty bent and helped me to my feet then turned me around. Suddenly my hands were free, and I was grateful her knife hadn't ended up in the lake along with Mitch's rifle. It was a few minutes before my arms started to work again, though not very well. I stuffed my bloody and ruined hands under my shirt into my armpits.

Still brandishing her knife at Mitch, Petty said, "Pull your pants up."

He did.

"Wow," I said. "You know what? You really are like Sarah Connor. Except without the crazy."

Petty gave me a strangely pleased and surprised look, then smiled at me, that beautiful, dimpled smile.

PETTY

I KEPT THE knife in Mitch's view as he yanked his pants up, zipped and buttoned them.

"Now walk toward the car." He did as he was told, and I followed with Dekker close behind me. He was unsteady, and I was concerned he was going to tip over into the pond. My shredded left calf muscle screamed in pain as I limped.

"Where's Randy?" I said.

"I took him to the hospital," Mitch said.

"No you didn't."

"He's gone," Mitch said, trudging toward the shore, holding his pants with one hand and his belt with the other. "He won't bother you anymore."

"Is Randy in the tailings pond?" I asked.

"Of course he is," Dekker said.

"Is my mother in there?" I said.

Mitch said nothing, and I realized I already knew the answer. I looked out over the pond, the gallons of acid within it, and watched the snow disappear as it touched the surface. I was overwhelmed by a compulsion to join the snowflakes, to dissolve and blend with them and my mother, who had vanished into those depths so many years ago.

But I had to live. I had to see that this monster got what was coming to him.

When we got to the Taurus, I turned to open the back door and suddenly heard a choking sound and scuffling behind me.

I turned back around, and Mitch was strangling Dekker with his belt with one hand while struggling to pull Baby Glock out of his pocket with the other.

I let go of my knife and gave Mitch an elbow shot to the chin, forcing him to release Dekker, who fell to the ground. Then I kicked Mitch in the groin, just like my dad had taught me. He dropped to his knees, and my gun popped out of his hand. I jumped on top of him, landing punch after punch, breaking teeth and bone, his and mine, head butting his face over and over, never wanting to stop—

thisisthesonofabitchwhokilledmymomandmademydadacrazy-motherfucker

—until I realized that Dekker was shouting in my ear and pulling me away.

I looked at my battered hands, my skull ringing, blood running down my face, and tasted it in my mouth. I hawked it back and spat it into Mitch's pulverized face. He panted and moaned, but didn't bother to wipe his face.

"You can't make me go with you," he groaned.

I picked up Baby Glock, pulled back the slide and aimed it at his head.

"You're going to get in your car," I said, "and we're going to drive you down to the hospital, where we're going to call the cops. And if you try to escape, if you try to run, I will shoot you, and I don't care if I go to jail for the rest of my life. My father, Michael Rhones . . ."

I could no longer speak. *My father*. I'd cursed him, even hated him, for most of my life, hated him for the endless drills and the training and the working out, his silences, his rules.

I'd asked myself *Why?* thousands of times, wondered endlessly why he'd raised me like he had. Somehow, he'd known this day would come, and he sacrificed his whole life to give me the tools he knew I'd need one day. Suddenly the love I'd felt for him as a little girl flooded me with such potency it nearly knocked me over.

I forced myself to stop crying and stood straight and tall as I faced the man who destroyed my family.

"Like Dekker said, Dad trained me for this moment. He trained me to kill. And I will kill you."

"She will," Dekker said.

"Get in the fucking car," I said.

I SAT IN the front seat facing backward, my gun pointed at Mitch.

"You're just like your mother," he said.

"Thank you," I said.

"It's not a compliment. She was a—"

"Did you not hear what she said?" Dekker asked him. He had to use the heels of his hands to drive because some of his fingers were broken and the skin looked gray. "You probably want to keep your fucking mouth shut."

"You're going to prison," I said to Mitch.

He tried to smile, his broken face looking like a watermelon dropped from the top of a ten-story building. "But I'll get out," he said. "No matter what you do, no matter where you go, I will find you."

I held his gaze silently for a moment. "Oh," I said, letting myself smile back at him. "You better hope to God you don't."

He stopped smiling and looked out the window. He didn't utter another sound the rest of the way to the hospital.

Dekker laughed. "You are such a badass."

He parked in front of the emergency room.

"You go on in," I said. "I'll guard him until the cops get here."

Dekker pointed to a black-and-white idling at the curb, exhaust fumes making clouds in the cold night. "They're already here." He got out of the car and knocked on the cruiser's window.

Inside the ER, the lady at the admissions desk did a double take when she saw the three of us accompanied by the deputy.

"Car accident?" she asked, jumping to her feet and picking up the phone.

"No," I said and pointed at Dekker. "He's got a head injury." I pointed at Mitch. "This guy tried to rape me and kill both of us."

Orderlies appeared and put Dekker into a wheelchair and wheeled him right in.

The admissions nurse said, "Are you all right?"

"No," I said. Then I collapsed to the floor.

Chapter 31

Saturday

DEKKER

I HOPED PETTY was okay.

"What did he hit you with?" the attending nurse asked me.
She was about my grandma's age, dressed in hot pink scrubs, her
dyed-blond hair cut in a pixie. Her name tag said Sally.

"His car, for one thing," I said. "And I think he might have
pistol-whipped me."

"Follow my finger with your eyes, please," Sally said, shining
a light into my eyes and moving her finger from left to right and
then up and down.

Moving my eyes didn't feel too good, but I didn't have any
problem tracking.

"We need to clean up those cuts on your scalp," Sally said. "See
if you need any sutures."

My head seemed huge, twanging with a dull, heavy ache.

My hands and feet felt sunburned, and four of my fingers were splinted.

"Can you help me make a phone call?" I asked her.

She picked up the receiver from the wall phone. I told her the number, which she punched in then gave me the handset. "I'm going to grab the antiseptic and some gauze."

She left the room as Uncle Curt answered the phone.

"Dekker," he said, his voice raw, sounding a lot older than he was. "Are you okay? Where are you? Did you get my fax?"

"We were already in Paiute by the time it came through. Randy King got it."

A pause. Then Uncle Curt whispered, "What?"

I gave him the short version, which he repeated to Aunt Rita as I told it.

"We just landed in Denver," Curt said. "We rented a car and we should be up there in a couple of hours."

"But wait," I said. "How did you know to—"

"When Rita got home she read the letters and put it all together—she's the brains in this outfit, as you well know—she figured out Michael Rhones didn't write them, and that you were headed straight for the place he never wanted Petty to go or even know about."

"Mitch shot Randy," I said. "He's dead." And just like that, I was crying hard. I was more tired than I realized.

"It's not your fault, Dekker," Curt said. "It's not your fault, and it's not Petty's fault."

I couldn't speak, and I couldn't stop crying for a good minute and a half. I blew my nose and averted my face when the nurse stopped in the doorway. She discreetly stepped away.

"I knew there was something weird about Mitch," I said, sniffling. "And I think Petty knew it too. But she wanted him to be her dad so bad she couldn't hear me, you know what I mean?"

"Yeah."

"I kinda wish you could have seen her though," I said, brightening a little. "This guy outweighed her by a hundred and fifty pounds and she kicked his ass. It was sick."

"I wish I'd been there."

I knew he meant he wished he'd been there from the time we left his house.

"Hey, listen," Uncle Curt said. "I need you to write down a number for Petty to call."

"Hang on," I said. I hollered toward the door, "Sally? Can you help me with something?"

She walked into the room.

"Can you write down a number for me?"

She found a pen and a pad of paper and wrote the number down as I repeated it.

"It's my lawyer buddy's private cell number," Uncle Curt said. "George Engle, remember? Can you have her call him? He said it doesn't matter what time it is."

"Hang on," I said. Then to Sally: "Can you take this to Petty for me and have her call this number? Tell her it's her lawyer."

"Sure," Sally said, and left the room again.

"We're on our way," Uncle Curt said. "Then we're going to bring you and Petty home. Love you, punk."

I choked up again. "Love you too, hippie."

"See you soon."

PETTY

I WOKE UP under blankets in a hospital room with an IV in my arm and my hands wrapped up like a mummy's. My face felt huge, and I remembered head-butting Mitch. When I opened my eyes, a police officer rose from a nearby chair and walked toward me holding the backpack we'd left at Mitch's cabin.

"I'm Officer Pearson," he said. "I wondered if I could—"

"Where's Mitch?" I said. "He shot Randy and hit Dekker with his car. You've got to—"

"He's in surgery right now and under guard," the cop said.

"Where's Dekker?"

"The other guy you came in with? He's in the next room," the cop said. He pulled the faxed papers from the backpack. "Are you Michael and Marianne Rhones's daughter? Anne Marie Rhones?"

"Yes," I said. "Well, I was. My dad changed our names."

"You've been missing a long time."

"Eighteen years," I said. "Wait. How do you know I've been missing?"

"Your mom's case was big news in this state," he said. "Then when you and your dad disappeared, it made headlines again. Your family raised money and offered a reward. They searched for you and your dad for a long time. Three years ago there was even fifteenth anniversary local media coverage."

"There was?"

"You can look it up online."

This astounding news had a strange effect on me. I pictured the quarter-mile radius of my former life—the tiny bubble of my existence—expanding to encompass Dekker's family, and the family I'd never known I had, and this cop and the whole state of Colorado.

"You up to giving me a statement?"

I was, and I did. It was the second time in two weeks I'd been interrogated by police. This time, though, I had a lot more to tell.

The cop scratched his balding head.

"So *you're* the one who beat the sh—the crap out of Mr. Bellandini?"

"Yes sir," I said. "Dekker was in restraints, so he wasn't able to assist much."

The cop shook his head. "Mr. Bellandini is not a small man."

"No sir," I said.

He reached into his pocket and pulled out a business card. He set it on a tray next to my bed. "If you think of any other details, please give me a call."

I took the card. "You've got to go up to the tailings pond at the Black Star mine. It's full of sulfuric acid," I said. "We think that's where Mitch disposed of Randy's body. And probably my mom's."

"Already done," he said.

I was breathless. "Did you . . . find him?" I knew they wouldn't find her, not after all this time.

The cop nodded. I started to cry. Randy was a bad guy. But I didn't wish him dead. Everything that had happened welled up in my eyes and ran over.

"I'm sorry," he said. "I'll be back soon."

He left the room and I let myself cry about everything. I didn't quit until I was done, spent and exhausted.

A nurse named Sally came in the room and checked my blood pressure. "How are your feet?" She lifted the blanket and took a look.

"They feel like they're against hot coals."

"First-degree frostbite," she said. "You're not going to lose any toes, but they're going to hurt for a while. You're also suffering from mild hypothermia and dehydration."

"I also pulled my left calf muscle pretty severely."

"Yup. It was very swollen, so we wrapped it up. When you get home you may want to visit an orthopedist."

Home. That word. What did it mean now?

Sally walked around to the left side of my bed and touched the bandage I hadn't noticed on my arm where I'd dug out the microchip. "We had to give you a few sutures here."

I nodded. "Is Dekker okay?"

"He's going to be fine." She held up a little yellow piece of paper with a phone number written on it. "He said you're to call this number."

She dialed it for me and handed me the receiver.

After two rings, a professional-sounding voice answered. "George Engle."

"This is Petty Moshen."

"Hi, Petty," he said, his voice more friendly now. "How are you doing? How's Dekker?"

"We're both going to be okay," I said.

"Good," George said. "I'm not going to take up too much of your time right now, but I wanted to ask you a couple of questions."

"Okay," I said.

"What exactly did you take from Keith Dooley's office?" He said the name with some contempt, and it made me smile.

It all seemed so long ago, another lifetime, although only a week had passed.

"I didn't take anything that belongs to Mr. Dooley. I took my dad's laptop, a photo album with pictures of my family, some letters, my mom's necklace, and an envelope with what I think is a psychiatric evaluation in it."

"Is that the envelope you left at Curt's?"

"Yes," I said.

"Curt opened it. I told him he wasn't supposed to, but he did anyway. It wasn't a psych eval. It was ten blank sheets of paper. It was a bluff."

I should have been angry but I wasn't. I was relieved. Dad was just trying to keep me safe, I knew that now. I believed it. I was grateful for it.

"Curt said you also took all the firearms out of your house. Everything in the house is part of the trust, so legally speaking, none of that is your property. But I'm confident I can persuade old Dooley to drop the theft charge because of the conflict of interest in regards to Randy King. Getting the will overturned is a formality."

"What about the—" I turned my face away from the nurse and cupped my hand over the phone receiver. "—murder charge?"

"The what?"

"Randy told me there's a warrant out for my arrest for murdering my dad. He said the autopsy showed someone held a pillow over his face and suffocated him."

George gave a bark of a laugh. "Rest in peace and all that, but I grew up in Niobe and I knew Randy when he was a little kid. He was always a bully, and that sounds like something he would do. I've got your dad's autopsy report right here. Cause of death: myocardial infarction."

"Heart attack," I said. "Randy had me halfway convinced that I'd killed my own dad." Relief mixed with sadness washed over me.

"Yup. Tox screen came back negative, of course. Randy was trying to scare you."

"It worked," I said.

"In any case," he said, "you should have a check from the insurance company within the month. Curt and Rita are on their way, and they said you can come back to Kansas with them."

I had the same feeling I imagined regular people would have knowing their parents were coming to get them.

"Mr. Engle?"

"It's George."

"Mitch Bellandini is going to say he was defending Dekker when he shot Randy, but he wasn't. He hit Dekker with his car. He was going to kill Dekker. And he attempted to sexually assault me. I'm afraid he's going to get away with it, just like he got away with killing my mom." I swallowed. "Is he?"

"Since he tried to dissolve Randy's body, he'll probably be charged with depraved indifference, which is a second-degree murder charge. You and Dekker will have to testify against him, unless he pleads guilty and there's no trial."

"Because if he doesn't go to prison," I said, "I'm going to be looking over my shoulder for the rest of my life."

"He'll probably get eight to twenty-four years for the second-degree murder charge, four to twelve each for the assault and attempted murder, and six to eighteen months for the attempted rape, so he's looking at a minimum of sixteen years in prison, potentially out in eight. But there are so many variables—depends on the judge, whether they'll consider his past criminal behavior, etcetera."

My heart sank. Only eight years?

"But we're getting ahead of ourselves. He's in custody, so you can rest easy for now. When you get back to Kansas, we'll get together and sign paperwork and so forth. I hear you kicked this guy's ass. Good work. What exactly happened?"

It took me fifteen minutes to tell him the whole story.

THE NEXT TIME I opened my eyes a different nurse was standing at the end of my bed and the sky outside was light.

"How you feeling?" she asked while taking my blood pressure.

"Okay," I said. "What time is it?"

"It's about one-thirty." The nurse took my temperature. "I was told to let your uncle and aunt know when you woke up. Do you want me to bring them in?"

"Sure," I said, not bothering to correct her. I figured that Curt and Rita had said they were family so they could visit. I wished I had time to take a shower, because I was pretty sure I didn't smell too good, but they'd probably understand.

"They're out in the waiting room," the nurse said. "I'll go get them." She vanished from the doorway, and I fidgeted while I waited.

I heard a knock on my door as it swung inward.

And there stood my father.

Chapter 32

PETTY

It was surreal.

"Dad?"

Even as I said it, I knew it wasn't him. But it could have been.

The man who looked uncannily like Michael Rhones—only better-fed and not haunted—came meekly into the room as if he were entering the cage of a Bengal tiger.

"Anne Marie?" he said.

I nodded.

"I'm your dad's oldest brother, Scott."

A woman followed him in.

"And this is your Aunt Gwen."

They stood side by side, staring at me, their mouths open. Scott's eyes were shiny with tears.

"My God," he said. "You look just like your mother."

"I know," I said. "And you look just like my dad."

Scott's tears ran down his face. Gwen wrapped her arms around him, crying herself.

She and Scott pulled chairs close to my bed and sat. Scott asked me where I'd been all these years, and I told him about my life in Kansas, and then about the past week.

"How did you know I was here?" I said.

"One of the police officers recognized your name," Gwen said. "He called the Jefferson County Police to tell them you'd been found, and they contacted us."

"I have so many questions," I said.

"I'll try to answer them," Scott said, wiping his eyes. His facial expressions, his mannerisms, were so like Dad's, if I squinted my eyes, I could pretend it was him, but in another, better life.

"What exactly happened with my mom and Mitch Bellandini?" I steeled myself for the answer.

Gwen pulled two tissues out of the box on the tray by my bed, handed one to her husband and blew her nose with the other.

"Before your folks dated," Scott said, "your mom went out with Mitch Bellandini one time. Once." He held up his index finger. "That was all. He proposed to her on that first date, said he knew they were meant to be together." He spat the words out, his disgust evident. "She tried to be nice and let him down easy, but he wouldn't take no for an answer, wouldn't leave her alone. Not after she and Michael started dating, not when they got engaged. Not even when they got married."

"Grandma Davis said Mom invited Mitch to the wedding," I said. "Is that true?"

"No," Aunt Gwen said. "He just showed up and made a total scene. He acted out *The Graduate*, screaming her name in the church."

I pictured the photo of Mom and Dad at the altar and Mitch crashing through that happy scene, ruining it for everyone.

"He seemed so normal when we first met him," I said, but I

didn't think that was really true. I'd just wanted him to be. Looking back now, I could see all the red flags I'd chosen to ignore.

"That's what your mom said," Scott said. "He was fired from the company where the three of them worked because his behavior became so crazy they couldn't ignore it anymore. He followed her everywhere. He tampered with your dad's car—loosened the lug nuts on his wheels. One tire came off on I-25. He wasn't hurt, but he knew who'd done it. They went to the cops lots of times, went to court, got a restraining order. He kept breaking it, paying fines, spending time in jail. But he would not stop."

An orderly came in with a tray of food and set it on the little adjustable table by my bed.

"Thank you," I said.

He smiled at all of us and then left the room again.

"How am I supposed to eat this?" I said, holding up my bandaged hands.

Gwen clucked and stood, removing the cover to the tray. "I'll help you," she said.

I wasn't hungry, but I didn't want to refuse this motherly attention. She picked up a big plastic mug and turned the straw toward me and held it to my lips. I drank gratefully.

"So Mitch wouldn't stop," I said.

Gwen cut up some colorless meat on the plate and held up a forkful. I obediently ate it.

"Right," she said. "The cops' advice to your parents was to move away."

"And then, Bellandini totally lost it when your mom got pregnant with you," Scott said.

I nodded. Dekker had read about the freak-out in Mitch's letter to my mom. "Why didn't they move away?"

"Your dad couldn't find another job," Scott said. "He tried. Your folks were so stressed out, but they did their best to keep up a good front for you. They loved you so much." He began crying again, and Gwen had to stop feeding me to wipe away more of her own tears.

This stoked my loathing of Mitch even further. The things he'd done had affected not just me and my little world, but these people and my other relatives too. Who knew how wide the ripples went?

"So how old was I when Mom disappeared?" I said. "I read one of the newspaper articles about it."

"You were two and a half," Gwen said, gently wiping my lips with a napkin. "Michael came home from work and found you wandering the house alone, naked with wet hair. Marianne had vanished. You kept saying 'game.'"

I gasped.

"You don't remember any of this, do you?" Scott said, incredulous.

"I actually remember Mitch holding me under the water in the bathtub."

Scott and Gwen looked at each other.

"Really," I said. "I think that's how he got Mom to go with him."

"I'm sure that's right," Gwen said. "The trial was about a year later, and after Bellandini was acquitted, your dad bought all kinds of guns and put bars over the windows and dead bolts on each door, but still he didn't feel safe."

Scott rose and walked to the window, looking out into the gray sky. "The last time I saw my brother, he showed me a letter he'd received in the mail with no return address. It said something like, 'No matter where you try to hide, I will find Anne Marie, and I will take her from you the way you took Marianne from me.'" He turned away from the window. "Michael took it to the police, but they couldn't prove it was from Bellandini."

"I can't eat any more," I said to Gwen. "Thank you."

She put the cover on the plate then hesitated before reaching out to smooth the hair beside my bandage. Tears clung to her lashes. "Your mom," she said, "was my best friend." Her chin quivered and she turned away to fuss over the food tray some more. *My mom's best friend.*

Gwen wiped her eyes, and sat down again. Scott came away from the window and sat next to her, holding her hand.

"So the cops started to treat your dad like some kind of conspiracy-theorist crackpot," she said. "He felt like no one could help him."

The day nurse came in and took my vitals while pretending not to listen.

"Not long after that," Scott said, "I called your house, but the phone had been disconnected. Tried your dad's cell phone. No such number. Went to the house. It was all unlocked. No forced entry. Not a single thing was missing. None of his or your clothes. His wallet and driver's license were on his dresser. Both cars in the garage. Your favorite toy in your crib. It was as if the two of you had been raptured right out of the house."

"We figured the two of you had finally gone into hiding," Gwen said.

Scott's eyes got shiny and he said, "I miss your dad so much."

He broke down crying again. I felt terrible for him. I now knew that people liked to be touched when they felt bad, so I reached out and took his hand as best I could with my gauze-wrapped one.

"He changed our names," I said. "His was an anagram of Michael Rhones—Charlie Moshen. And he called me Petty."

Gwen and Scott looked at each other and laughed and cried.

"Petty," Scott said, shaking his head.

"That was what your mom wanted to name you when you were born," Gwen said, wiping her eyes again. "Because she was a huge Tom Petty fan, and your dad loved Richard Petty the race car driver. But your dad decided it was too weird. No offense."

"It's okay," I said, and I meant it. He'd chosen my name to honor my mom. Anne Marie Rhones had disappeared forever the day that we had—eighteen years ago.

I was and would always be Petty Moshen.

Epilogue

Nine weeks later

PETTY

"Hello, Petty!" Mrs. Drake, the retirement facility director said when I walked into the lobby. "I just left a message for you at your Uncle Scott's house."

I must have looked concerned, because she smiled and said, "Just wanted to find out when you were coming in. Jeannie's been asking for you all morning. She's getting her hair done now though, so you can wait for her down in the game room."

I held up a bag. "I brought her some candy," I said. "Make sure she shares it with you all."

"Will do," she said.

"Thanks," I said. "See you later." I waved and walked down the hall.

I sat at a table in the game room, pulled out my new iPhone and dialed Dekker's number.

"Well?" he said.

"I passed," I said, and I couldn't keep the smile out of my voice. "Drove myself to Grandma's today. It was terrifying."

He let out a whoop. "I knew you could do it. I told you you could do it."

"How's summer school?" I asked.

There was a pause.

"I have to tell you again that I really can't let you pay my tuition," he said.

"It's already done," I said. "If it weren't for you, I'd be married to Randy. Or dead. So just deal with it."

"But I—"

"Let me explain how this whole gift-slash-gratitude thing works. You say thank-you, and you really mean it. I say you're welcome, but, like, please don't bring it up ever again. And you say I won't, and you really, really mean it. And then we move on."

He laughed. "Fair enough. Thank you."

"You're welcome."

We were quiet a moment.

"So have you gotten used to the decibel level there at your uncle's house?" he asked.

"Not really," I said. "Uncle Scott and Aunt Gwen's kids—my cousins—come over and play board games and laugh and holler at each other. I have to go up to the guest room and close the door sometimes."

"How much longer you planning on living with them?"

"I don't know," I said. "I want to spend as much time as I can with Grandma before the Alzheimer's takes her away from me completely. They've said I can stay as long as I want. But I am coming out for Uncle Curt's pig roast party." My heart pounded as I said this, knowing I'd get to see him soon.

"Woot," he said. "When will you be here?"

"July second," I said. "Roxanne's picking me up at the Kansas City airport and then we're heading down to Saw Pole. Then we'll swing up to your uncle's place. So we'll see you at his house that Friday, right?"

"Yup," he said. "You'll get to meet my other cousins too. It'll be a blast. And bring some earplugs because Uncle Curt's hired a band, and they're loud."

"Maybe you can play drums with them," I said.

"Can't really hold drumsticks yet."

"You will," I said.

"How's your leg?"

"Better. Can only run four miles at a time though."

"Yeah, me too—oh, wait. That's not me." He laughed. "How come you're going to Saw Pole? Are you selling the house?"

"No," I said. "I bought a new headstone for Dad's grave with his real name on it. It's going to say, 'Michael Rhones, son, brother, husband . . .'" I choked up a little, which surprised me. "'. . . and father.'"

"That's a great idea," Dekker said.

We were quiet again.

"So what's the latest word on Mitch's trial?" he said.

"Sometime next year. There are lots of motions and that kind of thing, so it's going to be a while." My faithful viewing of the *Offender* shows had prepared me for this. "I try not to think about it. You still having nightmares?"

"Yeah," he said. "I guess that's normal, huh?"

"What's normal?" I said.

He laughed. "Well, I'm late for class, so . . ."

I gathered my courage. "I've missed you, Dekker. A lot."

"I've missed you too," he said.

I could tell by the tone of his voice that he meant it the same way I did. I didn't even need a chart to figure it out.

"I can't wait to see you, Petty."

We hung up, and I was warm all over, imagining seeing him again at his uncle's house. I was sitting in a square of sunshine coming in through the big window, smiling at nothing when my grandma walked in.

"There you are! Are you ready to play some gin rummy today?"

"You bet."

She sat in the chair opposite me and handed me the cards. "You deal. I can't shuffle like I used to. I used to play bridge, you know. I was in tournaments. They used to call me Black Bart."

"They did?" I said, even though I'd heard this exact thing from her nearly every day over the past two months. It didn't bother me though.

I was still learning to shuffle, so the cards popped out of my hands in groups of three and four. I gathered them back up and tried again.

"Your hair looks nice," I said.

Her hand went up to it. "Thank you," she said. "Yours too. Did you get it cut?"

I mimicked her and touched my head. "Yes. You like it?"

"It's very flattering. You've always had a great head of hair, Marianne."

"Thanks, Mom," I said, and dealt the cards.

Acknowledgments

I AM DEEPLY grateful to the following people:

The brilliant, gifted Michelle Johnson of Inklings Literary Agency, who turned Super Bowl Sunday into my favorite holiday and changed my life forever in the best possible way.

The team at HarperCollins Witness Impulse and especially the genius editor, Chelsey Emmelhainz, who spurred me to take Petty to the next level and who made the editing process almost as fun as the writing.

The staff of the Hand Hotel in Fairplay, Colorado, for the long, productive writers' retreat weekends filled with great atmosphere, food, and wine.

Rocky Mountain Fiction Writers, Pikes Peak Writers, and Lighthouse Writers Workshop, who gave me the tools I needed to get here.

The members and staff of The Neighborhood Church, who acted as beta readers and lifted me up in prayer on a daily basis.

My small group, Dan and Lori Aguiar, Bob and Deirdre Byerly, Todd and Denise Lansing, and Kim and Michael Marks, who are my encouragers and cheerleaders.

Kathy Bradford, whose insight into the heart of my manuscript gave it what it needed to attract the perfect agent and the right publisher.

Bob Byerly, whose expertise in police procedure helped me keep it real.

John Rasmussen, whose legal counsel and road-trip oil cans were invaluable.

The late, great novelist and Lighthouse instructor Cort McMeel, whose enthusiasm and belief in my work gave me permission to believe in it.

My parents, Bob and Tanya Stormes, who encouraged me to dream big, and my siblings, Rob Stormes, Lori Malone, and Deveney Woodall Stormes.

My ridiculously accomplished and brainy cousins, Anne Marie Ross Mosqueda and Nancy Ross Dribin, whose confidence in me and this story made me feel accomplished and brainy too.

The world's greatest critique group, the Highlands Ranch Fiction Writers (aka Because Magic), who will not let me get away with lazy or corny writing, and who've spent countless hours with me dissecting literary theory, geek culture, and the meaning of life. They encourage me with their wit, talent, wisdom, and skill. Lynn Bisesi, Deirdre Byerly, Claire Fishback, Marc Graham, Nicole Greene, Michael Haspil, Laura Main, Vicki Pierce, and Chris Scena, you are not only my critique partners, but my dear friends, without whom none of this would have been possible.

My daughter Chloe, whose creativity, fearlessness, intelligence, and discernment hearten everyone around her and whose inner light illuminates every good thing it touches.

My daughter Layla, who's overcome more adversity in her

short life than most ever will, but who manages to create mind-blowing art, and inspires and challenges me daily.

Most of all, I want to thank my husband, muse, and brainstorming partner, Andy Hawker, who pushed me to take my work seriously, do my best, and never give up. I'll meet you out back.

About the Author

LS HAWKER grew up in suburban Denver, indulging her worrisome obsession with true-crime books, and writing stories about anthropomorphic fruit and juvenile delinquents. She wrote her first novel at fourteen.

Armed with a B.S. in journalism from the University of Kansas, she had a radio show called "People Are So Stupid," edited a trade magazine, and worked as a traveling Kmart portrait photographer, but never lost her passion for fiction writing.

She's got a hilarious, supportive husband, two brilliant daughters, and a massive music collection. She lives in Colorado but considers Kansas her spiritual homeland. Visit her Web site at LSHawker.com.

Discover great authors, exclusive offers, and more at hc.com.